# ALLEGRA

## A Novel Set in the Italian Renaissance

# C. DE MELO

# NOTE FROM THE AUTHOR

It has taken years of careful research in Florence, Italy to write this novel. Many of the dates, major events, and characters are historically accurate. One must not forget, however, that this is a work of *fiction*. This entitles the author to take certain artistic liberties—the greatest being the independence I have bestowed upon my female characters. In reality, women of good breeding had little or no freedom in the patriarchal society of 16th century Florence. There is speculation among historians on the facts surrounding the life of Bianca Cappello. As with many historical scandals, rumors have a way of becoming accepted truths with the passing of time.

# DEDICATION

Thank you, D.

*"Never was anything great achieved without danger."*

—Niccolò Machiavelli

# CHAPTER 1
## FLORENCE, TUSCANY
## OCTOBER 1547

The Tuscan landscape remained shrouded in gloom as a tempest unleashed its fury upon the city of Florence. Rain hammered against the windows of the spacious workshop where Vittorio Castagno sat repairing a gold necklace by the light of flickering candles. A servant entered the room to stoke the fire in the hearth.

"Fetch me some undiluted wine when you're done," he said, hoping to drive the chill from his bones.

"Yes, Signore."

He disliked fixing jewelry, but the exigent clients he'd inherited from his father were accustomed to the extra service. His father had transported exotic spices for a living for many years until Portugal undercut the Venetian spice trade by sailing around the Cape. With the need for middlemen eliminated, the resourceful businessman began moving precious metals and gemstones for the nobility who needed vast sums of money to fund wars. Jewelry served as portable wealth; a precious commodity always in high demand. Within a short period of time, his father had acquired a client base that spanned from the pope in Rome to the doge in Venice.

The door opened and, without looking up, he pointed to a vacant spot on the cluttered workbench. "Set the chalice there, girl."

"Vittorio."

He didn't expect to see his wife standing in the doorway. "Stefania."

"I am with child," she said flatly, her face expressionless.

He hesitated. "That's wonderful news."

"Is it?"

An awkward silence followed the question.

Averting her gaze, she said, "The hour is late. I'm tired."

"Sleep well, my love."

He watched her go before resuming his work with a heavy heart.

Gianna crept into the room shortly afterward. The faithful servant exchanged a meaningful look with her master. "The midwife is hopeful."

Vittorio pinched the bridge of his nose. "And the physician?"

"The dottore believes that perhaps *this time…*"

"Isn't that what he said last time?" He'd only caught a glimpse of the premature infant before the servants wrapped the tiny body in linens. The sight of his son's blue lips would haunt him forever.

The servant girl appeared, handed Vittorio a chalice of red wine, then swiftly departed. He took a long sip of the ruby elixir, grateful for its numbing warmth.

Gianna wrung her hands. "Signore—"

"Go now," he interjected. "Tend to your mistress. She could surely use one of your potent draughts tonight."

Without another word, Gianna slipped out the door, leaving her master alone with his troubled thoughts.

Meanwhile, Stefania surrendered to despair in the privacy of her bedchamber. She'd been poked and prodded all afternoon until she was sore. Both the midwife and the physician seemed positive, each promising to pray for the health of the unborn babe. By now, she could see through the veneer of false hope and empty words.

Sitting before a Venetian mirror on the dressing table, she studied her reflection in the mottled glass. A pale, weary face stared back at her. Where was the vibrant young woman who had accompanied her grandmother, Sabina Rossi, to Florence eight years ago? Oh, how happy and naïve she had been back then, pregnant with Cosimo de' Medici's lovechild. Her grandmother had tried to warn her of life's unexpected pitfalls, but she'd paid little mind to the old woman's unsolicited advice—until a bloody miscarriage, followed by Cosimo's betrothal to Eleonora di Toledo, shattered her idyllic world.

Gianna entered the room and handed her mistress a ceramic cup. "Best to drink it hot, Signora."

Stefania took a cautious sip. "What am I going to do?"

"What you always do. Pray."

"I don't believe it will be different this time. Do you?"

"Yes, I do," Gianna replied with forced conviction.

"I wish I had your spirit, Gianna."

"You possess more spirit than everyone in this household put together. I'll be praying for you—all of us will."

Stefania attempted a smile. "Thank you."

"The dottore said you need plenty of rest, so I bid you goodnight."

Stefania stared blindly into the distance as she slowly drank the herbaceous brew. Despite her anxiety and racing thoughts, she went to bed and eventually fell into a deep slumber.

Gianna went out of her way to glean as much helpful information as she could from the city's apothecaries and various midwives. She oversaw her mistress's diet with special care, stocking the kitchen with the finest quality wheat, non-acidic fruits, and dry red wine—all of which, supposedly, produced healthy boys.

After years of bitter disappointment and heartbreak, Stefania remained stoic in regard to her condition. She quietly submitted to her maid's dietary administrations and bitter green concoctions without complaint, and didn't raise any objection when Gianna began applying foul-smelling plasters to her abdomen once a week.

*\*\**

Invitations for the Medici Christmas banquet were distributed in early December. The most prominent members of Florentine society were expected to attend, including the Castagno family. Plagued by persistent nausea, Stefania had no desire to leave her home.

"Go and enjoy yourself, Vittorio," she urged. "Given my condition, you can easily make an excuse for my absence."

"Gianna will prepare a tonic to settle your stomach."

"None of them work."

"Then I will personally consult with every apothecary in the city until I find one that does."

"I am not well," she persisted. "I feel weak."

"Your cheeks are radiant and you've grown robust! The way Gianna frets over you, I'd wager you're the healthiest woman in Florence."

"I don't want to take any chances…"

"Stefania, I honestly believe it will be different this time."

"Dear God, I hope so."

Pulling her into his arms, he kissed the top of her head. "Why not take a respite from the constant worrying and celebrate the birth of our lord in high style? The Medici are generous hosts who always provide excellent food and entertainment."

"Eleonora is pregnant again."

Vittorio knew that Stefania's reluctance to accompany him to the banquet had more to do with the duchess's condition than her own. "We cannot refuse every invitation we receive during your pregnancy, my love. Especially from the Medici."

Stefania acknowledged his prudent words with a nod. Social occasions served as opportunities to keep a close eye on rival families while forging new alliances. "Very well. I will accompany you."

He smiled encouragingly. "That's better."

On Christmas morning, Stefania consumed the bitter elixir her husband had procured from the Santa Maria Novella monks. Thankfully, the expensive medicine diminished her nausea, allowing her to confront the day in relative comfort. Arrayed in a velvet gown matching the green of her eyes, she accompanied Vittorio to Santa Maria del Fiore cathedral for Holy Mass, then followed the Medici retinue to the Palazzo Ducale, formerly the Palazzo della Signoria. Transforming the government headquarters into his private domicile had proved a cunning strategy on Cosimo's part since it further solidified his power in Florence.

Stefania stood beside Vittorio and did her best to maintain a cheerful disposition. At one point, she discreetly studied Cosimo while he addressed a cluster of elderly magistrates. What was it like to embody such power? His marriage to Eleonora had secured an alliance with the formidable Kingdom of Spain, and his distant cousin, Caterina, had become Queen of France last March. The cards seemed to be in his favor.

Her eyes slid to Eleonora, who hovered near her husband in a costly gown of burgundy brocade. The growing mound beneath the luxuriant fabric drew many stares. Cosimo's broodmare was pregnant. *Again.* She had to admit, the woman's fecundity was impressive. By sheer coincidence—or God's cruel humor—she and Eleonora had been pregnant roughly around the same times throughout the years. One woman was blessed, the other, cursed.

Two ambitious courtiers drew Vittorio into conversation, compelling Stefania to wander off in order to afford them a measure of privacy. She walked toward an adjoining room where a few guests were congregated beneath the much-acclaimed portrait of Eleonora. Bronzino created the fine painting shortly after she had given birth to her fifth child. Dripping with gemstones and pearls to accentuate her royal status, the duchess was depicted in an exquisite black and white gown flaunting the pomegranate motif—a symbol of fertility.

*Eleonora, the perfect wife.*

At the sound of rustling fabric and footsteps, Stefania tore her eyes from the propagandistic portrait to see the duchess standing beside her. Surprised, she immediately inclined her head in greeting. "Your Grace."

"Bronzino's talent is impressive, is it not?"

"Most definitely, but it was aided by your natural beauty."

The corners of the duchess's lips lifted a fraction of an inch. It wasn't the first silver-tongued compliment she'd received that day, and it certainly wouldn't be the last. "I wish to have a word with you, Signora Stefania."

Many sets of eyes followed the women as they retreated to a quiet corner.

"I know how difficult it has been for you and your husband these last few years." Eleonora's eyes dropped to Stefania's belly. "Be assured that His Grace and I are praying for you and your unborn child."

"You are most kind, my lady."

Taking hold of Stefania's hand in an unprecedented gesture of friendliness, she said, "God will bless you." Although she didn't say the word 'eventually,' her tone implied it. "You must never give up hope."

"We never do."

She offered Stefania a genuine smile, then retreated to the main hall.

A moment later, Vittorio appeared carrying two chalices of mulled wine. Offering one of them to his wife, he inquired, "What did she say to you?"

"Everyone is staring at me," Stefania observed, ignoring his question.

"The most important woman in Tuscany has gone out of her way to speak with you privately," he pointed out. "Naturally, people are curious."

"She is praying for me and the baby."

\*\*\*

Vittorio departed for Rome in mid-February. The night after his departure, Gianna was startled from sleep by the sound of Stefania's cries. Scrambling out of bed, she uttered a quick prayer before grabbing a handful of linen cloths from the cupboard. Running to her mistress's bedchamber, she mentally prepared herself for the gruesome task ahead.

She pulled back the coverlet and froze. *No bloodied sheets?* "Wake up, Signora!"

Stefania sat up in bed. "Santa Madonna!"

"There, there, it was only a nightmare. Shall I fix you a draught?"

"I had a dream," Stefania said, her voice trembling with emotion. "I saw a baby girl seated upon on a bed of jewels, completely covered in gold dust. She even smiled at me!"

"God be praised."

"My baby is alive, I know it."

Gianna crossed herself before kissing the silver crucifix around her neck. "Thank the Blessed Virgin. This is an omen."

Stefania's hands flew to her belly and her eyes welled with tears of joy. "The baby moved inside of me! Another sign!"

"We should attend Holy Mass first thing in the morning to thank God for this miracle."

"I want you to summon the city's best astrologer as soon as possible."

Gianna almost recoiled. "Signore Vittorio would not approve of an astrologer coming here. Would it not be better to go to church, instead?"

Stefania's brow shot upward. "My husband will be none the wiser as long as the matter remains between us."

Nodding reluctantly, Gianna murmured, "As you wish."

Snuggling under the warm covers, Stefania went back to sleep with the mental image of her healthy, golden baby.

A few days later, a dark eyed man in a fur-lined cloak and orange doublet arrived at the Palazzo Castagno.

"Messer Mancini is waiting downstairs," Gianna said from the doorway of her mistress's bedchamber.

Stefania closed the lid of her jewelry chest. "Mancini?" she repeated with a furrowed brow. She'd heard the rumors about him and wondered if there could there be any truth in them. "Are you certain he's the best?"

"Everyone seems to think so. The Strozzi and the Pucci employed his services not long ago."

Pandolfo Pucci was one of Cosimo's close companions, a man of considerable influence within the Medici court. Stefania's curiosity was piqued. "Help me don this necklace, hurry."

The maid wrung her hands nervously before obeying the command. "It's not too late for me to send him away. We can still go to church."

"I shall meet with him in my sitting room."

A moment later, Messer Mancini's presence dominated the small, feminine room. Doffing his plumed hat with flourish, he

13

said, "Signora Stefania, I am at your service."

"Please, sit." She waited for the extravagantly dressed man to take a seat before inquiring, "Are your readings accurate?"

"*Certo*," he assured. "Perhaps you've heard that my father was a famous astrologer, as was my grandfather before him. I am proud to say that even the Medici children have benefitted from my expertise."

Surprised by this revelation, she said, "My maid mentioned the Strozzi and Pucci, but she said nothing about the Medici."

"I don't share that information with just *anyone*." The enormous topaz adorning his pinky finger flashed in the sunlight as he stroked his black goatee. "May I speak frankly?"

"You may."

"The duchess herself summoned me more than once," he bragged in a conspiratorial tone.

*If this astrologer was good enough for Eleonora's children...*

Stefania cleared her throat. "Can you perform readings on the unborn?"

"No one in Florence can do that." Sensing her disappointment, he added, "My mother's midwifery skills were legendary, and she taught me how to discern the sex of a child inside the womb."

"Can you see if my baby will survive the birth, too?"

"I can determine its progress," he replied cautiously.

Stefania hesitated, embarrassed. "My husband doesn't approve of such things. He's unaware of your visit today."

"I assure you, madam, that I'm the very incarnation of discretion." Messer Mancini slowly reached out his hands and paused two inches short of Stefania' midsection. "May I proceed?"

She nodded and the man pressed both of his palms against the bulge beneath her satin gown. After several seconds, she prompted, "Well?"

"You're carrying a healthy girl."

"Thank God and all the saints!"

The astrologer's eyes focused blindly on Stefania's gold

necklace as a crystal-clear vision unfurled in his head. "She'll be gifted; a blessing and a curse," he whispered unwittingly.

"A curse?" she repeated, alarmed.

"Forgive me, I misspoke," he lied, regretting his lapse of judgement.

"What did you see?"

Witchcraft was a serious offense in Florence. Performing a public Act of Faith or hanging from the gallows at Fort Belvedere held little appeal for him, so he replied blandly, "I saw nothing, Signora Stefania. Rest assured that she'll be a healthy child, fortunate to have such loving parents."

Stefania regarded him dubiously before placing some coins in his upturned palm. The moment her fingers brushed against his skin, his eyes grew wide. "Is something wrong?"

"Not at all," he lied again, hastily pocketing the coins. "Be sure to record the exact date and hour of your daughter's birth so that I can create an accurate astrological chart."

Stefania watched from the window as the astrologer exited the courtyard. He took a few steps down the street, stopped, then turned around to meet her gaze before disappearing around the corner.

## CHAPTER 2

On the seventh day of April in the year 1548, as the church bells rang under the midday sun, Stefania Rossi, wife of Vittorio Castagno, gave birth to a living infant. The delivery wasn't without serious complications, and the physician quietly informed the parents that this child would be their last.

Vittorio took a seat beside his wife and gazed in wonder at the baby in her arms. In that instant, Stefania was more beautiful than all of the Madonna and Child paintings in Florence.

"Look at our daughter, Vittorio. She's perfect, is she not?"

"Yes," he replied, gently stroking the downy hair on the infant's head. "Her hair is the color of burnished gold."

"I was told my mother had light hair." She paused, her expression serious. "I know you would have preferred a son."

"Hush," he chided, already smitten with the child. "I'm overjoyed to have a fine, healthy daughter."

Stefania and Vittorio reveled in their new roles as first-time parents—it didn't matter that she was twenty-eight years old or that he was thirty-two. As the days passed, the love they bore for their child grew, but so did their anxiety. What if something happened to them? Who would care for their precious little girl in their absence?

Stefania arranged a private audience with Cosimo soon after recuperating from the birth. A liveried page led her into one of the public rooms of the Palazzo Ducale where the Duke of Florence sat behind a desk.

"Thank you for meeting with me, Your Grace," she said once the servant had departed. "Regrettably, Vittorio could not accompany me today, but he sends his warmest greetings."

"I've told you before, Stefania, there's no need for such formalities when we're alone." He smiled broadly. "You look exceedingly well. I hear congratulations are in order."

"We're so happy, Cosimo. She's a healthy baby, thank

God."

Cosimo crossed himself. "Thank Him, indeed. My wife and I prayed frequently and fervently for the safe delivery of your child. She would have liked to congratulate you personally, but she and her ladies are at Santa Maria Novella with the Spanish ambassador." He paused. "Have you chosen a name?"

"She'll be christened Allegra."

"How fitting. I look forward to meeting her."

"Allegra is the very reason why I've asked to see you. As you know, I have no family and Vittorio is estranged from his brothers. If something were to happen to us, our daughter would be completely alone in the world."

"Are you asking me to be her godfather?"

"You're the only person I trust."

"Rest assured, Stefania. Should anything happen to you or Vittorio, I'll take Allegra into my household and protect her as my own daughter."

"My husband and I are forever in your debt."

An impish grin stretched across his face, instantly transporting her back in time to their youth. He stood. "Come."

"Where are we going?"

"It's a surprise."

She followed Cosimo into an antechamber where he summoned his valet and whispered something into the man's ear. After casting a glance at Stefania, the valet nodded and left the room.

Feeling giddy, she inquired, "What mischief is afoot?"

"You'll see."

They talked of idle things as they waited, but Stefania's curiosity was making it hard to concentrate. At length, the valet returned carrying a tray containing two painted ceramic cups.

"This was gifted to my wife by the Spanish ambassador," Cosimo explained. "I want to share some with you in celebration of your daughter's birth."

She accepted a cup from the valet with a grateful nod. The mysterious brown beverage gave off a strange but pleasant odor.

Cosimo held up his cup. "To Allegra's health."

Stefania took a small sip. The cold, bitter beverage was flavored with vanilla and spices. "What is this?"

"The best-kept secret in the Spanish kingdom. The Dominican monks who accompanied the Spanish ambassador to Tuscany call it *xocolatl*, and they claim it's good for your health, particularly the stomach."

"What is it made from?"

"Cocoa beans from the Viceroyalty of New Spain."

"From the New World," she whispered, intrigued.

"The beans are finely ground into a powder and serve as a base for this drink. You and I are the first Tuscans to taste it. What do you think?"

"It's very good," she said before indulging in another sip. "Adding a bit of honey or sugar may improve the flavor."

"You always did have a penchant for sweets."

***

Vittorio, who could barely tear himself away from his daughter's side, was obliged to visit clients in Venice during the last week of May. Stefania instructed Gianna to summon the astrologer the moment her husband left Florence.

Messer Mancini arrived at the Palazzo Castagno arrayed in red brocade and sporting a massive garnet on his forefinger. A black satchel with strange markings hung from his shoulder. "Felicitations, Signora Stefania."

"A healthy girl, exactly as you predicted," Stefania said, indicating the wooden cradle in the corner.

The astrologer gazed down at the pink-faced infant, then at Stefania. *Her first and last child.* He hastily lowered his eyes before she caught his impertinent stare. A servant entered with a tray containing two glass vessels and a bowl of dried apple slices.

Accepting a goblet from his hostess's hand, he said, "A toast to your daughter's continued good health." He took a sip. "When was she born?"

"On the seventh of April."

"And the time of day?"

"Noon. I heard the church bells ringing."

Messer Mancini sat down and opened his satchel. Inside were scrolls depicting the horoscope and astronomy charts, a journal, a few pieces of graphite for jotting notes, and a deck of tarot cards. At the very bottom was a heavy book bound in black leather.

Opening one of the journals, he wrote: *Allegra Castagno, 7 April 1548, noon.* "I need to consult with the almanac to make a few calculations."

Stefania watched in fascination as he flipped through the book and wrote down several numbers. "I know a bit about astrology…"

He continued writing without looking up. "Oh?"

"Allegra is in the House of Aries—the ram."

"Mmm-hmm."

"From what I hear, it's a good sign. A strong sign."

He turned a page and ran his finger down a column of numbers. "Stubborn would be a better description." He stopped writing and met Stefania's insistent stare. "Are you aware of the direct relationships between the signs of the zodiac, the planets, the stars, and the parts of the human body?"

"No."

"Your daughter is ruled by the planet Mars and her element is fire, which is powerful."

"Detrimentally so?"

"Fire can destroy, but it can also melt something hard in order to make it soft and pliable. With fire, things can be reshaped, *reborn*. It can be positive if used correctly." Leaning over his notes, he added, "I will draw up a chart indicating the most auspicious days for certain decisions or events."

"What about the unlucky days?"

"I will include those, too."

Pointing to the stack of tarot cards, she inquired, "Is it possible to see her future?"

"She's rather young for a reading."

"Do you know any other methods of divination?"

The desperation and fear in the woman's eyes startled him.

He had seen that look before. Miscarriages, stillborn infants, until—*finally*—a living, breathing baby…

Glancing at the closed door, he said, "Fetch the infant."

Stefania gathered Allegra from the cradle and placed her in the astrologer's arms. "Please, tell me anything you can."

Awakened from sleep, the baby stared at the strange man with a frown.

"Hello, little one," he said, caressing her plump cheek with his forefinger. "Aries rules the head and your daughter's eyes are as lively as I expected them to be." His gaze was drawn to the baby's perfectly formed hands, her greatest asset, capable of creating incredible things; pity she wasn't born male. "This child is strong and will live a long life."

A grateful smile tugged at Stefania's lips as she retrieved the baby.

He started collecting his items and placing them back in the satchel. "I'll have my servant deliver the completed chart to your home—"

"No!"

"If you prefer, you may dispatch one of your servants to collect it."

"That would be better," she said before placing Allegra in the cradle.

"Very well. It will be finished by the end of next week. As always, you can count on my discretion."

When he picked up the deck of tarot cards, Stefania asked, "Would you do a reading for me?"

He hesitated. "Perhaps another time."

"Please, I insist."

Although he already knew the woman's future, he reluctantly spread the cards face-down on the table. "Pick one."

Stefania selected a card, which he took from her hand without revealing its face, then placed it at the bottom of the deck. It was the Major Arcana, a skeleton upon a pale horse with sickle in its hand. *Death.*

"Please select another card," he instructed.

"What's wrong with the one I chose?"

"Nothing," he lied. "I have my own method." At least that was true.

The second card she selected depicted a cloaked woman and child seated inside of a boat with six silver swords standing upright.

Stefania's brow creased in worry. "What does it mean?"

"The Six of Swords represents a difficult past, which is now behind you," he replied. "The problem you've been grappling with for a long time has finally been resolved with the birth of your child."

Stefania breathed a sigh of relief before asking two predictable questions. The astrologer replied with two blatant lies.

*Unhappy clients were not good for business.*

# CHAPTER 3

Stefania insisted on feeding Allegra herself rather than follow her husband's suggestion of hiring a wet nurse. When the baby became colicky and her breasts failed to produce enough milk to satisfy the child's growing hunger, she begrudgingly accepted defeat.

Fortunately, procuring high-quality breast milk for babies was an easy task in Florence. Lactating women often advertised their services, and parents were cautioned to be extremely selective since it was widely believed that diseases and humoral qualities could be passed onto infants via breast milk. Some families sent their children to the Casentino Valley because the women from that region were supposedly healthier, and the pestilence-free air of the countryside enabled babies to thrive. Wealthier families maintained a wet nurse in their household.

Before long, little Allegra had her very own live-in wet nurse; a bonny young woman with a cheerful disposition and excellent, abundant breast milk. In a matter of weeks, the baby's weight doubled, much to the delight of her parents. In addition to this, Messer Mancini's astrological chart delineated Allegra's favorable alignment with the moon, which governed over the female sex.

The year 1548 may have brought good fortune to the Castagno household, but it left the opposite on the Medici doorstep. Eleonora gave birth to an unhealthy son in July. Little Antonio was hastily baptized and died shortly afterward. A year later, she gave birth to a healthy son and they christened him Ferdinando.

Eleonora birthed nine children so far, seven survivors. Many Florentines assumed she would stop bearing children, especially when her belly remained flat for the next three years. The duchess took advantage of this childbearing respite to improve their living conditions. After convincing Cosimo that their expanding family was too cramped in the Palazzo Ducale, she used her own funds to purchase the Palazzo Pitti in 1549.

Longtime rivals of the Medici, the Pitti family attempted to build the biggest palazzo in Florence with its very own piazza— a luxury normally reserved for civic or religious edifices. Their plan backfired when the grandiose project forced them into bankruptcy, thus allowing Eleonora to strike a bargain by negotiating a much lower price than the property's actual worth. The Boboli Gardens, specifically created for the duchess's pleasure, were conveniently located directly behind the palazzo, making it the ideal residence for the Medici family.

Plans were drawn up to enlarge the existing structure. The furnishings and artwork procured by Eleonora reflected her refined taste. The Medici continued residing in the Palazzo Ducale and their many country villas during the ongoing construction phase. When they began spending more time at the Palazzo Pitti, entertaining guests and impressing dignitaries, people nicknamed the Palazzo Ducale the "Palazzo Vecchio."

Members of the nobility followed the ruling family's example by purchasing property in the Oltrarno, making it fashionable to own a home in the greener part of town, away from the foul-smelling streets of the city center.

While Eleonora fussed over her new home across the river, Vittorio and Stefania fussed over their daughter. Allegra grew too quickly for Stefania's taste, and the initial joy she had experienced as a mother gradually faded as she became less needed by the child.

"She's getting so big," Vittorio said to his wife one day as they both watched Allegra play with Gianna in the sunny courtyard below.

Stefania sighed sadly and stepped away from the window. "I know. In a way it's such a shame."

Taken aback, he frowned at his wife. "You should be happy."

"I am, but Allegra grows too fast. She rarely sits on my lap anymore, and she doesn't allow me to coddle her."

"She prefers to run and play, which is normal for a child her age. Our daughter is blessed with robust health," he pointed out impatiently. "This is something to celebrate, not weep over."

"I'm not weeping…I want another baby."

"Not again," he said, pinching the bridge of his nose in annoyance.

"Vittorio, please."

"Are you mad, woman?"

"Don't be angry, husband. It's natural for women to want children."

"After years of disappointment, we finally have a perfect daughter. Why can you not be grateful for the gift God has bestowed upon us?"

"I *am* grateful, but Allegra isn't a baby anymore. She doesn't need me."

"Of course, she needs you!" Lowering his voice, he added, "Have you forgotten the difficulty of the birth?"

"I haven't forgotten, but I've prayed to God on the matter many times. He can help me deliver another healthy baby if I put my faith in Him." She paused, her eyes wild. "I need this, Vittorio. My heart is heavy and my mind is restless. Only a baby can cure me."

The bouts of melancholia his wife often suffered throughout their marriage had temporarily subsided after Allegra's birth, but they were gradually returning. As a result, their daughter spent many hours playing alone, usually under Gianna's watchful eye.

He paced the room. "You've inherited your mother's illness—"

"Stop!"

"It's happening again with more frequency."

She covered her ears. "Vittorio, I beg you."

Grabbing hold of her hands, he gently pried them away from her head. "She, too, suffered from this malady and took her own life because of it."

"Please, let's not talk of her…"

"I don't want the same thing to happen to you." In a gentler tone, he suggested, "Maybe you should go to church daily

24

instead of only twice a week. God's Holy Spirit will ease the restlessness within your soul and guide you toward peace."

"All the masses in Florence cannot help me."

Vittorio stormed across the room to close the door. "It's bad enough that I defy Holy Mother Church by wasting my seed in order to not impregnate you. Now you want me to commit the sin of murder?"

She recoiled. "Murder?"

"Lower your voice," he snapped. "Yes, *murder*. If you carry another child to full term, there's a good chance you'll die during the delivery. That's precisely what the physician told me."

"My body is still strong," she insisted. "We need to have faith."

"You should heed your own counsel, wife, and have faith in God's wisdom. If He wanted you to have more children, then He would have provided them."

"I know for a fact that I'm destined to be a mother many times over."

"How could you possibly know such a thing?"

She hesitated, debating whether or not to reveal her secret. Finally, she confessed, "Messer Mancini informed me that I would bear more children and enjoy a long life."

His eyes narrowed. "You consulted with him behind my back?"

"I invited him here shortly after our daughter's birth." Seeing her husband's expression, she quickly added, "You were away on business."

"You allowed that warlock into my home?"

"He is a respected astrologer."

"The practice of divination is clearly forbidden in the Holy Scriptures."

"I had him draw up Allegra's astrological chart, nothing more. Besides, he's been employed by various noble families, including the Medici." Vittorio's icy stare compelled her to add, "I refrained from telling you because I knew you wouldn't approve."

"You try my patience, Stefania."

"He read my cards," she pressed. "I asked him if I was destined for a long life and if I would bear more children."

"Whatever that unholy man told you—"

"He answered 'yes' to both of my questions."

"I will not hear any more on this matter."

"But, Vittorio…"

Vittorio left the room without a backward glance.

Meanwhile, Allegra had managed to escape Gianna's watchful eye and wandered into her father's workshop. Scattered upon the long workbench were several colorful gemstones sparkling in the sunlight. She climbed onto the chair, teetering precariously on its seat. The yellow gleam of a broken bracelet caught her eye.

"Gold," she whispered, her blue gray eyes wide with wonder.

Taking hold of the shiny bracelet in her chubby hand, she examined it with a studious expression before reaching for a set of small pliers. She aligned the links accurately and tightened them, exactly as she had seen her father do on many occasions.

Vittorio entered the workshop. "Allegra, no!"

"I fix it," the little girl cried triumphantly.

Surprised to see the bracelet properly repaired, he embraced his daughter and kissed her forehead. "Yes, you did."

Gianna appeared in the doorway, breathless with flushed cheeks. "There you are! This clever girl is getting too fast for me."

Vittorio attempted to hand Allegra over to Gianna, but she clung to her father. "Papa, no!"

Gianna put her hands on her ample hips. "Come along, child, your father has work to do."

Allegra's lower lip quivered and tears gathered in her eyes. Seeing this, Vittorio sighed and waved Gianna away.

"You'll spoil her, Signore Vittorio," the wise servant muttered.

"Perhaps," he conceded, setting his daughter down on a stool beside him.

In 1553, shortly after her fifth birthday, Allegra suffered a serious bout of fever. Stefania feared she would perish, but the fever broke by the end of the second day. After that harrowing experience, the child was immune to almost every ailment that befell the city, yet that did not stop Stefania from becoming an overprotective mother.

Eleonora gave birth to a girl around the same time, but little Anna did not survive long. Some people whispered that the duchess's birth canal was ruined; worn away from too much usage. After all, she already walked with a slight limp from damaged hips. Maybe it was time for her body to take a much-needed rest. Eleonora stopped the wagging tongues when she delivered her eleventh child, Pietro, in June 1554. He was a healthy boy who thrived, and the last child she would ever bear in her lifetime.

# CHAPTER 4

The last remaining rival left in Tuscany for Cosimo to conquer was the Republic of Siena. Their refusal to acknowledge Medici power in the region instigated a series of drawn-out battles that came to be known as the Italian wars. The Battle of Marciano in August 1554 marked the end of the fighting. Despite a valiant effort, Siena lost its independence to the Duchy of Florence. It was a humiliating defeat for the proud Sienese. Cosimo added insult to injury by affixing enormous Medici coats of arms throughout the city for all to see.

With all of Tuscany submissively under their rule, Cosimo and Eleonora could concentrate on forging and strengthening political alliances outside of the region. They hosted a party at the Palazzo Pitti in the spring of 1557 to celebrate the betrothal of their firstborn, Maria, to Alfonso II d'Este. The marriage was an attempt to seal a peace treaty between the Este family and Cosimo's ally, King Phillip of Spain.

Banquet tables groaned beneath the weight of delectable treats as minstrels performed enchanting ballads.

"Do you think Allegra is all right?" Stefania asked for the third time.

Vittorio sighed. "Can't we enjoy ourselves for one evening without your incessant worrying?"

"Forgive me, husband."

"Gianna will put her to bed soon, and she'll have sweet dreams." He brought her knuckles to his lips. "Now, let's eat. I'm famished."

They supped on roasted venison and wild boar stew accompanied by fresh vegetables and cheeses, followed by an array of sugary cakes and pies.

After the lavish meal, Cosimo approached Stefania. At age thirty-seven she was still a striking woman and, despite his devotion to Eleonora, he could not help but admire his former lover's beauty. "I'm happy to see you and Vittorio here tonight. I hope you're both enjoying yourselves."

"The party is wonderful." Looking at Maria, she added, "Your daughter seems pleased. She's such a lovely young woman."

Following her gaze, he said, "How quickly they grow up. I can hardly believe she's to be married." He paused. "Tell me, how is my godchild?"

"Allegra is doing well. She's a clever girl."

"I can't remember when I saw her last—or you, for that matter."

"Vittorio is away on business so often...I rarely go out."

"You must instruct him to remain in Florence." She laughed without humor, prompting him to add, "There's no reason why you can't attend our gatherings without him. We grew up together, Stefania, you're practically family. No one would dare speak ill of you for being present in my home without your husband."

"Thank you, but my daughter takes up most of my time. As you probably know, I'm completely devoted to her."

"She must get lonely."

Stefania lowered her eyes. "I wish I could have provided her with many brothers and sisters."

"God has his reasons, my dear. Be grateful that you have Allegra."

"We are, Cosimo. She's a source of constant joy to Vittorio and I."

"I don't doubt it." He paused. "There are several boys and girls from noble households who come to play in the gardens," he said with a sweeping gesture toward a nearby window.

In the Pitti family's attempt to outdo the Medici, the windows were designed to be as big as the front door of the Palazzo Medici on Via Larga. Well, at least that was the rumor. Regardless of whether or not this was true, they offered a pleasant view of the Boboli Gardens. Stefania's gaze fell upon pathways and fountains amid the expanse of greenery.

He continued, "I believe Eleonora is organizing something

for the children this week. Why not bring Allegra?"

She hesitated, unsure. "I don't know…"

"It will be good for her to play with other children."

Finally, she relented. "That would be lovely, thank you."

***

The young Medici hosts were charmingly dressed in red and gold, the colors of their family crest. Sections of the Boboli Gardens were decorated with festoons of yellow and white flowers, and the servants had set up a Maypole with multicolored ribbons. An assortment of tiny cakes and sugared fruits were prettily displayed on a nearby table.

Eleonora and a spattering of noblewomen fanned themselves beneath the shade of trees while servants kept a close eye on the children. Allegra dutifully kissed her godmother before two Medici girls, Isabella and Lucrezia, took her by the hand and led her to the Maypole. Stefania politely greeted her impeccably dressed hostess, smiled at the other noble ladies present, then took a seat among them.

Maria de' Medici, considered an adult after her betrothal, sat with the women. She appeared abnormally pale, coughing frequently into a lace handkerchief. Stefania couldn't help but wonder if she was contagious. The women indulged in harmless gossip until a liveried boy arrived with a tray of chalices containing diluted white wine.

"It's delightfully cold," one of the ladies commented after taking a sip.

"We store the bottles in our grotto," Eleonora explained as she waved her bejeweled hand toward the garden. Her gaze fell upon Stefania. "Signora Stefania, I'm glad you accepted our invitation. We have not seen our godchild in a long time."

"My apologies, Your Grace. Thank you for the invitation. Allegra was overjoyed at the prospect of playing with your children."

Eleonora glanced at the laughing children. "My husband should be here shortly. I'm sure he'll be pleased to see you and your daughter."

The eyes of the other ladies slid in Stefania's direction as

30

she replied, "It's always an honor to see His Grace."

"Signora Stefania and her husband, Signore Vittorio Castagno, grew up in the Mugello alongside the duke," Eleonora explained for the benefit of the curious women, although the majority of them were already aware of this fact.

Maria leaned forward in her chair. "Was my father a precocious boy, Signora Stefania?"

"Oh yes."

"Was he a troublesome lad?"

Eleonora frowned. "Maria."

Stefania smiled. "No more troublesome than any other child, my lady. Your father was exceptionally clever and well-read. It was clear to everyone that he was destined for greatness."

"You also knew my grandmother."

Stefania nodded. "We all held Signora Maria Salviati in the highest esteem. She was considered a moral pillar in the Mugello."

"Your grandmother was her good friend, isn't that so?"

"Yes, the two were rather close," Stefania replied as the memories of her joyful youth flooded her mind.

Eleonora rose, ending the conversation. "I think the children must be thirsty by now. Shall we, ladies?"

The ladies followed the duchess toward servants bearing trays of watered wine mixed with honey. Standing off to the side watching the children was the Medici heir, Francesco, accompanied by his faithful friend and mentor, Bernardo Buontalenti.

Francesco was quiet, awkward, and somewhat reclusive. His interests were as odd as his manner—alchemy, chemistry, astrology, and the occult. Bernardo, who was ten years older than Francesco, was admired for his many talents, which included painting, sculpture, and architecture. Taken under Cosimo's wing at the age of sixteen after losing his family in a terrible accident, Bernardo quickly became a favorite of the Medici court. He had received instruction from the very best Florentine masters—Bronzino, Michelangelo, and Vasari—and he loved to cook. Due to his passion for fine cuisine, one of

Bernardo's responsibilities at court was to plan sumptuous feasts, which were always highly praised events.

Maria, who had not accompanied the ladies to the banquet tables, sat alone beneath the trees. Seeing this, Francesco and Bernardo went to keep her company. They had the young woman laughing in no time at all.

Cosimo quietly exited the palazzo and surprised his three-year-old son, Pietro, by swooping him up into the air. The little boy squealed in delight.

Allegra greeted her godfather before running off with the other children. The blonde highlights in her hair shone brightly in the sun, creating a golden halo around her head.

"She's growing up to be a fine young lady. Pretty, too," Cosimo said, his eyes following the graceful movements of his willowy godchild.

Stefania smiled proudly. "Thank you."

"Does she ride?"

"No."

Cosimo met her gaze. "An accomplished lady should know how to properly handle a horse. I employ highly-trained grooms to teach my children. Every morning they ride to San Miniato al Monte and the countryside beyond. Why not have Allegra join them? I have plenty of horses in my stables."

*Allegra could fall off of the horse, break her neck, and die.* "I appreciate your generous offer, but..."

The fear that crept into Stefania's eyes did not go unnoticed by Cosimo. "I know you worry about Allegra—as you should—but your daughter isn't made of glass. Children are incredibly resilient. I should know, I have many. They fall and scrape their knees, but they get back up and run off as if nothing happened. You can't hide your daughter from the world forever."

"You're right, of course. I only worry about her getting hurt."

"Have you forgotten how much *we* enjoyed riding our horses? Why deprive Allegra of something that once brought you such pleasure?"

Stefania recalled the exhilaration of galloping through the

lush green hills of the Mugello with Cosimo at her side. They were young and carefree back then, oblivious to danger. The invigorating feel of the wind in her hair as the horse beneath her pounded his hooves against the earth was forever engraved into her memory.

"I miss those days," she admitted quietly.

They shared a brief, intimate look before he cleared his throat and turned away. "Speak with Vittorio and, if he agrees, Allegra can begin her riding lessons immediately."

Later that day, Stefania and Allegra described the party to Vittorio in vivid detail.

"Lucrezia called me her god sister," Allegra announced proudly.

Vittorio chuckled. "I hate to disappoint you, dearest, but there's no such thing as a god sister."

"Cosimo offered our daughter riding lessons," Stefania said. "He told me to speak with you and, if you're in agreement, she can begin at once."

Allegra added, "Lucrezia has already picked out a pony for me. She's gray and white, and her name is Dolcezza because she has a sweet temperament."

"Isabella and Lucrezia went out of their way to make our daughter feel welcome today," Stefania explained. "Since Lucrezia and Allegra are close in age, the two of them were inseparable this afternoon."

"Please say yes, Papa."

Vittorio nodded. "I think it's a fine idea." *One is never too young to form valuable alliances.*

The lessons commenced the following week. To her parents' surprise, Allegra's newfound interest in horses didn't diminish her passion for goldsmithing. Every afternoon, she sat beside her father and fashioned discarded scraps of precious metals into whimsical shapes.

On a hot August morning, Lucrezia said to Allegra, "I want to tell you something, but you must swear not to repeat my words."

"I swear."

"I'm worried about my sister."

Lucrezia wasn't prone to hysteria; she faced life with practicality and levelheadedness. For her to be worried, the situation must be serious, indeed. "Maria isn't getting better, is she?"

"I overheard my parents whispering last night. They said she may have contracted a serious illness. I fear she's going to die."

Allegra crossed herself. "Don't say such a thing."

Lucrezia crossed herself, too. "Forgive me, but her upcoming marriage is so important…Mother keeps telling us to pray to God for Maria's swift recovery." She paused, her eyes glistening with unshed tears. "If she dies, I'll be offered to Alfonso in order to salvage the peace treaty."

"Hopefully, it won't come to that."

"There's a good possibility that it will, and there's nothing to be done. Isabella was betrothed to the Duke of Bracciano against her wishes, but what can she do? What can any noblewoman do? My sisters and I have been groomed since birth to be the wives of men chosen by my father. In truth, I don't want to get married to anyone."

It was common knowledge that noble daughters were little more than political pawns to be used by ambitious fathers for the gain of money, lands, and military support. The stakes were even higher for the Medici.

Allegra thought for a moment. "You could claim sanctuary in a convent."

Lucrezia laughed bitterly. "One prison in exchange for another?"

"I'll continue to pray for your sister's recovery. Don't worry, God will answer our prayers."

"I hope you're right, dear friend."

By mid-September, Maria was bedridden. The best physicians were summoned, several cures were prescribed, but her condition worsened daily. The poor young woman was bled, forced to drink crushed pearls, and bathed in hot milk. Despite these measures, she died at the tender age of seventeen on the nineteenth of November.

Maria's funeral took place in the Basilica of San Lorenzo, where she was laid to rest in a gown the color of lilacs. Cosimo walked down the nave after the service and knelt on the circle of porphyry marble located directly before the high altar. Buried beneath the royal stone was his great ancestor, *Cosimo Pater Patriae*, whom the Florentines began referring to as *Cosimo il Vecchio* in order to distinguish between the man who currently ruled the city and his long-dead ancestor.

Crossing himself after uttering a brief prayer, he stood and walked toward his daughter's coffin. Eleonora and her black-clad ladies followed him at a slight distance like an undulating murder of crows. Heavily armed guards quietly accompanied the Medici retinue.

The church overflowed with mourners who had come to pay their respects, including the Castagno family. Allegra noticed that Lucrezia seemed particularly distraught, and she did her best to comfort her friend. Their attention was diverted by Bernardo, who came to stand beside Lucrezia. She looked up to him as one would an older brother.

"Do you see that man over there?" he asked.

Both young women followed his gaze. A richly-dressed nobleman stood on the far side of the church staring at them.

Lucrezia inquired, "Who is he?"

"Alfonso's uncle," Bernardo replied. "He's here to represent the Este family, as a gesture of respect for Maria."

"He's also studying me closely in order to offer an accurate report."

Allegra commented, "I'm sure your beauty and good manners will be highly praised." Bernardo snorted derisively and Lucrezia made a face, prompting her to add, "I'm sorry, did I say something wrong?"

"You lack deception," Bernardo observed. "Your naiveté is endearing, Signorina Allegra. You are living proof that there is hope in this world."

"Forgive me, Signore Bernardo. I don't understand…"

Lucrezia intervened, "The Este family isn't concerned with my beauty or my charms."

Allegra's brow creased in confusion. "I thought he's here to make a report on you."

Lucrezia narrowed her eyes at the man across the room, then said, "He's been sent here to make certain that I'm not sickly and frail like my sister, Maria. The only report Alfonso wants to hear from his uncle is that I look healthy enough to bear him sons. That man over there is the farmer, you see, and I, the broodmare."

## CHAPTER 5

In July 1558, Lucrezia wed Alfonso II d'Este. To her relief, she remained in Florence because her husband was off fighting a war in France.

"How does it feel to be a wife?" Allegra inquired a few days after the wedding. They were out riding their horses in the countryside.

Lucrezia shrugged. "My husband departed so soon after the ceremony, I've barely had time to adjust to my new role."

"At least the duke is young and handsome."

"I can't deny that," Lucrezia conceded. "Alfonso is quite good looking."

"He seemed pleasant toward you during the wedding celebration."

"Formal would be a better description."

"Maybe, in time, you two will fall in love."

Lucrezia studied her friend. "I believe you are a romantic."

Allegra blushed. It was true; she enjoyed reading stories of courtly love and poetry written by the great troubadours. "Is that a bad thing?"

"No, but it can be a dangerous thing."

"How so?"

"I'm a few years older than you, and have been watching the young men at my father's court since I was a child. Whenever there's a new young lady present, the competition among the men begins—lavish compliments, gifts, and declarations of love abound until the lady surrenders to one of them. Once she does, the man will inevitably lose interest and go on to the next conquest. If the lady is lucky, all she'll suffer is a broken heart. If the man in question is a cad, she may lose her good reputation."

Allegra's face paled. "This can't be true of all men."

"No," Lucrezia conceded. "But more often than not it is. I'm telling you this as your friend. You'll be presented to society soon, and you don't want to be like a lamb among the wolves."

"What advice do you have to offer?"

"Guard your heart and keep it safe, don't trust men."

The Medici celebrated another wedding in September of that same year. In an attempt to secure the Tuscan border, Isabella was given in marriage to Paolo Giordano Orsini, Duke of Bracciano. Unlike Alfonso, her charming and handsome brother-in-law, Paolo was stout, unattractive, and brash.

To Isabella's relief, her husband left the following day, leaving his bride and her sizeable dowry behind in Florence. Cosimo himself had insisted upon this unusual arrangement because he distrusted his son-in-law. His desire to keep his daughter close was a blessing in disguise to Isabella. As a married woman with plenty of money at her own disposal, she enjoyed considerable freedom and exercised control over her own affairs; much more so than was customary for Florentine women.

Freed from the clutches of their husbands, the Medici sisters attended parties and other social events with their maids and ladies as chaperones. They continued to ride their horses through the lush Tuscan countryside each morning, and Allegra was grateful for their company. She looked up to the two older girls as role models, and someday hoped to enjoy a similar liberal marriage arrangement.

\*\*\*

Two years later, Lucrezia broke Allegra's heart as they rode their horses along the city wall toward San Niccolò. "I received news last night of my husband's safe return to Ferrara."

Knowing her friend's departure was both imminent and inevitable, Allegra began to cry. She reigned Dolcezza to a halt, and watched her breath form vaporous swirls in the cold February morning.

Lucrezia urged her horse closer to the mare. "Don't cry, Allegra. We knew this day would come. At least Isabella will still be here in Florence. She's very fond of you."

"I have great affection for your sister, but she's not you."

38

"We can continue our friendship through correspondence."

"As much as your letters will gladden my heart, it's not the same as seeing you and hearing your voice," Allegra lamented, wiping the wetness from her face. "You'll be sorely missed."

"I'll miss you, too."

Allegra reached into the pouch at her waist and pulled out a sapphire ring. "I've been keeping abreast of the news and carrying this around for several months. I knew it was only a matter of time before Alfonso demanded your return. This is for you, something to remember me by."

Lucrezia gazed in awe at the ring before slipping it onto her middle finger. "What an unusual design. I love it, thank you."

"Can I tell you a secret?" Allegra waited for her friend to nod before confessing, "I made it myself."

Lucrezia stared at her incredulously. "You made this? How?"

"My father taught me. I've been making jewelry for years, actually."

"Does anyone else know about this?"

Allegra shook her head. "He told me never to tell anyone."

"Your father is right. Women aren't meant to do the work of men. The magistrates and the clergy would disapprove, not to mention the guilds. Don't worry, I'll never reveal your secret." Looking down at the fine ring, she added, "I'll treasure your gift forever."

The sadness Allegra experienced after Lucrezia's departure lasted weeks. During this time, she consoled herself at her father's side, sketching out new ideas and experimenting with new designs.

"I'm worried about our daughter," Stefania said to Vittorio one day.

"It's normal for her to miss her friend," he pointed out. "She'll be fine, you'll see. Come and take some fresh air with me on the terrace."

"I thought you had work to do."

"I have a moment to spare, and the day is pleasant."

They stepped onto the terrace and admired the vista. A sea

of terracotta rooftops stretched toward the Arno River. The water shimmered beneath the early afternoon sunshine while a balmy breeze caressed their faces.

Stefania closed her eyes and whispered, "When we were first married, I believed we would have a house full of children. Sometimes, when I'm alone and the house is quiet, I imagine the sounds of their laughter and running footsteps."

Vittorio took hold of her hand. "That was my dream, too. God must have had his reasons for denying us a bigger family." He paused. "Stefania, I've been thinking…You give alms to the poor, so why not spread your Christian charity to the Spedale degli Innocenti?"

"Our servants disperse bread and coins to the city's monasteries and convents on a daily basis, including that one."

"Yes, but I'm suggesting that *you* go to the orphanage to spend time with the orphans." When she continued looking at him askance, he explained, "Bestowing affection and attention on the needy children may ease your restless spirit, my love. Besides, I'm sure the nuns would appreciate the extra help."

It seemed foolish to Stefania that she had never thought of this idea before. She and Gianna set off for the orphanage located in the Piazza della Santissima Annunziata in a hired litter the following morning. When they knocked on the door of the Spedale degli Innocenti, a middle-aged nun with rosy cheeks opened the door.

"Buongiorno," Stefania said. "I would like to speak with whomever is in charge."

The nun waved them inside. "That would be me. I'm Sister Federica. How can I be of service, Signora…?"

Stefania motioned to Gianna, who handed the nun a heavy coin purse. "My name is Stefania Castagno. Please accept this gift on behalf of our household."

The nun inclined her head in gratitude. "God bless you and your family for this act of generosity."

Stefania eyes darted around the room. "Where are the children?"

"Most of them are learning their catechism right now."

"Perhaps I can see them afterward?"

Sister Federica's brow creased slightly. "The midday meal follows catechism, then the children are taught basic skills in order to be apprenticed to blacksmiths, butchers, and other tradesmen when they're old enough." She paused and added tactfully, "You can rest assured that your monetary gift will be put to good use."

Stefania did not move. "Actually, I wish to see the babies."

"Are you and your husband wanting to adopt a child?"

"Not exactly…I wanted to hold them, if possible." The nun's eyes narrowed and Stefania licked her lips nervously. "I'm unable to have any more children, and my daughter is almost a young lady. I thought that, maybe, I could help the nuns in caring for the orphaned infants."

"I understand," Sister Federica said as realization lit up her plain features. "I was married once—many years ago. I could not provide my husband with an heir, so he remarried and my family forced me into a convent."

"I'm sorry," Stefania offered.

"Christ is a *much* better husband, I assure you," the nun said cheerfully. "Come this way. We have a total of nine infants at the moment and we would gladly accept any help in caring for them."

Stefania and Gianna were led into a room full of tiny beds and mismatched cradles that were obviously donated. A young novice was trying to change a baby out of its soiled linens while pacifying another one who cried loudly. The sound awakened Stefania's maternal instinct, and she immediately took the fussing baby into her arms, leaving the novice to finish her messy task.

"There, there, little one. Hush now," Stefania cooed while gently rocking the infant. Soothed, the chubby blonde boy smiled, melting her heart in the process. "Sister Federica, I can come help you every day, if you wish."

The nun crossed herself. "God be praised."

Stefania developed a rigid daily schedule that began at dawn. She would spend the entire morning at the orphanage and arrive home in time for the midday meal. Sometimes, she returned in the evening if any of the children were ill or there was a shortage of available nuns. As Vittorio had predicted, the needy infants soon filled the emptiness in her life.

Gianna watched over Allegra in her mother's absence, deepening the already existing bond between the two of them. When Allegra's womanly flow began, the kind servant comforted the girl and concocted a tonic to ease her painful cramps.

Stefania came home later that day and found her daughter in bed. "What ails you, child?"

Gianna emerged from the antechamber followed by a servant carrying a basket of freshly washed linens. "Allegra became a woman this morning."

"It hurts," Allegra whimpered as she clutched her lower abdomen.

Stefania's eyes misted as she stroked Allegra's hair. "The pain only lasts a few days."

"Why does womanhood have to involve any pain at all?"

Stefania smiled without mirth. "This is only the beginning, my dear."

***

The year 1560 was a difficult year for Allegra. In addition to Lucrezia's departure from Florence, there were failed assassination attempts on her beloved godfather. Pandolfo Pucci, a longtime favorite of Cosimo, conspired with others to kill the Medici ruler after a heated argument. One of the plans involved waiting by the window of the Palazzo Pucci, and shooting Cosimo with a pistol as he passed on the street. Another plan was to hide gunpowder in Cosimo's bedchamber while he was at mass, then quietly ignite it when he went to bed. What later came to be known as the Pucci Conspiracy led to the decapitation of a few traitorous men, and Pandolfo himself being hanged from the window of the Bargello.

# CHAPTER 6

In April 1561, a little over one year after moving to Ferrara, Lucrezia de' Medici died. Cosimo and Eleonora were stricken by this unexpected news. Reports of their daughter suffering fever, severe weight loss, and constant nosebleeds were met with suspicion. Soon, the question was on everyone's mind: could Lucrezia have been poisoned?

Rumors spread quickly throughout the city. In light of the recent Pucci Conspiracy, Medici allies seized the opportunity to prove their loyalty to their ruler. Several noblemen met with Cosimo one night in order to broach the topic of vendetta. In hushed tones, they delineated an elaborate assassination plot against Alfonso. Reluctant to act precipitously, Cosimo shook his head at their ideas.

"Your Grace, someone must have poisoned your daughter," reasoned one of the men. "Signora Lucrezia's odd symptoms beg investigation."

Cosimo sighed. "Her body was thoroughly examined and there was no proof of poison."

"There was no proof of *arsenic* poisoning, but there are other less detectable toxins that can be obtained at an exorbitant price."

The gentleman at his side interjected, "And the Este family is wealthy enough to procure such rare poison."

"We can't allow this crime to go unpunished," said another.

Cosimo frowned. "I'm not fully convinced of my son-in-law's guilt in this matter."

"My lord—"

Cosimo banged his hand on the table, startling the men. "I will not shed blood and risk a battle between Florence and Ferrara on mere speculation." Narrowing his eyes, he warned, "If anyone acts against my authority by carrying out this scheme, he'll be sent to the gallows. Have I been clear?"

Wide-eyed and fearful, the men nodded.

Cosimo sat back in his chair and sighed tiredly. "God saw fit to pluck my eldest child in the prime of her life. Despite our best efforts, Maria died of illness, so why can't the same be true of Lucrezia?"

There was no more talk of vendetta after that night, and no proof of wrongdoing ever surfaced from the court of Ferrara.

News of Lucrezia's untimely death came as a devastating shock to Allegra. There was never any mention of illness in the letters she'd received from Ferrara, which was both unusual and worrisome. Did Lucrezia suspect someone of intercepting her correspondence? If so, what was she afraid of? Were the rumors true? Could she have been poisoned?

Shortly after learning of her friend's death, Allegra received a message stating that Dolcezza obtained an infection in her hoof, which spread to her leg. The mare had to be put down.

Allegra fell into a deep state of sadness. She barely ate, barely spoke, and spent most of her time closeted in the workshop mourning the loss of her friend and her horse.

"She'll get sick at this rate," Stefania said to Vittorio one evening after supper. "Have you noticed how thin she's become?"

"I'm worried about her, too. Maybe we should get her a cat or a dog," he suggested. "An animal companion would lift her spirits."

"Gianna has been administering her most potent tonics, but I don't see any improvement in Allegra's mood or appetite."

"It's time to call the physician."

Stefania shook her head. "He'll prod and poke her, then bleed her, which will only worsen her condition."

"What do you propose we do? Get her another horse?"

"There's only one thing in this world that offers Allegra both joy and consolation, and she needs it now more than ever. I wish to propose an idea."

Unable to sleep, Allegra went downstairs to select a book to read. Hearing her parents talking in the library, she cautiously peeked into the room.

Stefania continued, "I think it's time we secure an apprenticeship for our daughter. She needs instruction from a master goldsmith."

Allegra stepped back into the hallway and pressed herself against the wall, her heart racing with excitement.

"Don't be absurd," Vittorio chided.

"Have you seen her sketches lately? She has transformed the pain of loss into the most incredible designs I've ever seen."

"Her designs are extraordinary, I agree, but there isn't a single bottega in Florence that would accept a girl."

"We swore to deprive our child of nothing."

"Allegra has never been deprived of anything! She's been afforded a good education, she can read, write, and even speak Latin. There are male heirs in Florence who can barely spell their names."

"Allegra was born to be a goldsmith. She has the power to transform any scrap of metal you give her into something wonderful."

"Yes, she does," he agreed. "Had she been born a boy..."

Hearing this, Allegra ran off in tears.

Gianna stood at the top of the stairwell wearing a scowl. "Signorina Allegra, must I remind you that it's impolite to eavesdrop?"

Ignoring the reprimand, Allegra said, "I hate being a girl."

"What nonsense is this?"

"I want to be a goldsmith but my father won't allow it."

"Although you're extremely clever, you're still young—"

"I'm thirteen years old!"

"Your father knows what's best for your future. Now run along and go to bed. It's late."

Allegra could not stop thinking about her father's words as she lay in bed that night. *Had she been born a boy...*

The following morning, Vittorio announced his imminent departure to Rome. Hearing this, a plan unfurled in Allegra's head. The moment her father's carriage disappeared from view, she ran into the workshop and extracted careful measures of silver and gold from his supply. For the next few days, she worked arduously to create a pendant.

Gianna and her mother usually napped after the heavy midday meal. When the household grew silent, Allegra donned her plainest gown and a black cloak. Pulling the hood low to conceal her face, she hid the pendant in her bodice and crept outside. Luckily, no one was in the courtyard as she tiptoed to the gate. The moment she was on the street, she walked briskly toward the Palazzo Strozzi. The corners of her lips lifted at the thought of the goldsmith's possible reactions when he saw her work. Would he be surprised at her skill in relation to her age? Pleased? Perhaps even *amazed*?

A toothless man stepped into Allegra's path, causing her to gasp aloud in surprise. She was about to abandon her plan and run home when she noticed the man's milky eyes.

"Forgive me," he croaked while tapping his walking stick on ground.

Allegra sidestepped the blind man and slipped into the Piazza delle Cipolle where vendors sold melons, cabbages, and other foodstuffs. Pigeons and rats scurried around her feet foraging for scraps as she pressed between shoppers and market stalls. She stifled a giggle as an old woman balancing a basket of onions on her head collided with a man carrying a rickety cage of chickens. Flying feathers and cackling hens created a momentary ruckus before the two vendors cursed each other and went their separate ways.

Allegra crossed the market and headed for the small bottega located a few doors down from the imposing Palazzo Strozzi. The simple sign above the door read: ORAFO. The bottega itself was humble—certainly not the best in town—but it was the closest to her home. Taking a deep breath, she opened the door and went inside. A middle-aged goldsmith was in the process of demonstrating the technique for soldering silver when he noticed that none of his apprentices were paying attention to him. Following the curious gazes of the boys, he noticed Allegra.

He set down his tools and studied her with a quizzical expression. "Are you lost, child?"

"No sir." When he continued to stare at her expectantly, she said, "I'm here because I want to be a goldsmith."

Everyone gaped at her with a stunned expression before bursting into laughter. "I have work to do, girl. Stop wasting my time."

"I know how to make things with silver and gold. I can prove it to you." She reached into her bodice and pulled out the pendant. Holding it out for his inspection, she added, "I made this by myself."

He took a step closer and frowned. "That pendant is worth quite a lot of money. Where did you get it?"

"I—I told you, I made it."

Peering dubiously at Allegra, he demanded, "Did you steal it?"

"What?" This was definitely not the reaction she had envisioned.

"I'm going to ask you one last time—"

"I made it in my father's workshop."

"Not only are you a thief, you're a liar," he said, snatching the pendant from her hand.

"I'm telling the truth, I swear. Please, I need to be apprenticed to a bottega so that I can learn more things."

He smiled derisively. "Do you see any girls here?"

To Allegra's mortification, all the boys were staring at her with contempt in their eyes. Defeated, she replied, "No, I don't. I assumed you'd make an exception if you saw what I was capable of."

The goldsmith picked up his tools and turned his back on her. "Never assume anything of anyone. Go home, girl, before I have you arrested by the Otto."

The Otto di Guardia policed the streets and markets with the authority to arrest anyone who disturbed civil order. Allegra remained unfazed by the threat, however. "I'm not leaving without my pendant."

"I'm taking it to the authorities. They'll eventually find the rightful owner."

Allegra's hands balled into fists. "I *am* the rightful owner,

47

you fool!"

Resisting the temptation to strike the girl for her impertinence, the goldsmith eyed one of the boys and cocked his head to the side. A tall, thin apprentice with reddish hair ran forward, grabbed Allegra by the arm, and forced her outside. She struggled as he marched her toward the market.

"Let go of me! How dare you!"

"*How dare I?*" he sneered. "You barge into the bottega with a stolen piece of jewelry—"

"Are you deaf? I didn't steal it! I made it!"

The boy rolled his eyes. "Of course you did."

"Obviously, you're as thickheaded as your master."

"Go away, you stupid girl."

Furious, Allegra pushed the apprentice, who stumbled slightly but easily regained his balance. Angered by her provocation, he shoved her, causing her to fall to the ground.

Allegra fervently wished she possessed the physical strength to beat the boy senseless. Staring up at him from the slimy cobblestones, she choked back tears of indignation.

"Serves you right for stealing and telling lies," he snapped, evoking snickers from those within earshot.

A nearby cabbage vendor eyed her with a mixture of amusement and disdain. She wanted to hit him, too.

"Where are your parents, anyway?" he demanded, his eyes darting around the Piazza delle Cipolle. "I hope they administer a sound beating to teach you some manners."

*I should never have come here.* Had she been born male, none of this would have happened.

The apprentice gave her a withering look and mumbled under his breath before retracing his steps to the bottega.

No one spoke a single word of comfort or offered assistance as Allegra rose to her feet on shaky legs. To her dismay, the hem of her dress was soiled with horse dung. Feeling the heat of mocking stares, she tilted her head back and glared at the people in the market.

A flamboyantly dressed man strode across the piazza to where she stood. Doffing his plumed hat, he bowed, drawing

48

curious looks from passerby. "Ignore these simpletons," he advised, sotto voce. "They cannot possibly fathom the extent of your talent."

"I beg your pardon?"

The man straightened and smiled. "Allow me to introduce myself. I am Messer Mancini, and I'd be happy to escort you home, Signorina Allegra."

Eyeing him warily, she demanded, "How do you know my name?"

"I know everyone's name in Florence, my dear girl— everyone worth knowing, that is."

Allegra's eyes slid to the bottega. The goldsmith and the impertinent apprentice hovered in the doorway. "Do you know them, too?"

Following her gaze, he nodded in response to her question. "I also know that you're far more determined and clever than they'll ever be."

"I am?"

"Oh, yes. In time, you'll learn to hone those traits and use them to your advantage—like weapons." He offered Allegra his arm. "Shall we go?"

*Weapons against men*, she vowed, slipping her hand into the crook of his elbow.

They walked the short distance to the Palazzo Castagno in relative silence, and were ushered inside by a flustered servant. Stefania rushed into the main hall and stopped short at the sight of the astrologer.

"Buona sera, Signora Stefania," Messer Mancini said. "I came across your daughter in the Piazza delle Cipolle and took the liberty of escorting her home."

Stefania shot Allegra a reproving glance while taking in her disheveled appearance. "Thank you for your courtesy, Messer Mancini. The entire household has been searching for her."

Looking from mother to daughter, he said, "Well, I'm sure you two have much to discuss, so I'll take my leave."

"Please show him out," Stefania mumbled to the servant.

"There's no need, I remember the way. I can show myself

out. Good day to you both." He walked away, feeling extremely satisfied with himself.

"Mother, how do you know that man?"

"Never mind that now," Stefania snapped. "Have you lost your wits?"

"I can explain—"

"Explain? I've never laid a hand on you, Allegra, but you deserve a sound beating for this act of…of…sheer recklessness. Why did you sneak out like that? What were you trying to accomplish?"

"I didn't mean to cause any trouble."

Gianna appeared in the doorway looking both relieved and irritated. "There you are! I've been searching all over—" She stopped short as Vittorio's voice called out from the courtyard.

Stefania ran to the window. "Santa Madonna! Your father is here."

Allegra panicked. "I thought he was due to come home tomorrow."

"I thought so, too."

Gianna crossed herself. "What now?"

"Please don't tell him, Mother," Allegra pleaded.

Stefania shook her head. "There's no way I can hide this from your father. He'll find out sooner or later. People talk."

"Signore Vittorio will be furious," Gianna murmured.

Stefania turned to look at her maid. "And rightly so!"

Everyone tensed at the sound of Vittorio's footsteps on the stairs. When he entered the room and saw the scene before him, the smile vanished from his face. "What in God's name is going on here?"

"Our daughter crept out of the house to wander around the Piazza delle Cipolle alone," Stefania replied.

Vittorio frowned. "Is this true, Allegra?"

"Yes, Papa."

"You had better explain yourself immediately."

Allegra told her parents about making the pendant, sneaking off to the bottega, and being publicly humiliated by the apprentice.

Stunned, Vittorio demanded, "What possessed you to do all of this in the first place?"

"I heard you and Mother talking in the library," Allegra confessed. "You said that if I had been born a boy, you would apprentice me to a goldsmith. I wanted to prove my worth despite being a girl."

Stefania shot her husband a sharp look.

"You eavesdropped on our conversation," Vittorio said icily.

"I didn't mean to—"

He held up his hand to silence her. "Get cleaned up and meet me in the workshop."

"Papa—"

*"At once."*

Gianna offered her hand to Allegra. "Come on, let's get you cleaned up."

Stefania watched them walk away, then quietly followed her husband into the workshop. "Vittorio…"

"Stefania, not now."

"This is partly our fault, husband."

"Do not try my patience by attempting to defend her actions."

"I'm as upset as you are, but put yourself in her shoes."

"What Allegra did today was foolish and dangerous."

"Our child suffered disillusionment and humiliation for the *sin* of being a girl," Stefania pointed out gently. "Had she been born a boy—"

"But she was not!"

Undeterred by his anger, she persisted. "*Had* she been, however, she would have gained an apprenticeship immediately, I'm sure of it."

"You know this for certain without even seeing the pendant in question?"

"Don't you?"

"Yes," he admitted. "Allegra wouldn't have taken such a risk if she hadn't created something truly worthy."

Encouraged by her husband's words, she suggested, "What

if we hired someone to instruct her privately? Here, in our home?"

"Stefania, *please*."

"Are we to let our daughter's talent go to waste simply because she lacks the necessary parts between her legs?" Her vulgarity evoked a dark look from Vittorio, so she hastily added, "Forgive me."

"Leave me be, wife," he said tiredly.

"What are you going to say to her?"

"I don't know."

Stefania hesitated. "When I was carrying Allegra in my womb, I dreamt of a baby girl covered in gold dust and seated upon on a bed of jewels. I believe it was a sign."

"Why am I only hearing of this dream now?" he demanded angrily. "Why didn't you share this with me sooner?"

"What does it matter? Allegra is *only* a girl," she retorted coolly before stepping out into the hallway and closing the door on him.

Vittorio ran his hands through his hair. Stefania could be obstinate at times but, in this case, she was right. Had Michelangelo or Botticelli or Bronzino or any of the great artists been born female instead of male, the world would have never known their talents.

He picked up a stack of vellum sheets from the table and leafed through his daughter's sketches. Fantastic shapes, whimsical curlicues, intricate etchings—he'd never seen jewelry like this anywhere. The girl had unique ideas, but so did Brunelleschi. None of the city's architects took him seriously until Cosimo il Vecchio commissioned him for the interior of San Lorenzo basilica. After seeing what he was capable of doing, Brunelleschi garnered respect and admiration from the guilds. He later designed the cupola of Santa Maria del Fiore cathedral and became a legend within his own lifetime.

*Is it possible that Allegra possessed the same kind of artistic genius?*

A knock on the door forced him back to the issue at hand. "Enter."

Allegra stood in the doorway, scrubbed clean and wearing a fresh gown.

"Come in and close the door." He waited for her to obey before continuing. "Do you know how easily your chaste reputation can be ruined in this city?"

"I only wanted to prove my worth."

"By stealing my gold and wandering the streets like a peasant?"

"Please—"

"You went behind our backs! Did you honestly think you would gain an apprenticeship with your childish scheme?" He softened when he saw the pain and remorse in his daughter's eyes. "Your mother and I have provided you with the best life has to offer, but there are limitations. I've allowed you into my workshop because you exhibit exceptional skill, but I will not tolerate this kind of behavior."

"I'm truly sorry."

Allegra's sincere apology tempered Vittorio's anger, and he studied her for a long moment. "Let me ask you something. Would you have accepted an apprenticeship at that bottega?"

"I would."

"Why? It's not an establishment of great repute, nor is the master goldsmith particularly skilled."

"May I be honest with you?"

"You may."

"You can no longer teach me anything new."

Stunned by her reply, he couldn't deny it. Allegra's skill and talent had surpassed his own a long time ago. Turning his back on her, he wandered to the window and gazed at the sky.

"Forgive me if I've offended you, Papa."

"Your mother and I only want your happiness, my dear." Turning around to meet her eyes, he added, "I'll hire a goldsmith to privately instruct you here in our home. Consider it a secret apprenticeship."

Allegra hugged her father. "Thank you!"

Later that day, Vittorio retrieved the pendant from the bottega and was duly impressed by his daughter's handiwork.

## CHAPTER 7

Domenico Spinelli, one of the most respected goldsmiths in Tuscany, smiled at the sight of an old friend. "Vittorio Castagno," he said. "The last time I laid eyes on you was at your father's funeral. God rest his soul."

"Forgive me for not coming to see you sooner," Vittorio said sheepishly. "The business keeps me constantly occupied."

The old man chuckled. "Carlo's clients were many, if my memory serves me well, and difficult to please."

"They are exigent, yes."

"Your father was a good man. I miss him."

"I do, too."

After a silent pause, the old man inquired pleasantly, "What brings you to my bottega this fine morning?"

Vittorio removed Allegra's pendant from his pocket and placed it in Domenico's hand. "It appears that my—*child*—is destined to be a goldsmith."

"This is good work," Domenico commented while examining the pendant by the light of a nearby window. "Very good, indeed. Did you have any hand in its creation?"

"None whatsoever."

"A talented apprentice is always welcome here. How old is the boy?"

Vittorio cringed inwardly. "Thirteen."

"When can I meet the lad?"

The midday bells began ringing in the distance and Vittorio suggested, "We can discuss this matter further over a good meal and some wine. My servants are preparing a tasty peposo as we speak."

"I cannot refuse my favorite dish."

The two men navigated the streets from Domenico's bottega in the privileged Mercato Nuovo, which sold luxury goods, toward the Palazzo Castagno. Stefania stood in the main hall, waiting to greet their guest.

"Welcome to our home, Signore Domenico."

"Signora Stefania, you are as lovely as I remember."

"Thank you," she said. "Please, sit."

A servant entered and doled out chalices filled with watered wine.

Vittorio inquired, "How is your son? He must be a grown man by now."

"Bruno is twenty-three years old. He completed his apprenticeship a few years ago, and has been helping me run the bottega ever since."

"You must be proud of him," Stefania said.

"Indeed, I am." The old man's face lit up and he added, "He's to be married this summer."

"Congratulations."

"Thank you." Domenico glanced around. "So, where is your son? I'm looking forward to meeting my future apprentice."

Stefania shot Vittorio an accusatory look. "We don't have a son."

The old man appeared confused. "I don't understand."

"The student would be our daughter, Allegra," Vittorio confessed.

Domenico frowned. "A girl?"

"She knows how to cut metal, set stones, and solder the tiniest details with impressive skill. I haven't taught her how to cut and shape gemstones, only because I don't know how to do it myself."

"You're not a goldsmith," Domenico pointed out.

"True, but my father taught me a few rudimentary techniques." Vittorio looked down at his hands. "I'm clumsy, whereas my daughter is not. She has true potential. If you decide to become her instructor, you'll find an apt pupil, I promise you—perhaps even more advanced than the boys her age who are now in your bottega."

The old man's rheumy eyes lit up. "That's quite a claim, Vittorio."

"A claim that I stand behind with full confidence," he stated, earning a smile of gratitude from his wife.

Domenico rubbed his chin. "I never suspected you capable of such radical ideas."

"Before you make a decision, would you at least see her sketches?"

"I do not approve of women trying to do men's work," Domenico admitted, casting an uneasy glance in Stefania's direction. "No offense."

"None taken, Signore Domenico."

He continued, "But since I have always thought highly of you and your father, I agree to meet the girl and judge her potential."

"Thank you," Vittorio said, relieved.

Stefania dispatched a servant to fetch their daughter. Allegra entered the room a moment later with a pile of sketches in her hand.

Vittorio said, "Signore Domenico, this is my daughter, Allegra."

"Hello, Signorina. Your father tells me that you can design and make jewelry. May I see your sketches?"

Allegra nodded and handed him the stack of sheets. No one spoke as Domenico carefully studied each and every drawing.

Finally, he looked up. "You drew these by yourself?"

"I did," Allegra replied.

"Where have you seen such fantastic shapes?"

"In my head."

Domenico stared at the girl, perplexed.

"Well?" Vittorio pressed.

"I need to give it some thought."

Hearing this, Allegra did her best to hide her disappointment.

Domenico set off for the Palazzo Castagno to give his answer the following morning. Allegra, who barely slept that night, stood alongside her parents wearing an anxious expression on her face.

"I will instruct your daughter," Domenico said, his face and tone serious. "But it must never be made public knowledge.

Neither the magistrates nor the guilds can ever know."

*Or the Holy Church.* "Naturally, this matter will remain between us," Vittorio assured, tossing a glance in his daughter's direction.

Stefania added, "Our servants are discreet, so you need not worry."

"I'm glad to hear it, Signora." Turning to Allegra, he added, "I expect you to be ready to begin our lessons immediately."

Vittorio was surprised. "So soon?"

"If your daughter can set to paper what she sees in her head, I'm eager to discover what her hands are capable of doing."

"Yes, Signore Domenico."

"You will call me Maestro," he corrected.

"Yes, Maestro."

Domenico was shown into the spacious workshop where he and Allegra worked together for hours. At the end of the day, the goldsmith was duly impressed.

"I would like to leave you with a small gift before I go," Domenico said as he extracted a tiny bronze statue from the inside pocket of his surcoat. "Each of my apprentices has received one from me. I urge them to keep it close to their person at all times."

She examined the miniature figure. "Who is this?"

"Why, it's Saint Eligius, patron saint of goldsmiths."

"Thank you, Maestro."

\*\*\*

Allegra's hands worked tirelessly throughout the summer of 1561, curling strips of copper and silver to create pieces flaunting filigree and granulation. She learned about these styles from one of the books in the library. The classical tomes portrayed Hellenistic ladies wearing earrings and chokers mimicking the appearance of ornate lace. Inspired by the delicacy and elegance of this ancient jewelry, she set out to master the techniques.

Domenico was often astonished by Allegra's eye for detail and her ability to perform the most painstaking task with precision. His young pupil never complained, listened carefully to his instructions, and knew how to handle criticism. What's more, she used the latter to her advantage, improving upon her skills.

One day, Allegra casually inquired of Domenico, "Is your son like you?"

"What do you mean?"

"Is he a Maestro?"

"Bruno is quite skilled, but he has yet to achieve the level of master." The old man paused. "He lacks patience, you see."

"Will I ever meet him?"

"You'll meet him at the wedding."

"Does he know you're tutoring me?"

"No one knows, not even him." Then, as an afterthought, the old man inquired, "You haven't told anyone, have you?"

"No, Maestro."

"Good girl."

There was a long pause as Allegra stared down at her lap.

His brow creased. "What ails you, child?"

"Sometimes I ask God to turn me into a boy." The old man was taken aback by the unexpected comment. Regretting her confession, she hastily added, "Please don't repeat my words to my father."

Domenico searched his mind for something suitable to say; kind words to comfort his pupil. "Well, I'm glad you're not a boy."

"Do you honestly mean that?"

"Yes, I do. You're the only girl I've ever tutored, and I'm willing to wager that you're the only female apprentice in Florence. That makes you special on two counts."

Vittorio, who was walking along the corridor, paused in the doorway.

Allegra inquired, "Why must I remain a secret if I'm so special?"

The old man sighed. "The role of women is to wed, bear children, and give glory to God through their submissive and chaste behavior. Your indulgent parents have risked much on your behalf. Arranging a secret apprenticeship is no small thing.

Remember that many girls your age are already betrothed, some are even mothers."

"I'm aware of my good fortune, Maestro, but I also believe the world is an unfair place. I possess more talent than many of the city's goldsmiths—my father even said so."

"The world is quite unfair, I agree. And your father is correct, but perhaps he shouldn't tell you such things."

"Why not? It's true."

"Arrogance is most unbecoming, especially in women."

"Do you think I could someday be like you?"

"You possess extraordinary skill for your age, but only time will tell. Never forget that we live in an age where specialization is considered a virtue; it's the trademark of a master."

Allegra pondered his words with a serious expression.

Vittorio cleared his throat and walked into the workshop. "What have you accomplished today, Allegra?" he inquired while inspecting his daughter's current project—a bracelet of braided copper.

Turning his attention to Domenico, he said, "The last time I delivered gemstones to your bottega, Bruno asked me to do some repairs. I have them here in my pocket."

Domenico stood. "I was about to take my leave. I would be happy to deliver them for you."

"We can walk to your bottega together. I could use some air."

Allegra also stood. "May I go, too? I would very much like to see the Maestro's bottega and meet his son."

The men regarded one another before Vittorio inquired, "Do you have any objection, Domenico?"

"None at all," the old man replied.

Walking hand in hand with her father, Allegra absorbed the city's many sights. She noted the various styles of architecture and the gracefulness of outdoor religious shrines. When they entered the Mercato Nuovo, she was delighted by the sight of rich velvets and shimmering silks. The patterns and colors served as inspiration for future designs.

They stopped before a small shop with a single window. The

shutters were thrown back to reveal a wooden counter where a beautiful woman stood beside a set of scales. Glossy black hair framed a heart-shaped face that broke into a smile as they entered the bottega. Domenico patted her arm and mumbled a greeting before ducking into the back room to check on his apprentices.

"Buona sera, Signorina Anabella," Vittorio said cheerfully.

Allegra looked to her father in surprise. How did he know this woman?

"Buona sera, Signore Vittorio," Anabella replied in a melodic voice, her eyes focused on the girl at his side. "Is this your daughter?"

"Yes. Allegra, this is Signore Domenico's future daughter-in-law."

"It's a pleasure to meet you," Allegra said with a curtsy. She could not stop staring at the woman's pretty face and neither could her father.

Anabella smiled. "The pleasure is mine, Signorina. You're such a lovely and well-mannered girl. How old are you?"

"Thirteen."

"I'm sure many boys will want to dance with you on my wedding day."

Before Allegra could reply, a plump young man with a jovial face appeared in the doorway. His mischievous eyes were a combination of green and gold. "*Everyone* will be dancing at our wedding, my love."

"Bruno," Vittorio said. "How are you?"

"I'm well, thank you."

Domenico reappeared and placed a hand on his son's shoulder. "Vittorio has come to deliver your repairs."

"Good. My clients are eager for their jewelry." Bruno's eyes fell upon Allegra and he inquired, "Signore Vittorio, who is this beauty at your side?"

"My daughter, Allegra."

Bruno made an elaborate bow before kissing her hand. The gesture drew laughter from the adults, prompting Allegra to edge closer to her father. Surprised by the suspicion and distrust in the girl's eyes, Bruno paused for a moment. Intent on lightening her mood, he held up a finger, went into the back room, and emerged with both hands balled into tight fists.

"Pick a hand," he said.

Allegra did not move.

"Bruno, you and your silly games," Anabella chided.

Ignoring her comment, he prompted, "Go on, try and guess which hand conceals the treasure."

Allegra gazed deeply into Bruno's eyes and saw no malice or mockery in them. She pointed to his left hand and, when it came up empty, he made a comical sad face.

"I suggest you pick the other one," he whispered.

A reluctant smile tugged at her lips as she pointed to the right hand.

"Are you certain?" When she nodded, Bruno opened his hand to reveal a blue glass bead. Placing it in the palm of Allegra's hand, he said, "A pretty trinket for a pretty girl. Oh, look! It matches the color of your eyes."

"Thank you, Signore Bruno."

"You are most welcome, Signorina Allegra."

Later that day, Allegra soldered a gold loop to the bead and slipped it onto a gold chain.

*** 

Dressed in her finest gown of periwinkle silk, Allegra accompanied her parents to the church where Bruno and Anabella would exchange marriage vows before God. Throughout the ceremony, the happy groom stared at his bride in the same manner a puppy stared at its master.

Several other men stared at the bride, too.

A lively celebration followed at the Spinelli household. Diluted wine mixed with spices poured freely to refresh the thirst of merry guests as servants carried platters piled high with roasted meats.

Vittorio allowed his daughter to drink a bit more wine than usual, earning him a reproving look from his wife.

"Drink it *slowly*," Stefania admonished after Allegra's chalice had been filled to the rim.

Allegra obeyed, but the wine still went to her head, making her deliciously dizzy. Hired musicians struck up a lively tune, prompting her to tap her feet. A few girls came by the table and urged her to join them in a fast-paced jig. Forming a circle by holding hands, they turned and dipped, giggled and spun around in circles.

Later, some of the men sang ballads of courtly love to honor the bride. One even went as far as reciting a love poem he had written specifically for Anabella. The guests hooted at the sexual insinuations throughout the verse, whereas Bruno listened with feigned amusement.

"How inappropriate," Stefania whispered to Vittorio as she watched the lewd poet kiss Anabella's hand with tears in his eyes.

Allegra heard the comment and glanced at her father to gauge his reaction. Vittorio merely shrugged, pretending to be deeply interested in the contents within his chalice.

The musicians played for everyone's pleasure as the night wore on. Allegra felt someone touch her hand. It was Bruno and he reeked of wine.

"Dance with me, Signorina Allegra."

Before she could respond, he led her toward a cluster of dancers. Never having danced publicly with a man, she felt self-conscious.

Sensing her discomfort, he asked, "Are you enjoying yourself?"

"I am, thank you."

He spun her around. "Someday, you'll be dancing at your own wedding."

"I have no plans to marry," she said coolly while keeping pace with him.

Grinning, he teased, "Destined for the convent, are we?"

"No, sir."

His expression turned serious. "You don't like men, do you?"

Lucrezia's death had destroyed the literary heroes and poetic knights that she once held in high esteem. Men killed their wives. Men scorned girls and humiliated them in public. Men ruined the reputations of good women.

*Guard your heart and keep it safe, don't trust men.*

"No, Signore Bruno, I don't."

He chuckled in the face of her immature petulance. "You're too young to harbor such ill will towards us." Taking a step closer, he added, "The thought of boys may repulse you now, but, when you're older, you'll feel differently."

She recoiled from him. "Never!"

Bruno stared at her in stunned silence.

Mortified by her outburst, she said, "Forgive me, Signore Bruno."

He frowned. "Not all men are rogues, Allegra."

She blushed to the roots of her hair and said nothing. Anabella glided past them on the arm of a handsome man, and Bruno's eyes followed the laughing pair.

## CHAPTER 8

The cold, damp winter resulted in many Florentines getting ill and Domenico was no exception. The old man fell prey to fever and chills around Christmastime, and not even the joyous news of his daughter-in-law's pregnancy roused him from his sickbed.

Allegra fretted over her Maestro's condition daily. Stefania sent servants to his home with curatives, steaming broths, and healing elixirs at her daughter's insistence. Thankfully, his health was eventually restored and their lessons resumed in mid-February.

On the one-year anniversary of her apprenticeship, Allegra handed Domenico a simple wooden box.

"What have we here?" he cheerfully inquired.

"I've been working on this piece for a long time, Maestro. I would appreciate your honest opinion."

Domenico opened the box. Nestled on a square of red cloth was a filigree and granulation choker fashioned from silver. The old man walked to a sunlit window and held it up to the light for closer inspection. Each bead was perfectly executed, the size and shape identical to the naked eye. The twisted metal curlicues between the rows of beaded clusters were created with meticulous precision.

He stood by the window for so long that Allegra grew fidgety. "Well? Is it any good?"

Domenico's expression was one of puzzlement. He'd never seen anything like this—and from one so young! "It's marvelous."

"Marvelous enough to be displayed for sale in your bottega?"

The question, though bold, was valid. "Yes."

Allegra's grin was so wide he thought her face would split in half.

Three days later, Domenico presented Vittorio and Stefania with a heavy coin pouch. They were astonished at how quickly Allegra's necklace had sold, and the high price it had fetched.

*** 

Anabella gave birth to a healthy boy in June, and the new parents christened their son Agostino. Allegra eagerly anticipated playing with the baby as she accompanied her parents to the Spinelli household.

Anabella received her guests in an elegant gown and carefully coiffed hair. Bruno sat in a chair beside his wife, holding their tiny son. Plump and pink, little Agostino stared longingly at his mother, who practically ignored him. After exchanging pleasantries, Stefania went over to admire the baby.

"Such a fat little cherub," she gushed.

"God could not have bestowed a better gift upon us," Bruno said before kissing the top of his son's downy head.

Stefania turned her attention to Anabella. "You look well." Lowering her voice, she added, "I hope the birth wasn't too difficult."

Anabella's eyes welled with tears. "The pain was unbearable. Now, I'm fat and miserable because of having birthed a child."

"You are the most beautiful woman in the world," Bruno countered, his expression troubled.

"Be patient," Stefania advised. "I was much older than you when I delivered Allegra, and my figure returned quickly."

This seemed to cheer the distressed young woman. "Really?"

Stefania nodded. "You'll be back to your old self soon enough."

Allegra was about to ask if she could hold the baby when Agostino suddenly let out a piercing wail.

Anabella covered her ears and frowned. "Ugh, that noise!"

"He's hungry, my love," Bruno said, trying to soothe the baby.

Anabella rolled her eyes. "He's *always* hungry…Francesca!"

A corpulent wet nurse with damp streaks running down the front of her bodice entered the room and carried off the fussy infant. Disappointed at not having had the chance to hold the baby, Allegra quietly sighed and sat down in a vacant chair.

"Agostino is a fine boy," Vittorio commented.

"Yes," Bruno agreed. "Hopefully, he'll soon have a brother or sister to play with him."

Anabella shot her husband a hateful look that suggested otherwise. "Perhaps *you* should deliver the next baby."

Bruno's face fell in utter disappointment. "Darling, I know it must have been difficult—"

"*Difficult*?" she scoffed. "You have no concept of the tremendous pain a woman must endure to bring a baby forth into this world. I never want to suffer through that ordeal again."

Stefania winced at the young woman's lack of appreciation for having birthed a healthy child—on her first attempt, no less! A heavy silence filled the room after Anabella's outburst. Bruno's face was a mixture of shock and disillusionment.

Sensing that she had offended her guests, Anabella offered sheepishly, "Forgive me. I am tired and still recovering from the birth."

Stefania said tentatively, "You will forget the pain, Signora Anabella. Every woman does. Just *look* at your son—he's a miracle. God has truly blessed you both."

Anabella said nothing whereas Bruno gazed sadly at the floor.

***

Ferdinando de' Medici became cardinal at the age of fourteen in 1562. In October of that same year, Anabella and little Agostino fell seriously ill. Domenico and Bruno hired the best physicians that money could buy, but no cure seemed to work. Stefania sent curatives and Gianna's potent elixirs, but those also failed. Within a few short weeks, mother and son died of consumption. Miraculously, Bruno's robust health remained intact, but he was utterly devastated by the loss.

At the funeral, Bruno sat grim and motionless beside his

son's tiny coffin. The mourners spoke in soothing voices, trying to offer comfort to the brokenhearted father. Domenico, who had expressed so much joy over his clever grandson, stood near Bruno with red-rimmed eyes.

Allegra recalled the rosiness of little Agostino's round cheeks. They had reminded her of ripe plums...Now, the baby's face was ashen and devoid of expression. Bruno, once jovial and full of smiles, seemed as lifeless as his son. She had never seen him look so sad and hopeless. Would he ever know happiness again? *Could* he, after life had dealt him such a cruel blow?

Stefania leaned sideways and put her lips to Allegra's ear. "Do not stare."

Allegra immediately dropped her gaze. "I pity Signore Bruno."

"We all pity him. Losing a child is the most painful thing in the world."

Bruno suddenly cradled his head in his hands and gave into tears. The sight of such anguish made a few mourners cry, including Allegra.

It was later discovered that Anabella had contracted the disease from her lover before passing it on to her son. Her infidelity had caused the death of an innocent child. To Bruno, this knowledge was the final coup-de-grace, leaving him a broken man.

Domenico resumed his lessons with Allegra several weeks later, but he, too, had changed. At one point, he doubled over and silently wept.

Allegra set down her tools and gently patted his back. "It pains me to see you suffer, Maestro, I'll have Gianna make a draught to soothe you."

While she went in search of Gianna, Vittorio entered the workshop.

Sensing his friend's presence, Domenico hastily wiped his eyes. "Forgive me. Every time I picture my grandson's face..."

Vittorio placed a comforting hand on the old man's shoulder. "My prayers are always with you and your son. How is Bruno?"

Domenico shook his head sadly. "While that bastard still breathes my son will never know peace."

The man with whom Anabella had committed the crime of adultery not only survived the illness, but had fled the city to avoid legal repercussions. Bruno tried in vain to chase him.

"God will punish him soon enough," Vittorio assured. "You should be grateful that Bruno's life was spared."

"My son knew his wife had admirers, but he never suspected Anabella of being unfaithful. Oh, how he loved that stupid girl..." The old man's face contorted into a grimace. "We never thought her capable of such a vile deed. I hope she's burning in Hell right now."

"She was cursed with beauty and attracted too much attention."

"Vain, silly woman!" Domenico cried vehemently. "She forsook her loving husband and beautiful child—*for what*? Compliments, trinkets, and moments of stolen pleasure. The wanton whore."

There was an awkward silence before Vittorio said, "Bruno is young. In time, he will recover from this blow."

Domenico was about to reply when Allegra entered the workshop.

"Gianna said this will make you feel better, Maestro," she said, offering him a ceramic cup.

"Thank you, Allegra," he said before taking a sip of the warm liquid. Turning to Vittorio, he added, "My son is leaving Florence. He told me so this morning. He claims there are too many painful memories here."

Allegra inquired, "Where is Signore Bruno going?"

"A group of Portuguese dignitaries traveling from Rome stopped in Florence to pay their respects to the Medici. One of them, a respected navigator, came into the bottega to purchase gifts for his wife and daughter." Domenico paused, his eyes watering. "Bruno convinced the man to allow him to join his crew."

"Bruno isn't a sailor," Vittorio pointed out.

Domenico shrugged sadly. "I know. I've tried to talk him out of it, but there's no reasoning with him in his current state of mind."

"Who will run the bottega?"

"I will. A few of the senior apprentices will help me."

"You can count on my help. I'm here for whatever you need."

"I can help you, too," Allegra chimed.

Vittorio inquired, "When do the Portuguese depart?"

"Within a fortnight."

Later that evening, after the family had supped, Allegra crept into the workshop and went through her father's satchel.

Vittorio appeared in the doorway. "What are you doing, Allegra?"

"Where is that old compass you received as payment last year?"

"Why do you want it?"

"I'd like to remount it and offer it to Signore Bruno as a parting gift. He has suffered so much, I thought a token of our goodwill might cheer him."

"A compass is a most fitting gift for one is about to depart on a long journey. I'm sure he'll appreciate the gesture. Let me fetch it for you."

Originally from Germany, the mariner's compass fit perfectly into the palm of Allegra's hand. Its round face was composed of lapis lazuli and it boasted ivory coordinates. She sat at the workbench and carefully pried the delicate instrument from its dented brass casing.

In a matter of days, Allegra created a new casing for the compass in silver, etching an elaborate border along the edge. The center flaunted a meticulously rendered Florentine giglio.

Vittorio examined the finished piece with satisfaction. "Excellent work. You must think highly of Signore Bruno to put forth such an effort."

She felt the color rise in her cheeks. "I want him to have something special to remember us by. I hope he likes it."

"I'm certain that he will, but he must not know you made

it." Allegra nodded in understanding and he added, "I'm going to the bottega and can take the compass to him."

"I would prefer to say goodbye to him personally, if you'll allow it."

Vittorio regarded her thoughtfully. "Very well."

Allegra wrapped the compass in linen and tied it with a scrap of ribbon before accompanying her father to the Spinelli bottega. She was completely unprepared for Bruno's disheveled appearance. His thin, unshaven face failed to hide the gray pallor of his skin, and two dark smudges beneath his eyes revealed lack of sleep. His clothing was in bad need of laundering, too.

"Buongiorno, Bruno. It's good to see you," Vittorio said gently. "How are you these days?"

Bruno's eyes glistened. "I am alive, Vittorio."

Vittorio nodded solemnly. "Your father told us of your plan to go to Portugal. Although we're sorry to hear it, Allegra and I came to say goodbye and wish you well."

Bruno's eyes slid toward Allegra, and the pain reflected in his gaze almost made her wince.

She placed the parcel on the counter. "This is for you."

Slowly, he unwrapped the gift and stared at the compass before gently touching the silver casing with his fingertips. "It's a fine piece."

Allegra reached across the counter and boldly touched his wrist. "May it guide you well and bring you back to Florence."

Both men looked at her in surprise, causing her to blush.

Bruno leaned over the counter, closing the gap between himself and Allegra, then pointed to the giglio etched into the casing. "Did you select this design for me?"

His eyes twinkled and, for an instant, she saw a trace of the old Bruno.

"Yes," she lied.

"I shall never forget your kindness, Signorina." Looking to Vittorio, he added, "Or yours, Signore Vittorio. Thank you both for this fine gift."

"God bless you and keep you, my friend," Vittorio offered

before guiding his daughter out of the bottega.

Allegra looked over her shoulder to find Bruno staring after her.

***

Bruno departed for Portugal on the eleventh of November. Eight days later, the nineteen year old Bishop of Pisa, Giovanni de' Medici, died. Oddly, it was the same month and day as his sister Maria's death. Eleonora and Cosimo took this as a bad omen—and rightly so. Fifteen year old Garzia died less than a month later on the twelfth of December, followed by Eleonora's death on the seventeenth of December. She was forty years old. The reports concluded that the duchess and her young son had expired from malaria while visiting Pisa.

Cosimo was inconsolable. It was bad enough to have lost three of his children in such a short span of time, but his wife's death set him over the edge. The duke's beloved consort was laid to rest in a luxurious gown embellished with gold embroidery and gemstones. Great care had been taken with her final ablutions to make her appear as attractive in death as she was in life. The Florentines came to pay their last respects with tears in their eyes, including the Castagno family.

Stefania approached Cosimo to offer him words of comfort and he pulled her into an embrace. Vittorio moved to shield them from the eyes of curious onlookers as his wife whispered soothingly into the ear of her former lover. The intimate gesture should have made Vittorio jealous, but the only emotion he could muster toward Cosimo was pity.

Cosimo whispered, "What's to become of me, Stefania?"

"You'll go on, my dear friend. You're the ruler of Florence and the people need you."

*"Oh Eleonora..."*

Stefania stepped out of his arms. "Calm yourself, *Your Grace*. This is a public event and people are watching you like hawks," she warned, her tone gentle but firm.

Heeding her wise counsel, Cosimo cleared his throat and quickly composed himself.

She placed her lips to his ear. "My home is your home if you

71

need to mourn privately. No one will bother you there."

***

Isabella de' Medici wasted no time fulfilling her familial duties. She stepped into her mother's shoes as first lady of Florence, receiving guests and managing the family's villas and palazzos on her grieving father's behalf. Armed with an impressive aptitude for politics, she often discussed strategies with her father and brothers before they implemented any new policies. Francesco assumed a greater role in Florentine affairs since Cosimo shirked many responsibilities now that his wife was no longer at his side to guide him. It wasn't long before he acted as regent on his father's behalf.

Eleonora's death cast a shadow over Christmas that year, and the holy day was celebrated in solemn reverence by the majority of Florentines. Vittorio, who had business to conduct in the north, left for Venice shortly after Epiphany.

On a cold January evening, Gianna entered her mistress's private sitting room and announced, "There's *someone* here to see you."

Stefania looked up from her book expectantly. "Oh?"

Allegra, who sat beside her mother reading, closed her book. "Is it Domenico? Is he ill?"

"No, Signorina." Gianna gave her mistress a meaningful look. "*He* insists on seeing you privately, Signora Stefania."

Allegra stood. "Who is this person who refuses to announce his name? Mother, I'm going downstairs with you."

Stefania shook her head. "Stay here."

"But—"

"I said no, Allegra," Stefania said before following Gianna out the door.

She descended the stairs and found a man in a hooded cloak standing in the main hall surrounded by four heavily armed guards. *Medici guards*. When he pushed back the hood, Stefania took in the dark circles beneath his eyes, the unkempt beard, and sallow cheeks.

"Your Grace," she said with a respectful curtsy.

Cosimo's eyes were intense. "Signora Stefania, forgive this

72

intrusion."

Conscious of the four men staring at her, she said politely, "On the contrary, my lord. You honor my household with your presence."

"May I have a word? Alone?"

She nodded. "We can retire to the library, if you wish."

Cosimo motioned for his guards to remain behind as he followed Stefania into the library. After closing the door, she indicated a chair by the fire and coaxed the embers within the hearth with a poker. He sat down and stared into the growing flames. Kneeling at his feet, she took his icy hands into her own and rubbed his fingers vigorously in order to warm them. The familiar intimacy between them required no words.

A nostalgic smile eventually touched his lips. "You used to do that when we were children."

She returned the smile. "You used to like it."

"I still do." Suddenly, his face crumpled and tears streamed down his hollow cheeks. "I am lost…"

"I know how much you loved her."

He shook his head sadly. "Eleonora wasn't only my wife, she was my friend, my political advisor. She was *everything*." He heaved a weighty sigh. "I can't rule efficiently without her wise counsel."

Stefania's heart ached to see him in such pain. "Isabella and Francesco have been well-groomed for their roles in life, and they can help you. Right now, you must be strong for them and for the people of Florence." She stood and smoothed the creases of her gown. "Warm yourself by the fire while I have my servants fetch us some wine."

Stefania opened the door and came face to face with her daughter. Closing the door behind her, she whispered, "What are you doing here? I told you to remain upstairs."

"Those are Medici guards," Allegra said, eyeing the men in the other room. "Is my godfather here? If so, I would like to greet him."

"He is unwell and wishes to speak with me privately." When Allegra's face fell in disappointment, she added, "Don't be glum. Have one of the servants bring our best wine to the library and offer ale to the guards. Go, quickly."

A servant arrived in the library with a tray. Stefania waved the girl away, then poured wine into a silver chalice before handing it to Cosimo. "Our best vintage."

He took a sip. "Delicious. Thank you for receiving me like this."

She poured wine for herself. "As I told you, my home is your home."

"Everyone is watching me," he lamented. "Sometimes, I hear them whispering behind my back."

"Them?"

"Nobles, magistrates, people in general…"

"What are they saying?"

"One magistrate—I won't tell you his name—said, 'His Grace has become dangerously lost in his own bereavement.' "

*Insensitive bastard.* "You have the same right as any man to grieve the loss of loved ones."

Cosimo drained the contents in the chalice and Stefania swiftly refilled it. "I wonder if they even perceive me as human."

"Ignore them," she advised. "What do they know? They're nothing but fuddle-minded old men."

For the first time since his wife's death, the corners of Cosimo's mouth lifted slightly. "You've always been spirited and outspoken."

"If my memory serves me well, *you* were the one with a clever retort at the ready." She smiled slightly before taking a sip of wine. "The Castagno brothers were usually too slow to keep up with your sharp wit."

"You weren't too slow, that's for certain."

"Not everyone appreciates a sharp-tongued woman."

"I do." He sighed. "Vittorio is a fortunate man to have you at his side." When she lowered her eyes, he added, "Forgive me."

"There's nothing to forgive, my lord."

"Actually, there is." He followed this statement with a long, deliberate pause. "Have you ever forgiven me?"

She frowned slightly. "For what?"

Cosimo set down his chalice and walked to where she stood. "Where do I begin? I never apologized for breaking your heart, Stefania."

"It happened so long ago," she said dismissively with a nervous smile. "We were young and naïve."

"We were young and in love," he countered softly. "We created a child together."

Stefania stared into the ruby contents of her chalice. "I lost the child, and you married Eleonora for love."

"Political gain," he reminded her. "First and foremost."

"A strategic alliance that won your heart, nonetheless."

"Love was an unexpected surprise. You know that."

Stefania quietly sipped her wine as the memories she fought hard to suppress for so long bubbled to the surface. She wasn't prepared to deal with them. Not now. *Not ever.*

"Stefania?" he prompted.

"Eleonora made you happy."

"Yes, she did." He took a step closer. "So did you."

Stefania smiled sadly. "Our brief affair was nothing in comparison to your long, fortuitous marriage."

"Our time together was meaningful," he said, reaching for her hand.

She flinched from his touch. "Why are you here, Cosimo?"

"I needed to see you," he confessed. "I am…"

She nodded in understanding. "I know."

"I've had many women in my life, but I've loved only two of them. One is dead." He caressed her cheek. "The other stands before me now."

Stefania didn't recoil from the caress. Encouraged by this, Cosimo closed the gap between them and claimed her mouth with his own. The familiar rush of passion consumed them and, for a fleeting moment, they were young lovers once again.

Stefania pulled away and put a stop to the temporary madness. "I love my husband," she said firmly. "I've never been unfaithful to Vittorio and I don't intend to start now."

Out of the corner of her eye, she saw the library door close.

He spread out his hands in a gesture of helplessness. "Stefania…"

"Dearest Cosimo, I know you're lonely and in need of female comfort, but I can't take Eleonora's place in your bed."

His dark eyes bore into hers with a burning intensity, then he heaved a shuddering breath and looked away. "I should not have come here tonight."

"Don't say that," she countered, gripping his hand tightly for emphasis. "You're free to be yourself and speak your mind here. No one in this household will ever betray you, least of all me."

He met her gaze. "I appreciate your words more than you know."

They sat together before the fire, quietly drinking wine until Cosimo felt it was time to go home.

Stefania saw him out, then went in search of her daughter. She found Allegra reading by the fire. "Did you go downstairs to spy on us?"

Allegra closed the book. "I won't tell Papa what I saw."

"You have no clue what transpired between us."

"I have an idea, but I know it's not your fault. Cosimo de' Medici is not himself anymore due to his grief."

"Who told you this?"

"Everyone in Florence is saying it. Besides, the servants talk." Allegra studied her mother thoughtfully. "I'm relieved that you turned down his advances."

"I love your father and would never betray him."

"May I speak freely, Mother?" At Stefania's wary nod, Allegra continued, "What I don't understand is why my godfather would kiss you in the first place. I knew you two were friends in the Mugello…"

To Stefania's chagrin, she blushed. "You're very much like me when I was your age. Clever, outspoken, full of life…" *What happened to that lively girl?* Life and all its harsh reality gradually crushed her spirit.

"Mother?"

Stefania snapped out of her reverie and met her daughter's inquisitive eyes. Her grandmother had always been open and honest. Allegra, who was now a young woman, deserved the same courtesy. "I'll tell you the truth, but it must remain between us, agreed?"

"Agreed."

"Cosimo was more than my friend. He was my lover."

Shocked, Allegra asked, "When?"

"Before he met Eleonora and before your father and I were wed."

"You weren't a virgin when you married father?"

Stefania averted her gaze. "No."

"Does he know about you and Cosimo?"

"Yes."

"Did Eleonora know, too?"

"Not to my knowledge."

Mother and daughter regarded each other quietly. Finally, Allegra said, "I'm glad you told me this."

Stefania's brow creased. "Why?"

"I've always thought of you as perfect."

Stefania chuckled without mirth as she sat down beside her daughter. "No one is perfect, of that you may be sure."

They resumed reading and, every once in a while, Allegra would discreetly glance at her mother, who suddenly seemed different.

Plagued by loneliness, Cosimo eventually took on a mistress by the name of Eleonora degli Albizzi. The woman brought him some measure of comfort, but she lived under the indelible shadow of the late duchess.

# CHAPTER 9

In January 1563 Vittorio received a hefty commission. Domenico and Allegra worked arduously for weeks to create a stunning diamond necklace for one of his best clients in Venice. When the time came to deliver the merchandise, Vittorio suggested that Allegra accompany him.

Stefania, who was present when he extended the invitation to their daughter, said, "You must keep a close eye on her, Vittorio."

"You can keep an eye on her yourself," he countered. "It would please me greatly if you accompanied us as well."

Stefania shook her head. "I can't leave my babies for very long."

Allegra glanced uneasily at her father. "Please come with us, Mother."

Vittorio hid his impatience. "The children aren't going anywhere, Stefania. There will probably be more infants when you return."

"You've never been outside of Florence," Stefania said to Allegra, smoothing her daughter's hair while simultaneously ignoring her husband's comment. "How exciting this journey will be for you."

"Papa, will you show your clients my jewelry designs?" When Vittorio appeared doubtful, Allegra added, "I would appreciate an objective opinion of my work. We can say that Domenico or one of his apprentices drew them."

"She makes a good point," Stefania said.

He frowned. "I dislike the idea of lying."

"What harm can come of it, Vittorio?"

"Very well," he conceded. "I'll decide who sees them, however."

"Thank you, Papa," Allegra said, offering him a hug.

Stefania's devotion to the orphans prevented her from seeing

Vittorio and Allegra off the following morning. One of the babies was sick and she had gone to spend the night by the child's bedside. Gianna stood in the dimness of early dawn holding a candle and waving goodbye.

The journey was long, but they enjoyed decent weather. Vittorio booked two adjoining rooms at a respectable inn frequented by wealthy merchants. Since it was too early to retire, he hired a gondolier to take them for a ride. The late afternoon sun caused the Grand Canal to gleam like liquid copper.

"This is the most beautiful city in the world," Allegra said, admiring the gorgeous palaces along the water.

Vittorio chuckled. "I agree, but never say that aloud in Florence. I knew you'd love Venice—the colors, the exotic palazzos, the light. Hopefully, this trip will serve as inspiration for your future creations."

They glided past the enormous Piazza San Marco, which boasted the city's magnificent cathedral and the Palazzo Ducale, the doge's residence. The bells of the Campanile di San Marco rang as the tangerine sun initiated its slow descent in the sky. The gondolier continued rowing and eventually changed direction at a confluence where three canals convened.

Vittorio pointed to an imposing palazzo flaunting numerous lancet windows and three façades facing water, which was unusual. "That's the residence of Bartolomeo Cappello, head of one of the noblest families in Venice. We're going there tomorrow morning to deliver the diamond necklace to his wife, Signora Lucrezia Grimani. She likes diamonds and her young stepdaughter, Bianca, favors pearls."

"Pearls are the most prized jewels of Europe," Allegra commented. "Bianca must possess good taste. How old is she?"

"I suspect her to be about your age."

"I look forward to meeting her."

After breaking their fasts the next morning, they crossed the canal via gondola, then walked the short distance to the Palazzo Cappello.

A liveried page led them to a large salon boasting a marble

balcony overlooking the Grand Canal. Expensive tapestries graced the walls of the spacious room, and an incredible chandelier fashioned from blue and white glass hung from the center of a frescoed ceiling.

Two black gondolas glided upon the aquamarine water outside the open windows, capturing Allegra's attention. Across the canal, fancy balconies and Moorish windows graced the façades of colorful palazzos.

Their hostess, an attractive woman with lively eyes, entered the room and smiled at them. Although the style of her gown was somewhat conservative, it was cut from costly gold brocade.

"Signore Vittorio, it's always a pleasure to see you," Lucrezia said. "And who is this lovely young lady? Wait, I see a resemblance."

"This is my daughter, Allegra."

Allegra curtsied. "How do you do, Signora?"

Lucrezia inclined her head before addressing a nearby servant. "Tell Bianca that we have guests." To Vittorio, she added, "A pity my husband isn't home. He's meeting with the doge as we speak."

"A pity, indeed," Vittorio agreed.

An attractive girl with reddish blonde hair and creamy complexion entered the salon. Her hazel eyes were alert, taking in every detail of Allegra's face and clothing.

"There you are, Bianca," Lucrezia said. "You remember Signore Vittorio, and this is his daughter, Allegra."

"Hello. Do you often travel with your father, Signorina?"

"This is my first time," Allegra confessed.

Bianca smiled, the whiteness and evenness of her teeth matching the uniformity of the pearls circling her throat. "Welcome to Venice."

Vittorio placed an arm around his daughter's shoulders. "As you know, I have no sons. Allegra is of great help to me. She offers valuable advice to my clients."

Intrigued, Bianca inquired, "What kind of advice?"

"Allegra has an exceptional eye for color and form," he

replied smoothly. "She knows what gem and shape will complement each individual."

Bianca's hand flew to her throat and her fingertips caressed the pearls.

Seeing this, Allegra said, "Pearls are an excellent choice for you."

Bianca's eyes slid toward Vittorio. "Father only buys from the best."

Lucrezia rubbed her hands in anticipation. "I'm eager to see my new necklace. Has Domenico outdone himself again?"

"Most definitely," Vittorio replied.

Reaching into his satchel, he made quite a production of extracting a flat leather box. Nestled within a bed of black velvet was the diamond necklace, which he offered to the noblewoman with great flourish.

Lucrezia gasped as she held the necklace up to the sunlight. "Oh…"

"Look how the stones capture the light," Bianca said.

"The necklace is perfect," Lucrezia declared. "I can't wait to wear it tonight. The ambassador of Milan is throwing a masquerade ball in honor of Carnevale. It will be a lavish affair and everyone will be there."

"You'll be the envy of all the ladies tonight," Vittorio complimented dutifully. "I also have some new gemstones to show you."

Vittorio set a box of gemstones on the table, and Lucrezia's eyes dilated with pleasure as she fingered the biggest, shiniest diamond. Catching sight of the vellum scroll protruding from the inside pocket of his cloak, she inquired, "Are those orders for other clients?"

"No, these are sketches," he replied before unrolling the scroll.

"Jewelry designs," Bianca said, leaning forward to get a better look.

Lucrezia appeared puzzled. "This doesn't look like Domenico's work."

Vittorio and Allegra exchanged anxious looks.

Bianca pointed to a delicate filigree pendant set with a large center stone. "I've never seen anything like this."

"Who drew these?" Lucrezia demanded.

Thinking quickly, Allegra replied, "One of the Maestro's protégés."

Relieved, Vittorio added, "A talented young man."

"I want this pendant," Lucrezia stated, pointing to the sketch.

Allegra could barely contain her joy. One of the most prominent ladies in Venice desired *her* pendant! "Signora Lucrezia, may I suggest an emerald for the central gemstone? It would bring out the green in your eyes and compliment the rosiness of your skin."

Lucrezia was astonished. "I've never worn emeralds."

"What a shame," Allegra said, holding one of her father's best emeralds near the woman's face.

Bianca squinted. "I believe Allegra is correct."

Lucrezia turned to Vittorio. "I will follow your daughter's counsel."

Bianca turned to Allegra and inquired, "What about me?"

"Actually, there's a design here that would suit your elegant throat," Allegra replied, showing her a teardrop pendant suspended by two large pearls. "Not every lady can wear this piece."

"Yes, I want this one."

*Two commissions!*

Bianca seized Allegra's hand. "Would you like to see the ruby ring Father purchased for my fifteenth birthday?"

"You have not yet turned fifteen," Lucrezia reminded her.

Bianca tilted her head to the side. "I will in a few weeks."

"She insisted on getting her birthday present early and my husband indulged her," Lucrezia explained. "Can you imagine? Patience is not one of my stepdaughter's virtues." She turned to Allegra and inquired, "How old are you, Signorina?"

"I will turn fifteen in April."

"We're the same age!" Bianca exclaimed.

"Two beautiful girls with exceptional taste," Lucrezia said

indulgently. Turning to Vittorio, she added, "Shall we discuss prices over some wine?"

Bianca led Allegra to the stairwell. "Come on."

Vittorio caught his daughter's eye and said, "We do not intend to stay too long, Signora Lucrezia. There are other clients we must visit."

Allegra followed her young hostess upstairs, then down a long corridor lined with fine oil paintings. Bianca entered a bedchamber decorated in shades of pink, white, and gold. After sitting down at a mirrored vanity table, she opened a jewelry chest covered in floral motif.

"Father spoils me," she admitted while extracting a ruby ring.

Allegra took the ring and held it up to the light pouring in from an open window. "It's well-made and the stone is of excellent quality."

Bianca slipped the ring on her finger. "I'm glad to hear it. What do you think about these other pieces?"

Allegra studied the jewelry with the eyes of an experienced goldsmith, examining the craftsmanship as well as the imperfections. "You have many fine things, Signorina Bianca."

Changing the subject, Bianca inquired, "How long will it take to complete our commissions?"

"A couple of months, perhaps. My father will deliver the pieces as soon as they are finished."

"I can hardly wait!" Bianca curled a tendril of hair around her plump white finger. "It would please me if you came with him so that we may see each other again."

"I would be delighted."

"Since this is your first time visiting *La Serenissima*—the Most Serene Republic of Venice—I would like to know what you think of our fair city."

"I find it enchanting."

"Have you taken a gondola ride on the canal?"

"Yes. The palazzos are grandiose and colorful." Allegra gazed out the window. "It's strange, yet wonderful, to see streets made of water."

Bianca stood and walked over to Allegra. "I agree."

A barge glided slowly into view. Two young men on deck pulled up fishing nets. Naked from the waist up, their toned bodies were browned from the sun. Allegra instinctively hid behind the window casement in order to remain unseen. Bianca, on the other hand, didn't move, but waved coquettishly, drawing whistles and shouts from the men.

*"Che bella!"*

A moment later there was a knock at the door and Bianca rolled her eyes. "That will be my maid, Cattina."

A woman with a sour expression poked her head into the room. "Signorina Bianca, must I remind you not to linger at the windows? Your stepmother forbids it," Cattina chastised. "It's not fitting for a girl of your station to consort with commoners, let alone fishermen!"

"I wasn't *consorting* with anyone. It was an accident," Bianca lied. "My new friend and I merely wanted to breathe in some fresh air. I didn't notice the barge until it was too late."

Cattina frowned before retreating and closing the door. Bianca led Allegra away from the windows facing the Grand Canal to another window facing the street.

"My stepmother forbids *everything*," Bianca lamented. "Lucrezia is so strict. I miss my real mother."

"What happened to her?"

"She died three years ago."

"I'm sorry," Allegra offered.

"I miss her. Have you ever lost someone you loved?"

Allegra nodded. "My friend, Lucrezia de' Medici."

"She was your friend?"

"Her father is my godfather."

Bianca's eyes became round as saucers. "You're full of surprises, aren't you? The Duke of Florence is your godfather. How intriguing." She paused, her eyes narrowing. "Tell me, do you think the rumors surrounding Lucrezia's death are true?"

Allegra hesitated. "Between you and me, yes, I do."

"How terrible! Murdered at the hands of her own husband."

"Don't repeat those words. There's no proof."

"So why do you believe the rumors?"

"Lucrezia and I were friends. We corresponded frequently. Not once did she mention feeling sick or contracting illness in her letters. Don't you find that strange?"

"I would tell my friend everything if I had one."

Surprised, Allegra said, "I imagine a beautiful and pleasant girl like you has many friends."

Bianca's eyes glistened with unshed tears as she shook her head. "Most of the girls my age are envious, snobbish creatures who gossip behind my back. I can tell you're nothing like them. I'm an excellent judge of character, you know."

Flattered, Allegra confessed, "If it's any consolation to you, I don't have many friends now that Lucrezia is dead. I used to spend time with Isabella, her sister, but she's too busy fulfilling her late mother's duties."

Bianca reached out and took hold of Allegra's hand. "Let's be friends."

"I'd like that very much. On a happier note, I'm sure you'll have a splendid time at the ball tonight."

Bianca's face lit up. "Come with me!"

"Thank you, but I didn't pack any formal gowns."

"You're thinner than me, so I'm sure you can easily fit into one of my gowns." Bianca threw open the doors of her armoire and extracted a silk gown the color of seafoam. Intricate gold embroidery and tiny copper beads adorned the bodice and sleeves. Holding it against Allegra's body, she said, "This color suits you. Here, hold this. I have a mask, too."

Bianca fetched a copper eye mask decorated with sable feathers.

Allegra held it up to her face and said, "I've never worn a mask before. It feels strange on my face."

"You won't feel it after a few minutes."

"I must ask permission of my father."

"I'm sure we can talk him into it," Bianca said, setting the gown on the canopied bed. Going to the window, she inquired, "Have you seen what we're really famous for in Venice?"

"The Piazza San Marco?" Allegra replied as she went to

stand beside her new friend.

Bianca leaned over the ledge and giggled. "No, I mean our courtesans."

Allegra's brow creased in bewilderment. "I didn't see any."

"Sometimes they pass along this street," Bianca explained, swiveling her head from left to right in search of them. "There's a rich widower a few palazzos down from ours who employs their services on occasion." She looked at Allegra and, seeing her puzzled expression, added, "Men from all over the world come to Venice to consort with our courtesans."

"Why?"

"Why do you think?" Bianca shot back saucily.

Allegra blushed. "No, I meant what makes them so special?"

"Well, in addition to their *talents*, Venetian courtesans are considered to be the most highly educated women in Europe. They're well versed in philosophy and politics, speak several languages, and the majority of them are accomplished musicians and poets. The most popular courtesans are quite wealthy and dress more elegantly than some noble ladies."

"We have courtesans in Florence, but they're nothing like what you describe."

"Florence has prostitutes," Bianca corrected. "Venetian courtesans are fit to entertain kings. If you take another gondola ride, look out for them. The most famous ones live in palazzos and you can sometimes see them lounging on their balconies, fanning themselves as if they don't have a care in the world."

"They must work long hours," Allegra commented.

Bianca laughed. "No, their lovers are extremely wealthy and maintain them in high style."

"What about the courtesans who don't have wealthy patrons?"

"The less affluent ones stake out the fashionable areas of the city. They're usually flanked by two servants so they can walk properly."

"What do you mean?"

"Venetian law requires working courtesans to wear chopines in public." Allegra shrugged and she continued, "Chopines are shoes with high platforms that makes the wearer at least a full head taller. Courtesans must stand out from other women when walking the streets."

"What a concept," Allegra mused thoughtfully.

"Sometimes I envy them," Bianca admitted.

Taken aback, Allegra inquired, "Why?"

"They enjoy the same freedom as men, and no place in the city is banned to them."

"Even public buildings?"

"Yes."

Allegra couldn't imagine such freedom. They watched the Venetians below with detached curiosity until Bianca's face lit up. Following her gaze, Allegra noticed a plainly dressed young man in the street staring up at them. Bianca smiled at him before blowing him a kiss.

Astonished by her brazenness, Allegra asked, "Do you know him?"

"His name is Pietro Bonaventuri."

Pietro caught the invisible kiss in his hand and placed it over his heart.

Bianca selected a red rose from a floral arrangement on a nearby desk then paused in thought. "Not you, my lovely," she said to the flower as she opted instead for a white lily.

The angel Gabriel was often depicted offering a white lily to Mary in Annunciation paintings because the flower symbolized virginity. Bianca let the flawless lily fall from her hand.

*Was she promising Pietro her virginity?*

Pietro peered up at Bianca with an expression of awe and gratitude; a man hopeful of carnal pleasures to come. He waved and retreated into the alley, clutching the lily to his chest.

"There. That should keep him happy for a while." Noticing Allegra's discomfiture at having witnessed such a scene, she added, "You're very pretty, you know. I'm sure you have several admirers in Florence."

"Actually, no..."

"I find that hard to believe."

Allegra thought it imprudent to confess her disdain toward

men, so she said, "I'm so busy with my studies and helping my father that I barely have time for anything else."

"There's *always* time for love, my friend."

The comment, which was meant to make Bianca appear worldly and sophisticated, rang hollow to Allegra's ears. "Is Pietro your betrothed?"

Bianca sighed sadly. "He's a lowly clerk working for a Florentine banker here in the city. Father would never approve of such a match."

"Yet, you like him."

Bianca shrugged demurely as she rearranged the flowers in the vase. "He worships me. How can I not?"

A loud knock at the door made both girls jump away from the window. It was Cattina again. "Your father is leaving now, Signorina Allegra."

The two girls followed Cattina into the salon. Vittorio drank the remainder of his wine and Lucrezia seemed pleased—an indication that she had negotiated a good price for the gemstones.

"Signore Vittorio, would you and your daughter care to join us this evening?" Bianca asked without preamble.

"What an excellent idea," Lucrezia chimed.

Vittorio's face went blank. "To the ball? I don't think—"

Lucrezia held up her hand. "Oh, I *insist*."

"We don't wish to impose on you…"

"There's no imposition, I assure you. The host is a good friend of ours. He won't mind if we extended the invitation to you and your daughter."

Vittorio smiled. "That's very kind, but—"

Lucrezia cut him off again. "Think of how pleasurable it would be for your daughter." Turning to Allegra, she asked, "Have you ever been to a masquerade ball?"

"No, Signora Lucrezia."

Lucrezia met Vittorio's eyes. "Allegra could take home a very special memory of her first trip to Venice." Lowering her voice, she added, "You can use the occasion to widen your client base."

"Very well," Vittorio conceded.

Bianca clapped her hands. "Cattina, wrap up the gown and mask that I set out on the bed."

Cattina went upstairs and returned a moment later with a neat parcel, which Vittorio accepted with gratitude. He placed an arm around his daughter when they were outside.

"Well done, Allegra. Two commissions from your designs."

Allegra's face split into a grin. "I can hardly believe it. Thank you for accepting the invitation to tonight's party."

"We'll stay for a little while, then make a polite and *early* departure." His index finger shot upward to make a point. "Always leave a social event early. It's the surest way to maintain an excellent reputation and receive more invitations."

Later that evening, Vittorio and Allegra arrived at the ambassador's stunning residence by gondola. The white marble palazzo stood out dramatically against a red twilight sky. Guests sporting fantastic masks stood on the balconies, chatting gaily and drinking wine from delicate glass goblets. Music poured from the windows as they alighted the small vessel.

They cut through the courtyard and ascended the stairs to the main floor where several couples danced in the center of an enormous ballroom. Together, they marveled at the grandeur of beveled mirrors, each finely etched with floral designs. Venetians were masters when it came to the art of glassblowing, which explained the sparkling chandeliers suspended from the frescoed ceiling.

Allegra took her father's arm as he escorted her through the throng of guests. Vittorio noticed how the eyes of several men followed his daughter. With a deep pang of regret, he realized that she was no longer a little girl.

"This is your first social event," he pointed out. "Too bad your mother chose not to come with us." Not wishing to dampen the mood, he hastily added, "What do you think so far?

"Oh, Papa, this is a magical place."

"Would you honor your father with a dance?"

"With pleasure."

The musicians played one tune after another and the dancers

kept pace with the music. After the third melody, Vittorio suggested they rest.

Bianca approached them in a pink velvet gown, her signature string of pearls, and a golden mask sporting white ostrich plumes. "Allegra!" she cried. "Is this not the most wonderful party?"

"It's incredible," Allegra replied.

"Hello, Signore Vittorio."

Vittorio bowed. "Signorina Bianca, you are a vision of loveliness."

"Thank you."

"Where are your parents?"

Bianca indicated a group of people across the room. Lucrezia caught Vittorio's eye and inclined her head. The candlelight caused the diamonds at her throat to sparkle like stars.

"Dance with me," Bianca said, pulling at Allegra's wrist.

Allegra turned to her father. "May I?"

Vittorio nodded and kept an eye on his daughter while she and Bianca danced to the merry beat of a popular tune.

A gentleman eventually came over to Vittorio and said, "Men with pretty daughters are forced to play the role of watchdogs. I should know, I have three of them."

Vittorio chuckled, recognizing him as the husband of one of his clients.

The man continued, "Signora Lucrezia's diamonds are the talk of the evening. My wife has already hinted twice that I should speak with you, so here I stand. I wish to commission a necklace similar in style and equal in quality for my wife." He paused. "And another for my mistress."

*Thank you, Signora Lucrezia.* "I'm happy to accommodate your request."

"My wife also mentioned something about an apprentice creating unusual jewelry designs."

"Ah, that would be Domenico Spinelli's protégé..."

Seeing Vittorio deeply engrossed in conversation, Bianca grabbed Allegra's hand and led her away from the dancers.

"Come quickly, we don't have much time."

Glancing nervously at her father, Allegra asked, "Where are we going?"

"Pietro is here tonight," she whispered. "He slipped a note to the scullery maid who passed it along to me."

"Do you trust your servant?"

"I keep her quiet with sweetmeats and the occasional coin," Bianca explained. "Pietro will be waiting on the lower terrazzo wearing a black cape and bauta."

"There are many people wearing bautas tonight."

Bianca ignored the comment as she squirmed her way through the guests and descended the stairs to the lower terrace. Unlike the upper balconies, this part of the palazzo was dimly lit, affording more privacy.

"There's no one here," Allegra whispered.

Bianca searched the darkness in desperation, then pointed. "There he is."

Sure enough, a young man in a black cape and white bauta mask stood in a corner, beckoning them.

"Stay here and warn me if anyone comes." When Allegra hesitated, she added, "Please do this for me. I would gladly do the same for you."

"Very well," Allegra reluctantly agreed.

Bianca ran and threw herself into Pietro's arms. Allegra kept her eyes on the stairwell and did her best to ignore the sounds of lip-smacking and moans. At one point she peeked over her shoulder and saw Pietro's hands roaming freely over Bianca's bodice.

*"I love you, Bianca."*

*"Oh Pietro…"*

Allegra cringed in disgust and was tempted to sneak back inside, but she didn't wish to upset her new friend. After all, it was thanks to Bianca's invitation that she and her father were here. To her relief, a black and white checkered harlequin and a Greek goddess appeared at the top of the stairs. They stumbled and giggled, obviously drunk. Allegra cleared her throat loudly in warning.

*"Pietro, you must go before anyone sees you!"*

Bianca appeared a moment later, breathless and bright-eyed. The girls practically ran back to the ballroom where Vittorio was avidly searching for his daughter.

"I have to go," Bianca muttered, spotting Cattina across the dance floor. "Please don't breathe a word to anyone of my meeting with Pietro."

"Your secret is safe with me," Allegra promised.

"You're a good friend. I hope to see you soon."

Catching sight of Allegra, Vittorio approached her with a frown. "Where were you? I turned around to talk to someone and you disappeared."

"Forgive me, Papa. Bianca and I grew hot and tired from dancing so we stepped onto the balcony for a bit of fresh air," Allegra lied.

"I managed to acquire two more commissions tonight."

"That's wonderful."

"Let's celebrate with a bit of wine, then we must leave soon afterward."

Early the next morning, Vittorio dispatched a messenger to the Palazzo Cappello with Bianca's gown, the mask, a note of thanks, and a bouquet of flowers. Later, Allegra accompanied her father to another client's palazzo where he sold a sapphire, then to a goldsmith's bottega where he sold a decent quantity of gold and silver. By mid-afternoon they had concluded their business in Venice.

As they walked back to the inn to collect their belongings. Allegra spotted a woman teetering on the highest shoes she'd ever seen in her life—the chopines! In addition to holding a walking stick in each hand, two servants helped her remain upright. She wore an exaggerated amount of white face powder along with garish rouge and lip paint. The gown she wore, although made of costly red velvet, screamed of vulgarity. The tight bodice's neckline plunged so low that it exposed the tops of her rosy nipples, which were highlighted with gold dust. The overflowing breasts were heavily powdered, the delicate veins carefully traced with blue paint in order to draw attention to them.

Vittorio maneuvered his way through the crowded piazza, maintaining a wide berth from the courtesan. When he caught Allegra staring, he admonished, "Avert your eyes."

Allegra was tempted to repeat what Bianca had told her about Venetian courtesans, but she thought it best to hold her tongue. After all, girls of good breeding had no business knowing about such matters.

## CHAPTER 10

Allegra worked on her first official jewelry commissions with great care and diligence, prompting Domenico to supervise his pupil's work without interference.

Upon completion of the two pendants, the old man looked into Allegra's eyes and declared, "You no longer need me."

It was the greatest compliment she had ever received from him. "Thank you, Maestro."

"It's unfortunate that we live in a world where you can't take credit for your fine work."

"I wonder how people would react if they ever found out that your *mysterious protégé* is a woman."

"Banish the thought, Allegra. They must never know the truth."

She smiled sadly. "Don't worry. I'll never reveal the secret, I promise."

*** 

Lucrezia and Bianca were extremely pleased with their pendants. It was difficult for Allegra to remain aloof as they admired *her* handiwork while praising Domenico's talented apprentice.

"Such detail," Lucrezia said, astonished by the delicate intricacy of the filigree design. "I wish to know the goldsmith's name."

Vittorio paled. "I don't know his name."

"Does Domenico intend to keep this genius under lock and key forever?"

*Genius*. Allegra smiled inwardly as she pretended to be interested in a boat floating past the open window.

Vittorio shrugged apologetically. "The Maestro must have his reasons."

Several barrels were heaped upon the deck of the boat and, in order to distract herself, Allegra tried to imagine what they contained inside. *Wine, perhaps?*

Lucrezia's brow creased in confusion. "I would think a young man with talent like *this* would be ambitious and desirous of fame."

Allegra's tongue throbbed from the pressure of her teeth as she continued staring at the barrels. *Oil? Gunpowder?*

Vittorio laughed nervously. "I agree with you, Signora Lucrezia. Perhaps he's exceedingly shy or lacks social skills." He picked up his leather satchel. "Would you care to see the new opals I've recently acquired? I also have a pair of stunning sapphires."

"I would love to see them."

While the adults chatted over prices, Bianca led Allegra upstairs to her bedchamber. "I want to wear my new pendant," she said while sitting down at her vanity. "I've missed you, Allegra."

"I've missed you, too."

Bianca slid a strand of pearls through the pendant's loop then held it to her throat. "The masquerade ball was grand, was it not?"

"So grand that it seems like a dream now," Allegra replied as she fastened the clasp.

Bianca gazed at her reflection. "It's even prettier than the sketch. Please relay my immense satisfaction to Maestro Domenico and the young man who created this for me." She paused. "Your father has been conducting business with the Maestro for many years now, am I correct?"

"Yes. Although he provides gold and gems to other goldsmiths, my father prefers working with Maestro Domenico because he's an honest man and highly skilled. He refers all commissions to him."

"I met him only once, a long time ago. He came to Venice accompanied by a plump young man. A jolly fellow."

"That would be Signore Bruno, his son."

"I believe you're correct," Bianca said. "I imagine Signore Bruno must be envious of his father's talented apprentice."

"I doubt it. Signore Bruno left Florence a while ago."

95

Allegra didn't wish to recount the tragedy that led to his departure.

"Maybe this unknown pupil will someday come to Venice in his master's place," Bianca mused while touching the pendant at her throat. "A man who can create something so fine must have amazing hands...I wonder if he's handsome." Her eyes met Allegra's in the mirror's reflection. "You're blushing," she accused, turning around in the chair. "You've seen him. You know who he is."

"No," Allegra countered.

"Do you swear upon our friendship that you don't know the young man?"

Allegra's face grew hot. "No one knows who he is."

Bianca stood and peered out the window. "Surely, you must have reached the same conclusion..."

"And what would that be?"

"His hands are divine, so he must be a good lover."

"I...I wouldn't know."

"I'm a virgin, too," Bianca confessed. "Naturally, I allow Pietro to kiss me, but we've never..."

"I didn't think you did."

"Cattina often tells me that I'm far too spirited for my own good." Changing the subject, she said, "Pietro will love this pendant—he loves *all* of my jewels. He says they pale in comparison to my beauty, however. Isn't he sweet? Father is trying to arrange a marriage between me and the widower, Girolamo Priuli."

"Who?"

"Why, the Doge of Venice, of course." Her lip curled in disgust. "Ugh, I can't bear the thought of dancing with that wrinkled old man, or bedding him for that matter!"

*You could easily suffocate him with a pillow while he slept.* Allegra was shocked by her wicked thought. "How old is he?"

"Old enough to be my grandfather! Father talks of a daughter's duty, and bringing honor to our family, and maintaining one's status." Bianca sighed. "Listening to him go on and on is tiring."

"Your father could change his mind." Bianca shook her head then began to cry. Allegra hugged her and said, "Don't cry."

Bianca stepped back and wiped away a tear. "Pietro has no title and can't afford me." Attempting a smile, she added, "Let's speak of pleasant things, shall we?"

Hoping to steer the conversation to happier shores, Allegra said, "I spotted a courtesan the last time I was here."

Bianca's face lit up. "Did you see her shoes?"

"They were the highest shoes I've ever seen in my life!"

"Was she walking funny?"

"Teetering precariously."

The conversation soon became infused with humor as Bianca recounted the time she spotted a courtesan urinating beneath her window.

Cattina eventually came to the door to announce Vittorio's departure.

Bianca reached for Allegra's hands. "The time passes too quickly when we're together. I'm happy that we're friends."

"Me too," Allegra said sincerely.

"Promise me that you'll write."

"I promise."

***

When Vittorio and Allegra arrived in Florence, Stefania greeted them with smiles and embraces. "Welcome home."

"Everyone loved Allegra's creations," Vittorio proudly announced.

Noticing the lack of joy on her daughter's face, Stefania inquired, "What's wrong, dearest? Are you not feeling well?"

"I'm fine, Mother."

"Have Gianna mix a curative," Vittorio said. "Our daughter has been morose throughout the journey. I think she may be getting ill."

"I'm not ill," Allegra countered.

"Then what's wrong?"

"Standing by quietly while someone else received praise for my work was one of the most unpleasant things I've ever experienced."

Stefania sighed. "Your father has already explained…"

"I would shout your name from the rooftops if you were my son," Vittorio offered. "I would praise your work from Venice to Sicily."

Allegra fought back tears. "Am I to remain invisible and nameless my entire life merely because of my cursed sex?"

"Allegra!" Stefania exclaimed.

Vittorio's brow creased. "Is it fame and fortune you desire?"

"No, Papa."

"What do you want, then?"

"I want *recognition* and *respect*, same as any other artisan in the city."

Stefania placed an arm around Allegra's shoulder. "Your father and I admire your talent and dedication, so does Domenico."

"Your mother is right," Vittorio said. "Is it not enough to know that we're proud of you and your fine work?"

Allegra nodded for the sake of argument. Later that night, as she stared at the moonlit ceiling from the comfort of her bed, an idea came to her. She slipped into a dressing gown, crept into the workshop, and lit several candles. Quietly, she labored through the night to create a tiny metal stamp. Her surname, Castagno, meant chestnut tree, so a *castagna* (chestnut) would serve as her signature. The back of each pendant, each necklace, and each ring—everything she created—would bear a chestnut stamp from now on. It would be her mark of excellence.

Allegra's eyes grew heavy as the night wore on, and the hours of labor began to take their toll. She stifled a yawn as the gray light of dawn seeped through the crack beneath the door. Leaning forward on the workbench, she rested her head on her arms with the intention of closing her eyes for only a few minutes.

*"Allegra?"*

Allegra stirred at the sound of her father's voice in the hallway. The bright rays of morning sun permeated the room and smoke rose from the candle stubs. Groggy and stiff from sleeping in the hard chair, she rubbed her eyes. The door opened a moment later.

Taking in the scene, Vittorio demanded, "What are you doing?"

Stefania joined her husband in the doorway, accompanied by Gianna. "It's a bit early for you to be working, is it not?"

"You haven't yet broken your fast," added Gianna.

Allegra stretched. "I created a stamp for my jewelry."

"You worked throughout the night?" Stefania inquired, dismayed. "Vittorio, this is too much. She'll make herself sick."

"I had every intention of returning to bed, Mother."

Vittorio snatched the stamp from the workbench and smiled knowingly at his daughter. "It's a brilliant solution."

Stefania peeked over her husband's shoulder. "Why did she make a chestnut stamp?"

"Because an artist has the right to sign his—*or her*—work," he replied.

*** 

Allegra and Bianca corresponded regularly throughout the summer. One of Bianca's letters contained the account of a marvelous festival in Venice, describing in vivid detail a fleet of gondolas festooned with ribbons and flowers. She also wrote about Pietro and their forbidden affair, lamenting how her father was too old to understand the concept of true love. Allegra penned letters full of encouraging words in the hope that her friend might find some comfort in them.

When Bianca's letters stopped arriving, Allegra grew concerned for her friend. Hopefully, she wasn't locked up in the doge's palazzo after being forced to marry him.

## CHAPTER 11

Allegra continued to travel with her father under the false pretense of being his assistant. Together, they journeyed to Rome, Arezzo, Orvieto, Verona, and Bologna, obtaining a total of fourteen commissions from her wonderful sketches.

Throughout the fall and winter, Allegra created rings with clusters of multicolored stones, diamonds and rubies nestled within whimsical filigree pendants, strings of carved gems surrounded by granulation beads, and earrings with layers of tiny seed pearls. After completing her commissions, she sat back to take inventory of her handiwork and felt a deep sense of pride and satisfaction.

Father and daughter set out to deliver the finished products after Easter. The clients were extremely happy, and Vittorio collected a small fortune in payments.

Allegra's patrons proudly flaunted her unique jewelry in noble households and royal courts, resulting in many more commissions. People referred to the unknown goldsmith as *La Castagna* due to the tiny chestnut stamped on the back of each piece. Nobles from Rome to Venice praised "his" talent and skill, yet no one had ever met the reclusive maestro. Some people concluded that La Castagna was seeking fame in Rome and others believed he currently resided in Venice. There were those who claimed to have met the talented goldsmith abroad, while a few maintained that he was a hideously deformed genius who never left the sanctuary of his workshop.

***

On March 11, 1564 the body of the great artist, Michelangelo Buonarroti arrived in Santa Croce. Despite long negotiations with the Roman authorities, the artist's nephew was constricted to smuggle his uncle's body in the middle of the night to Florence, preventing its burial at St. Peter's Basilica. The artist, who had lived nearly eighty-nine years, would be mourned by many.

On the same day, a slovenly dressed messenger arrived with a note for Allegra written in Bianca's flowery hand.

*Dearest Allegra,*

*I hope this letter finds you and your family in excellent health. I'm currently living in Florence with my husband, and would be delighted if you paid me a visit. I would gladly go to you, but it's unwise for me to venture out in my current condition. – Your Friend, Bianca Cappello*

Stefania stood beside her daughter as she read the letter aloud, then asked, "Does she list an address?"

Allegra handed the sheet of parchment to her mother. "Yes, here."

"This is by the Piazza San Marco."

"Why didn't Bianca write about her marriage sooner? How strange that she didn't send me an invitation. May I go visit her?" When her mother hesitated, she added, "Please? I'm worried about my friend."

"Very well."

"You can come with me, Mother."

Stefania shook her head. "I would accompany you, but the babies are sick again. Gianna and one of the male servants will go with you."

Allegra left for the San Marco neighborhood the next morning with the two servants in tow. They were instantly accosted by the pungent odor of questionable meat boiling in a vendor's cauldron as they entered the piazza. The rancid smell, combined with the stench of steaming horse manure, compelled Allegra to place a rose-scented handkerchief to her nose. They eventually stopped before a dilapidated palazzo divided into various separate living quarters. Puzzled, Allegra checked the address twice.

"Allegra!"

She looked up to see Bianca waving from a window on the highest floor. The servants waited in the minuscule courtyard while Allegra ascended the stairs to her friend's new home. A slovenly dressed servant led her to a sparsely furnished room.

101

The threadbare rug and dusty old furniture made her cringe. A nearby wall sported a bad attempt at a pastoral scene, and there were chunks of plaster missing from the fresco.

Allegra did her best not to appear shocked by Bianca's appearance as she entered the shabby salon. Accustomed to seeing the Venetian beauty attired in costly fabrics and dripping in precious jewels, she was unprepared for the cheap satin surcoat with signs of wear in the fabric.

"Thank you for coming," Bianca said, self-consciously patting her improperly coiffed hair.

"How good to see you," Allegra said while embracing her friend. "I've been so worried."

"Forgive me for not writing sooner."

Noticing the fleshiness around Bianca's face and the mound beneath the fabric of her gown, Allegra inquired, "Are you with child?"

Bianca placed both hands on her protruding belly. "You knew the situation I faced in Venice...I had to do *something*. My father would never approve of our union, so Pietro and I were secretly married last December. I was too ashamed to tell you."

"You eloped with Pietro?"

"Who else?" Bianca replied, chuckling without mirth. "This house belongs to the Bonaventuri family."

Allegra looked around with renewed interest, her eye falling on a copper bowl in bad need of polishing. There was no possible way her noble friend could be happy in such a dismal place.

Bianca shook her head in disgust. "His mother and father still don't know what to do with me. You should have seen the way they gawked at me when I arrived!"

*They were no doubt shocked by Pietro's arrogance and ambition to marry so far above his station.* "What of your father and stepmother?" Allegra inquired. "Have you heard from either of them?"

"They refuse to speak with me and will not return my letters. Father is furious that I made him look bad in the doge's eyes.

As for Lucrezia, well, she was never my friend to begin with."

"I'm sorry to hear it."

Bianca's eyes glistened. "Oh Allegra, what have I done?"

Allegra put her arm around Bianca's shoulders in a gesture of comfort. "At least you and Pietro are finally together. Surely, he must bring you some measure of comfort."

"There's no comfort to be had by him."

"Does his family treat you well, at least?"

"Well enough by peasant standards, I suppose." Bianca wiped away a tear. "They're so poor!"

"Oh, Bianca…"

"I was a stupid, silly girl. I should have known. Pietro is so far below my station." Lowering her voice, she added, "My mother-in-law forces me do menial work—darn socks, pluck chickens—can you imagine?"

"Perhaps you could sell some of your jewels and—"

"I left my jewels behind in Venice."

Allegra stared at her incredulously. "Why did you do that?"

"Guilt. Father bought them for me as gifts and I betrayed him by running away and disobeying him." Bianca looked down at her wedding band. "This is the only gold I own now." She paused, her lip trembling. "Pietro was so angry with me. He screamed and called me terrible names. Now, I must endure endless tirades on my selfishness and stupidity. I'm with child and we need the money. My jewels are worth a fortune and he could have sold them. Pietro isn't the same man I fell in love with. Gone are the honeyed words, the terms of endearments, the promises…I've grown fat, according to him. I doubt he even loves me anymore."

*Pietro is a worthless charlatan, a scoundrel of the lowest character.* "You're carrying his child, my dear. How can he not love you?" Allegra countered with far more conviction than what she actually felt.

"I was once as naïve as you, my friend," Bianca chided. "I've arrived at the conclusion that men are deceitful liars."

Allegra had arrived at the same conclusion years ago. "I wish there was something I could do."

"Actually, there is." Bianca hesitated. "Would it be possible, I mean, could I please borrow some money? I'll pay you back as soon as I can."

Allegra immediately emptied the contents of her coin purse and placed the money in Bianca's hand. "Take this, and there's no need to repay me." Then, as an afterthought, she removed the pearl earrings from her earlobes and held them out to her friend. "Take these, too. Consider them a wedding gift. I know how much you like pearls."

"I cannot possibly accept the earrings, Allegra."

"I insist."

Bianca took the earrings. Noticing the tiny chestnut imprint on the gold mounting, she inquired, "What is this?"

"That's the symbol of the new goldsmith everyone is talking about," Allegra replied. "Remember Domenico's protégé, the one who made your pendant?"

"How could I forget? I miss wearing it!"

"His identity is still unknown, but people call him La Castagna."

"Ah, because of the chestnut," Bianca deduced. "How clever. The earrings are lovely, thank you, my *best* friend."

"I'm pleased you like them."

"I knew you would understand my plight and not judge me too harshly for my folly," Bianca said sheepishly.

Allegra thought of her mother's youthful romance with Cosimo de' Medici. "I would never judge you, Bianca. Once the baby is born, Pietro will surely come around and be sweeter than ever toward you."

Bianca seemed hopeful. "Do you truly believe that?"

"I do." Allegra felt guilty for lying, but what else could she possibly say under the circumstances? A pregnant woman should be made to feel secure and content in order to deliver a healthy child.

"Pray for me, will you?"

"I'll pray every day," Allegra promised.

Bianca settled on the window seat and glanced down at the Piazza San Marco, which teemed with Florentine commoners.

A child defecated in a corner, and a man piled hay into a cart while singing out of tune. "Do you remember the views from my father's palazzo in Venice?"

Allegra was overwhelmed by pity. "I remember them well."

Bianca picked up a scrap of fabric from a basket and started mending. "I'm relegated to the role of servant in this deplorable abode. Me, a *Cappello*, doing *this*." She shook the shoddy fabric in disgust and added, "Please come see me again soon."

"I will, you can rest assured."

Allegra left the house, relieved to be out in the fresh air. She told her parents of Bianca's dire predicament during supper that evening.

"I already knew the situation," Vittorio admitted.

"Why didn't you tell me, Papa?"

"I didn't want to upset you."

Stefania poured wine into his chalice. "What else are you not telling us, Vittorio? I have the feeling you're hiding something."

"There's a warrant for Bianca's arrest."

Allegra's hand flew to her chest in shock. "Whatever for?"

"She married without paternal consent. Her father is outraged, and rightfully so. Did Bianca not mention it to you?"

Allegra shook her head. "What will happen to her if she gets arrested?"

"Her father will most likely force her into a convent."

"For how long?"

"For the rest of her life."

Allegra couldn't imagine Bianca visiting a convent, let alone being imprisoned in one. "Mother, will you please speak with my godfather on Bianca's behalf? He could offer sanctuary in Florence and prevent the magistrates from making an arrest."

"Bianca Cappello is living in hiding," Vittorio stated icily. "Not exactly the type of person deserving of Cosimo's mercy."

Stefania ignored her husband's comment and studied her daughter. "Do you believe that Bianca deserves sanctuary after disobeying her parents and bringing dishonor to her family?"

"No, she does not," Allegra conceded to the relief of her

parents. "*But* she does deserve forgiveness for putting faith in a man's lies."

Vittorio frowned. "She had no right to go against her father's will."

"Bianca was only fifteen when Pietro convinced her to elope with him in December," Allegra reasoned.

"That's no excuse," he snapped.

Allegra frowned. "Pietro has lied and broken several promises, yet I'm sure no one will force *him* into a monastery for the rest of his life. He'll go on to marry another woman while Bianca's life is ruined."

"Sounds to me as if he tricked her," Stefania commented. "That lowly young man aimed too high; his arrogance is appalling."

"Pietro was angry and abusive toward Bianca when he discovered that she left her jewels behind in Venice," Allegra said.

Vittorio and Stefania exchanged meaningful looks.

Stefania asked, "Why would she do that?"

"Bianca said she felt so guilty about betraying her father that she couldn't bear to keep his expensive gifts. Surely, that says something about her character, does it not?"

Vittorio said, "It changes nothing, however."

"No," Allegra agreed. "But it's not fair, is it?"

Stefania sighed. "Life is not fair."

Vittorio regarded his daughter thoughtfully. "Do you truly feel strongly enough about this matter that you would have your mother trouble Cosimo de' Medici over it?"

"I do," Allegra asserted.

"Very well. Then you shall ask him yourself."

Surprised, Stefania asked, "Do you think that wise, husband?"

"Our daughter is old enough to make this decision." He shook his head and added, "Ah, the foolishness of youthful love. Do you see how it can lead you into an abyss of misery if you're not careful, Allegra?"

"Rest assured, Papa, I have no intention of eloping with

anyone."

"What your father is trying to say is that someday you'll fall in love," Stefania explained. "Don't break our hearts in such a hurtful manner."

Allegra took a sip of watered wine. "I never want to fall in love."

Stefania laughed softly. "I'm afraid you have no control over your heart."

"I despise men, Mother. They're cruel and dishonest. They mislead, humiliate and even poison women." Seeing the look on her father's face, Allegra amended, "I don't think that of you, Papa."

"I'm relieved to hear it," Vittorio said wryly.

Dismayed at her daughter's negative view of the opposite sex, Stefania said, "Not all men are like Pietro."

"I realize that, but it still doesn't change my opinion."

"Perhaps in the future, you should keep your opinion to yourself," Vittorio said. "I won't have my daughter spewing forth such radical ideas."

"As you wish, Papa." Changing the subject, Allegra said, "I gave Bianca my word that I would visit her again."

Vittorio set down his fork. "Allegra—"

"Bianca is lonely and sad. She's paying dearly for putting faith in the false sanctity of love and the lies of a dishonorable lout. I don't wish to punish her further by withholding my friendship. Besides, are we not under Christian obligation to forgive the sins of others and offer comfort to those in need?"

Stefania reached for her daughter's hand. "Your father doesn't wish for you to ruin your own reputation."

Allegra looked at her parents in turn. "I gave my word that I would see her again. Please don't make me break my promise."

Vittorio sighed tiredly. "You may visit Bianca, but your visits must be infrequent and preferably brief."

"Thank you," Allegra said. "There's one more thing I must confess to you. I gave her some money—a few coins—and my pearl earrings."

"You gave Bianca jewelry?"

"As a wedding gift," Allegra said.

"How very generous of you," Stefania interjected before her husband could disapprove of the gesture. "It seems we've raised a compassionate and kind-hearted daughter, Vittorio."

"May she never be a fool," he shot back, raising the chalice to his lips.

# Chapter 12

Shortly after Allegra's sixteenth birthday, Francesco de' Medici was betrothed to Joanna of Austria, daughter of the Holy Roman Emperor. Cosimo had managed to secure a powerful bride for his son, and a banquet was thrown at Palazzo Pitti to celebrate the brilliant match.

The event would serve as Allegra's official introduction to Florentine society. On the day of the party, Gianna helped her young mistress prepare by applying a facial treatment and styling her hair.

Stefania opened the door of Allegra's bedchamber and smiled from the doorway. "You look wonderful, daughter."

"Perhaps you'll find a husband tonight," Gianna teased, tucking an errant strand of hair into the neat braided coil at the base of her neck.

Allegra shook her head vehemently, causing the older women to laugh. Suddenly, Stefania stopped laughing and placed a hand to her brow, frowning as if in pain.

"Mother, are you all right?"

Stefania shook her head dismissively. "I'm fine, only a bit tired."

Gianna was instantly at her mistress's side. "You do too much, Signora," she murmured. "You should rest a bit before you go out this evening."

"You're wearing yourself out at the orphanage," Allegra added, urging her mother to sit down on the bed.

"I'll be right back with something to make you feel better," Gianna said to Stefania before slipping out of the room.

"The little ones are so helpless," Stefania explained. "The babies are sick and require a lot of time and attention. There aren't enough nuns to care for the older children."

"We don't have to go to the party, Mother."

"Nonsense," Stefania countered. "You've been looking

forward to this for so long. I'll feel better after one of Gianna's elixirs."

"There will be other parties."

"Listen to me. Men will wish to dance with you tonight, and you'll be expected to oblige them in order to not cause offense. If any gentleman takes liberties with you, come tell me or your father immediately. Also, don't wander off alone with *anyone*. Always remain within sight of others, do you understand?"

"Yes, Mother."

"It's easy for a young, inexperienced girl to lose her reputation if she isn't mindful at all times."

"Don't worry, Mother. I won't dishonor myself or our family."

Stefania smiled. "I know you won't. You're an intelligent girl."

Vittorio appeared in the doorway a moment later. "Stefania, we should stay home if you're unwell."

"I'm fine, husband. This party is Allegra's debut into society. Doesn't she look lovely?"

He glanced at his daughter, nodded, then walked away mumbling something about stubborn wives.

Stefania drank the tonic and felt better afterward. With Gianna's help, she donned her best gown and reddened her pale cheeks with rouge.

Vittorio frowned as Stefania descended the stairs. "We should stay home, Stefania. You're obviously sick."

"How I wish you would stop coddling me, Vittorio," she snapped. "Let's hurry lest we be late."

Without another word, the three of them set off for the Palazzo Pitti escorted by two armed guards.

The aquamarines set in silver at Allegra's throat contrasted with her rose gold gown—*ice and fire*. The unusual necklace drew many looks from noble ladies when she entered the main hall of the Palazzo Pitti. Music and gay chatter filled the air as servants passed around trays of food and drink.

Isabella de' Medici greeted the Castagno family warmly before embracing Allegra. "It's been too long since I've seen your pretty face."

Allegra smiled. "Hello Isabella, it's good to see you again."

Stefania inquired, "I take it your husband is well, my lady."

"Yes, he's in Rome as we speak." Isabella took a step closer to Stefania and added, "I know my father went to see you a while ago. Thank you for your discretion."

"His Grace is always in my prayers."

Isabella smiled gratefully before noticing Allegra's stunning necklace. "What an extraordinary piece." Turning one of the stones over, she smiled at the sight of the tiny chestnut stamped into the silver. "La Castagna. I should have known."

"You've heard of him?" Vittorio inquired, surprised.

"A number of ladies in Florence praise his talent, myself included. Given that you work closely with Domenico Spinelli, have you discovered the identity of this goldsmith?" Vittorio shook his head and she continued, "He shrouds himself in mystery, which only piques everyone's curiosity. A most clever strategy."

More guests arrived, and Vittorio and Stefania were soon pulled into conversations. Isabella wound her arm through Allegra's and said, "Seeing you reminds me of old times."

"I miss those days."

"Me too. I sometimes long for my youth and the company of my late siblings. They're all in Heaven with my mother." She smiled sadly, then added, "We should go riding together one day."

"I'd like that very much."

"Look at my brother," Isabella said, changing the subject.

Allegra spotted Francesco with Bernardo and several other noblemen. The future groom seemed somewhat dazed rather than enthusiastic at the prospect of marriage.

Isabella continued, "He's always been so sensitive."

Awkward would have been a better description in Allegra's opinion, but she refrained from saying so. "I've always thought of Francesco as kind."

"Yes, he's a kind man, I'll give him that. He's also like a little boy in many ways, and I'm worried that marriage might be hard for him." She sighed. "Come, let's get something to drink, shall we? I'm parched after greeting so many guests."

Allegra hesitated. "I'd like to speak with my godfather first, if you don't mind. It's rather important."

Isabella scanned the large space. "My father was here a moment ago...Ah, there he is. Go and talk with him, then come find me afterward."

Allegra nodded. "I shall return shortly."

Cosimo smiled as his godchild approached him. "I see a lovely rose before me. Hello Allegra."

Allegra blushed as she curtsied. "Your Grace flatters me."

"*Padrino* when we are in private," he corrected.

"I hope you're well and in good health, my lord."

"Well enough, thank you," Cosimo replied, offering her his arm. "It gladdens my heart to see you here today."

"As it does mine to see you." She paused, noticing many eyes following them. "I need to ask a favor of you."

"Already the courtier, I see," he teased.

"It's not for me, it's for another girl. Bianca Cappello."

"The Venetian who ran off with the Florentine."

"You're aware that her father has a warrant out for her arrest."

"Of course, I am."

"He intends to force Bianca into a convent."

"As he should. I would do the same if one of my daughters had behaved so unscrupulously."

Allegra hung her head in defeat. "Oh."

Cosimo grasped her chin and forced her to look at him. "With that said, I know the circumstances surrounding the elopement, and I'm aware of Pietro Bonaventuri's absurd ambition. That reckless young man deserves a sound beating." He searched her face and added, "You need not worry, for I've already granted Bianca Cappello sanctuary in Florence."

Allegra took hold of his hand and kissed it. "Thank you."

"How do you know Bianca?"

"I've accompanied my father to Venice twice. Bianca's stepmother, Signora Lucrezia, is one of his best clients."

"I see."

One of the city's magistrates came to stand beside Cosimo and whispered, "Your Grace, a word, please?"

Cosimo nodded to the man. "We'll talk later, Allegra."

Having been dismissed, Allegra sought Isabella's company.

"The conversation with my father seemed to flow in your favor," Isabella commented.

Allegra said, "I asked him to protect my friend, Bianca Cappello."

"Ah, that poor girl. I convinced my father to prevent her arrest. Besides, she's already paying the price for her rebellious act; Bonaventuri is a known rake and an adulterer."

*Adulterer?* Allegra was about to press Isabella for more information when a young man with curly brown hair appeared before them.

"Who is an adulterer?" he demanded, grinning mischievously.

Isabella quirked an eyebrow at him. "Signorina Allegra Castagno, allow me to present Troilo Orsini, my husband's cousin. He's charged with looking after me in Florence while Paolo tends to his many duties elsewhere."

Allegra inclined her head. "It's a pleasure to meet you, Signore Troilo."

Troilo bowed with flourish before bending over Allegra's hand and kissing her knuckles. "The pleasure is *all* mine."

Allegra retracted her hand and blushed when she caught her father watching the scene from across the room.

Isabella followed Allegra's gaze. "I'm certain your father is well aware that every eligible male in this room is aching to be introduced to you."

Troilo said, "Take my cousin, for example. He comes from a noble family in Rome. He's witty, possesses political savvy— good-looking, too."

"He wishes to meet Allegra?" Isabella inquired.

"From the moment she arrived," he replied. "I'll go and fetch him."

"Breathe deeply, Allegra," Isabella said. "Here comes your

father."

Vittorio came to stand beside his daughter. "Are you enjoying yourself?"

"Yes, Papa."

Bernardo joined them and complimented Allegra lavishly. "Signore Vittorio, your little girl has blossomed into a lovely flower." Vittorio inclined his head and he continued, "Given that this is your first time at court, Signorina Allegra, would you do me the honor of a dance?"

Allegra smiled. "With pleasure, Signore Bernardo."

Bernardo waited for Vittorio to nod his head before escorting her toward a group of dancers.

"I remember my first time at court. The clothes, the jewels, the intrigue…I'm practically an old man in comparison to you, but that day is still fresh in my memory." He paused. "You must be excited."

"I am."

He stood very straight and his movements were precise. Allegra did her best to follow his steps.

Bernardo smiled warmly. "You seem to have grown up overnight. Look at you, such a pretty girl."

"You are too kind."

"You know me better than that," he chided.

It was true. Bernardo was not one to flatter falsely.

He continued, "There are many young lords here tonight who will no doubt try to sink their claws into you. As someone who respects your family and has your best interests at heart, may I offer you some advice?"

"Any wisdom you wish to impart will be most appreciated."

"You already know this court is full of ambitious men who seek your godfather's favor." He waited for her to nod, then said, "Never reveal anything of importance, especially to these upstarts who believe themselves to be great men before they even grow hair on their chins."

At this, Allegra giggled. "I won't."

"There are no secrets at court. People talk. Mind what you say."

114

"Thank you, Signore Bernardo, I'll be sure to follow your good counsel."

"I know you miss Lucrezia as much as I do. Being the practical person she was, she would have offered you the same advice."

Allegra grew teary-eyed at the mention of her late friend's name. "She already did, years ago. Lucrezia told me to guard my heart, keep it safe, and not trust men."

Bernardo nodded. "You'll fare well in this city if you take her advice."

When the dance ended, Bernardo escorted her back to where Vittorio and Isabella stood, then excused himself. Troilo approached a moment later with an attractive young man in tow.

Troilo said, "Signore Vittorio, Signorina Allegra, I present my cousin, Cesare Orsini. He's visiting from Rome."

Cesare bowed over Allegra's hand, holding it only as long as necessary beneath Vittorio's watchful gaze. She couldn't help but admire his hair, which was a thick mane of gold.

Vittorio cleared his throat. "How long have you been in Florence?"

"Only a few weeks," Cesare replied. "It's a remarkable city."

"Cesare finds the art in Florence quite impressionable," Troilo added with a smile that implied a private joke.

"That's a common reaction when people visit our city," Vittorio said.

Cesare turned his attention to Allegra. "Do you have a favorite artist?"

"I admire all of them."

"Equally?"

"Yes."

Cesare grinned. "A most diplomatic reply."

Not wishing to appear dull, Allegra said, "Each artist has unique talents, but I do have some works that I favor more than others."

"Such as?"

"Perseus, for example, is one of the most ambitious and

brilliantly executed sculptures in the city. The sculptor is also a master goldsmith."

"Benvenuto Cellini's work is impressive," Vittorio conceded. "But let's not forget Michelangelo's David."

"Or Donatello, for that matter," Isabella said.

"Judith and Holofernes is my favorite," Allegra agreed.

"Because it represents God's divine justice?" Cesare inquired.

*No, because a powerful woman is giving an evil man exactly what he deserves.* Allegra smiled sweetly and replied, "Yes."

"A bit too savage for my taste," Troilo countered. "I still think Botticelli's Primavera is the finest painting in Florence."

"Wait," Isabella said. "I thought we were discussing sculpture."

They talked of Florentine art while the musicians struck a new tune.

Cesare looked at Vittorio. "Signore, would you grant me permission to dance with your daughter?" At Vittorio's wary nod, he bowed to Allegra. "Shall we, Signorina?"

Allegra allowed him to take her hand and they joined the other dancers. She could not help but admire the length and agility of the young man's body as it stepped gracefully to the music.

Cesare studied her face with an expression of approval. "You are Cosimo de' Medici's godchild, yet this is the first time I've seen you at court."

"I've been to the Palazzo Pitti several times, but this is my first public social event."

They spun around then came together, and he held her in his arms for a brief instant. "You should be punished, you know."

"Whatever for?"

"For depriving us of your beauty."

*So this is the game of young lords at court.* Allegra laughed derisively, which he found disconcerting.

Undeterred, his heavy-lidded green eyes dropped to her mouth. "Such rosy lips. Have you ever been kissed, Allegra?"

For some strange reason, the way he looked at her made her

feel giddy and angry at the same time. *Don't trust men...*

"No, sir, I have not."

*Santo Cristo! Virgin lips!* "If your father wasn't watching me like a ravenous hawk, I would steal a kiss from you right now."

Allegra was reminded of the shadowy terrace in Venice where Pietro stole furtive kisses from Bianca—kisses that eventually led to her current, miserable plight.

He took a step closer and her eyes narrowed. "You wouldn't dare."

"Oh, but I *would* dare!"

"Stealing kisses from maidens is the work of knaves."

"I would gladly suffer the insult to taste your sweet lips...And you would beg me to kiss you again."

"Perhaps in your dreams I would behave thusly."

"Oho! What a sharp retort for a girl with such an innocent face and gracious demeanor."

"I believe you lack proper manners, Signore Cesare," she said lightly, her sweet tone laced with a bit of venom. "You need a lesson in chivalry."

His eyes reflected genuine pain. "You wound me to the core. Your words pierce my heart like an arrow."

"I've made your acquaintance only a moment ago, yet I hold the power to wound you? Take care with that fragile heart of yours, sir."

Cesare placed a hand over his heart in supplication. "What? No honeyed words for your new admirer?"

"Unfortunately, I have no beehives to provide the honey..."

"Face of a goddess, tongue of a shrew," he said, eyes sparkling with excitement as she drew close.

Allegra placed her lips to his ear. "Face of a god, tongue of a charlatan."

Cesare was genuinely shocked. Up until that moment he assumed their verbal spar was all in good fun. Most girls behaved coquettishly, but gave in to his charms after a round or two of playful banter. Such was not the case with Allegra Castagno.

They continued dancing quietly as his mind raced to find something suitable to say that didn't involve teasing or shallow courtly phrases. Allegra deprived him of the chance, by curtsying and walking away the moment the music stopped. Stunned at being rejected by a lady for the first time in his life, Cesare stormed off the dance floor.

Allegra paused at the buffet table and scanned the room. Isabella danced with Troilo, her mother chatted with a group of ladies, and her father spoke animatedly with a man sporting a crop of reddish hair. Although he had his back to her, she could see the man's clothing was of good quality. Curious, she walked toward her father and regretted it instantly when the man turned his head and caught her eye. Her gaze shifted to her father, who was now obliged to make an introduction.

Vittorio said, "This is my daughter, Allegra."

Bending over her hand, the man said, "Matteo Vanusi, at your service." He searched her face, squinting his eyes. "I must say, Signorina, you look familiar. Have we met?"

Allegra's heart raced. "No, I don't believe so."

Vittorio looked from one to the other, perplexed. "It's highly unlikely that you know my daughter."

"I must be mistaking her with someone else," Matteo agreed. Noticing Allegra's necklace, he frowned. "May I inquire where you got that?"

"It's was made by the goldsmith, La Castagna."

A shadow crossed his face. "I hear his name more and more each day."

"I'm not surprised. His designs are unique and his pieces are expertly crafted," she pointed out, ignoring her father's warning look.

Matteo bristled. "You seem to be very familiar with his work."

"I've seen a number of ladies flaunting his creations."

"Yet you're the only one doing so tonight."

Vittorio gave Allegra a meaningful look and said, "Signore Matteo is swiftly gaining recognition in the city as a *goldsmith*."

"Is that so?" she inquired with feigned interest.

Matteo named his noble patrons in an attempt to impress them. To Allegra's satisfaction, the list was short. Smiling smugly, he added, "I doubt La Castagna will ride out the storm. Few of us do. People will tire of his audacious designs soon enough."

His arrogant words transported Allegra back in time to the Piazza delle Cipolle, when she was pushed to the ground. The sneering vendors, the horse dung, the humiliation...

Allegra's eyes narrowed. "Do you really believe that, Signore Matteo?"

"I most certainly do."

"And yet...Isabella de' Medici informed me only a moment ago that she commissioned a necklace similar to mine from La Castagna." It was her turn to humiliate him, and she did so with great satisfaction. "The storm you speak of is little more than gentle summer rain."

Matteo's face was deep red as he turned to Vittorio. "Spinelli still hasn't discovered who this man is?"

Vittorio's eyes were on his daughter as he replied, "No."

Allegra interjected, "I find it fascinating that a *genius* of his caliber would wish to remain anonymous. It shows humility, which is a cornerstone of excellent character, don't you agree?"

Matteo raised an eyebrow. "You obviously admire this man, Signorina."

"Oh, very much so."

Vittorio motioned to a nearby servant bearing a tray of silver chalices. "Let's have a bit of wine, shall we?"

They drank wine and the conversation veered toward safer topics like construction projects and the installation of public artworks. Matteo's attempts at garnering attention from Allegra through witty comments were met with monosyllabic responses.

Another gentleman approached them, eager to speak with Vittorio. Matteo seized the opportunity to dance with Allegra. This was her third dance of the evening. Was there a limit for the sake of propriety? Her mother hadn't mentioned a specific number. As they dipped and pranced to the melody, he did his best to charm her, but she remained aloof.

When the music stopped, he said, "You must let me call on you."

Allegra demurely lowered her eyes and headed to where Isabella stood.

"Who was that?" she inquired.

"Matteo Vanusi, the goldsmith."

Cesare and Matteo exchanged venomous looks as they crossed paths.

Isabella chuckled. "Your first time at court and two men are already fighting over you. I'm sure you're the envy of every girl present."

"The girls can have them both for all I care."

"You're not the slightest bit interested in either one?"

"Not at all."

"Which will only drive them—and other men—to pursue you more ardently. What a clever girl you are!"

Allegra was taken aback by the implication of her words. "That's not my intention, Isabella, I assure you."

"You're serious," Isabella observed, intrigued. "Lucrezia must have influenced you. She, too, had little patience for courtiers. Well, prepare yourself for unwanted attention; men are drawn to challenges."

"Oh no…"

Seeing the distress on Allegra's face, Isabella laughed aloud. "I'll wager that every girl here is on display for the marriage market."

"Not me. I find men to be boorish and arrogant." Fearing she spoke out of turn, she added, "Forgive me, I didn't mean to imply that all men are wicked."

"You need not explain yourself. In fact, I'm impressed by your prudence. The majority of girls have no concept of what courtship and marriage entails. Given the choice, I would not have married at all."

"At least you remained here in Florence under your father's protection after marrying the duke."

"I do enjoy more liberty than most wives, it's true. But it's

120

not the same as being free." A servant walked by with a tray full of wine goblets. Isabella snatched two of them and handed one to her friend. "To spinsterhood."

Allegra laughed at the jest before taking a sip, but deep down inside she believed spinsterhood to be the ideal subterfuge. A husband would surely put an end to her happy days of jewelry making.

Later in the evening, Cosimo pulled the Castagno family aside. "Be careful returning to your home, my friends," he warned. "The Otto found the body of a Milanese nobleman beneath the portico of Santa Felicita this morning. He'd been stabbed and robbed of his coin purse. The poor fellow was in Florence visiting his aunt."

"How terrible," Stefania said. "What is this world coming to?"

Cosimo shook his head sadly. "I've done everything within my power to curb violent crime. Alas, my efforts have failed."

"Crime is the bane of every city, Your Grace," Vittorio said.

"Francesco and I walk past Santa Felicita every day before crossing the Ponte Vecchio on our way to the Palazzo Vecchio," Cosimo said. "Easy targets for a pickpocket's blade or an enemy's assassination plot."

"God forbid," Stefania murmured, evoking a glance from Vittorio.

"I've already increased the number of my guards." Lowering his voice, Cosimo added, "My heir is about to marry a distinguished member of Austrian nobility. I don't want his wife to feel unsafe here in Florence. I can't bear to think what would happen if some ruffian were to attack us in her presence. Such an affront before a lady of her status would be disastrous."

"Pity you don't have an underground tunnel like the pope in Rome," Vittorio said. "His Holiness can easily traverse the route between the Holy See and the Castel Sant'Angelo privately and without fear."

"It would be difficult to create a tunnel with the Arno in the way," Cosimo mused aloud.

"Why not build a tunnel in the sky, high above the street?"

Allegra suggested. "You could walk over the rooftops."

Vittorio and Stefania chuckled at their daughter's outrageous suggestion. Cosimo, on the other hand, stared at Allegra with serious contemplation.

***

A colorful posy and a confection of marzipan wrapped in ribbon arrived at the Castagno household the next day. Stefania and Vittorio stood over their daughter's shoulder as she read aloud the notes attached to each gift.

"Last night you accused my heart of being fragile, but you're the one responsible for its weakened state," Allegra paused to stifle a giggle. "Please accept these flowers as a small token of my admiration. Cesare Orsini."

Stefania asked in a faint voice, "What does the other one say?"

Vittorio frowned. "You are unwell, wife."

"Father is right," Allegra agreed.

Stefania shook her head. "I'll be fine. Go on, read the other letter."

Allegra held up the other note. "Signorina Allegra, it was a pleasure meeting you and I look forward to our next encounter. Kind regards to your family, Your Servant, Matteo Vanusi."

"At least that one is free of melodrama," Vittorio commented drily.

Motioning to a nearby servant, Allegra said, "Place the flowers in a vase and set them out in the main hall. Dispose of these notes and take the marzipan to the kitchen."

Vittorio heaved an exaggerated sigh. "I'm sure more of these young men will start lining up at the door. Like flies to honey."

Stefania asked breathlessly, "Can you blame them? Look at our daughter, she's a prize to be had."

Allegra noticed that her mother's speech was labored. "You should rest, Mother. Please."

Her hand flew to her chest, her face white. "Perhaps you…are right."

Vittorio walked to where Stefania sat and took hold of her hand. "Come. I'll escort you to your chamber. Last night was too much for you. We should have stayed home." To Allegra, he added, "Send each gentleman a brief and formal note of thanks, nothing more."

"Yes, Papa."

Stefania stood and swayed. "Oh my…I feel…"

Vittorio caught his fainting wife before she hit the floor.

Allegra called for help. Gianna and a few servants came at once.

"Fetch the physician!" Vittorio cried. "Hurry!"

They carried Stefania to bed.

"You should not have ventured out last night," Vittorio chided.

Gianna's brow creased with concern at the sight of Stefania's white face. Touching her mistress's clammy forehead, she gasped. "She is burning with fever."

She hastily poured water from a pitcher into a basin, then soaked a cloth before applying it to Stefania's hot brow.

Stefania tried to speak through chattering teeth. "Get out. Babies…sick."

"Forget the babies," Vittorio snapped.

Allegra hovered nearby. "Gianna, what can I do?"

"Stay with your mother while I go to the kitchen to fetch some feverfew."

Stefania waved her hand at them and repeated, "Get out…*babies sick*."

Vittorio finally understood. He grabbed Allegra's shoulders and led her away from the bed. "I think she's trying to tell us that the children at the orphanage are sick."

"Could it be something contagious?" Allegra asked, alarmed.

"Let's hope not."

The physician arrived with disturbing news: the orphans at the Spedale degli Innocenti were battling the sweating sickness.

"How bad is it?" Vittorio demanded.

"Worse than the last time it raged through Florence," he replied while removing several bottles and unguents from his leather satchel. "I will do my very best to help your wife."

First, he administered an elixir consisting of coriander for fever and wolf's bane for Stefania's relentless headache, then he made her drink a fortifying tonic to regulate the humors. Before departing, he admonished Vittorio, Allegra, and Gianna to keep a vigilant eye on his patient.

They took turns sitting with Stefania throughout the night, periodically placing dampened cloths on her forehead as she tossed and turned with delirium. When her condition failed to improve, the physician was again summoned. This time, he resorted to bloodletting, which did little good.

"I'm going to die," Stefania moaned weakly.

"No, you're not," Allegra countered.

Stefania tossed and turned in bed, growing weaker by the hour. Unable to hold down any solid food, she subsisted on small amounts of broth and watered wine.

While Allegra remained optimistic in regard to her mother's condition, Vittorio didn't foster any false hope. It was common knowledge that those afflicted by the strange malady seldom survived. Some blamed foreigners from Africa for spreading the disease in Tuscany, while others claimed it came from consuming improperly cooked meats. A few implied it was a consequence of too much sexual activity.

Gianna acquired dottore masks, stuffing the long noses with potent herbs to prevent contagion. Allegra and Vittorio took turns reading to Stefania when she was lucid, and praying for her recovery when she was asleep.

By the end of the fourth day, the physician pulled Vittorio aside. "I've done everything within my power, Signore. Your wife is in God's hands now. I advise you to prepare yourselves for the inevitable."

Sickened with grief, Vittorio fought back tears. "How long?"

"A day, perhaps two."

The following morning when Vittorio entered his wife's bedchamber, he froze. Stefania's pallor was ashen. With a heavy heart, he knew she'd be gone before the day's end.

Seeing her husband's shocked expression, she said, "I'm

hideous."

"You're beautiful."

"Vittorio…My love."

"Oh, God, Stefania," he cried, his eyes filling with tears.

"Be strong for our daughter…"

"I will."

"Allegra must marry a man of her own choosing…for love, like us."

He nodded, taking her hand into his own. "She'll marry for love."

"Swear it," she insisted, her eyes fierce.

"I swear it."

"Let her make jewelry…"

"I will."

"Set her free." Stefania faded in and out of consciousness, then whispered, "Cosimo…"

Vittorio's mouth hardened into a thin line, but he immediately dispatched a messenger. "Tell His Grace that Stefania Rossi is on her deathbed."

Cosimo arrived within the hour and donned the dottore mask in order to say farewell to Stefania. Vittorio and Allegra reluctantly afforded him some privacy by vacating the room while Gianna remained discreetly out of sight in her mistress's antechamber.

Stefania smiled weakly. "You came…"

Cosimo sat in a chair by the bed, holding her hand. "Of course I did. I shall summon my best physicians and healers to help you."

She closed her eyes. "It's too late."

"I've already lost Eleonora, I can't bear to lose you, too."

Mustering all her strength, she lifted her head from the pillow. "Watch over Allegra and Vittorio. Promise me…"

He removed the mask and gazed into her eyes. "I promise."

"Thank you…" She closed her eyes. "Gianna."

Gianna ran out of the antechamber. "Yes, Signora?"

Stefania croaked through cracked lips, "It's time."

Gianna sent for the priest.

Cosimo's eyes filled with tears as he kissed her forehead. "God's grace be upon you, my sweet Stefania."

Vittorio and Allegra rushed into the room and surrounded Stefania, holding her hands. Cosimo retreated to the background and watched as his former lover struggled to pull air into her lungs. The priest was halfway through performing the last rites when Stefania heaved a final shuddering breath. The expression on her face was peaceful.

Vittorio threw himself upon the bed and wept for his dead wife. Allegra turned to Cosimo, who pulled her into his arms and soothed her with words of comfort.

# CHAPTER 13

Vittorio traveled to Rome three weeks after Stefania's funeral. Despite her father's urgings to accompany him, Allegra insisted on remaining in Florence. For the next several months, her emotional distress served as the impetus for creating remarkable jewelry. The loss of her mother had left a hole in her heart, and she attempted to fill it by immersing herself completely in her craft. Sometimes, the tears of grief mingled with the precious metals and gemstones. When she had finally exhausted herself, she carefully wrapped each exquisite piece in linen, placed them in a basket, and went to Domenico's house.

\*\*\*

The old man stretched as he slowly got out of bed. At his age, moving cautiously was a necessity. Brittle bones and aching joints—how much longer would God allow him to live? The sun had not yet risen and the sky was tinted gray-violet. The hungry cat scratched at the door, mewling loudly in her demand to be fed. The flea-bitten animal was sometimes a nuisance, but at least she was a loyal companion.

"Coming, coming," Domenico mumbled as he shuffled across the floor.

The orange feline rushed into the room as soon as he opened the door. Noticing the basket on his doorstep, he stepped onto the stoop and glanced around. A cloaked figure watched him from the end of the alley. The moment he bent to retrieve the basket, the figure disappeared around the corner. Fingering the linen cloth, he caught a glimpse of polished gold and immediately ducked back inside the house. After locking the door, he unwrapped each piece and spread them out on the table. His expression was one of incredulity as he stared at the fantastic jewelry.

This time, Allegra had truly outdone herself.

Matteo Vanusi called on Allegra after a respectable period of mourning. Hearing that his rival was trying to steal the object of his desire, Cesare Orsini also paid her a visit. The men sent gifts and flowers regularly, which Allegra passed along to the servants, who were more than happy to accept them. She treated both men coolly but politely, resisting their attempts at flirtation and physical contact.

Matteo Vanusi paid Vittorio an unexpected visit one afternoon. The men talked for a while in private before Allegra was invited to join them.

After polite greetings were exchanged, Vittorio said, "Signore Matteo informed me that he opened a new bottega on Via Roma, which is only a stone's throw from the Mercato Nuovo."

"A fine location," Allegra said. "I wish you success in your endeavor."

"Hopefully, you and your father can visit my establishment soon."

"We'd be delighted," Vittorio replied, ignoring his daughter's wry look.

The magnificent brooch on Allegra's bodice drew Matteo's gaze. "You flaunt La Castagna's jewelry often, yet it would please me greatly to see you wear one of my pieces," he said, producing a small box from inside his cloak. "Naturally, nothing my hands create can match your beauty, but this small token of my admiration will hopefully delight you."

Allegra hesitated, glancing at her father. "You should not have troubled yourself, Signore Matteo."

"Open it," he prompted.

Allegra opened the box to find a pair of sapphire earrings inside. They were well made, but common.

Matteo asked worriedly, "Do you like them?"

"Of course she does," Vittorio replied on his daughter's behalf. "This is a most generous gift, is it not, Allegra?"

"Yes," she said dutifully. "Thank you, Signore Matteo."

When Matteo departed, Allegra inquired, "What did he

want?"

"To see you, obviously," Vittorio replied drily. "You can't simply give those earrings to the servants."

"I don't want to wear them."

"Sweetheart, you can't go through life loathing men."

"His jewelry is common and dull."

Vittorio raised an eyebrow. "Matteo came here to propose a partnership. He's willing to split the profits with me if I can entice La Castagna to work exclusively for his bottega."

"Ha!"

"He tried to convince Domenico, too, but he wasn't interested."

"Matteo carries on as if he hates La Castagna."

"Oh, he does," Vittorio assured her. "Matteo is no fool, however. He can't compete with the best goldsmith in Tuscany."

***

Bianca gave birth to a girl, and named her Pellegrina, after her own birth mother. Allegra, along with a spattering of Pietro's friends, was invited to a modest celebration at the Bonaventuri home. After a mediocre dinner consisting of boiled capons and strained conversation, Bianca led Allegra away from the guests. They sat together in the far corner of the room, well out of earshot.

"Pellegrina is adorable," Allegra said. "You must be so happy."

"I am," Bianca affirmed. "She's given me a reason to live."

Allegra's brow creased in concern. "Don't say that, Bianca. You have so much to live for...Pietro is happy, too, is he not?"

Rather than reply, Bianca lowered her head and whispered, "There's something I must tell you."

"What is it?"

Bianca's eyes slid toward her husband and his friends, revealing unmasked contempt. "Pietro has a mistress."

Although Isabella had already referred to Pietro's adultery, Allegra feigned ignorance for the sake of her friend's dignity. "Are you certain?"

"I discovered a woman's leather glove in his pocket—perfumed, no less. It was tightly rolled and tied with a ribbon, like a love token."

"Did you confront him with this discovery?"

"Of course, I did! He said it was none of my concern."

Noticing the heightened color in her cheeks, Allegra said, "Calm yourself, you must retain your health and wits for little Pellegrina's sake."

"So much for my husband's love being restored once the baby is born."

"You were heavy with child," Allegra reasoned. "It's not uncommon for men to seek their physical needs elsewhere when their wives are indisposed by pregnancy. Pellegrina's birth was recent, and you're practically back to your old self again."

"Do you think so?" Bianca asked skeptically while examining herself in a nearby lusterless mirror. "Delivering Pellegrina has deprived me of my youthful vigor and beauty."

Hearing these words, Allegra was instantly transported back in time. Didn't Anabella utter a similar lament after birthing Agostino? Naturally, her mind wandered from Anabella to poor, devastated Bruno. *How was he? Where was he?*

"Do you agree?" Bianca demanded.

Allegra averted her eyes from Bianca's bulging waist. "Once your figure is fully restored, Pietro won't be able to resist the most captivating woman in Florence."

"You exaggerate because you're my friend."

"You were one of the most celebrated beauties in Venice, Bianca. The Florentines appreciate anything pleasing to the eye, including you."

Flattered, Bianca grinned from ear to ear. "You're so good to me, my dear. Let's go upstairs and sit by the window. We can watch the people below or we can discuss your new admirer."

Allegra shook her head in mock disdain as she followed Bianca down a short hallway and up a flight of stairs. "There's nothing to discuss."

Bianca twisted the tight-fitting wedding band around her

finger as she took a seat by the window. "I heard Matteo Vanusi is handsome."

"You heard correctly," Allegra conceded, sitting beside her. "What I want to know is from whom."

"The servants, of course. There's a gossip ring at the market, you know."

"I see."

"I also heard that he sends gifts on a regular basis. Flowers, sweetmeats, trinkets, and—if the rumor is true—a finely crafted lute gilded in silver."

"It's true. I have no musical ability but I own a gilded lute."

"You don't seem impressed." When Allegra shrugged, Bianca added, "Many women would swoon over a man who sends such lavish gifts."

"I'm not one of them."

"What does it take to soften your hard heart, Allegra Castagno?"

"I must reprimand my servants for their loose tongues."

"Harmless gossip, I assure you. Don't be too harsh with them."

"They have far too much time on their hands," Allegra countered. "I should assign extra chores to keep them busy."

Bianca tilted her head to the side. "I wish someone like Matteo Vanusi would court me like that. I would leave Pietro in an instant."

"He's trying to coax my father into a business partnership by showering me with gifts."

"Regardless of the reason, I highly advise you to enjoy the attention while you can. Someday, it may all end." Bianca gazed out the window, her eyes sad. "You don't want to end up like me."

\*\*\*

Michelangelo Buonarroti's public funeral was held on July 14, 1564 in the Basilica of San Lorenzo. The ostentatious affair was likened to a princely funeral, accompanied by great pomp and royal mourners. His coffin was displayed in the center of the nave, surrounded by his remarkable artwork and sculptures.

The entire city of Florence, from peasant to noble, came to pay their last respects to one of the greatest artists of all time. The coffin was then transported to Santa Croce, and Michelangelo's remains laid to rest in a magnificent sarcophagus designed by Vasari.

The marriage between Francesco de' Medici and Joanna of Austria took place the following year in December. To commemorate the grand event, Giambologna created a remarkable sculpture depicting Florence's victory of its rival, Pisa. The piece was housed in the Palazzo Vecchio where politicians and foreign dignitaries would see it.

The lavish wedding feast was celebrated with great pomp, lasting several days. Sumptuous dining, lively games, dancing, and various other forms of entertainment lasted throughout the afternoons and evenings.

Adorned in a gown of plum velvet, Allegra accompanied her father to the Palazzo Pitti in order to partake of the celebration. It was the first social event either of them had attended since Stefania's death. Torches illuminated the façade of the grandiose palazzo, and warm candlelight poured from the windows. Soft music filled the cold night air as they entered the courtyard.

Bernardo had outdone himself in planning the wedding supper. Roasted swans, peacocks, and pheasants were presented with their feathers carefully intact. Tender suckling pig and savory stews were served alongside delicate vegetable soufflés and spicy sauces. Finally, servants appeared with bowls of fruits that no one had ever seen before.

Bernardo took one of the bowls and presented it to Francesco himself. "From the Land of Amerigo to your table, my lord."

Francesco examined the reddish-yellow fruit before taking a bite. The juice and seeds dribbled down his chin. Wiping the moisture with his hand, he frowned. "Not very sweet, is it? The flavor is rather interesting."

Bernardo held the bowl out to Joanna. She tasted one, made a face, then set it down on her plate.

Francesco took another bite. "I like it. What are they called?"

"Pomi d'oro," Bernardo replied. "Golden fruits."

At the meal's conclusion, Bernardo dazzled the bride and groom with a magnificent castle made from thin sugar wafers. In addition to this, he had prepared his own special recipe of an icy vanilla custard that was both creamy and decadent.

Allegra had never eaten so much delicious food in one sitting. Afterward, as the guests began milling about, she became aware of three things: Cesare's hurtful glances in her direction, the suspicious looks on the faces of guests as they watched Troilo dancing with Isabella, and Francesco's immense disappointment. At one point during the celebration, she even overheard an odd exchange between the groom and his new bride.

"My father had the courtyard of the Palazzo Vecchio decorated *specifically* for you," Francesco explained, his voice tight with annoyance. "The lunettes were painted with murals of Austrian towns in your honor. Naturally, we're eager to show them to you."

Joanna's wan smile didn't reach her eyes. "Your father's gesture was most kind, but quite unnecessary. We have many painted lunettes and frescoes where I come from."

Being a sensitive man, Francesco took offense to his wife's lack of enthusiasm. "He did it to please you."

She sighed impatiently. "We have good manners where I come from, too. Rest assured, my lord, I shall thank him."

Changing the subject, he said, "Are you aware that we're planning on building our own private passageway above the city? Your feet need never touch the ground when crossing the Arno River."

"I heard that rumor," Joanna retorted dismissively.

"It's no rumor, I can assure you."

Ignoring him, she turned to speak to one of the ladies in her retinue.

Allegra could not help feeling sorry for Francesco as she watched him shuffle off like a dejected, hurt little boy. Joanna's snobbiness toward the Medici heir was appalling, to say the least. Isabella, who had also witnessed the newlywed couple's exchange, came to stand beside Allegra.

"What was *that* all about?"

"Your brother wishes to show his bride the lunettes in the Palazzo Vecchio, and she seems to have little interest in them. She wasn't impressed with Vasari's corridor, either."

"Austrian bitch," Isabella murmured as she exchanged an empty wine chalice for a full one. "I swear that woman has gone out of her way to be unpleasant to everyone from the moment she stepped foot in Florence."

"I'm sorry to hear it. Francesco is such a kind man."

Smelling the alcohol on Isabella's breath, Allegra wondered exactly how many of those chalices she had consumed.

Isabella took a deep sip and said, "My brother deserves better. I tried to warn my father, but he wouldn't listen...Joanna is the daughter of the Holy Roman Emperor, after all. Politically speaking, it's a brilliant match."

"Perhaps in time things between them will get better. Who knows? It may end up being a love match?"

Isabella laughed without humor. "Like my marriage?"

The sarcasm wasn't lost on Allegra. Isabella's union was obviously one of pure convenience. In fact, none of the Medici children were blessed with a love-match like the one their parents had enjoyed.

Isabella's eyes crinkled with mirth. "Look who's here."

Allegra spun around and found herself face to face with Cesare Orsini.

"Did you like the flowers I sent you yesterday?" he inquired.

"I did, thank you."

"I still have no idea what your favorite flower is, so I'll keep sending you different varieties until I do."

"Irises are my favorite, so you can stop now."

"Ah, the *giglio*, symbol of Florence," he said. "I should have known. I shall procure irises for you from now on."

"Pity you told him," Isabella said. "In time, he would have sent you an entire garden."

Allegra shook her head. "You shouldn't spend your money on me."

Troilo arrived and said, "You seem perplexed, cousin."

Ignoring him, Cesare stepped in Allegra's path as she started to walk away. "Don't deprive us of your company so soon, Signorina."

"I'm going to check on my father."

"Your father is deeply engrossed in a political discussion," Troilo said. "Now would not be the time to seek him out."

Allegra spied her father amid a group of old men wearing serious expressions. "Has something happened?"

"Only a new tax."

"Have at least one dance with me," Cesare interjected. "Please?"

The young man was persistent, Allegra thought as she acquiesced for the sake of politeness. Isabella and Troilo grinned mischievously as Cesare led her toward a group of young people forming a ring by holding hands. The dancers parted the circle to allow the newcomers, who quickly stepped in tune with the music. As the beat and tempo of the merry tune quickened, the dancers were forced to keep pace. Couples paired off and switched throughout the melody, and Allegra soon found herself having fun for the first time since her mother's death.

Allegra and the other ladies spun around and, when she was face to face with Cesare again, he said, "You're prettier when you smile. Perhaps now you'll finally allow me to steal that kiss."

"Stealing is a sin," she retorted with a wink.

Construction on the Uffizi wasn't yet finished when Cosimo commissioned Giorgio Vasari to create an elevated corridor connecting the Palazzo Vecchio to the Palazzo Pitti. Remarkably, it took only five months to complete the ingenious and highly ambitious project. Beginning on the south side of the Palazzo Vecchio, it joined the Uffizi and crossed the Lungarno degli Archibusieri, following the north bank of the River Arno over the Ponte Vecchio. The Mannelli family refused to sell or alter their ancient tower, so the corridor had to be built around it, employing the use of sturdy brackets. Covering part of the façade of the Chiesa di Santa Felicita—where an opening within allowed the Medici family to attend Mass privately—the corridor snaked its way over rows of houses in the Oltrarno, ending at the Palazzo Pitti.

The Medici could now traverse the route between the Palazzo Pitti and the Palazzo Vecchio without setting foot on the street. No more jostling between commoners or dodging the blades of bandits and pickpockets, either. More importantly, the corridor lowered the chances of assassination attempts on the Medici family.

# CHAPTER 14

To Francesco's immense disappointment, Joanna wasn't impressed with the Vasari Corridor. In fact, the only comment she made, while holding a perfumed handkerchief to her nose, was in regard to the offensive odor being emitted by the butchers and fishmongers on the Ponte Vecchio. To be fair, her complaint was valid. The Arno River was polluted with animal carcasses and entrails, and the foul stench of rotting meat and rancid fish could summon the bile to anyone's throat.

Later, when he showed her Giambologna's *Florence Triumphant over Pisa*, she remained stoic. When Francesco pressed her for a reaction, she peered down her nose at him and called the sculpture 'cheap propaganda.' This compelled the Medici heir to storm out of the Palazzo Vecchio, leaving Joanna alone with her ladies.

Despite Francesco's sincere efforts to please and impress his wife, Joanna remained standoffish toward him. In fact, every overture on the part of the Medici or other noble Florentines was met with Joanna's arrogance and poorly masked contempt. The nobles grew to resent her lack of charm and her constant rejection of their beloved culture. For example, her thinness resulted from a self-imposed diet that many found insulting, including the servants who worked hard in the kitchen. She turned up her nose at most of the Tuscan meals on the premise that they were too rich, too saucy, too spicy, and too unlike the plain, wholesome Germanic food to which she was accustomed.

Although she wasn't unattractive, Joanna's appearance was as harsh as her demeanor. Cosimo had commissioned the best Tuscan seamstresses to create new dresses for his daughter-in-law in current Florentine fashion, but Joanna insisted on the conservative fashions of the North, which were cut from dark-hued velvets covered with an exaggerated amount of heavy gold embroidery. Her refusal to acclimate to her surroundings only made her appear ridiculous. There was usually a sheen of perspiration on her pale wide brow thanks to the mild Tuscan climate and the burdensome nature of her cold-weather attire.

Over time, Francesco came to resent his wife and eventually ignored her altogether, encouraging others—courtiers and servants alike—to happily follow suit. It wasn't uncommon for him to spend long periods of time away from his wife and their marriage bed.

*** 

Allegra was deeply saddened by the news of Pellegrina Bonaventuri's sudden death. According to Bianca's heartbreaking message, the little girl had contracted a malady and expired during the night. Allegra attended the funeral, and comforted her grieving friend as best she could. The only good thing to have come from Bianca's marriage was now gone forever.

Pietro went back to his philandering ways only weeks after his daughter's funeral, while his grieving wife passed the time watching the world from the window, pining for her old life in Venice.

Concerned with her friend's state of mind and physical health, Allegra frequently visited Bianca. One day, the two women sat by the window in a pool of muted sunshine, chatting about mundane things as Bianca mended the hem of a dressing gown. Every once in a while, they'd glance at the busy piazza below. At one point, a brazen thief tore a gold earring from a woman's ear and ran away. The victim screamed as she held a hand to her bleeding earlobe. The thief, a pathetically thin boy who appeared to be no older than a dozen years, was quickly apprehended by a pair of burly men. The woman retrieved her earring and began administering blows on the boy's head.

"Can you imagine? He tore it right out of her ear," Bianca exclaimed, horrified. "The young have no respect nowadays."

As she cut the thread from the fabric with her teeth, two men on horseback stopped beneath the window. Bianca set aside her sewing to better study them. Curious, Allegra discreetly leaned over to see who had captured her friend's attention.

"That's Francesco de' Medici," Allegra whispered. "The other man is his friend, Bernardo Buontalenti."

Bianca did not flinch. "I know who they are."

Some of the people in the piazza curtsied and inclined their heads to the future ruler of Florence, but Francesco only had eyes for Bianca. Allegra hid behind the window casement to remain unseen.

Francesco urged his horse forward in order to get a better look at the lady in the window. "Forgive my impertinence, Signorina."

"*Signora*," Bianca corrected, her keen eyes taking in his costly attire.

"Signora…?"

"State your business, my lord."

Shocked by Bianca's impertinence, Allegra gasped. Even Bernardo cracked a smile at the woman's saucy demeanor.

Francesco continued, unfazed. "I glimpsed your face in the window, and had to make certain that you were mortal."

Bianca batted her lashes coquettishly. "Are you satisfied, my lord?"

"I see now that you are no mortal, but rather Venus herself."

A few of the peasant women in the piazza snickered as they watched the scene with wide eyes and gaping mouths.

Allegra risked a peek and saw that Francesco's expression was of a man suddenly smitten, struck unexpectedly by Cupid's arrow.

A slow smile spread across Bianca's face as she leaned over the window ledge to allow him a glimpse of her generous cleavage. "Are you always so generous with your compliments, Francesco de' Medici?"

"Never, Signora..?"

"Bianca Cappello."

***

Allegra paid Bianca a visit a few weeks later, and found a very different woman at the Bonaventuri household.

"Allegra!" Bianca cried, her face aglow with rouge and newfound joy. She looked resplendent in a gown of lilac velvet with costly lace embellishments. Garnets sparkled on her earlobes.

"Look at you! It's good to see you back to your old self, my dear."

Bianca ran her hands over the ornate bodice. "Isn't it divine?"

"I'm at a loss for words."

"Sit with me. I'll have my *maid* bring us wine."

A neatly dressed girl handed them two pewter chalices.

"Does this change of fortune mean that your father has finally forgiven you?" Allegra inquired before indulging in a sip of the fine wine. "Mmm, this is delicious.

"Unfortunately, no. I'm still dead to him."

"Did you inherit a fortune since we last met?"

Bianca laughed and waved the maid out of the room. When they were alone, she said, "You must swear not repeat my secret to anyone."

"My lips are sealed."

"These fine gifts are from my lover, Francesco."

Allegra's eyes became as wide as saucers. "Francesco de' Medici?"

"Oh, Allegra, he's *wonderful*." Bianca's face went from ecstatic to serious. "At first, I resisted, of course."

Allegra dutifully nodded. "Of course."

Bianca continued, "The day after your last visit, I received a lacquered box filled with marzipan and a note requesting to meet in private. I sent it back immediately."

"Rightly so. He's a married man."

"That's what I thought, too. A woman must not give in easily. The following day, however, a bouquet of roses arrived. *Pink roses*. How did he know they were my favorite? At that point, I thought Fate had intervened, so I agreed to meet with him."

"Oh, dear…"

"How could I refuse that sweet man?"

Seducing a desperately unhappy married woman with expensive gifts wasn't exactly a sweet gesture in Allegra's opinion, but she wisely kept that observation to herself. "Does his wife suspect?"

"I doubt she cares. Joanna treats him terribly. She doesn't love him, you know. He's as unhappy in his marriage as I am in mine."

"Then you both share a similar plight."

"*Exactly*, which is why I believe we're destined for each other. We are two halves of the same whole. I've never felt like this before about any man." She drew little hearts on her thigh with her fingertip as she spoke. "I simply cannot stop thinking of him."

Allegra placed her hand over the little hearts outlined on the velvety nap of the fabric. "As your friend, it's my duty to be honest with you, so I must ask you a serious question. Are you prepared to face the consequences if news of your relationship becomes public?"

"Francesco and I have resigned ourselves to the harsh reality of our predicament. So, yes, I'm prepared to pay the price for our love."

"If you're happy, Bianca, then so am I."

"I knew you would understand, Allegra. That's why you're my best and dearest friend."

"When do you and Francesco see each other?"

Bianca grinned, eager to share confidences. "He sends a messenger whenever he wishes to see me. Oftentimes, he lets a room at the city's finest inn, then orders the best food and wine. We spend the entire afternoon eating, drinking, and making love."

Allegra's face grew hot. "Bianca!"

Bianca chuckled, her eyes wicked. "Don't be prudish, my dear. What do you think he and I do together? Play chess?"

"No, but...I've never been married and therefore know nothing of such things."

"Someday you will."

Although the very thought repulsed her, Allegra said nothing.

Bianca's face lit up. "Oh! Let me show you what he gave me

last week."

She left the room in a rush of excitement and returned with a white brocade gown accented with pink embroidery.

Allegra touched the costly fabric. "It's lovely."

"I know. Francesco spoils me." She sat down and gripped Allegra's hand tightly. "This reversal of fortune is surely God's will. He's forgiven my sins and answered my prayers."

# CHAPTER 15

Two of Vittorio's best clients were in Florence at the same time, prompting him to honor the rich noblemen with a fine banquet. It was a way of saying "thank you" for their years of loyal service. Allegra was entrusted with planning the event and deciding upon the menu. She sent invitations to many of her father's friends and allies, including the Medici.

The Castagno household buzzed with activity on the morning of the event. Floors were swept and scrubbed, vases overflowed with early blooms, and the best table linens were aired for the occasion. The scents of sweet and savory tarts, roasted meats, and delicate soups permeated the air.

The late afternoon sun cast long shadows on the golden streets of Florence as noble guests made their way to the Palazzo Castagno. Domenico and Matteo were the first people to arrive.

Surprised, Allegra whispered to her father, "Why is he here?"

"Domenico extended an invitation to Matteo as a peace offering. I think he feels badly for rejecting the young man's business proposal."

Allegra groaned as the two men approached.

Matteo kissed her hand. "Such a pity that you're not wearing the earrings I gave you."

Allegra smiled apologetically. "I always wear my pearls with this particular gown. Excuse me, I must check on the servants."

Matteo watched in disappointment as she walked away.

The Medici siblings entered the main hall a while later with several armed men in tow. They were accompanied by Bernardo, Troilo, and Cesare. Cosimo was not among them.

"I'm sad that your father is not with you," Allegra commented after greeting Francesco and Isabella.

"He isn't feeling very well," Isabella explained.

"I hope it's nothing serious."

Francesco said, "You need not worry. He caught a slight chill."

"I'm relieved to hear it, my lord." Turning to Bernardo, she smiled. "It's always a pleasure to see you."

Bernardo bowed with flourish. "Likewise, Signorina."

Cesare bent over Allegra's hand. "You've ignored the last two notes I sent you." Catching sight of Matteo, he added, "Has another admirer captured your attention and made you forgetful?"

Troilo chuckled and pushed aside his jealous cousin. "*Admirers*. Plural."

"Some wine, my lords?" Allegra motioned to a servant carrying a tray of gleaming silver chalices.

Vittorio came over to greet the Medici entourage and made a point of introducing them to his clients, making them feel honored.

Allegra flitted around like a butterfly throughout the evening, sharing snippets of conversation with everyone. She noticed that Francesco's gaze frequently wandered toward the entrance, his expression impatient.

Bianca was the last person to arrive, demanding everyone's attention as she sauntered into the room in a gold and white satin gown. Jewels sparkled at her throat and the arrogant tilt of her head bespoke her noble lineage.

Vittorio appeared at Allegra's side. "I didn't know she was coming. There are rumors of her and Francesco—"

"The rumors are true, Papa, which is why I sent her an invitation."

Allegra smiled as Bianca walked toward them. "Dearest Bianca, you look magnificent. Thank you for coming."

"I was thrilled to receive your invitation. Signore Vittorio, how good to see you again. It's been a long time since we've crossed paths."

"Indeed it has," he agreed. "You have remained untouched by Time."

"You flatter me."

Vittorio nodded to them before joining a group of men.

Allegra whispered, "Francesco has been eagerly waiting for you."

"It's good to keep a man waiting," she said, deliberately not meeting his insistent stare.

The conversation flowed effortlessly as the guests dined on stewed hare, roasted suckling pig, and various fowls. Custards and cakes followed, along with fruits to cleanse the palate. The musicians played softly throughout the meal, but they picked up the pace as couples drifted to the main hall that had been cleared of furniture for the purpose of dancing.

At one point during the night Allegra spotted Bianca and Francesco sneaking off together.

"Will you dance with me?" Cesare asked, a half-full chalice dangling from his fingertips.

Allegra discreetly took the vessel from him and handed it to a nearby servant. "You should sit down for a bit."

"I think not," he said, gripping her elbow.

Cesare led her toward the other dancers and managed to keep up with them despite his advanced state of inebriation. When the music stopped, he insisted on cooling off in the courtyard.

"I'm drunk with love," he declared.

"You're drunk from wine."

"I'll fall down the stairs if you don't help me."

"It would serve as a fine lesson against overindulgence."

"Please?"

She sighed. "Very well, but only for a moment."

Before ducking into the hallway, Allegra caught Matteo watching them with a sad expression on his face. She followed Cesare down the long stairwell until the faint sounds of moaning and sighing made her stop in her tracks. Squinting into the darkness, she spotted Bianca and Francesco in a dark corner behind a potted lemon tree.

Allegra grabbed Cesare's arm before he could notice the amorous couple. "I have something to show you," she said, quickly retracing her steps and urging him to follow.

His eyes twinkled with mischief as he raced to catch up to her. When they were almost at the top of the stairs, he pressed Allegra against the wall. "I think I'll steal that kiss now."

Cesare's mouth came down on hers before she had a chance to reply. He tasted of wine and smelled faintly of citrus. When his insistent tongue broke through the barrier of her lips, the kiss became sloppy and wet.

Turning her head to the side, she freed herself of his mouth. "Stop!"

"Allegra, I adore you."

He was about to kiss her again when she pushed him away. "Cesare, no!"

She hastily ascended the remainder of stairs to get away from him. The instant she was in the hallway, Matteo stepped into her path, causing her to collide with him. His arms tightened around her.

"Steady, now," he said. "What's wrong? Did he do something to you?"

"Were you spying on me?"

"I only wanted to make certain that you were all right."

Allegra squirmed out of Matteo's embrace. "I'm fine."

Cesare came upon them a few seconds later. "Vanusi."

"Orsini," Matteo said, returning his rival's glare.

Allegra looked from one man to the other and rolled her eyes before abandoning them to their own ridiculousness. She entered the main hall and Isabella motioned for her to join their group.

Pulling Allegra aside, she whispered, "I had a pleasant conversation earlier with Signora Bianca. It's a shame she compromised her reputation."

"Pietro's treatment of her has been most unfair."

"Is any wife treated fairly?" Isabella countered. "I was distressed to hear of her child's death. I suppose it's expected that Francesco coddle his new mistress." She took a deep sip from the goblet in her hand and murmured, "God knows his haughty wife doesn't appreciate anything he does."

They stopped talking when Bianca entered the room with bright eyes and flushed cheeks. She was followed a moment later by Francesco, who joined the men in conversation.

"Well, well," Isabella commented under her breath.

Troilo appeared and swept Isabella into a circle of spinning dancers.

Bianca took the opportunity to pull Allegra aside. "Francesco told me that he wants no other woman in his life but me," she said, her voice verging on shrill. "My heart is racing!"

"When? Just now?"

"Yes, in the courtyard. He kissed me under the stars and confessed his undying love."

*He did much more than that in the courtyard.* "How wonderful."

"This may be the happiest night of my life."

Cesare approached them. "Signorina Allegra, a word, please."

"Please excuse me, Bianca," Allegra said before leading her troublesome guest to a quiet corner.

"Forgive me," he offered. "My lack of chivalry is inexcusable."

"I should apprise my father of your knavery," she scolded. "I'll overlook your offense only if you promise never to do that again."

"I promise," he vowed. "My intentions toward you are honorable."

"Cesare, *please*."

His expression turned serious. "Why do you reject me? Are you spoken for? Is Matteo courting you?" She ignored his questions and he pleaded, "Let me call on you tomorrow."

"I can't see you tomorrow."

"Why will you not allow me to properly court you and win your heart?"

"I'm not the woman for you." Ignoring his shocked expression, she continued, "Why not make the effort where you would achieve the best result? Look at Signorina Adelaide standing by the mantle there, or the young Countess of Pescara

147

who is now speaking with Isabella. They're both unmarried girls with parents seeking alliances with noble families."

Cesare's eyes never left her face. "I'm not interested in them. I'm interested in *you*."

"You know nothing about me. Now, if you'll excuse me…"

Allegra tried to leave but he took hold of her arm. "Wait."

She waited expectantly, but all he did was shake his head in defeat.

***

The demand for La Castagna jewelry compelled Domenico to broach the possibility of a business partnership with Vittorio. Allegra was invited to sit in on the meeting, which took place in the Palazzo Castagno.

"Only one thing concerns me, Domenico," Vittorio said. "If we display Allegra's jewelry in your bottega, as you propose, the demand for her pieces will increase even more."

The old man's eyes lit up. "My point exactly. More money for you, more money for me."

"My daughter couldn't possibly keep up with the high number of commissions. It's too much for one person."

"The senior apprentices could aid Allegra by doing the bulk of the menial work. After studying her designs, they would be responsible for the rough cutting and final polishing. Allegra would do the shaping and filing in order to add her trademark details, of course."

Allegra inquired, "Could I still stamp the pieces with my seal?"

"We're counting on it," Domenico replied, grinning.

"Allegra holds herself to high standards," Vittorio said.

"I understand that, Vittorio. Keep in mind that the master painters of Florence have been operating their bottegas in this manner for a long time. Whenever a painting is commissioned, the apprentices do the menial work: stretch canvases, mix paints, create background landscapes, and so forth. The master artist paints the principle figures in his unique style."

"You make a good point."

Domenico looked to Allegra. "You would continue to work

here under the guise of being my protégé, as you have all this time. Nothing would change."

Vittorio inquired, "How would we transport the finished pieces?"

"Carefully, secretly, trusted servants…"

Vittorio looked to his daughter. "Allegra, do you agree to this?"

"I have one condition. I wish to see the workshop in your bottega, Maestro, and meet the apprentices who would be aiding me. I'd like to examine their work."

Domenico was taken aback. "Do you doubt their abilities?"

"No, but—"

"You're the mysterious and talented La Castagna who's being praised as a genius in Tuscany and beyond. Those boys are in awe of your talent."

Allegra stared at him. "Yes, but they believe I'm a man."

Domenico looked down at his folded hands. "As they must."

"Isn't it enough that Domenico wants to sell your jewelry in the Mercato Nuovo?" Vittorio demanded. "Only the finest goldsmiths are invited to ply their trade in that privileged location. The city's luxury goods are sold in that area, attracting wealthy clients. Imagine the possibilities. Soon, you'll enjoy unprecedented fame. You should feel honored, Allegra."

Allegra merely nodded.

# CHAPTER 16

In 1566 Joanna of Austria gave birth to a daughter, but it did nothing to improve her marriage with Francesco.

Since Isabella welcomed any excuse to throw a party, a celebration was arranged at the Palazzo Pitti in honor of her brother's firstborn child. She greeted the guests with Troilo at her side and, although she was known for being free-spirited, the close relationship between the duchess and her husband's cousin attracted several unsavory speculations.

Allegra and Vittorio attended the event bearing gifts and well-wishes.

During the festivities, Isabella took Allegra aside and the two women indulged in a bit of gossip. Eventually, she inquired, "Do you still visit Signora Bianca Cappello?"

"Not as often as I used to. Bianca is busy with your brother these days."

They passed a buffet table, which offered an array of delectable treats. Isabella popped a bite-sized meat pastry into her mouth, then inclined her head in greeting to a few courtiers. Suddenly, she smiled. Allegra followed her friend's gaze and spied her father speaking with an attractive, impeccably dressed woman.

"Your father is still a handsome, virile man," Isabella pointed out.

Allegra nodded. "I'm aware of that."

"How long has it been since your mother passed away?"

"Just over three years."

Both women watched as Vittorio played the courtier. The woman laughed and placed a dainty hand on his arm.

Allegra inquired, "Do you know her well?"

"Well enough. Her name is Lavinia, and she's the widow of the late Conte Montello d'Asti. A wealthy woman with a pleasant countenance. Your father could do much worse."

"Is she a good person?"

"I've never heard anything unflattering about the countess." Isabella sighed. "It's not easy to see your father with another woman, I know."

"Who am I to deprive him of happiness and pleasure?" Allegra had not seen her father smile so readily in years.

Isabella's eyes turned mischievous. "Changing the subject…Do you know what some of the courtiers are calling you?"

"No."

"The Venus Fly Trap."

"Why on earth would they call me that?"

"You do to men what the plant does to insects—lure and destroy."

"I do not *lure* men."

Isabella's brow shot upward. "You may not realize it, but you do. Your obvious disdain for the male sex is somehow an aphrodisiac. There are gentlemen at this party begging for an introduction despite the fact that you broke the hearts of Matteo Vanusi and Cesare Orsini."

"It's a horrible comparison."

"You're correct. Ice Queen would be a more apt description."

"That would imply that my heart is frozen."

"Is it not?"

A tall, pretty girl with a porcelain complexion and light brown hair came to stand beside Isabella. "Dear cousin."

Eleonora di Garzia di Toledo was first cousin to the duke's children, and many people at court called her Dianora. This was her first season and she was full of life and gaiety.

"Dianora," Isabella said. "What mischief is afoot?"

"None, yet," the girl replied, eyes twinkling.

Despite the budding breasts beneath Dianora's costly gown, there was a layer of childish fat still clinging to her cheeks. Known for her prettiness and courtly manners, there were rumors that she would someday be the bride of Pietro de' Medici, Cosimo's youngest son.

The minstrels struck up a lively melody and Dianora clapped her long, white hands. "I like this tune!"

"Then you should be dancing," Isabella said.

"It's a shame your brother isn't here."

Pietro's reluctance to participate in the revelries at the Palazzo Pitti was due to his bizarre personality.

Isabella smiled. "I see a handsome young lord looking at you from across the room. Why not dance with him?"

Troilo arrived and bowed before Isabella, who took his proffered arm. Allegra noticed that several eyes followed them, including Cosimo's.

***

The houses of Spinelli and Castagno merged together, and the bottega in the Mercato Nuovo soon flaunted a new, freshly painted sign that read: *Spinelli & Castagno Orefici*. Allegra did her best to create the most wonderful pieces for the sake of their new enterprise. Predictably, the demand for her pieces increased considerably after being on public display.

Domenico arrived at the Palazzo Castagno one morning and informed Allegra of a new commission: a gold filigree pendant flaunting a single, perfect pearl.

"A flawless pearl is costly," Allegra said. "Who is commissioning this?"

"The person refuses to reveal himself and sent a messenger with half the payment upfront."

Since keeping secrets in Florence was nearly impossible, it wasn't uncommon for noble husbands to maintain anonymity when purchasing expensive gifts for their mistresses.

Allegra went into the workshop and started on the project. Hopefully, her father would locate a suitable pearl. She remembered the flawless string of pearls Bianca flaunted when they had first met. It seemed so long ago. Come to think of it, Allegra had not seen her friend in months.

Bianca's reversal of fortune, albeit impressive, came with a price. The pair had recently attended a public holy day festival and were harshly criticized for their indiscretion. They often hunted together in the countryside, too, which inevitably incurred negative speculations. News of the couple's displays of affection had a way of spreading throughout the city like wildfire. Even the most discreet households couldn't control the wagging tongues of idle servants and giddy daughters.

Allegra didn't share the views of the common people or the vicious courtiers who, due to sheer boredom, killed the time by speaking ill of others. On the contrary, she was happy for Bianca and Francesco.

She even envied them on occasion.

*Ice Queen…*

"Ow!" she cried as she dropped her steel file.

Vittorio, who happened to be nearby, popped his head in the doorway. "Is everything all right?"

Allegra sucked the blood on her cuticle. "I'm clumsy today."

"I may have located a suitable pearl. I'm leaving now to procure it."

"I can hardly wait to see it."

Later that night, Allegra held a flawless, opalescent orb in the palm of her hand. The pendant was finished before the week's end and Domenico was summoned to pick it up.

"Excellent," he said, admiring her handiwork.

Pointing at the pendant, Allegra said, "That pearl came all the way from Margarita Island, off the coast of America."

"It boggles the mind to think that men crossed Plato's Sea of Atlantis to obtain it," Domenico said, awed by the concept. "I hope the recipient of this gift truly appreciates the effort that went into creating it."

The glimmering white orb had the power to entrance. "I'm sure she will."

The next morning, Vittorio entered the workshop with a worried expression on his face. Allegra set down the ring she was working on. "Papa, what ails you?"

"That pendant you created for Domenico's client…"

She eyed her father expectantly as he handed her a black lacquered box. "What's wrong with it?"

"Open the box."

She did as she was told. Nestled within a bed of satin was

the pendant she had created. "I don't understand."

"Turn it over."

Allegra turned over the piece. The gold had been carefully melted and smoothed over to conceal her signature chestnut. She stood, visibly upset.

"Matteo Vanusi approached me this morning while I was leaving the bottega. He expressed his desire to court you."

"He asked for my hand in marriage?"

"Yes." Vittorio hesitated. "He claimed to have made this pendant for you as a token of his love, and asked that I give it to you when I inform you of his intention and affection toward you."

Allegra's face turned white as she balled her hands into fists. Not wanting to utter profanity in her father's presence, she pressed her lips together tightly and went to stare out the window.

After several minutes, Vittorio prompted, "Allegra?"

She sat down and resumed working. "Tell Matteo that my answer is no."

"Is that all you have to say?"

"Tell him to give the pendant to another woman." When her father did not budge, Allegra set down her tools and regarded him expectantly.

"Maybe you should consider his offer." At the sight of Allegra's frown, he quickly amended, "At least think on the matter before refusing him."

"Why would I do that?" she retorted. "Obviously, the man is dishonest and lacks moral fortitude."

"Try to see this from his point of view. Matteo wanted to give you the best while trying to impress you. He's desperate for your approval. It's not as if he's selling your pieces as his own."

"Are you suggesting that I be flattered by his deception?"

"Actually, yes."

Allegra laughed without mirth and shook her head disdainfully.

Vittorio continued, "Don't you wish to marry and start a

family?"

"Not today." She paused. "Or tomorrow."

"There's more to life than making jewelry."

"I know."

"You could do a lot worse than Matteo Vanusi. He's a good man from a respectable family, and he's a successful goldsmith."

***

Shortly after Allegra's twentieth birthday, Domenico arrived at the Palazzo Castagno with an important announcement. "The time has come for a second sign to hang outside our bottega." He produced a small wooden sign boasting a meticulously painted *castagna d'oro*—a golden chestnut.

Allegra's eyes welled up with tears. "I'm honored, Maestro Domenico."

"You deserve it, *Maestra* Allegra. Given that two thirds of all our sales are La Castagna pieces, it seems fitting to flaunt your name, too."

Vittorio placed an arm around her shoulders. "I'm proud of you and I know your mother would be, too."

"Papa, how much gold do you have on hand?"

"A sizeable measure, why?"

"I wish to celebrate this occasion by creating a pendant for myself."

Vittorio frowned. "But you already have so many of them."

"Not like this one," she countered with eyes full of mischief.

"Very well, take what you need and make note of the exact measure so that I can deduct it from my supply."

Several days later, Vittorio noticed a long gold chain around her neck, but the pendant itself was tucked inside her bodice.

"Is this your newest creation?" he inquired, puzzled.

"Yes."

"The pendant is hidden. What's the purpose of wearing it if you're not going to flaunt it?"

"*I* know it's there."

Allegra pulled out the chain and a solid gold chestnut about

155

half the size of a real one dangled from the end of it.

Vittorio took the tiny chestnut into his palm. "It's flawless; a most unusual piece for a most unusual goldsmith."

# CHAPTER 17

"Don't go yet, my love," she implored, wrapping her arms around him.

"The sun is rising and your ladies will be here soon for your toilette."

He pushed back the coverlet and made to leave, but she held fast. "I'll send them away. It's chilly outside, but it's warm beneath the covers."

Glancing at her curvaceous body, Troilo was tempted to give in to his lover's request. "Isabella, you know that I cannot." He kissed the tip of her nose before adding, "Although the Lord knows how badly I want to. You could tempt the devil himself when you employ that sweet tone."

Isabella giggled and let go of him, then watched in amusement as Troilo dressed in haste. "Why are you in such a hurry?"

"I'm expected."

She leaned up on her elbow. "By whom?"

"Have you forgotten? Your brother invited me to go hunting."

She flopped back on the pillows and sighed. "I remember."

"We've been taking far too many risks lately," he commented while fumbling with the buttons of his suede doublet.

Isabella pouted prettily. "I'm sure Bianca will be there. It's not fair that Francesco can parade his lover openly whereas I cannot."

"You know it's different with men."

"I know," she agreed with a sigh. "Don't worry. Everyone is well aware that we're good friends. After all, we're family."

He raised an eyebrow. "I doubt they see our affection as familial."

Isabella reached out to give his bottom a playful slap.

"*Cousin* Troilo."

He frowned. "I'm serious, sweetheart. We need to be cautious. If my cousin ever discovered—"

"He'll never know," she interjected. "Besides, what does he care?"

"You obviously don't know your own husband."

"How can I? Paolo rarely sets foot in Florence. We hardly ever spend time together. It's obvious to everyone that ours is a marriage of political strategy and convenience."

"Still…"

"Do you honestly think your cousin is living chastely?" she challenged. "I'm sure he has several mistresses to keep him warm at night."

"A man can have mistresses. A woman must remain virtuous because she's responsible for bearing children," he pointed out. "You'll someday be the mother of Paolo's legitimate heir. No man wants to be a cuckold or raise a bastard."

"So I'm to remain alone and untouched, like a statue."

"That's not what I meant, my dearest."

"Are you tired of me? Is there another lady vying for your affection?"

"The answer to both questions is no."

She crossed her arms. "I promise to be more careful."

Troilo winked at her before slipping out of the bedchamber.

*** 

"Did you hear about Isabella?" Bianca asked. "She miscarried. *Again.*"

Allegra accompanied her friend on an afternoon stroll. Peeking over her shoulder to make sure the servants were out of earshot, she replied, "It's quite sad."

"Paolo Orsini visits his wife in Florence on occasion, does he not?"

"Most certainly."

The obligatory coupling for the procreation of children was expected, and Allegra knew that Isabella submitted to it with as much dignity as she could muster.

They passed a cartolaio advertising Vasari's *Lives of the*

158

*Artists*. The art historical canon was first published in 1550, but the book had just been recently revised with new editions.

"Wait, please," Allegra said, indicating the book.

"Francesco obtained a copy for me last week when the revised version was first released."

They walked into the cartolaio where Allegra made her purchase.

Bianca, who browsed the generously stocked shelves, returned to the former topic of conversation. "One cannot help but speculate on the paternity of these doomed infants."

Allegra cast a nervous glance at the bookseller as he handed her the leather-bound book. To the man's credit, he pretended he hadn't overheard Bianca's careless comment.

"Thank you, Signorina," he said. "Please keep me in mind for any other books you may wish to acquire for your library."

Allegra smiled at the man. "I shall." The moment they were outside, she said to Bianca, "I can't believe you said that in front of the bookseller."

Bianca raised an eyebrow. "I didn't mention any names."

"I'm sure he could easily guess."

Bianca sighed in annoyance. "I believe he and every other Florentine has drawn the same conclusion by now."

Unfortunately, she was right. Isabella had suffered a series of miscarriages, and some people wondered if they were deliberate attempts at abortions.

"We should never repeat such gossip," Allegra chided. "Isabella is my friend and adultery is a serious sin."

"You're telling *me* this?"

"Forgive me, Bianca, I didn't mean to offend you."

"I know you didn't. Oh, look!"

Allegra followed the direction of her friend's bejeweled finger. They were nearing the arches of the Mercato Nuovo's loggia, and Bianca headed toward a bolt of patterned brocade.

A few months after her outing with Bianca, Allegra received news of Isabella's pregnancy. The duke had visited Florence only once since her last miscarriage, and the people harbored serious misgivings in regard to the child's paternity.

The sun descended in a rosy sky, reflecting its golden light on the majestic dome of St. Peter. The good people of Rome were winding down from their daily activities and looked forward to the evening's rest.

Cardinal Ferdinando de' Medici, beloved prince of the Catholic Church, reposed in his fine palazzo while awaiting the evening meal. His exalted position within the Vatican came with many privileges: wealth, women, and power. What more could any man desire? His home was lavishly furnished with many works of art and quality furniture. Sighing contentedly, he poured wine into a crystal goblet with a golden stem, admiring the exquisite vessel.

A page peeked his head into the room. "Your Eminence, he's here."

Ferdinando took a sip. "Send him in."

A decently dressed man with a sword at his side entered the room. He stood tall with his hands clasped in front of him. Ferdinando had always admired the discipline of well-trained soldiers, and Michele had been one of the best in the Roman army. Wounded in battle a decade ago, he now worked exclusively as a highly paid spy. Ferdinando liked Michele; he was honest, loyal, and a man of few words.

Ferdinando asked, "Is it true?"

"It is, my lord."

"Would you like some wine?"

"That would be most gracious of you, thank you."

Ferdinando poured wine into a silver chalice and Michele took a sip. His tongue rarely came into contact with anything this good.

The cardinal sat in a gilded chair with velvet cushions, then motioned to a stool beside the hearth. "Sit down and tell me everything."

Michele took a seat. "They've been together for quite some time."

"Is he discreet, at least?"

"At first, yes, but your brother has grown bold," Michele

replied. "Rumors abound in Florence of Francesco's Venetian mistress."

Who would have guessed his brooding, alchemy-obsessed brother capable of such folly? "Have those rumors reached Joanna's ears?"

"I'm almost certain they have, yes."

"Does Joanna know the identity of her husband's mistress?"

"I believe so."

Ferdinando slammed his fist against a nearby table top. "Francesco is married to the Holy Roman Emperor's daughter; a more advantageous match could not have been possible. He foolishly jeopardizes our family's position in Europe. And for *what*? A romp with a Venetian whore."

Michele cleared his throat. "I did confirm that Bianca Cappello was a virgin when she eloped with Pietro Bonaventuri, as you requested."

"Thank God for small miracles," the cardinal drawled. "What of the cuckold?"

"Pietro Bonaventuri currently resides with Bianca in the same household for the sake of propriety (Ferdinando guffawed at this), but he's as much of an adulterer as she is, and turns a blind eye toward his wife's infidelity."

"They're both damned to eternal hellfire," Ferdinando spat. "What manner of girl disobeys her father to marry a commoner? A stupid, gullible, disobedient one. What can we expect of Bianca's character given her tawdry past?" He paused and pinned Michele with a cold stare. "Let this be a lesson to you. Woman is the very incarnation of evil. Bianca should have been arrested, whipped, and forced into a convent."

Michele looked up sheepishly. "It was your father who intervened on her behalf, Your Eminence." He paused. "And…"

*"And?"*

"Apparently, your sister, Isabella, supported Bianca's cause and had great influence on your father's decision."

Ferdinando rolled his eyes. "Of course. My sister, the rebel."

"She and Bianca have become well-acquainted, my lord."

The cardinal cursed under his breath. *Has madness crept into the Medici line?* "My father has grown soft since my mother's death, God rest her soul. His fat mistress coddles him far too much for my taste. While my father neglects his duties, my lovesick brother is too distracted to fulfill his own obligations." He narrowed his eyes. "What are they saying about us, Michele? Be honest."

Michele respectfully averted his gaze by pretending to pick at something on his sword hilt. "There are a few jokes in Florence regarding Medici adulterers." He hesitated before adding, "The jests are not only aimed at Francesco's indiscretion."

*That only left Isabella.* "You refer to my sister."

"It seems that she and Troilo Orsini have become *friendly*."

Ferdinando shook his head in disgust. "God have mercy on the souls of those two fools. Isabella has been given far too much freedom. A married woman's place is beside her husband and away from wagging tongues."

"Your father doesn't trust the Orsini duke, which is why she resides in Florence under the eye of his cousin, Troilo."

"Yes, I know." *His sister was under more than merely Troilo's eye, apparently.* If she became pregnant and there was any doubt of the child's paternity…Ferdinando drank deeply of his wine and chased the possibility out of his head. "Isabella has yet to fulfill her duty and provide a male heir."

"She miscarried again, my lord."

*God's punishment for her sins, no doubt!* Ferdinando gazed down at his bejeweled hand and a sinister thought crept into his head. "Do you think that she—" He stopped himself. To even say the words aloud would be disastrous to the family's reputation. Adultery is a common enough sin, but abortion is blasphemy in the face of God's grace.

"Do I think what, my lord?"

"Is she as beautiful as the troubadours describe her to be?" the cardinal improvised. "Bianca Cappello, I mean."

"Her beauty was renowned in Venice."

"What do you think?"

Michele shrugged. "I prefer women with dark hair, my lord."

The cardinal said nothing as he reached for one of the oranges nestled inside an enamel bowl. The gemstones on his fingers flashed brilliantly in the fading sunlight.

After a long moment of silence, Michele prompted, "What would you have me do, Your Eminence?"

"For the time being, nothing. Return to Florence. Keep your eyes and ears open, and send a message if anything of importance happens."

Michele stood and placed the silver chalice on the tabletop.

The cardinal continued, "Take the chalice as part of your payment."

Michele grinned in appreciation. "Thank you, my lord."

\*\*\*

In August of 1569, Pope Pious V bestowed the title of Grand Duke of Tuscany upon Cosimo de' Medici. Throughout the thirty-two years Cosimo had been Duke of Florence, he'd done many things for the betterment of the city and its inhabitants. Although this news evoked little response internationally, the Florentines celebrated the elevated status of their ruler with honor and merrymaking.

Shortly afterward, Isabella gave birth to a healthy girl in 1570. She was christened Francesca Eleonora. Paolo came to Florence for the birth of his first child, and remained for several days while his wife recuperated from the ordeal in their country villa. The duke stared at the child for long periods of time, noting with relief that Francesca bore a great resemblance to himself. Maybe the rumors were untrue, he thought. After all, the Medici had many enemies.

Francesco de' Medici did not dismiss Isabella's possible infidelity as easily as his brother-in-law did, however. He harbored secret doubt regarding his niece's paternity, but not enough to deter him from attending the celebration in her honor.

Isabella became pregnant a mere two months after bearing her first child, and people hailed it a miracle. Another girl was born in 1571 (christened Isabella) and another gathering was held at the country villa to celebrate the birth of the second Orsini daughter.

When Isabella became pregnant immediately afterward, eyebrows rose. Thankfully, those wagging tongues stopped when little Isabella died in the summer of 1572.

The completion of Francesco's Studiolo in that same year served as little consolation after the death of his niece. The barrel-vaulted room was completely covered in frescoes and paintings depicting religious and mythological themes. Nestled within the Palazzo Vecchio, away from prying eyes, Francesco conducted experiments in alchemy and chemistry. Although he possessed a curious mind, he was neither a scientist nor an alchemist, and the Studiolo served mainly as a sanctuary from the outside world, away from his wife, the court, and the problems of life.

***

Pietro Bonaventuri squinted against the glare of the morning sun. When he heaved the woman's weight off of him, she stirred, moaning slightly in her sleep. His current lover was almost as fat as his wife. He sniffed the bedsheets and grimaced; they needed washing.

"Morning already?" the woman purred, her eyes still closed.

"I have to go," he said, throwing off the covers.

She nuzzled her face into the pillow. Light brown curls fell on her plump cheeks, which still bore last night's application of rouge. Pietro dressed and went downstairs. His lover's maid sat snoozing in a chair in the kitchen.

"Wake up, bag of bones," Pietro snapped. Startled, the girl sat upright. "I'm late for work. Fix me something to eat and be quick about it."

The maid scrambled around the kitchen procuring bread, cheese, and a few hard apples. Pietro sat down to eat. When she brought over a tankard of ale, he pulled her onto his lap and fondled her breast. She resisted his flirtation until he produced a shiny coin from his pocket. The girl hesitated for only an instant before snatching it from his hand and tucking it into the top of her bodice.

Pietro took a deep swig of ale before standing up. Taking the girl by the waist, he bent her over the table and lifted her skirt. She cried out when he entered her roughly from behind, so he clamped his hand over her mouth.

"Shut up, you fool," he snapped. "Your mistress is asleep."

The girl gripped the table's edge, enduring the hard thrusts.

When Pietro had finished his business, he lifted an apple from the table and bit into it. "Wash the bedsheets," he admonished. "They stink almost as much as you do."

The maid shrugged indifferently and adjusted her clothing as Pietro slipped out the back door into the early spring sunshine. The remnants of winter nipped the air and he shivered as he walked to the Palazzo Pitti.

Francesco de' Medici paid him a small fortune to perform a menial job while turning a blind eye to his affair with Bianca. The stupid cow had done well for herself, but she was treading on thin ice. Rumors of another lady in Francesco's company circulated and, given that Bianca had grown corpulent and argumentative, he wasn't surprised. It was only a matter of time before the Medici heir rid himself of his tiresome Venetian mistress.

Pietro turned the corner and collided with a man. A sudden icy sharpness assaulted his side. "What the...?" When he saw that the man held a knife, he cried out for help.

No one assisted Pietro as he was violently stabbed to death in the street. Someone eventually found his body and reported it to the Otto. Supposedly, the murder was a dire consequence of some amorous intrigue, which wasn't surprising given the fact that Pietro had several lovers. People suspected that Bianca and Francesco were somehow involved in the plot.

Regardless of the rumors, Bianca donned a fashionable black satin mourning gown and attended her husband's funeral with a solemn face. Allegra, who stood by her friend's side, noticed that Bianca failed to shed a single tear.

# CHAPTER 18

Virginio Orsini, heir to the duchy of Bracciano, was born in September 1572. Paolo was grateful for a son who could carry on the family name, and Isabella was relieved to have finally fulfilled her obligation to the duke.

"I'm thinking of hosting a party in honor of the Orsini heir at one of our villas," Francesco said to Bianca a few weeks after his nephew's birth. "Maybe I could incorporate a hunting trip for the men."

They were alone in his Studiolo. Bianca stood in a corner toying with a small magnifying glass while Francesco poured over astronomy books.

"Let's have a *real* party at the Palazzo Pitti, my darling." Sensing his anxiety, she added, "Don't you like the idea?"

"I do, but…Joanna may be in residence."

"Send your wife to the countryside," she suggested in a sweet tone laced with venom.

"I can't send my wife away. Besides, her presence will be expected."

"Which clearly means that mine will *not*!"

Francesco rubbed his temples. "Bianca, please understand—"

"I understand *perfectly*, Francesco," she fumed. "My presence is only *expected* when the Prince of Tuscany wishes to crawl between my thighs!"

Francesco bit back an angry retort. He was becoming increasingly weary of her frequent tirades. "You cannot expect me to parade my mistress right under my wife's nose. God's teeth, woman! She's the daughter of the Holy Roman Emperor."

"I'm the daughter of Bartolomeo Cappello and Pellegrina Morosini! Two of the oldest and noblest families in Venetian aristocracy!"

166

"I know that, dearest, but—"

"But, what?" she challenged. "To hear you speak, one would assume I'm a mere commoner—a peasant!"

Francesco took a step forward and placed his arms around her thick waist. "Sweetheart, don't be angry," he implored. "Why do you insist on arguing with me?"

Bianca tilted her chin in a petulant manner as Francesco planted ardent kisses along her white, perfumed throat. "I'm more Isabella's friend than Joanna will ever be."

"Of that there is no doubt."

A servant was on her knees in the next room, busily washing the terracotta floor. Every so often, they heard the sound of the wooden bucket scraping across the tiles.

She halfheartedly pushed him away. "Your kisses won't mend this rift."

"Oh, no?" he countered while fondling her breast.

She pouted prettily. "Not this time."

Francesco's hands slipped under Bianca's brocade skirt and found their way to her buttocks. He caressed and grabbed the meaty mounds until she moaned with pleasure.

*"Francesco…"*

The servant stood, wiped her hands on the grubby apron tied around her waist, and picked up the water-filled bucket. She walked down a long corridor and through a secret passageway to reach Francesco's private refuge. She shivered; she didn't like this room full of unholy instruments. The Medici heir tried to play God with his scientific experiments and attempts to make gold. Taking a deep breath, she took hold of the door handle. Someone had to keep it clean! Placing an ear to the Studiolo's door, she heard nothing. Assuming the room was empty, she entered with the intention of washing the floor and tidying up. At the sight of Bianca sprawled on the wooden table with her skirt hitched up to her waist, and Francesco bucking like a stallion between her legs, the girl quietly closed the door and went on to the next room, shaking her head and muttering prayers to the Madonna.

\*\*\*

Allegra received a strange commission from Domenico, this time for a silver medallion boasting a scorpion in its center.

Her eyebrow shot upward as she inquired, "Matteo Vanusi again?"

"I admit, a sinister scorpion with a stinger ready to inflict pain would be the perfect gift from a rejected suitor," Domenico teased.

"Maestro…"

"Rest assured, Allegra. The woman commissioning this piece is none other than Signora Paolina Gori. I'm sure you've heard of her."

Allegra chuckled without mirth. "Who hasn't? The widow is shameless in her endeavor to bed every man in the city."

"Well, this is a gift for her current lover."

"Will this man still be her lover when the pendant is finished?"

Domenico tried to frown in disapproval at Allegra's facetiousness, but couldn't keep from smiling at her sharp wit. "Let's hope so. Either way, she has already paid upfront and even created the design."

She took the scrap of vellum from his hand. "This sketch is quite good."

"Yes," he agreed. "She wants it completed before the end of the week. Can you do it?"

"I believe so."

Allegra created the piece within the allotted time. The finished product matched the sketch, and Signora Paolina was happy.

A few days later, an invitation to celebrate the arrival of Virginio Orsini arrived at the Palazzo Castagno. Allegra looked forward to seeing her friend, Isabella, and the baby. On the night of the party, she wore a spectacular gown of gold and blue brocade, which flattered her slim figure.

Vittorio noticed how his daughter captured the eyes of several men as they crossed the courtyard and ascended the stairs. At age twenty-four, Allegra was considered a spinster, but that didn't stop potential suitors from approaching him with intentions of courtship. Flowers, sweetmeats, and other tokens still arrived with notes expressing admiration, but her heart belonged to La Castagna and her beloved craft.

They entered the main hall where Isabella and Paolo sat side by side. Allegra greeted the duke and duchess, then cooed over the infant until he was taken away to be fed. A group of gentlemen approached Paolo. A handsome man in black with dark hair and a trimmed goatee handed the duke a wooden box.

"A gift from America, Your Grace."

Paolo's face lit up. "Tobacco!"

The man smiled. "You know it?"

"Oh, yes," Paolo replied, waving to one of the nearby servants. "You there! Find my valet, tell him to bring my pipes."

A while later the entire area was filled with pungent smoke as men drew on wooden pipes and exhaled white vapor through their mouths or nostrils. Unlike the smoke produced by fire, this had a distinct odor.

Isabella stood and slipped her arm through Allegra's. "I hate it when Paolo partakes of tobacco. The smell makes my head ache."

"I find it almost pleasant, even if it is a bit cloying."

Isabella shivered in disgust. "Come, let's take a stroll in the garden. I need to clear my head."

The fresh air tasted sweet after having inhaled the tobacco smoke.

Isabella said, "I've been away from Florence much too long."

"It took the birth of an heir to bring you back," Allegra said, admiring Isabella's maternal glow. "It gladdens my heart to see you." Her eyes slid to Paolo, who watched his wife like a hawk. "Your husband seems content."

"Men value male children. He barely grieved when Isabella died, and rarely spends time with his surviving daughter." Seeing the expression of dismay on Allegra's face, she quickly added, "Eleonora wants for nothing, of course. Paolo is most generous."

"Of that I had no doubt."

They walked along a pebbled path toward a fountain. Isabella recounted stories of her children, and it was obvious that she loved them. When she spoke of Paolo, the joy left her face. Allegra couldn't help feeling bad for her friend, and felt suddenly grateful for being a spinster. They returned to the main hall where a servant offered them chalices of wine.

Isabella took a long sip and said, "Marriage is not easy, my friend."

"I imagine it's not."

"The only way I could have escaped my fate is by dedicating myself to God. A cloistered life in a convent isn't very appealing, now is it?" She held up her vessel. "At least there's wine, which is no small comfort."

"A toast to small comforts."

Allegra felt instantly mellow after taking a sip. Staring into the chalice, she noticed the deep burgundy shade with surprise. The wine steward should have added more water to properly dilute the wine.

Cesare captured their attention and inclined his head in greeting.

Isabella inquired, "Still not interested?"

"No."

"He's been breaking hearts these last few years."

"I'm surprised he hasn't yet chosen a bride. There are so many accomplished ladies from noble families seeking husbands."

"His father is holding out for an advantageous match. None of the available women are rich or powerful enough for his taste. You would have been the perfect bride. Pretty, wealthy, clever—" Isabella suddenly straightened and whispered, "Oh, here he comes."

Allegra took a fortifying sip of wine, causing her head to swim.

Cesare brought her knuckles to his lips. "Signorina Allegra, how my eyes delight to see you. How are you?"

"Very well, thank you."

"It's been a long time since you've been at court. You

shouldn't deprive us of your beauty and charm."

"Your courtly manners have improved, I see. Let me see your tongue—is it silver or gold?"

He chuckled at the jest. "You won't refuse at least one dance with me?"

"I can agree to *one*. Would you excuse us, Isabella?"

"Certainly."

"The last time you and I danced together at the Palazzo Pitti was during Francesco de' Medici's wedding," he pointed out. "If my memory serves me well, you enjoyed it immensely."

"I did."

He led her toward a group of dancers spinning in circles and she stopped in her tracks. "I'm not familiar with this dance," she confessed.

"It's English, and quite popular in Queen Elizabeth's court," he explained. "Come on, you must be quick. Spin, step, spin, step. Like this…"

Cesare's ability to dance and move gracefully had always impressed Allegra, who did her best to follow his lead. *Spin, step, spin, step.*

"There now, you already know it."

Allegra giggled softly. "It's so fast!"

"Why don't you come to court more often?"

"I've already told you before, I'm not a courtier."

They spun round and round again, only this time Allegra grew dizzy. The combination of the strong wine with the frenzied dance threw her off balance. When the melody changed and the spinning stopped abruptly, she staggered and fell into a pair of strong arms. She closed her eyes to steady herself and when she opened them, both of her palms were against black velvet covering a hard expanse of a male chest. The open collar of a linen shirt revealed a glimpse of sun-kissed skin and a silver scorpion medallion. Gasping softly in surprise, she lifted her gaze. A pair of warm hazel eyes stared down at her from an attractive face sporting defined features.

"Hello," he said in a deep voice.

Mortified, Allegra offered, "Forgive me."

A faint smile tugged at the man's lips. "Dancing with exuberance never requires an apology, my lady."

To her surprise, he smelled faintly of cinnamon and leather, a most pleasing combination. She also detected a trace of tobacco. Suddenly, she remembered him as the man who presented Paolo with the wooden box. The woman beside him cleared her throat. It was Paolina Gori.

Directing his gaze toward the dancers, the man said, "I believe your *suitor* awaits your return."

Cesare watched her from a few feet away with a bewildered expression. To her chagrin, she still had her hands on his chest. Wriggling out of his arms, she murmured another apology and hurried toward Cesare.

"Are you all right?" Cesare inquired.

"I'm usually not prone to such clumsiness."

"Nonsense, you're a graceful flower."

"Even when I collide with courtiers?"

"I went to a banquet in Pistoia recently, and the lady of the house was so inebriated that she fell head-first into a tray of oysters. She provided better entertainment than the hired troubadours."

Allegra laughed aloud. "Surely, you jest."

"I do not."

"Thank you," she said sincerely.

"The pleasure was all mine. Now, if you'll excuse me…"

Allegra watched as Cesare walked toward a group of young men and women. She headed for a servant bearing a tray of sweetmeats and helped herself to one.

Vittorio appeared beside his daughter. "Are you enjoying yourself?"

"Yes, Papa. Are you?"

"I am." He looked around and smiled. "There's always a jovial mood surrounding the birth of male heirs."

"I learned a new English dance. You spin until you become dizzy."

"Obviously an invention of the young. It seems that—"

Vittorio froze, compelling her to follow his gaze. Her heart

172

jumped when she saw him staring at the mysterious man in black velvet.

"I don't believe it," Vittorio said incredulously.

The man walked toward them with confidence that verged on stealth.

For some absurd reason, Allegra's face grew hot. "Do you know him?"

Vittorio looked at her askance. "You don't remember?"

Allegra studied the man as he drew closer.

"Signore Vittorio, how good to see you again." Taking a step back, the man peered at Allegra. "This cannot be your daughter."

Vittorio patted the man's back in a gesture of male camaraderie. "It's good to see you back in Florence. Yes, this is Allegra."

The man reached into his pocket and pulled out a silver compass. It was a bit dented and scratched from use, but still in good condition.

Allegra gasped softly. "*Signore Bruno?*"

"At your service." Bruno bowed before kissing her hand. "It's a pleasure Signorina—or is it now Signora?"

"Signorina," she replied breathlessly.

Bruno's face grew serious. "I was saddened by your mother's death. She was a good woman, a true lady in every sense of the word. My condolences to you both."

After thanking him, Vittorio said, "Your father made no mention of your return to Florence."

"He doesn't know I'm here."

"Oh…?"

"I arrived barely a fortnight ago and wanted time to settle in before seeing him. I know that may sound strange to you, but I have my reasons."

Allegra lowered her eyes. *Paolina Gori.*

Vittorio inquired, "What brings you here?"

"The invitation to celebrate Paolo Orsini's heir."

Allegra expressed surprise. "You are friends with him?"

"He's one of my customers—or rather, *was*, until my ship

sank."

Now it was Vittorio's turn to appear surprised. "*Your* ship?"

"I was promoted to captain after my fifth year at sea, and given my own ship to command. I've been sailing up and down the spice route with the Portuguese, importing products from India to Europe."

"How exciting," Allegra commented.

"It was for a while." A shadow settled across his features. "My ship sank during a vicious storm a few months ago. I lost eight of my crewmembers."

Vittorio shook his head sadly. "I'm sorry to hear it. Your father never told me you were promoted to sea captain."

"He wasn't aware of it," Bruno admitted. "I've not been a very good son, Signore Vittorio. My letters to my father have been few and far between."

"Domenico loves you very much. He'll be overjoyed by your return."

"Ten years is a long time. In his last letter, my father stated that he wanted me to come home and manage the bottega. Is he ill?"

"He's fine aside from the common aches and pains of old age." Vittorio replied. "We would welcome your help in the bottega."

Bruno's brow creased in confusion. "We?"

"Your father and I are business partners. I thought you knew." When Bruno shook his head, he explained, "Domenico came to me a while back and suggested that we work together. He's getting along in years..."

"I know he is, and you did the right thing."

"I hope you've returned with the intention of staying a while."

"I'm giving it serious thought." Bruno's eyes slid to Allegra. Holding up the compass, he said, "Your gift aided me on many occasions, Signorina. It even saved my life once."

Pleased by his attention, she inquired, "How so?"

"I got lost in a jungle a few years ago. Thanks to my trusted compass, I found my way back to my ship."

174

"I'm glad to hear it," she said, finally glimpsing the Bruno she remembered in the golden green depths of his eyes.

Vittorio interjected, "When will you see your father?"

"I plan to visit him tomorrow."

"You and your father should come and sup with us next Saturday."

"That's most kind, thank you."

A new melody drew several dancers to the center of the large room.

"Signore Vittorio, may I dance with your daughter?" At Vittorio's nod, Bruno added, "Signorina?"

Stunned, Allegra accepted his proffered hand and followed him. He said nothing as he led her in the dance with surefooted ease. She did her best to be discreet when comparing the man before her to the one in her memory. The old Bruno was plump and jovial with eyes expressing mirth. This man was lean, muscular, and intimidating with eyes expressing...*nothing*.

Turning his head abruptly, he caught her staring at him. The corners of his lips lifted a fraction of an inch as he watched her face redden with shame.

"You dance very well, Signore Bruno," she said, attempting to smooth over the awkward moment.

"As do you, Signorina Allegra, when you're not spinning off the dance floor into the arms of strangers."

"Oh, I'm so embarrassed..."

"I'm only teasing you. I found it rather charming."

Allegra smiled shyly. Dancing with an older man was vastly different than dancing with a man her own age. Bruno's movements were elegant and confident; she was overwhelmed by his masculinity.

Bruno's eyes swept over the swell of Allegra's firm breasts and the smooth curve of her throat. Like Helen of Troy, the young woman's face possessed the kind of classical beauty that could drive men to madness.

"I can't believe how much you've grown, Signorina. Such a drastic change from the child I remember."

"You are also much changed, Signore Bruno."

"More than you know," he muttered. "How old are you, if I may ask?"

"Twenty-four."

"Twenty-four," he repeated, peering at her closely. "I hope your betrothed isn't *too* jealous."

Allegra followed Bruno's gaze to where Cesare stood watching them and said, "Cesare Orsini is not my betrothed."

"Your admirer, then."

"He admires every woman at court."

"You are widowed."

"No."

Bruno spun her around, seizing the opportunity to pull her close. "A beautiful twenty-four year old woman with no husband or suitors? You are a rarity, Signorina," he said in a tone that was oddly flat.

"I have no interest in suitors."

"Yet, you've had your fair share of them, I'm sure."

"My father is a widower with no sons. I help him with his business, which keeps me too busy to pursue courtships."

His expression was a cross between satisfaction and relief. "I must confess...I've thought of you many times throughout the years."

"Oh?"

"Don't look so surprised." The music ended, and he silently led her back to where Vittorio stood. After bowing to them both, he said, "Thank you."

***

Bruno Spinelli haunted Allegra's thoughts for days afterward. In an attempt to clear her head, she accompanied Gianna to the market.

"You've been quite pensive as of late, Signorina Allegra," Gianna commented while selecting vegetables. "What ails you?"

"Nothing. I'm fine."

"Signore Bruno Spinelli is back in Florence and he's dining with you and your father this Saturday."

"Yes."

176

Glancing slyly at her mistress, she inquired, "Why didn't you tell me?"

Allegra felt the color rise in her cheeks. "I must have forgotten."

"I see. Are you going to tell Bruno the truth about you?"

"Father and Domenico don't want him to know."

"Why on earth would you keep La Castagna a secret from the man who will inherit the bottega when Domenico dies?"

"I agree with you, but I must obey their wishes."

"I think it's ridiculous to—" Gianna stopped what she was doing and stared across the square. "Will you look at that? It's been years since I've seen that charlatan."

"Who are you referring to?"

She pointed. "There."

It was none other than Messer Mancini. His black hair was streaked with gray and he walked with a cane, but he still wore fashionable clothing. Rubies and emeralds sparkled on his fingers. Catching Allegra's eye, the astrologer grinned and winked at her. She smiled at him, grateful for the kindness he'd shown her all those years ago.

"The audacity," Gianna muttered as she returned to the task at hand. "I'm surprised to see him wandering the streets after his arrest."

"What?"

"Did you not hear? He was accused of witchcraft."

"When?"

"A few months ago. Thanks to a powerful nobleman whose wife had recently employed Mancini to create astrological charts for her children, he was set free. It's only a matter of time before the accusation resurfaces."

"How do you know this?"

"We servants know *everything* that goes on in the city. Anyway, men like Mancini have enemies."

"Why didn't you tell me this sooner?"

Gianna shrugged. "I didn't think he was of interest to you."

"You thought incorrectly."

"I tried to dissuade your mother from summoning him when

she was pregnant with you, but she ignored me."

"What are you talking about?"

Moving from the onions toward the melons, she replied, "Your mother had him draw up your astrological chart."

"Mother never mentioned it. Do you know where it is?"

"I know where to look for it."

Later that day, Allegra read the astrological chart that Messer Mancini had created shortly after she was born. Her element was fire, which seemed fitting for a goldsmith. She had never forgotten his prophetic words on that fateful day in the Piazza delle Cipolle: *Ignore these simpletons. They cannot possibly fathom the extent of your talent.*

\*\*\*

Domenico and Bruno made their way to the Palazzo Castagno beneath the silvery light of a waning moon. The father and son reunion, which took place earlier in the week, had been bittersweet. After a long, heartfelt talk, they vowed to put the past behind them.

Bruno promised to stay in Florence for an extended amount of time. Overjoyed, Domenico showed his son the new merchandise in their bottega. Bruno examined the ledgers and inventoried the stock.

"Their cook is excellent," Domenico said as they arrived at the gate.

Bruno smiled indulgently at his father. *He did not come for the food.*

A servant opened the door and led them inside.

"Do I detect the scent of peposo?" Domenico inquired, sniffing the air.

"Yes," Vittorio replied. "I had the cook prepare your favorite dish. Welcome, gentlemen."

Allegra's gaze instantly rested on Bruno, who looked dashing in a black suede doublet with slashed sleeves.

"Signorina Allegra," Bruno said, bowing over her hand. When he noticed the blue glass bead at her throat, he smiled wistfully. "You still wear it."

"Sometimes."

178

Bruno straightened, staring deeply into her eyes. "The color matches your eyes perfectly."

"That's what you said when you gave it to me." Allegra turned to Domenico to hide her discomfiture. "You must be very happy to have your son home."

"I am," the old man replied. "God has finally answered my prayers."

Vittorio patted Bruno's back. "Hopefully, he will stay in Florence."

"He promised that he would."

"Let's hope he keeps it."

"Did you hear, Vittorio? There's been another murder in the city." The old man shook his head. "Another visiting nobleman. The Otto found him with severed fingers."

"Thieves," Allegra said.

A servant doled out chalices of wine.

Bruno took a long sip, his eyes never leaving Allegra's face.

She continued, "The number of peasant farmers moving into the city increases each year. Work is scarce, and many of these men are forced to beg in order to feed their families. Unsurprisingly, the number of robberies in Florence corresponds with the rise in population."

Bruno's eyes narrowed. "Most women pay little heed to such matters."

"I'm not like most women, Signore Bruno."

During dinner, the conversation verged on tedious as the two older men discussed politics. Bruno and Allegra pretended to listen while exchanging furtive glances.

Upon hearing the name of a certain official, Bruno said, "I came across that name in one of our ledgers. The last three pieces he purchased for his wife were designed by La Castagna."

"Ah, he's a good customer," Domenico said. Turning to his hosts, he added, "This peposo is delicious."

Bruno continued as if his father hadn't spoken. "In fact, most of the sales coming into the bottega are from La Castagna commissions."

"Yes, my son."

"His symbol hangs from our door."

"The golden chestnut is widely known as a mark of excellence."

Bruno quietly demanded, "Who is this man?"

"I've already explained the situation."

Vittorio interjected, "La Castagna wishes to keep his identity secret."

"Why all the mystery, I wonder?" Bruno mused.

Domenico regarded his son impatiently. "Who knows? Who cares?"

Bruno would not be put off so easily. "I care."

"Perhaps society would not accept him otherwise," Allegra suggested in an innocent tone, incurring nervous glances from Domenico and Vittorio.

Bruno frowned. "What do you mean?"

"What if La Castagna is disfigured? Or a cripple who cannot walk?"

Vittorio cleared his throat and gave his daughter a warning look.

"Do you truly believe all this secrecy is due to a physical deformity?" Bruno inquired, amused. "It's an interesting theory, I'll give you that."

"It's a practical one," she shot back. "For all we know, he could be hideously scarred or perhaps even a dwarf."

Bruno turned to his father. "We need to come up with something to rival La Castagna's designs."

Exasperated, Domenico set down his spoon. "Bruno—"

"Father, please! I certainly can't fault you for cutting a deal with this unscrupulous goldsmith while I wasn't here, but I'm back now, and it's my duty to prevent you from making further mistakes."

Allegra regarded Bruno steadily. *Unscrupulous? Mistakes?*

Bruno continued, "Our apprentices toil to create an outsider's designs. It doesn't make any sense."

"It makes perfect sense," Domenico countered. "La Castagna gives us a handsome percentage on each item sold.

I'm old, and these gnarled hands can no longer keep up with the number of commissions we receive."

"Every La Castagna piece that leaves our bottega is one less Spinelli piece sold," Bruno pointed out, his eyes hard. "If he abandons us for a better deal elsewhere, we're ruined."

Feeling uncomfortable, Allegra motioned to a servant. "More wine."

Bruno continued, "Do you not see my point, Signore Vittorio?"

"I understand your concern," Vittorio conceded for the sake of argument. "But you should view this arrangement with La Castagna as an amiable collaboration, not a competition."

"Forgive me if I don't agree with you." To Allegra, he added, "Nor do I agree with your theory. La Castagna's designs are not the work of a dwarf or a deformed individual, but rather a man suffering from the sin of pride."

"Pride?" she repeated, taken aback.

"Have you ever truly *looked* at his jewelry?" he challenged. "In addition to being ostentatious, it screams of desperation."

Allegra's fury bubbled to the surface. "La Castagna's pieces are finely executed, his designs unique."

"From what I've seen of his work, you're correct. No goldsmith in the city would dispute his skill—it's flawless," Bruno conceded. "However, this is a man who wishes to exalt himself above others; a man who doesn't care about those he crushes underfoot."

"I think you're being a bit harsh, my son," Domenico muttered with an apologetic glance in Allegra's direction.

"Forgive me if I don't share your opinion, Father."

Noticing his daughter's distress, Vittorio inquired, "Are you suggesting that La Castagna is deliberately ruining the lives of our fellow citizens?"

"Based on the rumors, yes."

Allegra said, "Signore Bruno, you sound as if you loathe La Castagna."

"I do," he affirmed icily.

She dropped her gaze and hid her trembling hands in her lap.

"Initially, I had doubts about La Castagna, too," Vittorio said to appease Bruno. "So far, he's not given us any reason not to trust him."

Allegra regained her composure and stared at Bruno. "That's an interesting medallion around your neck. Did one of the Spinelli apprentices make it or did you acquire it abroad during your travels?"

Her reckless comment earned wary glances from Domenico and Vittorio.

"It's a recent gift from a *friend* who knotted it around my neck as I slept."

Bruno's intimate confession resulted in an awkward silence. Undeterred, Allegra stood and walked toward him.

"Allegra," Vittorio said in a warning tone.

Ignoring her father, she touched the medallion, her shaking fingers brushing against Bruno's hot skin as she flipped it over. "Oh, it bears La Castagna's stamp."

Without a word, he removed a knife from his belt and cut the leather cord around his neck. The medallion fell to the floor and rolled under the table.

"Bruno," Domenico chided. "Is this really necessary? Our hosts don't deserve such disrespect."

"Signore Vittorio, Signorina Allegra, I apologize," Bruno offered. "Father, you believe this reclusive goldsmith is your friend, but he is not."

Shaken by the vehement act, Allegra returned to her seat and said nothing more. Domenico took the opportunity to steer the subject back to the safer shores of politics and banking.

After dinner they retired to the library where honeyed wine and cheese awaited them. Vittorio and Domenico settled by the fire and continued their political debate, affording Bruno the opportunity to speak with Allegra.

"Forgive me for upsetting you earlier," he said quietly.

"There's no need to apologize, Signore Bruno."

"I hate seeing my father's kindness being taken for granted by an upstart that I know nothing about."

"You're a good son for worrying about him."

"I'm a terrible son who abandoned my father when he needed me most."

"Signore Bruno—"

Holding up his hand, he continued, "I'm determined to make up for my negligence. It's a wonder he accepted me back into his good graces."

She gently touched his arm. "Your father is happy to have you back—we all are." Bruno glanced at her hand, compelling her to add, "Forgive me if I spoke out of turn."

"You did warn me that you were different than most women." His eyes twinkled mischievously. "I confess that I've never had a woman fall into my arms until you came along."

"How mortifying…"

"How intriguing," he countered. "That English dance has become…"

She glanced at his arms as he spoke, recalling their warmth and strength. Her gaze slowly drifted to his broad shoulders and she wondered what they looked like beneath his doublet. He leaned closer and she caught a faint whiff of cinnamon. *Did his skin taste spicy, too?*

"Did you notice that as well?" he asked.

The question broke her reverie. "What?"

Bruno's eyes swept over her before a knowing smile touched his lips.

*Santa Madonna!* What was wrong with her? "Forgive me, Signore."

"So young, so powerful," he whispered.

Embarrassed, she averted her gaze. "I don't know what you mean."

"I think you do…"

The room grew suddenly hot. "Would you care for more wine?"

Ignoring her attempt to change the subject, he said, "You can have any man in Florence eating out of the palm of your delicate hand."

"You flatter me."

"And flattered women make bad decisions."

183

*Anabella.*

Allegra made no reply and he cursed softly. "How rude of me."

"I understand why you feel the way you do."

"How could you? You were so young back then, a mere child."

"I remember the suffering of a good man who didn't deserve the terrible fate bestowed upon him."

Bruno's mouth formed a taut line as he extracted the compass from his pocket. "Your thoughtful gift and well-wishes made me believe that some light still existed in this dark world. In my saddest moments, I would often recall the innocence and sincerity in your eyes when you said farewell."

"You had always treated me with kindness and respect, so I wanted to give you something to remember me by. It pleases me greatly that you're so fond of my gift."

His eyes glistened. "I miss my son every day."

The simple admission pained her heart. "I'm so sorry."

"Unfortunately, the past cannot be rectified; we can only move forward." He sighed. "Enough of this unpleasantness. Let's talk of other things."

"Why a scorpion?"

"The medallion?" She nodded and he continued, "The person who gave it to me is obsessed with astrology. I was born in the House of Scorpio, and my element is water. She also created a chart for me."

"*She* must care for you a great deal."

"Maybe she does but, to me, she is only a friend."

Obviously, their definition of friendship differed greatly. "I recently discovered that I, too, have a chart. I'm Aries and my element is fire."

"The ram is known to be stubborn and headstrong," he said. "Do you fit that description, Signorina Allegra?"

"Those who know me well would probably say yes."

"I remember dancing with you on my wedding day. You said you'd never marry."

"And I never have."

# CHAPTER 19

On a chilly October morning, Allegra set out for the market in search of hair ribbons and fabric for a new cloak. It wasn't often that she shopped for such frivolities, but with Christmas being only a few months away, she wanted to be prepared for any social events. She could have easily dispatched a servant to procure these items, but the last few commissions had kept her housebound, and she needed to breathe a bit of fresh air.

Gianna, who accompanied her, stopped before a stall flaunting several bolts of brightly dyed fabrics. "This one here would bring out the blue in your eyes," she said, indicating a plush blue velvet shot with silver thread.

Allegra nodded thoughtfully. "What about this one?"

"Red is nice, too." Then as an afterthought, Gianna added, "While we're out, we should stop by the Loggia del Pesce in the Piazza dei Ciompi. Your father would relish a good fish stew when he comes home from Orvieto."

"Yes," Allegra agreed distractedly as she gravitated toward another vendor selling brocade in periwinkle blue with gold patterning.

A male voice said, "The colors are perfect for you."

Allegra and Gianna turned around to see Bruno standing behind them.

"Buongiorno," he said cheerfully.

Allegra inquired, "What are you doing here so early in the day?"

"Shopping, like you." He pointed to the fabric. "I meant what I said. This color compliments your eyes, Signorina Allegra."

Wearing a knowing smile, Gianna quietly shuffled to the next stall to give them a measure of privacy.

"How are things at the bottega?" Allegra asked, despite knowing everything that goes on there.

"Business is good. The apprentices are busy."

"And your father is well?" Allegra saw Domenico yesterday when he came to the Palazzo Castagno with a new commission.

"Yes, thank you. I hear your father went to Orvieto."

She nodded. "He's expected back tonight."

An awkward silence followed. Gianna, pretending to look at sewing needles, strained her ears to eavesdrop on them.

Bruno took a step closer and said softly, "I must confess something. I can't stop thinking of you."

Paolina Gori suddenly stepped out from behind one of the stalls. Dressed in an elegant gown of copper satin, she looked pointedly at Allegra with a cold smile on her face. Placing a proprietary hand on Bruno's arm, she said, "Did she fall into your arms again, *mio amore*?"

Although the comment was meant as a jest, there was no mistaking the animosity in the widow's eyes.

"Not this time," Bruno replied, his tone laden with regret.

"Signora Paolina, how do you do?" Allegra said politely. "I believe we have never been formally introduced."

"No, we have not," she replied coolly. "Although I have commissioned work from La Castagna through your father, whom I admire."

*Small wonder you have not attempted to bed him.* Allegra vanquished the wicked thought. "I'm pleased to hear it, Signora."

"Shall we go?" Paolina suggested to Bruno.

Bruno nodded. "It was a pleasure seeing you again, Signorina Allegra. Send my regards to your father."

"Thank you."

Gianna came to stand by her mistress. "It seems you have a rival."

"Nonsense," Allegra snapped. "I have no interest in Signore Bruno."

"I was under the impression that you liked him."

"Only as a friend, nothing more." When Gianna stared at her in disbelief, she grew annoyed. "Let's purchase this fabric and go home."

186

"What about the fish?"

"We can send a servant."

Gianna smiled inwardly and said nothing more.

***

Christmastime meant gifts, and the demand for Allegra's jewelry had increased due to the season. Domenico, Vittorio, and Allegra held a meeting to discuss ways to efficiently handle the various commissions received at the bottega. They were seated in the library and looked up in surprise when Gianna appeared in the doorway with Bruno in tow.

Confused, Domenico said, "I thought you said you had errands to run, my son."

"I changed my mind." Looking to Vittorio, Bruno added, "I hope my presence is welcome, Signore."

"Most definitely. Gianna, have the servants bring out some refreshment."

Noticing Allegra, Bruno regarded her with unabashed curiosity. To her dismay, his eyes begged the question: *what are you doing here?*

Bruno sat down beside his father. "I want to discuss a few ideas with you and Signore Vittorio that will help sell more Spinelli pieces."

"We have more commissions than we can handle right now," Domenico pointed out. "We can barely keep up!"

"Yes, but they're mostly La Castagna's," Bruno countered.

"The bottega will profit greatly, thanks to those commissions."

"Signore Domenico is right," Allegra said.

Bruno looked at her, surprised. "Do you often voice your opinions on matters of business, Signorina?"

"Allegra aids me greatly in my work," Vittorio explained.

Intrigued, Bruno leaned forward in his chair. "How so?"

"I help my father with client orders and accounting," she replied, cringing inwardly at the coldness in his eyes.

Vittorio said, "Allegra also advises the ladies when she travels with me."

Bruno's eyes never left Allegra's face as he cocked his head to the side. "Advise them on what, if I may ask?"

"She has a keen eye for style and proportion," Vittorio replied. "She helps our clients select the metals and gemstones that work best for them."

"How do you advise them?" Bruno pressed. "Do you describe the pieces before they're even created?"

Annoyed by his son's impertinence, Domenico blurted out, "She sketches them."

Allegra stiffened and Vittorio shifted uncomfortably in his chair.

Bruno's look went from surprised to accusatory. "Father mentioned something about La Castagna being provided with sketches. I had no idea they came from you."

"What? No," Allegra protested, looking to her father for help.

"Well, it's not quite like that," Vittorio said.

Bruno frowned in confusion. "Please explain."

Allegra swallowed hard. "Well, I...er...I provide a *rough* sketch. Basic shapes, mostly."

"Yes, shapes," Domenico chimed. "La Castagna embellishes greatly on Allegra's *rudimentary* ideas."

Bruno grimaced. "It's unfair that your daughter's talents are being used to the exclusive benefit of the enemy."

Allegra's mouth fell open. *Enemy?*

"It's not like that, Signore Bruno," Vittorio countered.

"Very well," Bruno conceded. "If we are to continue doing business as partners, then I expect Signorina Allegra to provide sketches for *me*. I want to see more Spinelli commissions coming into the bottega, and less La Castagna. Is that agreeable to you, Signore Vittorio?"

Vittorio gave little more than a curt nod.

A servant entered the room carrying a tray. While she doled out tankards of ale, Allegra caught Bruno staring at the aquamarines adorning her throat.

"May I take a closer look at your necklace, Signorina?"

His request made her heart sink, but how could she refuse? With trembling fingers, she undid the clasp and reluctantly gave him the necklace.

He turned it over and frowned at the sight of the familiar chestnut stamp. "Did La Castagna give this to you?"

"The woman who commissioned it died before it was completed," Allegra replied, hoping the hastily constructed fabrication sounded true.

Vittorio added, "Why let a good piece of jewelry go to waste?"

Bruno's face darkened as he handed the necklace back to its owner. "I find it hard to believe that none of you suspect this man's identity."

"I send the sketches via courier and receive the finished product in the same manner," Vittorio said. "The messengers never divulge anything. I imagine they are paid well by their master to keep quiet."

"Not to mention fear of getting whipped," Domenico added for good measure.

Looking at Vittorio and Domenico in turn, Bruno said, "I wish to speak with you about our apprentices and their working environment. I believe we can make several improvements." Glancing at Allegra, he added, "Surely, Signorina Allegra doesn't need to be present for such boring details."

Allegra bit back an angry retort as her eyes flashed in outrage. To add insult to injury, neither Domenico nor her father said anything to contradict Bruno's blatant dismissal. Reluctantly, she left the room. To her chagrin, the men resumed speaking only after she'd closed the door. Appalled by her conflicting emotions, she closeted herself in her bedchamber.

Gianna poked her head into the room a moment later. "Signorina?"

"Did you hear him, Gianna? The audacity!"

"Keep your voice down."

"Signore Bruno is an ogre!"

"There, there. It's not like you to get so worked up."

"First he hates La Castagna and now he hates *me*."

"I can assure you that Signore Bruno does not hate you."

Allegra's eyes welled up with tears. "He was quite rude to

me…"

"He flattered you the other day at the market."

"I'm sure he's equally flattering to Signora Paolina."

Gianna stifled a smile at Allegra's display of jealousy. "His dalliance with that tawdry woman will soon come to an end, don't you worry."

Allegra sniffed. "Do you think so?"

"Only a blind person would fail to see the admiration in his eyes when he looks at you."

The affirmation made Allegra smile as she wandered to the window. The sun shone brightly in the sky, warming the courtyard below. "I think I'll take advantage of this fine weather and read outdoors for a bit."

Gianna smiled. "A splendid idea."

Allegra wrapped herself in a wool cloak, selected a book, and sat in the sunshine. Her mind raced, making it difficult to concentrate on the printed words. Bruno's temperament was like a pendulum, going from one extreme to the other; brooding one moment, charming the next.

She read quietly, the warm sun making her drowsy. *I'll close my eyes for only a few minutes…*

The sound of Vittorio accompanying the Spinelli men down the outer stairwell startled her. She must have fallen asleep. Quickly, she smoothed the creases from her skirt and sat up straighter on the bench. As they crossed the courtyard, Bruno caught sight of her and paused to speak with Vittorio. At the latter's nod, he walked toward her.

"Signorina Allegra?"

She shaded her eyes to peer up at him. "Yes?"

"I underestimated your value at the bottega. I wasn't aware of how much work you did until our fathers educated me. Please forgive my lack of chivalry toward you earlier."

"You may rest assured, the matter has already been forgotten."

He looked down at his feet. "You must think me an uncivilized beast."

"I wouldn't go as far as calling you a beast, sir."

190

He winked mischievously. "That's because you don't know me yet."

The look in his eye and the insinuation of his words made her breathless.

"I wish you a pleasant day, Signorina Allegra."

"Likewise, Signore Bruno."

Later that afternoon, an urgent message arrived from Bianca. Allegra went to see her Venetian friend early the next day.

Adorned in rose satin with several strands of pearls around her neck, Bianca announced, "I'm heading out to purchase something delicious."

Puzzled, Allegra said, "You asked me to come see you today."

"Yes, I want you to come with me. Francesco loves panforte."

Allegra's gaze fell on one of Bianca's maids. "Why not have one of the servants fetch some?"

"The weather is good and I feel like going out," Bianca replied with an innocent smile before planting a swift kiss on Allegra's cheek. "I *insist* that you accompany me."

"Very well."

"Shall we come too, Signora Bianca?" inquired one of the servants.

"No. Fetch my cloak." The servant came out with a red brocade cape lined with miniver and placed it over Bianca's shoulders. She caressed the luxuriant fur as they descended the stairs. "Gorgeous, is it not?"

"Fit for a queen," Allegra replied, for the cape was truly stunning.

"A gift from my beloved."

"Francesco has excellent taste."

"The very best." Once they were outside in the sunshine, she took Allegra's arm and whispered, "We're going to meet him now, in fact."

"I thought we were—"

"Hush, my dear. There's plenty of panforte where we're going. I didn't want to say anything in front of my servants because I can't trust anyone these days. Oh! The gossip, the rumors…"

Bianca maneuvered through the crowded piazzas and back alleys with the expertise of a pickpocket on the run. She finally stopped at a doorway. They were unescorted and far too well-dressed to dally in the street.

Allegra looked around apprehensively. "We should go inside."

Three sharp raps and the door opened into a richly furnished chamber. A discreet servant removed their cloaks. A crystal decanter of wine beckoned them from a table in the center of the room. Bianca motioned to the maid, who poured the ruby liquid into two delicate Venetian glass goblets.

"Where are we?" Allegra asked, admiring an intricate tapestry depicting two naked lovers embracing in a flower garden.

Bianca dismissed the servant and handed a goblet to Allegra. "We're in a private hideaway—one of several that Francesco and I use in the city."

Allegra took a sip of the wine. "This is superb."

"It comes from Poggio a Caiano, one of Francesco's villas in the countryside." Bianca waved her hand. "Well, what do you think?"

The room was small but exquisite. On closer examination, Allegra noticed a round table in the corner, its surface made of inlaid marble. The skillful intarsia depicted a maiden with seashells covering the nipples of her bare breasts. In the center of the table sat a plate of pink marzipan shaped into little hearts, along with a generous slab of panforte.

"I'm overwhelmed," Allegra replied.

Bianca popped a heart into her mouth. "These are divine. Have one. They make the color from rose petals. You can taste the flower, too."

Allegra dutifully tried a little pink heart and smiled. Her eyes wandered around the room, marveling at the beauty and costliness of the furnishings. On the mantelpiece was a silver and enamel clock, its tiny mechanisms whirring away behind a glass case. Directly behind the clock was a magnificent Venetian mirror etched with a floral motif along the edge. Above their heads was a Venetian chandelier fashioned from red glass.

She beckoned for Allegra to follow her into an alcove. "Oh, but you haven't seen the best room yet."

Allegra stepped through a tiny hallway that opened into a spacious bedchamber. All four walls and the ceiling were frescoed with life-sized figures painted in vivid flesh tones. The undulating scene depicted a Bacchanalia in an idyllic garden full of exotic flowers and birds. Nymphs, centaurs, and humans frolicked and took delight in various forms of carnal pleasure. Allegra spun around slowly and tilted her head upward to admire the frescoed blue sky where Cupid and Venus looked down upon the celebration. In the center of the room stood a massive canopied bed hung with sheer linen. She also noticed mirrors set into the painted scene at certain angles so that whomever was upon the bed could be reflected into the revelry. It was a room created specifically for the physical acts of love.

To Allegra's chagrin, she imagined Bruno naked upon the bed, beckoning her to join him. The inappropriate thought made her ache with a peculiar longing that was totally unfamiliar— *and exciting.*

"Well?" Bianca asked, her expression eager.

Although the room was undoubtedly vulgar, the artwork had been executed with tremendous skill. "Remarkable," Allegra replied, surprised at herself for not being shocked by the erotic scenes.

Bianca hugged her friend. "I told you that Francesco is good to me. He let me decorate these rooms by myself. I knew you'd like them."

"Who painted the frescoes?"

"Pontormo," Bianca replied, admiring one of the naked male figures.

Allegra became uncomfortably aware of the intimacy that took place within this room—intimacy that had nothing to do with her.

"Come, let's sit in the other room," Bianca said. "Francesco will be along any minute and he wants to speak with you."

"Oh?"

"That's why we're here."

"Why does he want to speak with me?"

"I don't know," Bianca replied. "He wouldn't tell me, no matter how much I begged." The sound of horseshoes on cobblestones echoed throughout the alleyway outside. Giddy with anticipation, she went to the tiny stained glass window. "We'll soon find out."

The door opened and Bianca flew into Francesco's arms. Feeling uncomfortable, Allegra turned her face away as they kissed.

"Signorina Allegra, how good of you to come," Francesco said, striding into the room in a smart doublet of red wool trimmed with silver thread.

"My lord," Allegra said with a respectful curtsy.

"Has my beloved given you a tour of her latest project?" he inquired, spreading his hands out to indicate the space around them.

Allegra nodded. "It's magnificent."

He sat down and Bianca placed her hands on his shoulders. "Signorina Allegra, what do you know about La Castagna?"

"Only that he's talented and in high demand. We've always dealt with him through couriers."

"I see," he said, rubbing his chin. "Anyway, there's a rumor that you provide La Castagna with sketches. Is that true?"

"Only rough sketches of what clients want, then he greatly embellishes on them," Allegra lied. Where was this leading? Had someone complained to the magistrates?

"I want to commission a necklace." Allegra almost sagged with relief as he continued, "It must be spectacular and unlike anything you've ever seen. This is why I thought it best to meet with you in private. Discretion is imperative."

Bianca's eyes were wide with surprise.

"You may rest assured, my lord," Allegra said. "We are exceptionally discreet. I assume this necklace is to be a gift."

"A Christmas gift, yes."

Bianca's eyes grew impossibly wider.

"May I ask who is to be the receiver of this fine gift? Knowing the lady will aid greatly in creating the design."

Francesco took one of Bianca's hands and kissed it. "It's for my one and only true love, Bianca Cappello."

"Oh, my darling!" Bianca exclaimed before hugging him. "Thank you!"

"I will get some sketches to you as soon as possible," Allegra promised.

"I can't wait to see them," he said between Bianca's fervent kisses.

Allegra inquired, "Shall this necklace be fashioned from gold or silver? I also need to know which gemstones to use, or would you prefer pearls?"

"Diamonds and gold," Bianca replied on her lover's behalf. Turning to him, she added, "I already have so many pearls, dearest."

"You may choose whatever you like," he replied indulgently.

"You're so good to me," Bianca whispered before claiming his lips.

Francesco pulled her onto his lap, his hands on her hips.

Sensing the mounting passion between the two lovers, Allegra went to the door. "Perhaps I should take my leave now, my lord."

Bianca peeked over her shoulder and smiled as Francesco said, "One of my guards will see you home safely, Signorina Allegra. Thank you."

Allegra fanned her face when she got outside. Several guards lolled about, looking at her from head to toe. She straightened her shoulders and announced, "One of you must see me home safely."

They fought each other for the privilege of being her escort, and the winner was a burly man with an easy smile. Oddly, on the way to the Palazzo Castagno, he chatted about wild hares and the various ways to eat them.

Allegra started on the sketches the moment she got home. Taking a piece of graphite into her hand, she sat down and stared at the blank sheet of vellum on the table. Picturing Bianca's face and neck, she began to draw a choker. One row of small diamonds, then a space of delicate gold filigree, then another row of diamonds. The next row in the same order, only bigger stones, followed by a third row with the biggest stones she could obtain. Finally, a scalloped border of tiny diamonds. Only Bianca could effortlessly carry off such a bold piece.

To avoid appearing arrogant, Allegra created a few more sketches and waited several days before seeking an audience with Francesco de' Medici. Predictably, he chose her first design.

Vittorio set out to obtain the diamonds while Allegra cut, shaped, and curled the gold filigree with painstaking care. She set out to create her finest necklace yet, and worked diligently for many weeks. At one point, she fell asleep on the workbench from sheer exhaustion.

With Gianna's help, Vittorio put his daughter to bed. "I've told her to stop working so hard lest she become ill."

"She'll kill herself at this rate," Gianna lamented. "You must stop this."

"Do you remember how stubborn her mother was?"

"Vividly."

"Well, add my stubbornness into the equation."

"Lord help us," Gianna said under her breath.

Vittorio woke up early in the morning the following day and went into the workshop where his daughter was already working. Two dark smudges beneath her eyes stood out in stark contrast with her pale skin.

"Papa," she said, startled.

"You cannot continue to work at this pace, Allegra. It's unhealthy." She was about to protest and he placed his hand up to silence her. "I know this commission means much to you, but nothing is more important than your health. Take a rest today."

"I can't, I must finish—"

"No, Allegra. Today you will rest."

## Chapter 20
## Christmas 1572

"I sent a note to Domenico and Signore Bruno, inviting them to join us today," Vittorio said to his daughter while the two of them broke their fasts in a stream of muted sunlight. "There's no reason why the four of us can't celebrate the holy day together."

"Perhaps Signora Paolina has other plans for Bruno." Allegra regretted her words the moment she saw the look on her father's face.

"Domenico mentioned that his son has broken off with her," Vittorio said with forced nonchalance. "Bruno Spinelli is an eligible bachelor."

"Well, there are plenty of ladies in Florence for him to choose from."

"Including yourself."

"He hates La Castagna, remember?"

"Yes, but he doesn't hate *you*."

"We are one in the same."

"You can always retire…"

Allegra stared at her father with a mixture of shock and hurt. "Being a goldsmith is what I live for."

"I realize that, my dear, but there are other joys in life."

"Like marriage? My friends Bianca and Isabella were terribly matched, and let's not forget poor Lucrezia, poisoned by her own husband."

"Allegra, you must learn to control that tongue of yours. The temper, too. Not all men are rogues."

"That's exactly what Bruno said to me when I was a young girl, yet who did he run to when he arrived in Florence? Paolina Gori, the whore."

"Allegra!"

"Forgive me, Papa, but I only speak the truth."

"Your mother and I indulged you too much. Being our only child, we wanted to please you. Were we wrong in allotting you so much freedom?"

"Please don't think that."

"You and I will attend Christmas Mass together, then Bruno and Domenico will join us for supper. I expect proper comportment befitting a lady this evening."

"Yes, Papa."

Later that day, Allegra chose to wear the gown the seamstress had created from the splendid periwinkle blue fabric she had bought at the market. The sky had grown dark and several menacing clouds drifted low on the horizon. Bruno and Domenico arrived with the first drops of icy rain. The servants stoked the fire in the hearth, then set out trays of spiced wine and roasted chestnuts. Vittorio led the men into the warm, candlelit library.

Bruno presented their hosts with a small wooden box containing cinnamon, cardamom, and nutmeg.

"Thank you for this fine gift," Vittorio said, holding out the box so that Allegra could examine its contents.

Inhaling the spicy scents, she added, "This is most generous."

He smiled slightly. "I'm glad it pleases you."

Vittorio and Domenico helped themselves to spiced wine and chestnuts while diving into a heated debate over which of the city's *quartiere* would win next year's calcio match. Rather than take the opportunity to speak with Allegra, Bruno joined the men. In fact, as the evening progressed, he barely spoke to her at all.

The conversation throughout the tasty meal of roasted venison and vegetables revolved around harmless court gossip. Domenico brought up Cesare Orsini's upcoming marriage, and Bruno's eyes slid to Allegra in order to gauge her reaction.

"I wish him and his bride much happiness," she said. "Who is she?"

"A Roman girl from a noble family," Domenico replied. "Apparently Ferdinando de' Medici had a hand in arranging the marriage."

Allegra had not seen Ferdinando since he left for Rome at the age of fourteen to become a cardinal. The mention of his name stirred childhood memories. "I wonder how Ferdinando is doing these days. Isabella rarely speaks of him."

"That's because he criticizes his sister's marital arrangement," Bruno interjected. "A married woman should be at her husband's side."

"True, but it was Cosimo who insisted she stay behind with her dowry," Vittorio pointed out.

Domenico looked at Allegra. "Forgive the indelicacy of what I'm about to say, but it's also common knowledge that Ferdinando does not approve of his brother's affair with your friend."

"Regardless of whatever gossip you may have heard, Signore Domenico, I can assure you that Bianca Cappello is a good-hearted woman," Allegra asserted passionately in her friend's defense. "The poor thing has suffered greatly in life."

To her irritation, Bruno chuckled and said, "By her own choice."

"I beg your pardon?"

"Had she obeyed her father, her life would have been much better."

"Would it, really?"

Bruno leaned back in his chair. "I believe so, yes."

"Bianca's father was negotiating her marriage with the Doge of Venice, a man old enough to be her grandfather."

"All the more reason why she should have gone along with his wishes. She would have lived her life as a great lady and a respected member of the nobility, rich beyond her dreams. Besides, the doge was so old she would have outlived him in a matter of a few years."

The servants cleared the dinner plates and brought out spiced cake.

Domenico bit into a piece and smiled. "This reminds me of the spiced cake my mother used to bake for me when I was a child."

Vittorio and Bruno smiled at the old man. Allegra, who still had much to say on the topic of Bianca Cappello, remained silent.

Noticing his pretty host's annoyed expression, Bruno inquired in a mocking tone, "Did I say something to offend you, Signorina?"

"Bianca did not love the doge," Allegra stated firmly, ignoring his question. "So, although she would have been a great and wealthy lady, as you say, she would not have been a happy one."

"Love led her to scandal and ruin. She and Pietro Bonaventuri lived in misery," Vittorio reminded her.

"Yes, Papa, she did live poorly for a time due to Pietro's treachery," she conceded. "But look at her now. The future Grand Duke of Tuscany has bestowed favor, love, and riches upon her in abundance."

Bruno leaned forward in his seat and pinned her with a cold stare. "The woman is known throughout the city as the *Venetian trollop*. The Florentines openly despise her. As for Francesco, he's being mocked by his subjects for shamelessly flaunting his—and I quote—*fat whore* in public. Anyone who associates with Bianca does so at his or her own risk."

Vittorio set down his knife and turned to look at his daughter with worrisome eyes. Domenico refilled his goblet and drank deeply.

"Are you insinuating that I should not be friends with Bianca?"

"Signorina Allegra, you are a grown woman and can associate with whomever you please. Be aware that some people may start turning their attention, along with their wagging tongues, on you."

"I don't care what other people think," she snapped.

Bruno looked down at his plate and said nothing.

"Anyone up for a game of chess?" asked Vittorio, breaking the silence.

Domenico beamed. "A fine idea, my friend!"

As they retired to the library, a servant entered with a

wrapped parcel. "This just arrived for Signorina Allegra."

"Hand it to me," Vittorio said. "There's no card. Who sent this?"

"The messenger at the door said it's from Signore Matteo Vanusi."

Vittorio handed the parcel to his daughter. "Well, open it."

Feeling the weight of Bruno's hostile stare, Allegra quickly unwrapped the gift. It was a small jewelry box fashioned from copper and silver. Nestled inside was a single chestnut.

Seized by panic, she snapped the box shut and immediately handed it to the servant. "Place this in my bedchamber."

Vittorio appeared puzzled. "Was there anything inside of it?"

"No," she lied.

"Matteo Vanusi is one of our biggest competitors," Bruno observed. "How peculiar that he'd send you a Christmas present, Signorina Allegra."

"I remember when Matteo used to shower you with gifts," Domenico said to Allegra. "Oh, how that young man tried to woo you. All in vain."

"That was a long time ago," Vittorio said. "I've not seen or heard from him since my daughter rejected his marriage proposal."

Allegra flushed to the roots of her hair as she went to stand by the window. Bruno's eyes burned into her back, but she had a bigger problem to think about: *Matteo Vanusi knew her secret.*

When Vittorio and Domenico sat down to play a game of chess, Bruno approached Allegra and said quietly, "It's becoming increasingly apparent that I'm a source of irritation to you."

"We do seem to disagree quite frequently."

"Fire and water," he said. "Opposites, yet we're very much alike."

"How so?"

"Neither of us trusts the opposite sex." Stunned at hearing this, Allegra looked away. He continued, "My reason is clear. As you well know, my adulterous wife caused the death of my

201

son."

"Signore Bruno…"

Undaunted, he continued, "But your reason is a mystery to me. Did some young man break your heart? Did you love him, but he only had eyes for another? What made you despise us so?"

"I do not despise men."

"Yes, you do."

"I love my father and Domenico, and…" She caught herself. "I admire you, too, Signore Bruno." It took all of her courage to confess that to him.

"Do you, now? Well, I'm grateful to be in your good graces, my lady," he teased. "Admiration from a woman like you is as precious as gold."

"Perhaps admiration from a woman like Signora Paolina is more valuable. She admires *all* the men in the city."

Bruno stared at her in shocked silence before bursting into laughter, drawing curious looks from the two older men.

Furious, Allegra clenched her fists and resisted the urge to slap him. "Do you find me amusing, Signore Bruno?"

"I find you more invigorating than the cold morning rain, Allegra." Taking a step closer to her, he added, "Yes, I also find you amusing, intelligent and beautiful in every way. If I merited your affection, I would be a happy and fortunate man, indeed."

Allegra's heart beat out of control as he spoke these words. She placed her hand against the nearby wall to steady herself. "You mock me, sir."

"I promise, I do not," he said softly, his eyes dropping to her mouth.

As she gazed into his eyes, she fought the urge to trust him. "I'm feeling a bit weary. I should leave you gentlemen and—"

"No," he said, reaching for her hand. "Please stay."

"Signore Bruno, I don't wish to argue with you."

"That makes two of us," he said, his expression sincere. "Come, let's sit together. I'll tell you about the time I came face to face with a tiger in India."

Intrigued, Allegra allowed him to lead her to the chairs by

the fire. They sat down and he regaled her with stories of his travels.

***

Allegra set out to see Bianca a few days after Christmas with a confection of honeyed hazelnuts. A servant led her into a bedchamber where Bianca sat at a dressing table in a gown of yellow and white striped satin. Around her neck was the stunning diamond necklace by La Castagna.

"My dearest friend!" Bianca cried when she saw Allegra reflected in the mirror. "How thoughtful of you to bring me a gift, thank you. I adore honeyed hazelnuts."

"I know you do." Dropping her gaze, Allegra added, "La Castagna has outdone himself."

"Look at how it sparkles in the light. He is a genius!"

"And Francesco is a generous man."

Bianca smiled wickedly. "I'll wear it for him tonight with nothing else."

"Bianca!"

"Stop being so prudish, dear."

"I'm not prudish."

"Oh no? Half the men at court lust after you, yet I've never seen you on the arm of any of them. Why is that?" Realization suddenly lit up her painted face. "Are you still a virgin?"

Allegra averted her eyes and said nothing.

Bianca shook her head in awe. "You can have any man of your choice."

"I don't want any of them."

One of the servants stood in the corner, listening to their conversation. Bianca frowned at her. "What are you gawking at, girl? Go on, get out." She waited for the young woman to leave before speaking again. "Forgive the indelicacy of this question. Do you prefer the company of women to men?"

"I'm not a lesbian."

"Good. The less complications in life, the better. So what is it?"

"The thought of being a wife fills me with dread," Allegra confessed. "One never knows how a man will act once the

203

marriage ceremony is over."

Bianca smiled wryly. "You're referring to me."

"It's not only you. I know of others who have been led astray by love."

"I agree that matrimony comes with certain risks and a fair amount of drudgery, but you're not getting any younger, Allegra. The bloom of youth will fade from your face before you know it, and men won't want you."

"I don't want them."

"Fine. You don't need to marry, but, at the very least, take on a lover before it's too late," Bianca advised. "Please know that I say this as your friend who cares for you. I don't wish to see you grow old alone."

***

Vittorio, who had been corresponding with Lavinia for a long time, finally mustered the courage to ask for her hand in marriage. The countess said yes. Eager to share the news with his daughter, he entered the workshop where Allegra was diligently working on a new commission.

She looked up from her task. "I thought you were out running errands."

"I have something to tell you," he said. "Lavinia and I are to be wed."

Allegra stood to embrace him. "This is wonderful news, Papa. When?"

"We will marry in the spring."

"Then we must plan a grand event to celebrate the auspicious occasion."

Vittorio looked down at the workbench, which was full of precious metal strips, gemstones, and tools. "Why not take advantage of the afternoon? The sun shines brightly and it's warmer than usual today."

"I have just begun this commission."

Vittorio waved his hand. "You work too hard and deserve a day of rest. On my way to the bottega this morning I noticed a new vendor at the market selling trinkets form the Far East.

Allegra set down her tools. "I'll fetch my cloak."

She left the house with Gianna in tow. Her thoughts had been heavy for days ever since receiving the jewelry box from Matteo. How had he discovered her secret? What was his objective? Blackmail? She only realized that she was approaching the Mercato Nuovo when she glimpsed the twinkle of gold from the windows.

"I had a feeling we would end up here," Gianna commented smugly.

Allegra admired the gleam of the golden chestnut in the sunshine. Gianna urged her toward the Spinelli-Castagna bottega and they went inside. The apprentices could be seen in the back room, busily working on her pieces.

*If they only knew…*

Bruno appeared in the doorway. "Signorina Allegra," he said, surprised. "To what do I owe the pleasure?"

His cool demeanor caught her off guard. "I was…I mean, I came by…"

"We picked up a few things at the market and stopped by to say hello," Gianna replied on behalf of her stuttering mistress.

Bruno smiled. "How thoughtful. Would you like to see the adjustments I've made to some of your designs?"

He motioned for them to follow him into a small antechamber, which served as the office. Rather than accompany her mistress, Gianna stayed behind, pretending to admire a tray of pendants on display. Two ledgers sat open on a wooden desk, and off to the side was a small bookshelf with several leather-bound volumes. An armillary sphere and an astrolabe were positioned on a shelf, and she paused to admire them.

"From my seafaring days," Bruno commented while unrolling a sheet with two different styles of rings sketched out in charcoal. "These are variations on your original design. Which do you prefer?"

She studied the images before inquiring, "What stone do you plan on using here in the center?"

"Ruby."

"Gold or silver?"

"Gold."

"I prefer the design on the right."

Bruno reached across her for a quill to make some notes. Overwhelmed by his nearness, Allegra's breath hitched. When his eyes dropped to her mouth, her heart raced uncontrollably. Slowly, he lifted his finger and caressed her cheek before resting his fingertip on her bottom lip.

"I'm pleased that you came to see me today," he said huskily.

Allegra did not trust herself to speak under his smoldering gaze. Slowly, he closed the gap between them. She did not move, she did not breathe. For a brief, blissful moment she was engulfed in the scents of spice and leather as he pressed his lips against her own. The chaste kiss ended much too soon.

"I should go," she said, flustered.

"Have I offended you?"

"No, I...I shouldn't have come. I'm sure you have work to do."

The flame which burned so brightly in his eyes went out abruptly, leaving only cold ash in its wake. "Thank you for your opinion, Signorina. Please send my warmest regards to your father."

Gianna followed her mistress out of the shop, then said quietly, "Signore Bruno is in love with you...I know you love him, too."

"Love is a luxury I can't afford."

"My dear child, you're depriving yourself of happiness."

"*You* never married."

Gianna smiled without mirth. "No, but my reasons for abstaining from men are far different from yours." When Allegra stared at her askance, she added, "My father was nothing like your father. I eventually ran away and learned how to be a lady's maid. Fate smiled on me the day I met your mother." She paused, sheepish. "I've spoken out of turn. Forgive me."

"There's nothing to forgive." Giving Gianna's hand a reassuring squeeze, she added, "I'm grateful that you're part of our family."

"As am I."

"There's something I haven't told anyone. The box Matteo Vanusi sent me for Christmas contained a chestnut inside of it."

"Santa Madonna! Do you think he knows?"

"There's only one way to find out."

They stopped at Matteo Vanusi's bottega on Via Roma on their way home. He smiled at the sight of Allegra.

"Buongiorno," he said.

Allegra placed both hands on the counter that stood between them. "I came to thank you for the gift, Signore Matteo."

"I'm flattered that you came in person when a note would have sufficed," he said. "Do you like the jewelry box?"

"It's lovely, yes."

"Did you notice what was inside?"

"A chestnut."

"Yes!" He smiled expectantly.

*Was this a game?* Allegra glanced warily at Gianna.

He continued, "I thought you'd appreciate it."

"I don't understand."

"Allegra *Castagno*," he said. "I thought it would be humorous to place a castagna in the box. It's a play on your name, you see."

Matteo's face was guileless, his eyes sincere.

The corners of Allegra's lips finally lifted. "How clever."

"I'm to wed soon and the jewelry box was meant as a parting gift," he explained. "It's my hope that you foster the same good will toward me that I foster toward you."

"Rest assured that I do, Signore Matteo," she said honestly, the years of resentment dissolving in that instant. "Felicitations to you and your future bride."

## Chapter 21

Bruno arrived at the Palazzo Castagno the next day, intent on speaking with Vittorio. Hearing his voice, Allegra crept out of the workshop and tiptoed down the hallway. She listened from the top of the stairs as the men retreated into the library. Luckily, her father did not bother to close the door.

"Signore Vittorio, I've come to discuss a delicate matter."

"You may speak freely."

"It involves your daughter."

Hearing this, Allegra's heart fluttered like a trapped bird in her chest.

Bruno continued, "Is she promised to another man?"

Vittorio hesitated. "No."

"I'd like your permission to court her."

"I see…"

"I assure you that my intentions are serious, and I can provide Allegra with the lifestyle to which she is accustomed. My navigational exploits with the Portuguese have enabled me to amass a considerable fortune."

"I've known you since birth and hold you in the highest esteem. I made a promise to my late wife that our daughter would marry a man of her own choosing, and I intend on honoring that vow. If Allegra will have you, then you have my permission to court and wed her."

"Thank you, Signore Vittorio. May I speak with her now?"

"Yes, of course. I'll have the servants offer you refreshment while I go and fetch her."

Allegra fled into the workshop and frantically paced the room. She could barely breathe from the combination of anxiety and excitement. The moment Vittorio entered the room, she confessed, "I heard everything."

Vittorio didn't know what shocked him more, the fact that she had eavesdropped on him or her reaction to Bruno's request of courtship. Up until now his daughter had treated every suitor with disdain, sometimes contempt. *Could it be possible...?*

"Oh, Papa..."

"Do you care for him?"

"I do," she admitted.

"Signore Bruno is a mature man of the world, not some foolish young courtier." Vittorio paused to let his words sink into his daughter's head. "He wants you to be his wife."

"What if I told him the truth?"

"No. Domenico and I are in accord on this issue." At her crestfallen face, he added, "There *is* a way you can marry him without hurting anyone in the process."

"I cannot give up my craft. My need to create is like my need to breathe. I'll never stop being La Castagna."

Vittorio felt a mixture of respect and frustration. "Very well. He's waiting to speak with you in the library. The choice is yours to make."

"I'm not being offered a choice," she countered bitterly. "This is an ultimatum."

"Don't look at it that way."

"As I see it, I can either continue being La Castagna and spurn Bruno, or marry him and give up everything I've worked so hard to achieve. Tell me, Papa, how is this fair?"

"Life is not fair, Allegra."

"Especially if you are cursed with womanhood," she retorted before storming out of the room.

She found Bruno staring out the window. "Buongiorno, Signore Bruno. You asked to see me?"

He turned around and walked to where she stood. "Signorina Allegra, I hope I'm not disturbing you."

"Not at all. You and your father are well?"

"Yes, but that's not why I'm here." Taking hold of her hands, he looked deeply into her eyes. "Allegra, I foster deep admiration for you, and that sentiment has grown into something more substantial. Your father has given me permission to court you, and it would please me greatly if you would allow me to do so."

Allegra wanted nothing more than to be held in his arms and taste his lips, but La Castagna chastised her heart. She witnessed Bruno's silent inner struggle as he awaited her response.

"I'm flattered, Signore Bruno," she said, gently retracting her hands. "Regretfully…"

Stricken, he took a step back. "I was under the impression that you were fond of me."

*More than I care to admit.* "I *am* fond of you. My father and I consider you a close family friend."

His mouth hardened. "Ah."

"As I've told you before, my father is a widower with no sons," she said, hoping to soften the blow. "I aid him greatly in his work, and have little time to myself."

An awkward silence followed. Bruno frowned pensively, then suddenly gripped her wrist. "I know you care for me. I see it in your eyes every time you look at me. Tell me who did this to you. Who hurt you?"

Allegra shook her head quietly.

"Is it Paolina?" he pressed. "She means nothing to me, she never did. I admit, I used her only as a diversion after being alone for so long."

"Please, stop."

"I broke off with her soon after I met you. You haunted my thoughts day and night. You're the only woman I want."

"My answer is no," she whispered. "I'm sorry."

Smiling without humor, he retorted, "Not as sorry as I am."

"I didn't mean to—"

"I won't take up any more of your time. I bid you good day."

Defeated, Allegra watched his retreat with tears in her eyes.

Vittorio entered the library a moment later. "Is La Castagna truly worth this much sacrifice?"

"Yes," she replied before bursting into tears.

Vittorio left for Arezzo the following week. Allegra remained in Florence during her father's absence in order to finish her commissions. She dispatched a messenger to Domenico to let him know the pieces were ready for delivery, and instructed him to pick them up the following morning. Oddly, he never showed. She sent another message at midday. Nothing. By late afternoon, one of his servants arrived at the Palazzo Castagno.

"Signorina Allegra, I was sent here by my master."

Alarmed, Allegra demanded, "Where is he?"

"He woke up feeling ill and is still in bed," the young woman replied, wringing her hands. "My master told me to come here and fetch your maid, Gianna, because she's well versed in flower lore."

"Why didn't you come sooner? Have you informed Signore Bruno?"

"He had business in Fiesole and Careggi, and departed at dawn. He's not expected back until this evening."

Allegra ushered the girl out the door. "Go home, put a cold compress on your master's head and sit with him. We'll be along shortly."

Gianna, who heard the exchange from the doorway, said, "I'll gather my herbs and roots."

Allegra donned a cloak, grabbed the leather pouch full of jewelry, and hesitated at the sight of the setting sun outside her window. Should she risk delivering the pieces herself? Although it wasn't the normal protocol, she tucked the pouch in the inner pocket of her cloak and left the palazzo.

As the two women hastily made their way to Domenico's house, Gianna said, "You should convince the old man to tell his son the truth about you."

"Neither he nor my father want that."

"I know about Bruno's visit and his proposal of marriage. That man loves you. End this charade for the sake of your happiness."

"Do not concern yourself with this matter, Gianna."

Gianna stopped in her tracks. "Do not concern myself, you say? Me—who has known and cared for you since birth, who loves you like a daughter?" She shook her head, her expression sad. "I've always known my place, but enough is enough, Allegra. You hardly eat, you hardly sleep. I will not stand by and watch you waste away. It would be an affront to your dear mother's memory, God rest her soul."

Gianna crossed herself and Allegra followed suit. "You're right, Gianna. Forgive me. Now come, we must hurry!"

***

Bruno stared at the ledger until the letters and numbers blurred before his eyes. He had met with clients in Fiesole and Careggi earlier, and returned to Florence much earlier than he had anticipated. For over an hour he'd been poring over the books, unable to concentrate. The late afternoon light was fading, so he lit a candle. His head ached from lack of sleep, causing him to rub his temples. Lately, his nights consisted of tossing and turning in his bed. During the day, all he could think of was Allegra Castagno.

He was certain that her desire and affection matched his own, yet she had rejected him. Why? Her excuse, although reasonable, rang hollow to his ears. Something—or someone—held her back.

*Matteo Vanusi?*

Sighing in frustration, he pushed himself away from the desk, grabbed his cloak from the peg, and stormed out of the office. "I shall return shortly," he said to the apprentices before exiting the bottega.

He'd stopped trusting women after Anabella's treachery, keeping his heart under lock and key. He had spent the last decade sailing to various ports throughout Europe, Asia, and twice to the sandy coast of the New World. He bedded many women, enjoying their bodies while cautiously avoiding any emotional commitments. The mere mention of the word *love* had him running in the opposite direction. Perhaps that explained why he preferred the company of whores who expected nothing from him except money.

While his mind wandered, his feet betrayed him. Without realizing it, he headed for the Palazzo Castagno. Would Allegra turn him away at the door?

He strode briskly along Via Roma, cutting through the crowds of laymen and merchants trying to sell the last of their

212

wares. Two prostitutes lurked in a gloomy alley attempting to convince a drunkard to part with his coin. He turned right onto the Piazza del Duomo, casting an appreciative glance at the majestic edifices that brought glory to Florence. As he veered in the direction of the Palazzo Castagno, he spotted Allegra and Gianna heading toward him. The two women walked arm in arm, deeply engrossed in what appeared to be a serious conversation.

Bruno ducked into a narrow alley so that neither woman noticed his presence. Where were they going so late in the day? Without a second thought, he followed them. To his surprise, they walked straight to his father's door.

***

A cat hovered on the stoop, waiting for a chance to dart inside the house. The opportunity presented itself when one of the servants opened the door. Allegra and Gianna were led straight to Domenico's bedchamber, which stank of vomit.

"I'll be quick about it," Gianna said as she set about preparing a curative.

"These stupid girls are trying to kill me," Domenico said weakly from his bed. "Thank you for coming."

Allegra set the leather pouch containing the jewelry on the bedside table and went to Domenico's side. Pointing to the bucket containing the vomit, she said to the servants, "Make yourselves useful. Fetch me an empty bucket and clean out this one. Fill a basin with water and bring me a cloth. Hurry!"

"Yes, my lady."

The old man put his face into the empty bucket and dry heaved several times. Allegra leaned forward to place an arm around his frail shoulders, unwittingly causing the chestnut charm to escape from the confines of her bodice. Bruno entered the room at that moment, surprising everyone.

"What's going on here?" he demanded.

"Your father's been sick all day and his servants only waited until now to fetch me," Allegra replied. "Gianna is mixing a curative for him."

Bruno's face suddenly contorted into an expression of

shock. Following his gaze, Allegra noticed the exposed chestnut charm dangling from her neck. Quickly, she tucked it back inside of her bodice.

Gianna hurried into the room at the sound of the old man's cough. "Here, Signore Domenico, drink this."

Domenico initially recoiled at the smell of the herbaceous elixir, but he forced it down by sipping it slowly.

"I should fetch the physician," Bruno said.

"I would wait," Gianna advised. "These days they resort to bloodletting for the slightest ailment. Your father cannot afford to lose any blood in his weakened state." Turning to the servants, she asked, "How long has he been vomiting?"

"Since midday," one of the girls replied.

Gianna sighed. "He needs a good broth, some bread, and an invigorating tonic to restore his stamina."

"Gianna has a healing touch," Allegra said softly. "If she can't make him better, then we'll call the physician."

Bruno nodded in agreement and Gianna got to work. Allegra helped as much as she could while Bruno sat with his father, applying cold compresses to the old man's forehead. Before long, Domenico's breathing grew even and he fell asleep.

"Thank you," Bruno said to Allegra and Gianna. "I can take over now."

Allegra gently touched his arm. "Please let me know if you need anything else." She was about to reach for the leather pouch on the bedside table, but he snatched it away from her. Appalled at his boldness, she put out her hand. "Signore Bruno, that pouch is mine."

Bouncing it on his palm, he demanded, "What's this?"

"Please give it back."

Ignoring the request, he emptied the pouch's contents onto the table before fixing her with an accusatory glare. "You personally deliver La Castagna's jewelry to my father's house?"

The ensuing silence was broken by Domenico's loud snore. Gianna slipped out of the bedchamber to await her mistress in the adjoining room.

Allegra's mind raced to construct a convincing lie. "The courier who normally delivers La Castagna's pieces to the bottega is sick today, so a new courier delivered it to my father's address by mistake."

Unconvinced, Bruno demanded, "Did he also deliver the chestnut charm hanging from the chain around your neck?"

"Another commission that we never received payment for," she replied, amazed at her propensity for fabricating untruths.

He looked at her incredulously. "Someone commissioned a chestnut?"

"We're not the only Castagno family in Tuscany."

"Do you know what I think? Not only do you know La Castagna's identity, you're enamored of him."

Allegra blinked in disbelief. "What did you say?"

"That love token around your neck is proof. Perhaps Matteo Vanusi made it for you. Is *he* La Castagna?"

"My life is not nearly as intriguing as you think, I assure you."

He cursed himself for speaking like a lovesick fool as she walked out of the room without saying a word.

Later, Allegra paced the floor of the workshop. Keeping busy was the surest way to get Bruno off her mind. Feeling inspired, she took charcoal to vellum and implemented arabesques into a few sketches. She then set out to obtain the opinion of the only person who would wear such fanciful jewelry.

Bianca received Allegra in her sitting room. "What a pleasant surprise! I love it when you visit me." To the maid hovering in the corner, she said, "I told you to wash my linens."

The girl looked at her mistress askance. "I washed them yesterday."

"You did a poor job of it," Bianca snapped. "Every piece must be rewashed. Fetch some sweet wine for us, then set your hand to the task." Turning to Allegra, she whispered, "Francesco expects my undergarments to be pristine. It's so hard to find good help these days. Tell me, what brings you here, my best and dearest friend?"

Allegra removed the sketches from a satchel. "La Castagna drew these and Maestro Domenico asked for my opinion on them. Since I don't possess half of your sophistication, I thought I'd show them to you."

Flattered, Bianca put on her most serious face as she studied the designs. "These are unusual," she commented, peering closely at one in particular.

"Do you like them?"

"Unique and bold, like many of his other pieces."

"Yes, but are they any good?"

Bianca looked up. "Good? They're wonderful! The man never ceases to amaze me. Is he accepting commissions for these?"

Trying to hide her excitement, Allegra replied, "I'm certain Maestro Domenico can convince him to create a few of them."

Bianca indicated two sketches. "I simply *must* have these in gold."

"Don't you wish to consult with Francesco first?"

"He'll approve, I'm sure."

"How is he these days? It's been a while since I've seen him."

Bianca smiled a bit too sweetly. "Our love grows daily."

## CHAPTER 22

*"Mio figlio!"*

The anguished cry was immediately followed by screams. Allegra ran to the window as Gianna burst into the workshop.

Allegra hastily removed her leather work apron. "What happened?"

"Something bad by the sound of it."

They flew downstairs and pounded on the outer gate of the palazzo across the street until a stricken servant opened the door.

"We heard Donna Luisa's screams. Is everything all right?"

"Young Master Osvaldo is dead," the girl explained.

Allegra and Gianna shoved past the girl, closing the door on the curious onlookers gathered in the street. The servant led them upstairs to the boy's bedchamber where the lady of the house was being revived from a swoon in the arms of her maid. Young Osvaldo stared up at the ceiling from his bed with lifeless eyes and bluish lips.

"How did this happen?" Allegra demanded of the maid.

"We have no idea, Signorina," the woman replied. "He was as fit as a bull yesterday…"

"Where is your master?"

"In Calabria." Donna Luisa stirred and, when she opened her eyes, she began screaming again. "I must prepare something to calm her."

"Stay and comfort your mistress," Allegra said. "My maid will do it."

The woman looked at Gianna and inquired, "Do you know how to make a strong draught?"

After years of administering draughts to Stefania Rossi, Gianna knew how to make them potent enough to send a horse into oblivion. "I do," she replied. "I'll return shortly."

Donna Luisa freed herself from the arms of her servant and

threw herself over her son's body. "My son!"

Allegra patted the grieving mother's back while staring at young Osvaldo's face. She had glimpsed the healthy adolescent through the window less than a week ago.

As if reading her thoughts, the maid whispered, "Yesterday was his thirteenth birthday."

It was late afternoon by the time Allegra reentered the workshop. She donned her apron, but it was impossible to concentrate on anything after seeing young Osvaldo's lifeless body. *Thirteen years old.* Unknown cause of death. Could she, too, simply die for no apparent reason? The possibility made her suddenly and uncomfortably aware of her own mortality.

With a heavy heart, she removed the apron and set it on a chair. Bruno inevitably came to mind. He had accused her of being in love with La Castagna the other day. The irony of the situation was enough to make her laugh and cry at the same time. His jealousy had thrilled her to the core, however.

Leaning on the sun-warmed windowsill, she gazed at the terracotta roofs of Florence. The Arno glittered under the coppery light of the late afternoon sun as boats glided to and fro upon its placid surface. The city teemed with life, yet she'd been cooped up in the workshop, drowning in work.

*Drowning in order to forget Bruno's kiss...*

Bruno would still be at the bottega this time of day. Overwhelmed with a desire to see him, she set out for the Mercato Nuovo. She knew it was unwise to go out alone, but after seeing Osvaldo's body...

*Life is fragile and short.*

Pickpockets and cutthroats lurked in dark corners as she wove through the busy streets of the city center. The sun dipped toward the horizon, creating elongated shadows in her path. Allegra veered toward the Mercato Nuovo and hesitated before entering the bottega. Only two older apprentices were still working in the back room at that late hour, and they froze at the sight of her in the doorway.

"Buona sera," she said. "I'm here to see Signore Bruno."

One of the apprentices motioned to the office door, which

218

was closed. "The master is…*indisposed*."

Female laughter erupted from behind the door and the faces of the young men turned red. Sickened by the sound, Allegra forced herself to knock. Bruno opened the door, his face blanching at the sight of her.

"Forgive my intrusion," she said, her eyes locked on Paolina Gori.

The widow stood by the desk wearing a mocking smile. Bruno stepped out of the office and shut the door behind him. "I wasn't expecting you."

Allegra took in his untucked shirt and the smudge of lip paint on his jaw.

"You came here alone?" he inquired with a frown. "At this hour?"

"I…I…" she trailed off, feeling foolish, angry and hurt. Osvaldo's death prompted her to mend the rift between them. Now, she regretted having acted so precipitously.

"Has your father returned?"

"Not yet," she replied. When he continued to stare at her askance, she said, "I came because…I wanted to see you."

Bruno's expression softened in the light of her honest confession.

Paolina opened the door and stared at them. "Shall we invite Signorina Allegra into the office for a drink?"

"Thank you, no." Allegra turned to leave. "I have to go."

His hand clamped down on her arm. "Wait."

"Let go of me," she snapped. To her horror, tears welled up in her eyes.

"Allegra, please…"

Paolina chuckled softly as Allegra wrenched herself free of his grasp and ran out of the bottega. "What an unstable young woman."

"She shouldn't be out alone at this late hour," he said, heading for the door. "I'm going to escort her home."

"If you go, I won't be here when you return."

Bruno ignored her comment as he ran out into the crisp evening air. It didn't take long for him to catch up to Allegra.

219

"Wait."

"What are you doing? Go away."

Taking hold of her elbow, he replied, "I'm accompanying you home."

"I don't need your company," she snapped, trying to free herself from his vice-like grip. "Let go of me."

Bruno looked straight ahead, forcing her to keep pace. They turned down a narrow street, then he yanked her into a dark alley. When they receded far enough into the shadows, he pushed her back against the wall.

"Allegra—"

"You must not dally," she interjected. "Paolina awaits your return."

"I've already told you. She was my lover once. Not anymore."

Allegra laughed bitterly. "I may not be as worldly as you are, Signore Bruno, but I'm not stupid."

"I know how it must look," he agreed softly. "But I assure you there's nothing going on between us."

"Is that why her lip paint is on your face?"

"Porca miseria." Frowning, he wiped his face with the back of his hand. "She came to the bottega begging for me to take her back. When I said no, she threw herself at me."

"Why should I believe you?"

Allegra felt his hand at the nape of her neck as he lifted the golden chain, revealing the chestnut charm. "Why should I believe you when you say you're not in love with La Castagna?"

*Touché.*

Suddenly, he claimed her mouth. Shock, confusion, joy, and fear shot through her in that instant. She slid her arms around his neck when his insistent tongue slipped into her mouth and coiled against her own.

Bruno's hand circled her waist as he pulled her against his strong, lean body. Allegra's knees almost buckled when his manhood hardened against the joining of her thighs. Cupping the hair at the base of her neck, he pulled it back in order to expose her throat. As his mouth traveled from her lips to the smooth skin of her neck, she whimpered in pleasure. He marveled at his body's response to Vittorio's daughter. Not even the prostitute in Cape Verde—who had pleasured him in ways that no European woman ever had—was capable of coaxing such fire in his loins. He had never wanted a woman so badly in his life.

Not even Anabella.

"Your body does not lie, Allegra." Tightening his hold around her waist and pulling her closer for emphasis, he demanded, "What prevents you from being mine?"

Allegra found it difficult to breathe, let alone think. His delicious scent, his power, his voice…Never before had she experienced such desire—*such lust*. She wanted nothing more than to offer him her maidenhead, right then and there, like a common trollop!

*Oh God, what am I doing?* "Please," she pleaded. "Signore Bruno…"

He pulled away and, despite the dimness of the alley, she could see the fire in his eyes. "Bruno," he corrected. "Say it."

*"Bruno."*

He released his possessive grip but continued to hold her in his arms. "My precious girl," he said, his lips against her temple. "You drive me to the point of madness."

The sound of footsteps startled them.

Allegra noticed a moving shadow over Bruno's shoulder and caught a glimpse of a twisted mouth with missing teeth. "Watch out!"

Bruno unsheathed the dagger at his side with lightning speed and placed the blade to the pickpocket's throat. As he shuffled back against the wall with his captive, his head turned left and right to make sure there were no other ruffians in the vicinity. Allegra found his stealth intimidating.

"I'm unarmed," the man cried. "I didn't mean to interrupt your—"

"Shut your mouth," Bruno snapped. Giving the man a hard shove, he added, "Be on your way."

The man shuffled off but his eyes were still glued to the glittering gemstones at Allegra's throat. Bruno clasped her wrist and urged her out into the fading sunlight of a busy street. They didn't speak until they arrived at the gate of the Palazzo Castagno.

Finally, he said, "I apologize for my lack of restraint."

"I shouldn't have gone to the bottega."

"Your father will marry soon enough," he said with a twinkle in his eye. "I am a patient man."

***

Lavinia had an extended family and Vittorio did not, which meant that their marriage would take place in Asti. Vittorio, Allegra, and Gianna traveled to the Piedmont region in April 1573 for the celebration. Domenico and Bruno had planned on accompanying them, but the old man became ill again, and his son was obliged to remain in Florence to care of him. Allegra worried constantly about Domenico, whose bouts of illness were becoming alarmingly frequent.

The bride wore a splendid gown of satin encrusted with pearls, and the couple's faces glowed with contentment throughout the church ceremony. A great banquet followed at Lavinia's villa in Asti.

While dancing with her father, Allegra said, "I haven't seen you smile this much since mother was alive."

His eyes misted at the thought of Stefania. "Do you think she's looking down on me from Heaven with resentment?"

"On the contrary," she assured him. "Mother loved you. She wouldn't want you to remain alone."

Vittorio's eyes slid to where the attractive countess stood chatting with a group of ladies. "She's a good woman and I love her."

"I wish you both all the happiness in the world."

"If only I could gift some of it to you."

Allegra shook her head. "I'm content with my life."

"Bruno pines for you, and I know you love him, too." Gauging her reaction, he added, "He would make a fine husband."

"I'll never sacrifice La Castagna for the mediocrity of marriage."

"Allegra—"

*"Never."*

"I won't force your hand." The music stopped and Vittorio led his daughter to a quiet corner. "There's something I need to tell you."

"Papa, your expression frightens me."

"Actually, you may like the idea. Lavinia wants to remain here."

"I thought your intention was to live in Florence."

"That was the original plan, but we came to a new agreement yesterday. Lavinia and I will spend the spring and summer in Asti, the autumn and winter in Florence. This is a fair arrangement for both of us. Now, I must decide what to do with you."

"What do you mean?"

"I can't leave you alone in Florence for six months."

"I have Gianna and a houseful of servants to keep me company."

"It would be unseemly."

"You would have me live in Asti half the year?" she demanded, horrified by the thought. "What about my commissions? The bottega?"

"You can work on them when you're in Florence."

"But not in Asti?" When her father remained silent, she added, "Lavinia doesn't know yet, does she?"

"No. I intend to tell her soon, however."

"I can't agree to this arrangement, Papa."

"Allegra, I have indulged you for many years—"

"If I refuse to give up my craft for Bruno, the man I love, what makes you think I'll denounce La Castagna for the countess?"

Vittorio stared at his daughter incredulously. "What will people say if I simply abandon my daughter and go away for half a year?"

"Your daughter is a grown woman; a spinster, in fact."

"That's not the point." He glanced at the guests. "No father in his right mind would leave his unmarried daughter alone and unprotected for months at a time. It's neither safe nor proper."

"If I was a man, you'd have no issue with it," she retorted bitterly.

"That's true, but irrelevant."

"Have you forgotten that my godfather is the Duke of Florence?"

Vittorio shook his head dismissively. "Cosimo is a lost cause."

"If it makes you feel better, Domenico can act as my legal guardian."

"He's too old. Until I find a viable solution to this problem, you'll stay here in Asti with us."

"For how long? When are you going back to Tuscany?"

"September."

Fuming inwardly, Allegra said nothing more. Assuming she had given into his wishes, Vittorio went off in search of his wife. The wedding celebration continued well into the night. When the majority of guests were inebriated, Allegra crept into the bedchamber Lavinia had assigned to her and locked the door. There, she finally gave into tears.

Gianna, who occupied the small antechamber, went to sit by Allegra. "Why are you crying on this joyous day?"

Allegra repeated the conversation she'd had with her father earlier.

Gianna nodded in understanding, her face serious. "This is indeed an unpleasant predicament. Give it some time. He may change his mind."

"If I stay, you must remain here until September, too."

"I suppose I must."

"How do you feel about that?"

Gianna shrugged. "At my advanced age, my only concern is to be well fed and comfortable while making myself useful. It's lovely here and, to be honest, it's thrilling to see new faces and eat new foods. Lavinia is pleasant and so are her servants. I have no complaint."

"Perhaps I should try to be as compliant as you are."

"It can't hurt, my dear. Life is easier when you simply go along with its current. Now, get some sleep. You'll feel better in the morning."

As the days passed, Allegra was forced to spend time with other ladies who did little more than gossip and needlepoint. Her only consolation was the villa's library which, although limited in size, contained decent tomes. Despite feeling melancholic, she did her best to appear cheerful for the sake of her father and his new wife.

She missed being alone in her workshop doing what she loved best, but most of all, she missed Bruno. In Florence, there were opportunities to see him. In Asti, there were none.

By the end of the second week, Allegra approached her father and said, "Please let me return to Florence, Papa."

Vittorio frowned. "Are you not happy here?"

"My fingers itch to make jewelry again."

"Let me think on it."

Allegra waited three days before broaching the subject again.

Irritated, Vittorio snapped, "You will remain here for the time being."

Allegra spun on her heel and walked away.

During supper that evening, she smiled and chatted with Lavinia's relatives. When it grew dark, she wrote a letter of apology to her father, donned a plain black cloak, and exited the villa with a purse full of coins. She selected a young mare from the stables and headed south to Genova, where she spent the night.

After an entire day of riding, she spent the night at an inn, and continued her journey toward Tuscany the following day. Exhausted and in desperate need of a bath, she arrived in Florence well past curfew. The city's gates were locked, and two armed guards stood watch outside the massive studded door while another held a crossbow in the lookout tower.

*Three men. One woman. Darkness…*

Seeing the cloaked figure on horseback, one of the soldiers

cried, "You'll have to find shelter outside the gates."

Allegra pushed back the hood of her cloak and her hair spilled over her shoulders in waves of gold. As the men stared in admiration of her face, she said in an authoritative tone, "Open the gate."

The soldier in the tower made a lewd comment. The one below chuckled and said, "Well, my pretty, perhaps we could let you through *for a price*."

The man in the tower shouted, "She wouldn't deprive us of some fun."

"I am Signorina Allegra Castagno, godchild of Cosimo de' Medici." She tilted her chin. "*Open* the gates."

"A noblewoman riding alone at this hour of night?"

"I'm under no obligation to explain the nature of my business to anyone except His Grace."

The two men on the ground mumbled to each other, then pushed open the heavy door. One of them mounted his horse and silently escorted her to the Palazzo Castagno. Allegra had never seen the streets of Florence so dark and silent. It was a great relief when she finally entered the courtyard of her home. She handed a few coins to the soldier, then dragged her sore body upstairs, fell upon the bed fully clothed, and slept.

The sun shone feebly through wooly clouds the next day. Allegra stirred at the sound of someone knocking on the door. She covered her ears at first, but whoever it was refused to go away.

She got out of bed and glanced in the mirror. Her clothes were dusty and crumpled, her hair a mass of tangles, and two dark smudges sat beneath her eyes. The pounding continued, drawing her attention away from the mirror's reflection. It was no doubt a messenger, sent by her father.

*He must be livid.* Allegra descended the stairs. "Calm yourself," she said, running across the courtyard to unlock the gate. "Stop banging on my—"

She froze at the sight of Bruno wearing a scowl. He held up a letter for her inspection, and she instantly recognized her father's handwriting.

226

"You traveled from Asti to Florence *alone*?" When she refused to answer, he bellowed, "Have you lost your wits?"

She recoiled at his tone. "When did you get this?"

"A messenger delivered it to the bottega less than an hour ago. Your father must be sick with worry, not to mention furious." His face settled into a mask of disapproval. "Do you have any idea what could have happened to you on the way here?" When his eyes swept over her, she felt terribly self-conscious. "When did you arrive?"

"Last night. I was so exhausted that I simply fell upon my bed."

"I'll dispatch a messenger to Asti at once." He paused. "Vittorio is a good man and he doesn't deserve to suffer such anguish so soon after his wedding day. You behaved selfishly, Allegra."

Shocked by his chastisement, she conceded, "I'll send him an apology."

As he turned to go, Allegra grabbed his arm. "Wait." He stopped and stared down at her hand. "Please don't be upset with me."

"Your father's message made me sick," he retorted angrily. "A young lady traveling alone on horseback...The road from Tuscany to Asti is littered with vagrants and bandits. You could have been ravaged or killed. Why in heaven's name would you take such a risk?"

"My father wanted me to stay in Asti until September and I wanted to return to Florence. There was no reasoning with him, so I took matters into my own hands."

"You could have at least made decent travel arrangements rather than sneaking off in the middle of the night, unchaperoned and unprotected.

Her lip quivered. "I didn't think..."

His expression softened at the sight of her tears. Gathering her to his chest, he held her tightly. "No, you did *not* think, did you? The dangers that could have befallen you are enough to make me tremble with fear."

Allegra felt safe in the circle of his arms and winced

inwardly when he let her go. "I didn't mean to cause you or my father any alarm."

"Yet that's exactly what you've done."

"I know, and I'm sorry. It won't happen again."

He calmed down in the face of her contriteness. "I'm relieved to hear it."

"I missed Florence and...I missed seeing you." When he said nothing, she asked, "Would you like to sup with me this evening?"

Studying her intently, he inquired, "Would that be wise?"

His husky tone and smoldering gaze caused her heartbeat to race. "Are you suggesting it's unwise to break bread with a friend?"

Bruno took firm hold of Allegra's chin and stared wistfully at her mouth. When her breathing grew shallow and her eyes fluttered shut in anticipation of his kiss, he chuckled softly. "*Friend*, you say?"

Turning on his heel, he headed back to the bottega.

Shaken, Allegra stared after him with longing. Sighing heavily, she went in search of her servants to prepare a bath. While soaking in the fragrant water, she tried to think of a solution to her problem. She wanted Bruno *and* La Castagna. Squeezing her eyes shut, she filled her lungs with air and immersed her head underwater. After a lifetime of resenting and avoiding men, she lacked feminine wiles. She was also ignorant on many issues pertaining to love and courtship.

Breaking through the water's surface, Allegra inhaled deeply and slicked her hair back from her face. She needed advice on love, courtship, and everything these rites entailed. There was only one person she could talk to about such things; only one person she could trust.

A couple of hours later, Allegra was seated in the privacy of Bianca's sitting room. After exchanging pleasantries and describing her father's wedding in Asti, she said, "I came here today because I need your advice."

"Something is troubling you," Bianca commented.

"Yes."

Bianca walked to the sideboard and poured wine into two chalices. "Wine usually helps. What ails you, my friend?"

Allegra took a deep sip of wine for encouragement. "As you know, I've never courted any man. I'm ignorant on males and matters of the heart and, since I have no siblings or mother to turn to, I've come to you for advice."

"You did the right thing."

Relieved, Allegra smiled hesitantly. "I need to ask you a question of a personal nature, and I'm counting on your discretion."

"Of course, my dear. Ask me anything."

"How do you prevent pregnancy?"

Bianca's head tilted back as she let out a hearty laugh. "Who is he?"

"I don't think you know him."

"I know everyone." Bianca studied Allegra's face then gasped. "You love this man! Cupid's arrow has struck you at last!" Her face grew serious. "I only hope he's worthy of you, my best and dearest friend."

"He is, I assure you."

"Does this mean that you and he…?"

"No, never."

Bianca smiled slyly. "But you want to."

Allegra's face burned under her friend's scrutiny. "Yes," she confessed. "You will help me?"

"Of course! First of all, there's no need to fret. What happens between a man and a woman is the most natural thing in the world." She grinned. "You still haven't told me the gentleman's name."

"Bruno Spinelli."

Bianca's face lit up. "Maestro Domenico's son? He's *quite* handsome. I can see why you want him."

"No one knows my secret, Bianca."

"Don't worry. No one will find out."

"Thank you."

"The carnal act of love is the most natural thing in the world. I'm certain that Bruno Spinelli has considerable experience in that area." Lowering her voice, Bianca added, "You must protect yourself from any unwanted consequences, of course. My servants will prepare the emmenagogue for you as a precaution."

"Forgive my ignorance, but I don't know what that is."

"It's a potent concoction of various roots and herbs including cloves, periwinkle, mugwort, parsley, and a bit of strong wine. After you make love with Bruno, which I hope happens soon, you simply drink it and it will cause you to bleed." Bianca paused to allow the implication of her words to sink in. When Allegra continued to stare at her askance, she explained, "It forces your menstrual blood to flow."

"To prevent pregnancy."

"Precisely. Or you can have Bruno pull out his manhood before he spills his seed into you, but, I warn you, this method is a bit tricky. Otherwise, you can simply become pregnant and force him to marry you, which is ultimately what you want is it not?"

"Bruno already wants to marry me, but I refused his offer."

"Oho! The plot thickens," Bianca said, simultaneously amused and shocked. "Here you are, a *virgo intacta* well over marrying age, wanting to prevent pregnancy with a man whom you wish to seduce, but have no intention to wed."

"You make me sound so *wicked*."

"Allegra, you're surprising me at every turn! What prevents you from marrying this handsome, rich man?"

Embarrassed, Allegra buried her face in her hands. "I can't tell you."

"Why ever not?"

"I…I simply cannot. Please, don't question me further. It's taken all of my courage to confess this much to you already."

"I respect your privacy," Bianca said gently. "I'm always here if and when you wish to unburden yourself."

"You are a true friend."

Allegra gratefully accepted the tiny bottle containing the emmenagogue and went home. She busied herself in the workshop until sundown, then changed for dinner. There was no sign of Bruno. Feeling like a fool, she sat at the dining table alone. She was in the middle of sipping broth when one of the servants appeared at the door with him in tow.

"You came," Allegra said with a smile.

He walked toward the table. "How could I stay away?"

A servant quickly set a place at the table and retreated into the kitchen. A moment later, a steaming bowl of broth was set in front of Bruno.

He ate a spoonful, then said, "You mentioned that your father plans on staying in Asti until September."

"They plan on living six months in Florence, six months in Asti."

"That's not unreasonable. In fact, it seems like a good compromise."

"I suppose it is," she agreed. "Asti is lovely."

"So lovely that you fled from it in the middle of the night."

"The thought of remaining in the north for so long made me sad."

"Why?"

She was relieved when a servant arrived with a platter of braised rabbit. As the girl served them, she said, "Please taste the rabbit and let me know if it's to your liking."

Bruno took a bite. "It's delicious." Leaning back in his chair, he eyed her steadily. "You haven't answered my question."

"I didn't want to be away from Florence for so long."

"Why am I here, Allegra?"

The direct question caught her off guard. "I enjoy your company."

"I can't help but wonder what your father would say if he walked into this room right now."

"He would disapprove."

"Any father would. You've invited a man to sup with you alone, without a chaperone. Servants talk, you know."

"I know."

"Yet you risk your father's displeasure on my behalf." He paused for effect. "So again I ask you, *why am I here*?"

Allegra met his gaze and her eyes revealed desire. Seeing

this, Bruno stood and walked to where she sat. She stood and boldly kissed him.

"Your kisses are sweet as honey," he whispered when she pulled away. "Tell me in words what I see in your eyes."

"Bruno, please…"

Gripping her shoulders, he repeated, "Tell me. I want to hear it."

"I want you."

"You reject my offer to court you, yet claim to want me?" he asked, panting with desire. "You are an enigma."

Ignoring his comment, she kissed him again, this time pressing against him as her arms slid around his neck.

"If we continue like this…"

Paying no heed to the warning, she repeated, "I want you, Bruno."

*So be it.* "Take me to your bed."

The moment they were alone, he pushed her against the wall and kissed her slowly, sensuously. His hands caressed her throat and breasts as his tongue devoured her mouth.

Pulling away, he said, "Say you'll be mine."

"I *am* yours."

"Oh God," he whispered. With nimble fingers, he undid the laces of her gown, marveling at the smoothness of her naked shoulders. When Allegra's face expressed apprehension, he froze. "What is it, sweetheart?"

She pushed him away gently. "It's nothing, it's only that I…"

When she said nothing more, he frowned in confusion "One moment you want me, the next you reject me."

"I'm sorry."

Something about her expression made him wary. When she began to cry, realization lit up his features. "You're a virgin."

"Yes, of course."

*Yes, of course?* "Mother Mary in Heaven."

"What's wrong?"

"Cover yourself."

"What have I done?" Confused and humiliated, she lifted the

gown to cover her breasts. "I don't understand. Why are you angry? I thought you wanted me..."

"I want you more than anything in this world, my love, but I was under the impression that you...I thought you had more *experience*." He shook his head and mumbled incoherently as he headed for the door. "I should go."

Allegra didn't know whether to feel insulted or flattered. "You don't want me because I lack experience? Because I'm a virgin?"

"Yes, exactly."

"Why?"

He stared at her in disbelief. "Dear God, woman, I have no intention of deflowering you like some villain in a tawdry novel—in your father's house, no less! I do possess *some* moral character."

"Bruno, I want you to make love to me."

"If that is indeed true, then marry me."

She turned her face away. "I can't marry you."

"Your father has wed and will be spending half the year in Asti. You can no longer use him as an excuse."

"Believe me when I say that it's best if we do not wed."

Frustrated, Bruno threw up his hands. "I'm at a loss, Allegra! You're begging me to bed you, yet you refuse to be my wife. I find that offensive."

"You shouldn't feel offended."

"*No?* How should I feel, then?"

"Wanted and loved," she replied sincerely.

Bruno's eyes narrowed as he searched her face. This woman loved him, quite possibly as much as he loved her. "Say it again."

"I love you, Bruno."

"Then stop this stupid game and be my wife, bear my children." When she shook her head, he pounded the wall in frustration. "Tell me why!"

"I wish I could."

"Who's preventing you from doing so?" When she refused to answer, he said gently, "What are you afraid of?"

233

Shaking her head, she looked away. A long, tense silence followed.

Defeated, he opened the door. "I'm done with your games, Allegra," he said icily. "I've already suffered enough in life because of a woman."

"Bruno, please."

"I won't risk my heart only to have you break it."

He stormed out of the room and out of her life.

# CHAPTER 23

Allegra woke up the next morning with swollen eyes from shedding so many tears. Bruno's last words still hung in the air. Had she lost him forever? She washed and dressed, then broke her fast without appetite.

A servant came into the room. "Signora Paolina Gori is downstairs."

*This early in the day?* Allegra made her way to the main hall where the impeccably dressed widow stood waiting by the window. "Signora Paolina. You wish to speak with me?"

"My apologies if I have disturbed you, Signorina Allegra," Paolina said in a tone that implied otherwise. "I'd like to speak with you in private."

Allegra led her into the library. "What is this regarding?"

"I'm here to deliver a warning."

"A warning?" Allegra repeated, surprised.

"My servant followed Signore Bruno last night. It seems he came here."

"I don't see how that's any concern of yours."

"I know your father isn't in residence…"

Allegra's patience ran thin. "Why have you come here, Signora?"

"I know who you are."

"I beg your pardon?"

The widow smiled smugly. "La Castagna."

The blow was hard, direct, and completely unexpected, but Allegra managed to maintain a cool demeanor.

Paolina continued, "Don't bother denying it. The clever spies whom I employ have been watching you and Domenico Spinelli for months," she replied. "I know you made the medallion that I commissioned for Bruno."

Hearing this, Allegra's face blanched. "Have you told anyone?"

"Not *yet*."

"What do you want?"

"I'm in love with Bruno and you're in my way."

"He doesn't love you."

"He was in the process of doing so until you fell into his arms," she retorted, rolling her eyes. "I warn you, if you continue to play the coquette with him, I shall expose you to the magistrates."

"You have no proof."

Paolina's eyebrow shot up. "Oh no? There are laws in Florence that govern the guilds, and you're in violation of every single one of them. If I were to expose you, an investigation would follow. The ensuing scandal would ruin your reputation, and your father's as well." She stared at her young rival in triumphant satisfaction. "I'll leave you to your thoughts, Signorina Allegra. Good day to you."

Paolina exited the library, leaving Allegra alone and defeated.

Vittorio arrived later that day, accompanied by Gianna. After a thorough tongue-lashing from her father, Allegra offered him a sincere apology.

Vittorio wouldn't be placated so easily, however. "Do you realize the danger you put yourself in? Lavinia's entire household searched for you." Pinching the bridge of his nose, he added, "I was so embarrassed."

"Papa, I'm truly sorry," she said, "Bruno delivered a harsh lecture when he came to check on me."

"Good," he snapped. "Someone should point out your foolishness." Taking a deep breath, he said gently, "I've been thinking, Allegra."

"Please, don't…"

"It's time for you to stop being a goldsmith and live your life."

"I *am* living my life."

"La Castagna is sucking you dry. It's time for you to leave him behind."

"No!" she countered. "*Please*, it's all I have, I beg you."

236

"You're coming back to Asti with me. Pack whatever books and items you wish to take."

"I'll be miserable there."

Vittorio's mouth formed a hard line as he walked to the window and stared outside. He thought of Stefania's last day on earth, and, most importantly, her last words. *Set her free.* He had made a vow.

"Papa?"

He glanced at his daughter's anxious face. Heaving a tired sigh, he turned away from the window. "I'll concede to your wishes, albeit reluctantly. Gianna will remain here in Florence, and I will have Domenico and Bruno keep an eye on you."

Allegra fought back tears at the mention of her beloved's name. She wanted to tell her father about Paolina's threat, but she'd already caused him enough trouble. "Thank you."

"I'm going to the bottega. I'll be back before supper."

No sooner had Vittorio left the Palazzo Castagno, than Gianna appeared in the doorway. "We were all worried, you know, including the countess."

"Forgive me, Gianna, I didn't mean to cause any grief."

"You should have told me."

"So you could alert my father?"

"I could never go along with such a dangerous and foolish plan."

"I'll write a letter to Signora Lavinia and ask her forgiveness."

"I know why you came back. The reason is as plain as the nose on your face. Wouldn't it be better to follow your father's wise counsel? Let La Castagna die quietly. Bruno Spinelli is a good man."

\*\*\*

Vittorio remained in Florence until the end of the week before returning to Asti. Several days later, a servant from the Bargello arrived at the Palazzo Castagno.

"What I have to say is for the ears of Signorina Allegra Castagno only," he said to Gianna, who hovered over Allegra's shoulder.

Miffed, she retreated into the next room.

The young man cleared his throat and said, "A man by the name of Mancini paid me to inform you that he's been imprisoned for witchcraft. His execution is scheduled to take place this Friday."

Allegra frowned in dismay. "Is there anything else?"

"No, my lady."

The messenger left and Gianna rushed back into the room. "There's nothing you can do, Signorina. It's a lost cause."

"Were you eavesdropping?"

"Of course," Gianna replied shamelessly. "Your father urged me to keep close watch on you."

"I can't ignore Messer Mancini's plea for help."

"You can't go to the Bargello, either."

"Why not?"

Gianna's face expressed incredulity. "It will seem suspicious. They can easily accuse you of being Mancini's accomplice. Besides, your father is not here to accompany you."

"I'll go alone."

"You'll do no such thing."

Allegra ascended the stairs to fetch her cloak. "I won't stand idly by while an innocent man is sent to the gallows."

Gianna chased after her mistress. "He's a warlock."

Allegra paused on the stairs. "My mother would not have employed a warlock to create my astrological chart. Besides, Mancini has been working for the nobility for years."

"You're as stubborn as your mother," Gianna chided. "I'll go with you."

They walked to the imposing civic building, which also served as the city's jail, and were shown inside by one of the guards.

"Wait here," the man said.

"Coming here was a mistake," Gianna whispered.

Allegra ignored her as she waited for one of the officials. When someone arrived, she said, "My name is Allegra Castagno. I've come on behalf of the astrologer, Messer

Mancini."

The man's eyes hardened as he looked the lovely young woman up and down. "Signorina Allegra, regretfully, there's nothing I can do."

"Then I would speak to someone who can, sir."

"My superior is indisposed at the moment."

"I'm happy to wait," Allegra said, sitting on a nearby chair.

The man did little to hide his irritation. "What is this prisoner to you, if I may ask?"

"Messer Mancini is an acquaintance."

"You do realize he's being held for the crime of witchcraft."

"He's innocent of the charge of which he has been accused."

"How can you assure me of that?"

"The *many* noble families of Florence wouldn't dare employ the services of someone with a dubious reputation. I, too, have an astrological chart designed by Messer Mancini."

Understanding the meaning behind her words, the man smiled tightly. "Perhaps Mancini wasn't dabbling in the dark arts when he worked for those respected members of our society, your family included, of course."

His mocking tone annoyed Allegra. "I demand to know what proof you have of this man's guilt."

"And who are you to demand anything?"

"Someone who has witnessed firsthand Messer Mancini's kindness and fine moral character. He came to my aid years ago when I was being wrongfully harassed in public."

"Why were you being harassed in public?"

Seeing the wicked gleam in the man's eye and knowing Allegra's quick temper, Gianna took hold of her mistress's hand. "Come Signorina. We should return home."

Ignoring Gianna's wise advice, she said to the man, "That's neither your concern nor the point. Again I ask you, sir, what proof do you have?"

"Forgive my mistress's impertinence, sir," Gianna interjected. "She's young and prone to hotheadedness."

Appalled, Allegra said, "Gianna!"

"If you'll excuse me, I have work to do," he said before

mumbling something about hysterical women.

"I beg your pardon, sir?"

"Go home you daft girl."

"How dare you?!" Allegra spat. "You ignorant, small minded—"

"Guards!"

Gianna tried to urge Allegra toward the door but her mistress was too busy hurling insults at the man.

Two officers took hold of Allegra. "Get your hands off me!"

They dragged her away kicking and screaming, and locked her in a cell located on the ground floor. Reserved for the nobility, the tiny chamber contained a window, a desk, a chair and a small cot. The cells below, which were used for commoners, were entirely different.

"Please, sir, you cannot keep my mistress here," Gianna pleaded.

"My superior will decide what to do with that shrew," he retorted. "Go home now, unless you want to join her."

Gianna walked outside in a troubled daze. What a predicament! She thought of her next move, then made her way hastily to the Mercato Nuovo. She found Bruno in the back room of the bottega.

"Signore Bruno, I need your help."

"Gianna! Where's Allegra?"

She told him what had happened.

Uttering a curse, he hastened to the Bargello with Gianna at his heels. Once inside, he demanded to see the person responsible for Allegra's imprisonment. The man deliberately took his time coming down, which only made Bruno's blood boil.

Looking at Gianna, the man said, "I told you to go home."

"She fetched me, instead," Bruno said. "I believe my ward, Allegra Castagno, was here earlier. It seems that her lack of comportment earned her a visit to one of your cells. I'm here to collect her and take her home."

The man smiled without humor. "Your ward?"

"Her father, Vittorio Castagno, is currently in Asti and

requested that my father and I keep watch over her in his absence. I am Bruno, son of Domenico Spinelli."

"I see. Well, Signore, your *ward* came here on behalf of a man accused of witchcraft and heresy."

"What of it?"

"We must prove she's not a witch, too."

"Mancini was apprehended on a similar charge a while ago and a nobleman's wife spoke on his behalf. Did she have to undergo the same treatment?" Sensing the man's outrage, he added in a gentler tone, "I can assure you that Signorina Allegra is no witch. Besides, everyone knows that Mancini is a harmless astrologer. This whole thing is nothing more than a terrible misunderstanding."

"If what you say is true, then your ward will be set free when my superior returns in two days."

*Two days?* Bruno frowned. "I have no intention of walking out of this building without Allegra Castagno."

"You have no other choice," the man said icily. "Good day, Signore."

"Very well," Bruno conceded. "Perhaps you will be so kind to have one of your officers accompany Signorina Allegra's maid to the Palazzo Pitti."

"The Palazzo Pitti?"

"Why, yes, of course. Signorina Allegra's godfather must be apprised of this matter immediately," Bruno said coolly. "Gianna, tell His Grace—"

The man's face paled. "His Grace?"

"What's your name?" Bruno asked. "I'm sure Cosimo de' Medici will want to know the identity of the man who imprisons innocent women."

"Signore Bruno, shall I also mention Messer Mancini's imprisonment?" Gianna inquired, playing along with the farce.

Bruno nodded. "Yes, especially since his own daughter, Isabella, recently employed the astrologer's services for the Orsini heir."

"Perhaps I've been too hasty," the man said, motioning to the officers in the background. "Free the woman."

"And Mancini?" Bruno demanded.

The man nodded reluctantly. A moment later, the bailiff emerged with Allegra, who blushed when she caught sight of Bruno. No one spoke a word as they waited for Mancini. The astrologer's eyes bespoke sincere gratitude as he crossed the courtyard toward them.

"I owe you my life, Signorina Allegra," Mancini said the moment they were outside. "Thank you."

"It's Signore Bruno whom you should thank," Gianna pointed out.

"Yes, thank you, Bruno," Allegra said.

Messer Mancini bowed. "I am in your debt, Signore."

"I'm glad I could be of service," Bruno said with a lingering look in Allegra's direction. "Now, if you'll excuse me, I must return to my bottega."

Allegra watched him walk away before inviting the astrologer to the Palazzo Castagno for the midday meal. Famished, Messer Mancini readily agreed.

"Florence is no longer safe for you," Allegra said as they sat at the dining table eating stewed capon. "Is there somewhere else you can go?"

"No, but I'll find a solution." The astrologer paused, then said, "He loves you—Signore Bruno, I mean."

Allegra set down her knife, stunned.

He continued, "And you love him, but you won't risk courtship lest he discover your secret."

Her eyes grew wide. "How do you…?"

The astrologer gave her a measured look. "Have you forgotten my profession? I knew you were meant for greatness the moment you were born. I've known for quite some time that you're La Castagna."

"La Castagna means everything to me."

"It certainly must if you allow a man like Bruno Spinelli to slip through your fingers." At her incredulous look, he added, "I know all about him, too. He's a good soul who's suffered tremendously in life."

"Messer Mancini, may I ask you an indiscreet question?"

"The answer to your question is yes," he replied, his dark eyes glittering in a way that made the hairs on the back of her neck stand on end. She was about to ask him if he practiced witchcraft.

"The accusation brought against you is true, then?"

"It is," he replied. "Are you frightened?"

"Yes," she admitted. "But I know you have no intention to harm me."

"None whatsoever."

"I'll never reveal your secret, I promise."

"Nor I yours."

"You must leave Florence, Messer Mancini," she reiterated. "It's only a matter of time before they arrest you again."

"And you must allow Bruno into your heart, Signorina Allegra."

## CHAPTER 24

"You haven't replied to any of my messages, so I felt compelled to check on you," Bianca explained. "You look pale and thin."

"Your concern is appreciated," Allegra said.

The two women sat in the shade of a potted lemon tree in the Palazzo Castagno's courtyard.

"How is your gentleman friend, Bruno Spinelli?"

"I haven't seen him in weeks."

"Why not?"

Allegra shook her head sadly, prompting Bianca to take hold of her hand. "It pains me to see you like this. What happened? Has he lost interest?"

"I don't know," Allegra replied, her eyes glistening with tears. "He won't see me or reply to my messages."

Bianca stared at her askance. "I'm confused. I thought he loved you and wanted to marry you."

"I think he still does. It's a long story…"

"Yes, well, isn't that always the case with love? Long, convoluted stories abound in poetry and literature, each one dedicated to that deliciously complicated emotion."

Allegra finally gave in to tears.

Shocked by the sudden outburst, Bianca embraced her friend. "Let's go inside, shall we?" she whispered. "The servants shouldn't see you like this."

They climbed the courtyard steps and entered the palazzo. Bianca ushered Allegra into a small sitting room and shut the door. "Tell me what's wrong, my dear. I've never seen you so distraught and it worries me so."

"I can never have Bruno."

"Why not? What prevents you from acting on your heart's desire?"

"A secret."

Bianca hesitated. "Are you deformed *down there*?"

"What? No!"

"A hermaphrodite, then?"

"It's nothing like that, I assure you."

"Then what in the world are you hiding from this man?"

Allegra paced the room, casting wary glances at Bianca every so often. "Can I trust you?"

"Implicitly."

"Do you swear never to reveal my secret?"

"Allegra, you're frightening me. What are you hiding?"

Allegra quietly took her friend by the hand. "Follow me."

"Where are we going?"

"You'll see."

They walked into the workshop. Bianca wandered around the room, puzzled. "Why did you bring me to your father's workshop?"

Allegra pulled the golden chestnut from inside her bodice. "Look."

"Such a pretty little charm."

"It's much more than a mere charm, Bianca. It's my signature. And this isn't my father's workshop. It hasn't been for a long time."

Bianca's brow creased in confusion, then she noticed the tiny chestnut stamp on the workbench. Picking it up to examine it closely, she said, "This is La Castagna's workshop?"

"Yes…it's also my workshop."

Bianca stared at Allegra in disbelief then shook her head. "Are you telling me that you...?"

Allegra sat down and started curling thin strips of gold.

"My diamond necklace, the one Francesco gave me for Christmas?"

"I created that one and many others."

Delighted, Bianca squealed. "All this time *you* were Domenico's mysterious protégé?"

"Yes."

"The sketches my stepmother and I leafed through in Venice when we first met—that was *your* work?" When Allegra nodded, she exclaimed, "You're a genius!"

"My story is long if you're inclined to hear it, but we should retire to my study where it's comfortable. I'll have a servant bring refreshments."

Bianca eagerly nodded and followed her friend upstairs. They settled comfortably and Allegra finally unburdened herself of the secret she had been carrying for years.

"Why not share this information with Bruno?" Bianca suggested. "Surely, he'll understand. You possess exceptional talent, and I doubt he'll blame your parents for indulging you. As you said, had you been born male, there would be no issue."

"But I'm not male, and Bruno loathes La Castagna for stealing Spinelli profits. He has no tolerance for dishonesty, either."

"I can understand why after what he went through with his wife," Bianca murmured. "He would understand your particular situation, no?"

"Perhaps, but there's another, more serious reason why I must abstain from the man I love, and her name is Paolina Gori."

"The rich widow? How does that vixen enter into this story?"

Allegra informed her of Paolina's threat.

"Bruno must know the truth about La Castagna," Bianca stated firmly. "Regardless of what that stupid woman said to you."

"What of Paolina? If she exposes me to the magistrates, it will ruin my father's reputation. There will be legal repercussions. I can't take the risk."

"Do you trust me, Allegra?"

Allegra nodded. "I would not have confided in you otherwise."

Bianca gripped her friend's hand. "Then leave everything to me."

***

A dull ache crept up the nape of Bruno's neck and settled at the base of his skull. His father's health was deteriorating at an

246

alarming rate, Vittorio wasn't expected to return to Florence until September, and he had not seen Allegra since the incident at the Palazzo del Bargello.

*Allegra...*

After the *misunderstanding* in her bedchamber, he had vowed to keep his distance, yet the moment she needed his help, his resolve had melted away. He would do anything for her, truth be told. The tantalizing image of her smooth flesh and the taste of her sweet lips tormented him daily.

A knock on the door ended his fantasy. "Enter."

"There's a lady here to see you," the apprentice said before ducking into the back room.

Bruno stepped out of his office and froze. Flanked by two servants, Bianca Cappello stood in the center of the bottega in a sumptuous gown of red and white velvet with slashed sleeves. Diamonds sparkled at her throat and rubies dangled from her pink earlobes.

"Signora Bianca," he said, surprised. "How may I be of service?"

Her red painted mouth puckered slightly at the sight of him. "I'm in need of pearls, Signore Bruno, and since I'm a friend of Allegra Castagno, I thought to purchase them from this bottega. I believe Signore Vittorio is still the best gem and gold merchant in Tuscany."

"Indeed he is, and it will be my pleasure to assist you in selecting the most perfect pearls. Right this way."

Bianca motioned for the servants to remain behind as she alone followed Bruno across the expanse of the shop.

"How many pearls do you require?" he asked while removing a tray full of gleaming white orbs. "Enough for a necklace? A bracelet?"

Bianca leaned across the counter and met his eyes. "Signore Bruno, you must forgive my boldness, but I'm here on a noble cause."

"By all means, state your business, madam."

"Not here," she said, her eyes shifting to the alcove that led to the office.

He nodded and she followed him into the small room. She sat down and he took a seat behind the desk. "How may I help you, Signora?"

"It's my hope to help *you*, sir," she replied with a slight smile. "Allegra Castagno is one of my dearest friends, and she cares for you a great deal."

Bruno frowned slightly. "I appreciate your concern, but I'm not prepared to discuss this topic with you."

Bianca's hand darted like a snake across the desk. Taking firm hold of his wrist, she said, "I *repeat*, she cares a great deal for you, and I believe the feeling is mutual."

"Regardless of my feelings, Signorina Allegra has no serious intention toward me," he muttered while reclaiming his hand.

"She loves you, Bruno."

"I believed that, too, once." He stood, walked to the door and added, "Not anymore. To Allegra, I'm just another admirer to be spurned."

She stood. "Oh, how wrong you are."

Ignoring her comment, he said coolly, "I'm happy to help you select a pearl, Signora Bianca, otherwise…"

"Remember, Signore Bruno, things are not always as they seem. There is so much you don't know."

Before he had a chance to respond, she pointed to the largest pearl in the case, then reached for the money pouch at her waist. He conducted the transaction in silence, then watched as Bianca exited the shop.

The Venetian's words haunted him throughout the remainder of the afternoon. When he could no longer tolerate the confines of the bottega, he went outside to wander the streets. His initial intention was to get some air and clear his head, but his feet led him straight to the Palazzo Castagno. Staring at the gate, he debated whether or not to knock.

A moment later, he said to a servant, "It's imperative that I speak with Signorina Allegra." The girl hesitated, her eyes going to the candlelit window of Vittorio's workshop. Someone was inside. Seeing this, he added, "Is your master back from

Asti?"

"No, sir. As for my mistress, she said she's not to be disturbed."

Bruno's mind raced. "Would you be kind enough to fetch me something to drink before I go? I'm parched."

The girl nodded, albeit reluctantly, and led him through the courtyard into the main hall. "Please wait here, Signore Bruno."

The moment she left the room, Bruno ascended the stairs and headed to Vittorio's workshop. Quietly, he pushed the door open. Allegra leaned over the workbench studying a gemstone with a lens. Unaware of being watched, she moved the stone closer to a candle flame as she searched for defects.

"What are you doing in your father's workshop?"

Allegra gasped, dropping the gemstone. "I was only doing a few repairs for my father's clients," she lied. "What are you doing here?"

"Vittorio taught you how to use his tools?"

She blew out the candle and went to him, intercepting his progress toward the workbench. "You know he's a practical man."

"Bianca Cappello came by the bottega today."

The servant appeared in the doorway, flustered. "Signorina Allegra, I told him you were not to be disturbed."

Allegra lifted a hand to silence the girl. "Everything is fine. Leave us."

After the girl had gone, Bruno continued, "She told me things are not as they seem where you're concerned. What did she mean by that?"

She wrung her hands. "I don't know."

"I believe you do."

"Are you insinuating that I'm a liar?"

"No, but I do think you're hiding something."

"I don't have time for these games."

He gripped her shoulders. "You attempted to seduce me recently, and now you accuse me of wasting your time?"

Lowering her gaze, she whispered, "I made a mistake."

"Look me in the eye and tell me you bear no love for me."

"Why did you come here?"

"Say the words and I'll trouble you no more. Look at me!"

Reluctantly, she met his gaze. "Bruno…"

Pulling her into his arms, he urged, "Sweetheart, tell me this terrible secret that keeps you from being by my side where you belong." He kissed her face, her lips. "Tell me, please."

Allegra pushed him away before he melted her resolve. "I don't want to hurt you or anyone else."

"What have you done that's so horrible? Have you killed someone?"

"No!"

"Are you a spy from another kingdom? A thief?"

This made her chuckle. "I'm neither."

He also cracked a smile. "You have a good reputation in this city, your father indulges you, the Medici favor you, and I love you like I've never loved any other woman—*what is your dark secret*?"

Allegra studied him for a long time. Finally, she said, "Ask your father."

"My father?" he repeated, shocked. "What the hell does he have to do with this?"

"Everything."

\*\*\*

Domenico Spinelli lamented the fact that his life was coming to an end. Death had finally come knocking, and it was only a matter of time before he'd be forced to open the door. He'd begun feeling ill a few days ago and, this time, the old man knew his body wouldn't recuperate from the ordeal.

Bruno's face appeared in the doorway. When Domenico opened his mouth to greet his son, it evoked a coughing fit. Bruno quickly poured water into a cup and put it to his father's lips.

"Thank you, son."

"Are you feeling any better today?"

"A bit," the old man lied. "What ails you?"

"How do you know there's something wrong?"

"I know you better than anyone else, Bruno."

250

"I confronted Allegra today. I know she loves me, yet she refuses to follow her heart. It makes no sense, does it?"

"Women can be fickle at times."

"Allegra may be many things, but fickle is not one of them. I tried coaxing answers from her, but…" He hesitated. "She advised me seek them from you, instead."

Domenico lifted his gnarled hand to his forehead and shook his head.

*"Father?"*

The old man heaved a tired sigh. Protecting La Castagna's identity was causing more harm than good at this point. The two young people he loved most in this world were suffering because of a mere farce. Did he truly want to die and leave things in such a state of disarray?

"I haven't been honest," Domenico confessed. "At the time, hiding the truth from you seemed like the right thing to do. Now, I'm not so sure."

"What truth are you referring to?"

"I know who La Castagna is…I've known all along."

"How does he enter into the equation?"

*"She,"* the old man corrected.

Bruno's expression was one of total disbelief at first, then it gradually hardened into one of fury. "Allegra."

"She's been displaying her God-given talent from the moment she became my pupil many years ago. The girl was born to be a goldsmith."

"You took on a female apprentice?" Bruno asked incredulously.

"None of our male apprentices can match her skill or compete with her unique designs."

Bruno paced the room. "How does Vittorio play into this web of lies?"

"He arranged the apprenticeship for his daughter. I admit, I was skeptical when he proposed the idea, but once I saw what the girl was capable of, I agreed to tutor her privately. I harbor no regret for doing so."

"Is it my destiny—*my curse*—to fall in love with deceitful

women?"

"Before you make assumptions, let me assure you that Allegra never wanted to live a double life."

"Yet she does a fine job of it."

"Vittorio and I forced her to maintain this secret. The Church, the guilds, the magistrates—there was no way she could create and sell her own jewelry openly as a woman. La Castagna was born of necessity, not choice."

"There are reasons why we have laws banning women from guilds."

"Enlighten me, my son, because I can't think of a single one. In my opinion, Allegra is a true maestra who should be running her own bottega."

"I can't believe this," Bruno murmured half to himself.

"Allegra wanted to tell you the truth but I forbade her from doing so. I also convinced Vittorio to uphold my decision."

"Why would you do that? Why keep me in ignorance? I'm your son!"

"You returned to Florence and immediately expressed your loathing of La Castagna. I refrained from telling you because I didn't want to jeopardize our fragile relationship." Domenico licked his dry lips. "I was also afraid of how you'd react, what you may have said or done. Reputations were at stake, not to mention legal consequences.

Bruno pounded the wall. "I'm a fool."

"Don't think such a thing. Nothing has changed where Allegra's feelings for you are concerned."

"*Everything* has changed," Bruno said before storming out of the room.

Feeling dejected and betrayed by those whom he loved, he walked aimlessly through the streets in the early evening gloom. His thoughts were like the tumultuous roiling waves of an angry sea. La Castagna's coquettish style, the delicate, intricate designs. It made perfect sense that a woman— *Allegra*—was behind the creation of those outrageously stunning pieces. How could he have been so blind to the obvious?

He turned onto Via Roma, the setting sun causing a riot of colors in the twilight sky. Some of the market stalls were already empty, and torches were being lit in preparation for the oncoming night. As he crossed the piazza with distracted steps, pigeons and rats scurried out of his way.

Bruno now understood why Allegra rejected his advances, and those of other suitors for that matter. She could never hide the truth from a man with whom she was intimate.

"I can make you forget your troubles, sir."

The female voice caused him to turn his head. A whore beckoned to him from the shadows, offering temporary release from anguish. His eyes flickered to her sagging breasts and rouged cheeks.

"I'm one of the best," she added with a smile that lacked a few teeth.

"No, thank you," he replied, hastening his steps.

Bruno walked straight to the Palazzo Castagno to confront Allegra.

*Again.*

The initial resentment and anger that burned within him a while ago melted away as he recalled his father's words: *Allegra wanted to tell you the truth.* She had kept the secret from him out of love, not malice.

Bruno glanced up at the workshop window. Candlelight shone from the panes and he imagined Allegra arduously working on a piece of jewelry. *La Castagna jewelry.*

The anger surged through him again and he turned to go, then stopped. *What did it matter?* She loved him, she wanted him, and she was a good woman. What more could a man like him possibly ask for in life? Taking a deep breath, he knocked on the door.

"You've come back, Signore Bruno," said the servant who had opened the door for him earlier. "My mistress is still in the workshop."

Pushing past the girl, he ran upstairs. Allegra gasped as he burst into the workshop for the second time that day. Without further ado, he pulled her into his arms, kissing her hungrily.

At length, he whispered, "Tell me the secret you chose to share with Bianca Cappello but not with me, the man who loves you."

She placed her palms against his hard chest, relishing the feel of his muscles. "If I tell you, things will never be the same."

"If you won't tell me, then allow me to guess."

"Bruno, please…"

Putting his lips to her ear, he whispered, "You are La Castagna." When she stiffened, he tightened his grip. "My father told me everything, so don't attempt to deny it."

A heavy silence followed, then tears filled her eyes. "Are you angry?"

"I'm angrier with our fathers for forcing this heavy burden on you." When she leaned against him and sobbed with relief, he gently lifted her chin with his fingertip. "According to my father, you wanted to confess the truth to me."

"I did. My heart has been heavy with guilt and sadness for so long."

"You need not suffer anymore."

"Will you forgive me?"

He pressed his lips to her temple. "Only if you marry me."

"Will you allow me to continue making jewelry?"

"Yes."

Overjoyed, she threw her arms around his neck and covered his face with sweet kisses. "I love you, Bruno!"

The close, physical contact evoked a hunger within him that had not been roused in a long time. "Nothing prevents you from being mine."

Standing on her tiptoes, she kissed his lips. Bruno swept her up in his arms and headed straight for her bedchamber. After setting her upon the bed, he locked the door and began removing his clothing.

Allegra's emotions were a jumbled mess—desire, apprehension, confusion, surprise, fear, love—*above all, love*. Bruno's lean naked body inspired admiration and lust as he approached the bed. His fingers began to undo the laces of her bodice, revealing the golden chestnut hidden between her breasts. His eyes were glued to the charm.

"Funny how life is," he said. "I have loathed La Castagna up until now." Burying his face in the softness of her neck, his hands explored her nubile body. "I've hungered for you from the moment you fell into my arms like an angel from the sky."

"And I, you," she whispered. "Be patient with me, for I'm naïve when it comes to the carnal act of love."

A slow smile stretched across his handsome face. "We can take all the time you need, dearest."

Bruno's warm lips trailed kisses along her jaw and neck. When his mouth traveled from her throat to her breast, she gasped in pleasure. An aching need began to grow deep within her core. Running her hands slowly along his back, she arched against him with burning need.

Bruno shivered under her touch. "Naïve, you say?"

"I please you, then?"

Allegra's eyes grew wide when he slid his rock hard member against her inner thigh. "Does *that* answer your question?"

"Will it hurt?"

"I'll be gentle," he promised.

No woman—not even the whores he had lain with in the past—had ever talked to him in bed. Anabella never looked him in the eye during copulation, let alone speak tender words. Allegra's candidness during lovemaking not only surprised him, it stoked his passion. Carefully, he tempered each thrust with patience until her body instinctively responded to his own. They continued in unified rhythm until coming together in a powerful crescendo.

*"Mia Donna,"* he whispered as he held her possessively in his arms.

"Stay with me tonight."

Exhausted, he nodded with closed eyes. "As you wish, my love."

Before long, they were both fast asleep. Gianna, who had been looking for her mistress, peeked her head into Allegra's room. When she saw the naked couple fast asleep in the twisted sheets, she immediately closed the door and crossed herself.

Santo Cristo! Thank God and all the saints that Vittorio was far away in Asti. Smiling indulgently, she walked away with a light step. The Castagno household would soon be hosting a wedding celebration.

Domenico became teary-eyed when his son and Allegra arrived at the house hand in hand the following morning. Bruno was truly happy for the first time since his arrival in Florence, and Allegra seemed joyfully unburdened of her dark secret.

*** 

Vittorio and Lavinia arrived one month ahead of schedule in order to help with the wedding arrangements. In the days that followed, Bruno and Allegra could not get enough of each other. They made love furtively and frequently. Bruno even took his lovely betrothed on top of his desk on a sunny afternoon in early September while the oblivious apprentices worked in the bottega. He was forced to cover Allegra's mouth to keep her from crying out in pleasure.

"I swear you are half goddess, half human," he whispered, holding her tightly. "My desire for you grows daily."

"You have never experienced this?" She hesitated before adding, "Not even *before*?"

Bruno held her gaze as he shook his head. "You refer to Anabella. She and I had a different kind of relationship."

"I remember she was quite beautiful."

"Yes, but she was also vain, selfish, and arrogant." He paused, adjusting his clothing. "Anabella *tolerated* me. She never *wanted* me."

Allegra slid off the desk and smoothed the creases in her gown. "Why did she marry you?"

"Her family was poor...I believe she did it for convenience, not love."

An urgent knock on the door startled them.

"Enter," Bruno said.

One of Domenico's servants stood at the door wringing her hands. "Signore Bruno, your father..."

"Is he all right?"

The girl's eyes glistened. "He's dead."

Bruno's shoulders sagged with grief. "When?"

"Maestro Domenico had a coughing fit and the water pitcher was empty, so I went to fill it," she explained. "By the time I returned, he was no longer breathing."

"Dear God," Allegra whispered as she crossed herself. "Oh, Bruno..."

"May his soul rest in peace," he said softly.

# Chapter 25

Domenico's funeral was a respectable affair. Several people came from all over Tuscany to pay their last respects to the famed goldsmith. Most were peers and former apprentices. Allegra grieved alongside her betrothed. She would miss her maestro and longtime friend.

Bruno and Allegra got married after a respectable period of mourning. Their wedding ceremony took place in the Basilica di San Lorenzo, where the bride's mother and great-grandmother were buried. Brunelleschi's smooth white walls and elegant pietra serena columns provided the perfect backdrop for the joyous affair.

Allegra, dressed in a splendid gown of cream silk with gold embroidery, held her lover's hand as they exchanged heartfelt vows. The guests followed the couple to the Palazzo Castagno where Vittorio had spared no expense to celebrate his daughter's marriage. Roasted meats, spicy stews, rounds of aged cheese, delicate pastries, custards, dried fruits, and plenty of fine wine delighted the many guests. Minstrels entertained everyone throughout the evening and well into the wee hours of the night.

Isabella congratulated the couple, then took Allegra aside. "Matrimony suits you, after all," she said with a wink.

"Who would have imagined it?"

"Farewell to the Ice Queen," she teased. "Bruno is a good man. Felicitations to you both."

Troilo and Bernardo also offered their congratulations.

At one point during the merrymaking, Bianca approached the bride. Leading Allegra to a quiet corner, she said, "I'm so happy for you."

"Thank you, Bianca. You were right about so many things."

A devilish smile played upon the Venetian's lips. "Life is too short to deprive yourself of carnal pleasures."

Allegra laughed. "Yes, it is."

"On a more serious note, I had a little chat with Paola Gori a while back. I made it clear that if she causes you or Bruno any trouble, she'll have to answer directly to Francesco."

Allegra had been secretly worrying about the widow's threat for so long that she visibly sagged with relief. "I'm in your debt."

"Nonsense, my friend. I only repaid the kindness you've shown me many times throughout the years." She smiled. "Consider it a wedding gift."

Later, as the guests laughed and danced, Bruno swept his bride into a shadowy corridor to steal a passionate kiss. "I'm the happiest man in Florence today."

Allegra snaked her arms around his neck. "And I, the happiest woman."

"Thank you for marrying me."

"I've done more than that, my love."

"What do you mean?"

Allegra took hold of his hand and placed his palm against her belly.

He stared at her in confusion, then realization lit up his features. "Are you…?" When she nodded, he picked her up and spun her around. "My precious girl. Does anyone else know?"

"Only Gianna. I told her this morning."

Bruno's eyes filled with tears as he remembered his late son, Agostino.

*Another child.*

A second chance at life, at love, at fatherhood; he experienced a moment of perfect bliss.

\*\*\*

Vittorio and Lavinia were present when Allegra went into labor in April 1574. When the midwife appeared in the main hall to announce the birth of a healthy boy, Bruno crossed himself and uttered a prayer of thanks to God before entering the bedchamber. The sight of his lovely wife resting against the pillows with a healthy infant in her arms evoked pure joy.

*His son.*

259

Bruno approached the bed and kissed Allegra's forehead. The infant stared at him with wonderment and his heart swelled with love. "I wish to call him Domenico, if that's agreeable to you."

"I was thinking Domenico Vittorio."

Bruno grinned before taking the baby into his arms. Walking to the window, he allowed the milky sunlight to kiss his son's new skin.

"Our great city awaits you," he whispered. "I regret that my father isn't here today to meet you, but you'll bear his name."

Two days later, a messenger arrived with the tragic news that Cosimo de' Medici was dead. Allegra mourned the man who had been her godfather. She and Bruno attended the spectacular funeral to pay their last respects to the noble ruler who had done so many good things for the city of Florence and its proud citizens.

No sooner had Francesco de' Medici succeeded to the grand duchy, than he installed Bianca in the palazzo he'd purchased for her on Via Maggio. Located steps away from the Palazzo Pitti, the elegant residence screamed of decadence after having been remodeled by the talented Bernardo. Francesco had commissioned his friend to reconstruct and design the existing edifice, and Bernardo exceeded all expectations. The entire façade boasted ornate sgraffiti, and the coat of arms above the door depicted a hat—or *cappello*—in honor of its noble inhabitant. The Palazzo Bianca Cappello came to be seen as an architectural accomplishment of the highest degree.

With Bianca only a stone's throw away, Francesco began openly parading his mistress under the nose of his outraged wife.

When Cardinal Ferdinando's spy apprised him of the situation in Florence, he called Bianca Cappello an "adventuress" and an "interloper," then cursed her for good measure.

## CHAPTER 26

By the time Vittorio and Lavinia returned to Florence in the autumn of 1574, La Castagna was almost a distant memory. The roles of wife and mother took priority in Allegra's life, and she fulfilled her responsibilities with a grateful heart. Little Domenico, who came to be called "Nico" thrived under Gianna's solicitous care. The old servant doted on the boy as if he were her own grandson.

As for Bruno, he was kind, and affectionate toward her. Although he displayed jealousy on occasion and was prone to occasional brooding, he was a fine husband.

One day, Bruno came home from the bottega and announced, "There are rumors that La Castagna is dead."

"For once, the rumors are true," Allegra replied, her eyes glued to her son as he suckled hungrily on the breast of his wet nurse. "My life is now devoted to you and Nico."

"Sales have plummeted, and people are demanding La Castagna pieces."

Allegra searched his face before leading him away from the wet nurse. "Are you suggesting that I create jewelry again?"

"That's precisely what I'm suggesting, my love."

"What of Nico? I can't devote as much time to my craft as I once did."

"We have a house full of servants who can help you with the baby."

Allegra grinned. "I love you, Bruno Spinelli."

\*\*\*

In July 1576 news of Isabella de' Medici's sudden death spread through Florence. Shocked and deeply saddened, Allegra tried to piece together the fragmented stories relating to her friend's demise. Supposedly, while hosting a hunting party in the Medici villa at Cerreto Guidi, Paolo Orsini found Isabella on her knees. According to him, she'd been washing her hair and spontaneously died; the reason of death unknown.

Later, several servants stated that they had witnessed Paolo strangling his wife for committing adultery with his cousin, Troilo.

Were the rumors true? Did Paolo kill his wife? Like the mysterious death of Lucrezia several years beforehand, there wasn't enough evidence to incriminate the husband.

Allegra and Bruno were heartbroken at the sight of the Orsini children crying copiously at Isabella's funeral. Paolo, on the other hand, failed to shed a single tear. Oddly, Troilo, who had shadowed Isabella's every step when she was alive, wasn't present to pay his last respects.

Bianca's presence was also missed at the funeral. Word soon spread that Francesco's mistress was recuperating after having given birth to Antonio de' Medici, their bastard son.

Allegra set off to visit Bianca and the baby a few weeks later. The Palazzo Cappello was as spectacular on the inside as it was on the outside. Frescoed ceilings and intarsia marble floors graced the spacious rooms. A well-dressed servant led Allegra to Bianca's boudoir, where she sat with her newborn son. Dressed in a loose fitting gown of sumptuous gold patterned silk, she resembled an empress.

"Allegra, come and meet my son."

Allegra placed a small basket of flower-shaped marzipan on a nearby table before presenting her friend with a gold bracelet for the baby.

"Thank you," Bianca said, slipping the bracelet onto her son's wrist.

"Congratulations. Antonio is perfect little boy."

Bianca sighed contentedly. "I know. Oh, look what Francesco gave me yesterday," she said, holding out her hand to show off a new emerald ring.

"How lovely," Allegra commented. "Francesco must be overjoyed."

"*Of course*. I've done what his wife is incapable of doing."

It was true. Between 1566 and 1575, Joanna had given birth to a total of six daughters, but only three survived infancy. The

Medici dynasty required a male heir, and the Austrian princess had failed in her duty.

Bianca continued, "What use are all those daughters? I've finally given Francesco what he so desperately wanted and needed—*a son*."

Allegra refrained from reminding her that Antonio, despite bearing the Medici name, could not be in line for the grand duchy of Florence. "How are you feeling?" she inquired, tactfully changing the subject.

Bianca placed a hand on her forehead. "The birth was unpleasant, but I'm recovering rather well. God wanted me to have this child."

Allegra dutifully crossed herself and smiled. "Thank the Madonna. It warms my heart to see you looking so well and happy, my dear."

"Me, too!" Spreading her arms wide, she inquired, "Well? What do you think of my new home? I've recently decorated my boudoir."

Like her bedchamber in Venice, the elegant room was decorated in shades of pink, white, and burnished gold. Fat cherubs draped in roses graced the frescoed ceiling and large paintings of bucolic pastoral scenes adorned the walls.

"Splendid, like you," Allegra replied.

\*\*\*

Allegra soon developed a schedule, splitting her time between creating jewelry and caring for Nico. One afternoon, Allegra received an urgent message prompting another trip to the Palazzo Cappello.

"Thank God you came to see me," Bianca said, obviously distressed.

"I came as soon as I received your message. Is it Antonio?"

"My darling son is the picture of good health," she said, crossing herself. "Not here. Come, I don't wish the servants to overhear our conversation."

They entered Bianca's private sitting room and Allegra waited until she closed the door to inquire, "Is Francesco well?"

"Oh he's well, all right," Bianca snapped. "Joanna is

pregnant."

"You know it's their duty to produce an heir," Allegra said gently.

"Whose side are you on?"

"Yours, of course. I'm merely stating that you shouldn't be upset with him for fulfilling his obligation to the people of Florence."

Bianca placed her face in her hands and wept. "What if that cow gives birth to a boy this time? Francesco will cast me aside!"

"Don't even think such a thing. Have you forgotten how much he despises Joanna? It will take more than a son to make him leave you," she said, hoping this was indeed the case.

"Do you believe that?" Bianca asked, sniffing and wiping her tears.

"You've given Francesco the boy he wanted. He loves you for that."

"Yet he refuses to acknowledge our son. I've begged, but it's no use."

Allegra said gently, "If Francesco openly acknowledges Antonio as his heir, and Joanna gives birth to a boy, imagine how humiliating it would be for you when the claim is rescinded."

"I suppose you're right."

"In his heart, Francesco may wish to do one thing, but his position forces him to do another. Surely, you understand this."

"I know he loves me and Antonio."

"Of course he does."

Feeling somewhat appeased, Bianca changed the subject. "How are you? Nico is well? Bruno, too?"

"We're all healthy and doing fine."

Bianca peered at her friend for a long time. "Oh, that I could taste a bit of your happiness…"

\*\*\*

On May 20, 1577 Joanna of Austria bore Francesco de' Medici a son. A grand celebration at Palazzo Pitti ensued for the boy whom they christened Filippo, in honor of the boy's godfather, King Phillip of Spain.

Bruno and Allegra partook of the celebration at the Palazzo Pitti and, along with hundreds of other guests, offered their congratulations to the ruling couple. Naturally, Bianca wasn't present for the festivities. She appeared at the Palazzo Castagno a week later wearing a black gown with a black veil to hide her tear-stained face and bloodshot eyes.

Allegra led her distraught guest into the library. "You look as though you're in mourning."

"That's because *I am*," Bianca replied dramatically as she took a seat by the hearth. "My life is ruined."

"You mustn't let Francesco see you like this," Allegra warned. "He's ecstatic over the birth of his son, and this comportment on your part would be offensive to him."

Bianca recoiled. "You're the last person I ever expected to reprove me."

"I'm not reproving you, dearest, I'm speaking as a true friend." Allegra reached for her hand. "Babies are innocent beings, free of sin. Don't worry. Francesco will love Antonio as much as he loves Filippo."

Bianca nodded, no doubt recalling the love she felt for her late daughter, Pellegrina. Nico came running into the room to show his mother the bright green grasshopper he caught in the courtyard. Bianca couldn't help but smile at the chubby three year old and open her arms to him. At first, Nico retreated to his mother's side but, at Allegra's urging, he shyly approached the elaborately dressed woman.

The moment the boy got close enough, Bianca snatched him up and sat him on her lap. "Let's see what I have here," she said, reaching into the drawstring purse at her waist. "I think there may be a bit of candied orange rind in this little tin."

Bianca opened the tin and offered it to the boy. Nico wasted no time in stuffing the sweet treat into his mouth.

A young woman appeared in the doorway. "Time for your nap, Nico."

Nico wriggled off Bianca's lap and ran to his nurse.

"I envy you, Allegra," Bianca said wistfully.

# CHAPTER 27

On April 10, 1578 the grand duchess woke up in a foul mood. "Bring me my chamber pot!" Joanna bellowed from her richly canopied bed.

Two maids scurried into the room. "Good morning, Your Grace."

Heavily pregnant with her eighth child, Joanna feared her full bladder would burst if she didn't relieve herself immediately. "Make haste!"

The young women helped their cumbersome mistress squat over the chamber pot. When she finished urinating, one of the maids went off to empty the pot while the other assisted with the morning's ablutions. Standing naked in the middle of her bedchamber, Joanna placed both hands across the pale expanse of her stretched skin. Hopefully, it would be another boy to act as a guarantee against her sickly son, Filippo.

Two males would secure the Medici dynasty.

A servant came in with a breakfast tray and Joanna cast a cool, disapproving eye at the aged cheese and fennel sausage served alongside boiled fruits and fresh bread. She picked at the fruit and ate a morsel of bread before waving away the tray.

*Damn these Florentines and their unpalatable food.*

"It's warm today, my lady," said one of the maids. She held up a cool linen maternity gown created by one of the court seamstresses.

Joanna waved the garment away in favor of a black velvet Austrian gown she had taken out to accommodate her large belly. The maids eyed each other quietly before helping their mistress dress for the day.

"I want to wear my pearls," Joanna said as she doused a silk handkerchief with rose water before applying it to her face.

She studied her reflection in the mirror. Strands of fine blonde hair stuck to her damp forehead, so she brushed them back with her hand. At age thirty-one, her alabaster skin was still smooth and firm. She hated the thought of growing old here in Florence with a husband who disliked her as much as she disliked him, but what choice did she have as a woman?

When her toilette was complete, Joanna went into the chapel to take communion, then sat in the loggia to enjoy the morning sunshine. She opened a prayer book and focused on the small printed page.

Francesco, who happened to be passing by, stopped at the sight of his wife. Her white skin and light gold hair literally glowed in the sunlight. Sometimes, she was almost pretty. It was a shame they didn't get along well. It would have made the perfunctory couplings a bit more palatable. Sensing his presence, she stiffened.

"Buongiorno, Joanna."

Without looking up from her book, she replied tartly, "A bit early in the day to visit your whore, is it not?"

Francesco's face reddened with anger. "What I do, where I go, and whom I see is no concern of yours, *wife*."

This drew a sharp look from Joanna. "You disgust me," she muttered the moment he walked away.

"The feeling is mutual, my lady," Francesco shot back over his shoulder.

Irritated by the distasteful encounter, she decided to take a calming stroll in the Boboli Gardens. The baby inside of her kicked as she crossed the breezy loggia and headed toward the stairwell. Descending the stairs, she caught a whiff of perfume and heard the rustle of silk.

*"Die, you bitch."*

"Who—"

Joanna didn't finish the sentence. She tried desperately to grab onto anything to stop her fall. Two scullery maids were on their knees, scrubbing the floor in the other room. Hearing Joanna's scream, they came running to her aid. One of them alerted her lady's maid, who in turn alerted Francesco, who was in the courtyard speaking with a groom. While everyone ran toward the stairwell, a cloaked figure crept along the shadows of the palazzo before darting into the Boboli Gardens.

Moaning with pain, Joanna was carried to her bed where she eventually bore a premature infant. Cannons fired for the birth of the second Medici son, but the child died shortly afterward. The following day, Joanna also perished. While the bells of the cathedral tolled for the death of the grand duchess, Bianca sat at home alone shedding tears of relief.

Cardinal Ferdinando was instantly suspicious when he learned of his sister-in-law's demise. "How exactly did she die?" he demanded of his spy.

"The servants said Her Grace fell down the stairs," Michele replied.

Ferdinando rubbed his chin. The spy clasped his hands behind his back and looked down at his feet. He knew better than to offer any insight or opinion unless specifically asked to do so. Ferdinando motioned to a servant to fill his goblet and offer one to Michele. The spy smiled gratefully as he accepted the fine wine, then watched as the cardinal paced back and forth before an open window. The majestic dome of St. Peter's filled its frame.

Ferdinando stopped. "What are the people saying in Florence?"

Michele shrugged in a calculated manner. "Everyone is shocked and saddened, but no one has made any accusations...."

The unspoken 'yet' made the cardinal frown. "What of the courtiers?"

"May I speak freely, my lord?" The cardinal nodded and he continued, "A few people have insinuated that Bianca Cappello and your brother conspired to kill Joanna."

Ferdinando winced. "I must scan the marriage market to find a suitable bride for Francesco before that vixen sinks her claws into him. Return to Florence at once and keep me apprised of their every move."

"Yes, Your Excellency."

"God help us if that fool marries Bianca..." After a long pause, he added, "I should have been firstborn."

***

Gianna passed away in her sleep shortly after Easter in the year 1579. The entire household was saddened by her death, and Vittorio insisted on providing a respectable funeral. Allegra became sick with grief by the loss of the beloved woman whom had cared for her since birth.

A month later, Bianca visited the Palazzo Castagno accompanied by armed guards and two ladies. Allegra embraced her friend.

"What a pleasant surprise, Bianca. You've brought quite an entourage with you."

"Actually, they must travel with me everywhere I go."

"Oh?"

"I've come to share good news with you, but it must remain a secret between us." She held out her hand and pointed to the gold wedding band gleaming on her plump, white finger.

"Does this mean that you and Francesco...?"

"We were married in secret a few days ago. Cardinal Ferdinando doesn't know. He's trying to arrange a marriage for his brother—can you imagine?" Bianca rolled her eyes. "Francesco couldn't bear another unhappy union like the last one, so he married a woman of his own choosing—*me*!"

Flabbergasted, Allegra inquired, "When is the announcement?"

"When it's the right time," she replied. "For now, we're simply reveling in our own little secret."

"Congratulations," Allegra offered, pulling Bianca close for another embrace. "Long life and good health to you both."

"I'll invite you and your family to the wedding celebration when our marriage becomes public."

"You can expect our attendance," Allegra promised.

On June 10, 1579 Francesco de' Medici announced his marriage to Bianca Cappello, and publicly acknowledged their son, Antonio. Two days later, Bianca was crowned Grand Duchess of Tuscany at the Palazzo Vecchio. Arrayed in a gold brocade with several strands of pearls round her neck, she received her new title with head held high.

A great celebration ensued. Long tables laden with delicacies beckoned hungry guests while wine stewards ran around filling silver chalices. The presence of official dignitaries alluded to Bianca's reinstated political status, but the low number of noble guests present at the festivities suggested that she was still very much despised by the Florentines.

"This is the happiest day of my life," Bianca confessed to Allegra at one point during the magnificent event.

"You deserve it," Allegra assured her. "Oh wait, I must now refer to you as *Your Grace.*"

"Only in public."

Both women chuckled, but they stopped the moment some courtiers approached to congratulate Bianca.

Allegra moved to stand beside her husband.

"I'm impressed," Bruno admitted quietly, his eyes focused on Bianca.

"Grand Duchess of Tuscany is no small feat."

"Especially for a woman who caused a scandal by rejecting the Doge of Venice in favor of a penniless boy."

"Not only that," Allegra whispered. "Running off with the boy, escaping arrest, becoming Francesco's mistress, and bearing his illegitimate son."

"While Ferdinando busily scoured the European kingdoms to find a noble bride for his brother, Francesco married his mistress in secret," Bruno commented. "There will certainly be repercussions for this rebellious act."

"I disagree," she countered. "All will be forgiven in time."

Bruno smiled. "My wife, the idealist." He looked around and added, "Perhaps you're right. The palace is crawling with Venetian dignitaries."

Having put aside their resentment, the political leaders of *La Serenissima* welcomed Bianca back into their fold. After all, her marriage to Francesco strengthened the link between Tuscany and Venice.

"I would say Bianca has done well for herself," Allegra said.

"Feeling envious?"

"No," she replied. "I wouldn't trade my life for hers."

Bruno gazed down at his wife, who looked splendid in a crimson silk dress. A gorgeous diamond and ruby pendant sparkled against her elegant throat. "What about your husband?" he asked while tracing the line of her clavicle with his fingertip. "Would you trade him for such a grand title?"

"I wouldn't trade my husband for the world."

***

Bianca settled into the role of grand duchess with great apprehension due to the precarious nature of her position. Whenever she and Francesco's heir, Filippo, were in the same room together, she carefully studied him. Despite being fed the best food that money could buy, the boy was puny for his age. The physicians poked and prodded him, prescribing every sort of tonic to encourage growth and stamina, but nothing worked.

It didn't go unnoticed by the courtiers that the Medici heir was a runt in comparison to the hearty Medici bastard. Bianca's smug pride at this fact was blatantly obvious, too. There was only one problem: even though Antonio was openly acknowledged by Francesco, he had been conceived out of wedlock and therefore barred from inheriting the duchy. Furthermore, Bianca still had plenty of enemies, including her own brother-in-law who now openly despised her for ruining his plans of securing a noble marriage for Francesco. As a result, Cardinal Ferdinando was made to look like a fool in the eyes of European nobility.

The first few years of marriage were not easy for Bianca, but everything changed in the year 1582. After a particularly long bout of fever, the little Medici prince died. Filippo's death propelled Francesco to take swift action. He commanded his solicitors to draw up the necessary documents to legitimize Antonio and make him heir to the duchy of Tuscany. Luckily, King Phillip of Spain backed Francesco in this endeavor, thus speeding up the process.

Bianca could breathe a bit easier now that she was the Medici heir's mother. She had a legitimate claim to rule as regent should Francesco die before Antonio reached adulthood, and this garnered some respect from both courtiers and members of the Medici family.

***

In 1583, Giambologna's *Rape of the Sabines* was installed in the Loggia dei Lanzi, located in the Piazza della Signoria. The stunning white marble statue was a testament to the sculptor's talent and eye for form. It served as yet another public artwork designed to bring glory upon the city and instill a sense of civic pride.

Allegra continued to take great pleasure in creating jewelry. As the years passed, she did her best to keep up with the changing tastes in fashion. There was a new goldsmith in Florence making a name for himself with daring new styles, and La Castagna pieces gradually lost popularity with younger nobles.

Rather than feel resentful, Allegra took a step back and allowed the ambitious maestro to step into the limelight while she devoted time to her son's education. Shortly after Nico's fifth birthday, she discovered that she was pregnant.

When Allegra informed Bruno, he became ecstatic and took her into his arms. "My heart rejoices with this news," he said, touching her belly. "God's greatest gift."

Bruno kissed her lips and, before long, their passion drove them into the bedchamber where he made love to his wife with the utmost tenderness.

In May 1580 Allegra gave birth to a healthy baby girl whom she named Sabina in honor of her great-grandmother.

Bruno was under his daughter's enchanting spell the moment he held her in his arms. "Sabina," he said. "I like the name."

Knowing her mother's misfortunes with pregnancies, Allegra felt extremely blessed to have birthed two healthy children in a row without complications. Little Sabina grew into a precocious child who demanded attention. With two children to raise, Allegra stopped making jewelry and concentrated on being a mother. Occasionally, she would venture into her workshop and work on something for pleasure, then set it aside for her daughter to wear when she was older.

The years passed in this peaceful, pleasant manner. When Vittorio and Lavinia came to Florence, they devoted the majority of their time to Nico and Sabina. Allegra mourned the fact that her mother wasn't alive to enjoy her grandchildren; she would have doted on them, too.

The Grand Duchess of Tuscany loosened the lace collar around her neck as she dabbed the perspiration from her brow with a silk handkerchief. The intense heat of the summer lasted well into late September, compelling the rulers of Florence to remain in their country villa of Poggio a Caiano.

After the delicious midday meal, her husband and son had decided to nap while she sat on the terrace beneath the shade of a potted persimmon tree. Scanning the sun-scorched landscape, she reached for her fan to cool her flushed face. The lovely villa and the land surrounding it was hers. Olive trees and vineyards stretched out as far as her eyes could see, and this was only one of the many Medici properties.

It was during these rare moments of solitude that Bianca congratulated herself on her achievements. At fifteen years of age she was married to a pauper. Now, she was the wife of the most powerful man in Tuscany. Her life wasn't perfect by any means, but it was good. *Very good.*

The heat made her drowsy and her eyes slowly closed.

Francesco wandered onto the terrace with a letter in his hand.

Bianca, who had fallen asleep in the chair, stirred. "How was your nap, my love?"

Ignoring her question, he announced, "Ferdinando is on his way here."

She sat up and pursed her lips in disapproval.

Seeing this, Francesco held up the piece of vellum in his hand. "His words are friendly, even affectionate. Perhaps Ferdinando has finally come to the realization that he was wrong about you—about us."

"Perhaps," she conceded in a tone that suggested otherwise.

Bianca suffered a great humiliation last year after undergoing a false pregnancy. In an attempt to spite his sister-in-law, Ferdinando circulated a vicious rumor that Antonio wasn't her son, but rather the son of a serving girl who'd been smuggled into Francesco's bed. The insult still stung.

Francesco planted a swift kiss on his wife's forehead. "Don't be cross, my love. He's my brother, after all. This visit could lead to reconciliation."

Bianca caught a whiff of female scent on her husband's clothing. The dainty young kitchen maid she acquired recently would be tossed out first thing tomorrow morning. Only unattractive women would be hired from now on.

"Darling," she cooed. "Let's sup under the stars this evening like we used to do when we were younger."

"I have a pile of legal documents to sift through, and each one requires my signature. Another time, perhaps."

Bianca smiled, but her eyes were hard. She would send the wench packing *tonight*. "You're always so busy. I worry about your health, Francesco. You must make time to rest."

He smiled hesitantly. "Yes, you're right."

\*\*\*

On the last day of September, Allegra received a tragic message from Asti. Lavinia and Vittorio had been hunting when he suddenly fell off his horse. The letter assured her that her father's death had been immediate.

"He did not suffer, my love," Bruno said gently in an attempt to soothe his inconsolable wife.

"My dear, sweet father…"

"Hush, now. I'll take care of you. I'll take care of everything."

True to his promise, Bruno arranged for Vittorio's body to be transported to Florence. He provided his father-in-law with a fine funeral, and did everything possible to comfort his grieving wife. He even sent a message to the grand duchess, who interrupted her sojourn in the countryside to comfort her friend in Florence.

Bruno and Allegra received Bianca like a queen, and they

enjoyed a wonderful dinner together. Afterward, Bruno retreated to his personal study to allow the women a chance to visit privately.

"I'm so glad you came to see me," Allegra said as the two women sat sipping sweet wine in the Palazzo Castagno's library. "Thank you."

Bianca reached out and took hold of Allegra's hand. "Your father was a good man. I'm sorry I missed his funeral, but I couldn't come any sooner."

"You're here now, which is all that matters. How long can you stay?"

"I must leave in the morning." Bianca paused, her expression anxious. "Ferdinando is coming to Tuscany."

"You seem worried, my friend."

"I am."

***

Bianca and Francesco welcomed Cardinal Ferdinando's arrival in Tuscany with a sumptuous feast. Roasted wild boar and pheasants, along with pies in fanciful shapes, graced the dining table. The October sun shone brightly, but there was an autumnal nip in the air. Ferdinando regaled his hosts with tales of Roman nobility and Vatican intrigues.

In the days that followed, Bianca noticed the Medici brothers frequently engaged in conversation. They even went hunting together on a few occasions, laughing like boys as they forced their horses into a gallop. Perhaps her husband was right; the cardinal's visit was a step toward reconciliation.

One day, Francesco and Bianca felt ill. The symptoms were abrupt and harsh, and they both died eleven days later, a few hours apart. It was later reported that the grand duke and grand duchess had suffered tremendously, their pain agonizing.

Ferdinando's behavior during his brother's final days—and after his death—raised suspicion. The cardinal made it a point to minimize the gravity of their medical conditions in his messages to the Vatican, stating that Francesco's illness was due to unwise eating habits and that Bianca, who worried so much over her husband's condition, became physically ill herself. He was fully aware of how the situation appeared once their deaths were confirmed, so he promptly ordered medical examinations of the bodies to divert any speculation of his involvement in their demise.

The cardinal promptly transported his brother's corpse to the Basilica di San Lorenzo in Florence, where a dignified funeral befitting the grand duke took place. Ferdinando expressed his contempt for Bianca by arranging for her body to be unceremoniously buried in Santa Maria a Buonistallo, a church near Poggio a Caiano. Four terracotta jars containing the viscera extracted from the autopsied bodies of Francesco and Bianca were buried in the crypt of that church.

When news of the sudden deaths of Francesco and Bianca became public, rumors of Ferdinando poisoning his brother and sister-in-law circulated in Florence. With his brother out of the way, the cardinal immediately stepped into the role of Grand Duke of Tuscany. Any rumors of his culpability were quickly met with the explanation of malaria being the official cause of death. In an attempt to appear magnanimous, he allotted considerable land and wealth to his orphaned nephew, Antonio.

\*\*\*

The late November wind blew across the Tuscan countryside with impressive force. Several dark clouds clung near the horizon, signaling the possibility of an oncoming storm.

Allegra shivered as she alighted the carriage, her gaze resting on a pile of autumnal leaves swirling in a frenzied dance. In her hand was a single white rose. Bruno moved to follow his wife, but she stopped him by placing a gentle hand on his arm. "I would rather go inside alone, if you don't mind."

"As you wish, my love," Bruno conceded before settling back into the warmth of the carriage. "Take as much time as you need."

Crows called out to one another from nearby cypress trees as Allegra crept up the pebbled pathway leading into the old stone church. The damp and dimly lit interior was empty, and her footsteps echoed as she crossed the flagstone floor.

An elderly priest emerged from the sacristy and inclined his head in greeting. Allegra closed the space between them with brisk steps.

Placing coins in his hand, she said, "A small gift for your church."

"Thank you." Indicating a nearby wooden confessional, he added, "Do you wish to unburden yourself, Signora?"

"Actually, I'm here because…" Even now it was difficult to say the words. As her eyes prickled with tears, she quietly inquired, "Would you kindly tell me where Bianca Cappello is buried?"

The priest frowned in thought. "Ah, yes."

The old man shuffled toward the rear of the church and stopped before a grave marker that was far too humble to contain the remains of a woman who had possessed such flamboyant style and fiery passion—much less the Grand Duchess of Tuscany.

When the priest disappeared into the sacristy, Allegra knelt and placed the white rose on simple tomb. "I miss you, Bianca. Rest in peace, my best and dearest friend."

# EPILOGUE
## APRIL 1594

Ferdinando de' Medici left the Church and allied himself with France by marrying Christine de Lorraine in 1589. They settled into the Palazzo Pitti, transforming it into a fashionable residence according to his wife's French tastes.

In time, he proved himself to be a shrewd ruler. One of the ways he obtained more taxes from the Florentines was through a decree in 1593 prohibiting the *arti villi*, or vile arts, from being conducted on the Ponte Vecchio. This meant that butchers, fishmongers, sausage and cheese vendors would have to ply their trades elsewhere. The only business allowed to exist on the city's oldest bridge was the making and selling of gold and gemstones.

In 1594 Ferdinando's decree was put into effect. The clever goldsmiths were quick to use their privileged location on the Ponte Vecchio to their utmost advantage. Whenever the female members of the Medici family and their friends crossed the bridge via the Vasari Corridor, they seized the opportunity to show off their wares. The ladies peeked through the small windows to admire the sparkling trinkets being held up for their perusal. Some of the bolder goldsmiths would call out to a lady by name, claiming that their newest creation was made especially for her slender finger or delicate earlobes. More often than not, these flattering exchanges resulted in profitable sales.

On a fine April morning, Allegra and Bruno stood on the Ponte Vecchio before a quaint shop with mullioned windows and ornate door hinges. The sign above the door read: NICO SPINELLI: ORAFO.

"Happy birthday, Nico," Bruno said, holding out a key.

At age twenty, Nico was as handsome as his father and already a highly trained goldsmith. He accepted the key with a grateful nod. "Thank you, Father, Mother. I'll make you both

279

proud, I promise."

Sabina stood by her brother's side. She had inherited her mother's talent for drawing, inspiring Nico to create fine jewelry based on her wonderful designs. The Spinelli name was held in the highest esteem among the goldsmiths of Florence.

"Hopefully, I'll obtain as many commissions as the famed La Castagna," Nico commented while fumbling with the lock on the door. "I heard that people are paying great sums of money for the late goldsmith's pieces. Collectors are going around to royal courts and making ridiculous offers to any lady flaunting his jewelry."

Allegra and Bruno exchanged a meaningful look.

"What do you think, Father?" Nico pressed. "Do I possess that kind of creative potential?"

Allegra took it upon herself to reply. "Of course you do."

"To this day, his identity is still a mystery," Sabina said, looking at her parents. "All those years he worked in Florence and no one knew who he was? Neither of you had any suspicion?"

Allegra shook her head. "None whatsoever."

Bruno caught his wife's eye and shrugged. "Well, I did hear that he was stubborn, headstrong, secretive, and competitive."

Allegra slyly added, "Well, I heard he was a genius."

"Yes, he was most definitely a genius," Bruno agreed, staring into the depths of his wife's blue eyes.

"Let's go inside, shall we?" Nico said, pushing the door open.

The five of them walked into the small bottega and admired the view offered from the back window. The blue sky and lush green hills in the distance served as the perfect backdrop for the imposing San Niccolò tower. While everyone gaped at the scenery, Bruno took hold of his wife's hand and gave it a squeeze, his eyes reflecting nothing but love and admiration for the woman who had once been the greatest goldsmith in Florence.

# AUTHOR NOTE:

According to the *Episcopal Diocesan Archive of Pistoia, the Book of Marriages and Deaths, Year 1587*, kept by Monsignor Bernardo Baldovinetti:

**Original Text:** ["... addì XIX di Ottobre 1587: tra le 4 e le 5 hora di notte morì il Serenissimo Francesco Granduca di Toscana et addì 20 detto mese e anno morì la Serenissima Gran Duchessa Bianca sua moglie et le loro intestine furono (po)rtate a santa Maria a Buonistallo in quattro mezzine (lei?) morì in martedì mattina a'hora circa 15 fu intervallo tra l'uno e l'altra circa 12 hore (Di)o li dia requie."]

**Modern Translation:** "The day of October 19, 1587 between 4 and 5 am His Serene Highness Francesco Grand Duke of Tuscany died and, on day 20 of the same month and year, Her Serene Highness Grand Duchess Bianca, his wife, died. Their viscera were brought to Santa Maria a Buonistallo in four jars. She died on Tuesday at 3 pm, the interval between their deaths being about 12 hours. May God give them rest."

Did you enjoy this novel? The author would appreciate your review on Amazon. Thank you.

The intrigue of Renaissance Florence and the Medici family continues with the exciting prequel: SABINA. Turn the page for a sample.

# SABINA

## A Novel Set in the Italian Renaissance

# C. DE MELO

# Chapter 1
## Lucca, Tuscany
## August 1, 1477

*"Let all Italy know, and all Christendom too, of the power, the strength, and the glory that the Florentines have at present in Tuscany."*

– Historian Benedetto Dei describing
"Florentie bella" in the book:
*La cronica dall'anno 1400 all'anno 1500.*

It was the first day of August and mercilessly hot. Not a single drop of rain had fallen for nearly a month, causing the crops, livestock, and Tuscans to suffer. Sabina Rossi sat on a stone bench outside her father's villa quietly reading a book, its pages well-worn from frequent use. It was a special book, and she took great pains to keep it hidden from her father's prying eyes.

Placing her fingertip on the page, she looked up at the cloudless sky. The endless expanse above her head was lapis lazuli, the noble blue favored by artists when painting the Madonna's cloak. She gazed into the distance, visually tracing the uneven line of Monte Pisano, the mountain separating Lucca from its rival city, Pisa. According to legend, God had deliberately placed it there to prevent the *Lucchese* from looking at the *Pisani*.

The distant bells of San Michele broke her reverie, and she recalled to mind its colonnaded façade. At the church's pinnacle, flanked by two angels, stood a large statue of St. Michael spearing the great dragon. Each metal feather of his sculpted wings quivered in the wind, making it seem as if the archangel could take flight at any given moment.

The crow at Sabina's feet hopped around to capture her

attention. Throwing another crumb from the chunk of stale bread in her lap, she inquired sweetly, "Still hungry, Mendi?"

The savvy bird visited her about the same time every day in order to receive a free meal, so she eventually nicknamed it Mendi—a shortened version of *mendicante*, or beggar.

"Sono disgraziato!"

Startled by the sound of her father's voice, Sabina tossed the book into a nearby rosemary bush as Mendi flew away with an agitated cry.

Don Antonio strode into the courtyard. "Where are you?"

"Here, Papa," Sabina replied.

The old man stomped toward his daughter with a scowl on his face. "Why do you disgrace us? Have you no shame?"

"What's wrong?" she asked, her face as innocent as an angel's.

"You continue to swim naked after I strictly forbade you to do so! People will think you're a common slut!"

"No one was around, so I decided to take a quick swim."

"No one was around, eh? Donna Francesca saw you on her way home from the market. She was so shocked that she dropped her basket. What were you thinking?"

"It's so hot, Papa. Who wouldn't relish the feel of cool water on their skin on a day like this? I didn't mean to offend anyone."

"Sabina!" Cecilia exited the villa carrying a potted plant with her three year old son, Paolo, in tow. "Did you pluck the leaves from my basil plant?"

Sabina regarded her older sister with disdain. Since the death of her husband, Cecilia had ceased to care for her appearance and had gained weight. The twenty-three-year-old widow looked tired and matronly.

"Well? Did you?" Cecilia pressed, frowning at the bare stems.

Don Antonio peered at Sabina suspiciously. "You're not still concocting silly love potions for those stupid village girls, are you?"

Although she remained silent, he saw the familiar look of guilt on her face and proceeded to administer a sound beating.

Sabina cringed from the assault as Cecilia attempted to placate their father.

The old man eventually regained his composure and balled his hands into fists. "What am I going to do with you, Sabina?"

Paolo spotted the book in the rosemary bush and picked it up.

Cecilia moved toward her son. "What do you have there?"

Sabina immediately snatched the book from her nephew's hands and placed it behind her back. "It's only a silly book of poetry."

"Let me see it," Don Antonio demanded.

Sabina shook her head and his face darkened in anger. Knowing her father's temper, she relented.

He leafed through the pages. "A book of poetry, eh?"

"Papa—"

"Not only do you sit here reading books of witchcraft, but you lie to *me*—your own father!"

"It's not witchcraft, it's botany."

"Botany, my elbow! You should be reading the Bible or reciting prayers or anything that may save that soul of yours, which I'm certain is bound for Hell!" Turning to Cecilia, he added, "Why didn't you stop her from committing such mischief today?"

"I was gone for most of the afternoon," Cecilia explained. "Donna Filomena is sick, so I helped her look after the baby."

Don Antonio sighed tiredly, then narrowed his eyes at Sabina. "When you're not writing silly poems, you're reading silly books."

"You simply lack appreciation for literature, Papa."

"I *do* appreciate literature," the old man corrected. "What I don't appreciate is a rebellious daughter. Why can't you be like Cecilia? She goes to church willingly, while you have to be forced. She engages in Christian works, while you mix potions. Cecilia has never given me reason to worry, but you give me nothing but grief!" He paused, his face a mask of anger. "As God is my witness, I will see you married before the month's end. I've already begun discussing the arrangements."

"Arrangements?"

"I'm planning your future," he said, calmly adjusting his sleeve.

Sabina smiled, unfazed. "Very well."

"You're going to marry Signore Tommaso Caravelli."

The exceptionally wealthy widower lived in Florence. Twice married and still without an heir to inherit his sizeable fortune, he was one of the most sought-after men in Tuscany.

Sabina stood, the smile vanishing from her face. "That's quite funny, Papa...I almost believe you."

"You *should* believe me."

"I would rather you marry me off to a Pisano than to that old Florentine! He's almost old enough to be your father!"

"Bite your tongue, girl! Signore Tommaso is several years younger than I am, and strong enough to keep you in line."

Despite the harm done to her precious basil plant, Cecilia interceded on her sister's behalf. "Father, you cannot be serious. Signore Tommaso is in his fifties—he's far too old for Sabina."

"He's exactly forty-nine."

Cecilia winced. "That's a thirty-year age difference."

The old man snorted. "I'm getting too old for your sister's constant mischief. She needs a husband—not a foolish young man with his head in the clouds—but a strong man with worldly experience who won't tolerate her impudence." When Sabina shook her head defiantly, he added, "If you refuse to marry him, I will personally escort you to the convent of your choice."

"I'll be good, I promise," Sabina said. "I'll never swim naked or do anything that upsets you."

He crossed his arms. "You will be obedient and do as I say."

Sabina crossed her arms, too. "I will not marry him."

"Do you realize how wealthy he is? Or the kind of life he can provide for you? There are countless women who would jump at the chance of marrying such a man."

"Then let him choose one of those women for his bride."

"You stupid, foolish girl! I should beat you until some good sense enters that hard head of yours."

Sabina's chin began to quiver. "Please, Papa..."

Don Antonio almost felt pity, then he remembered how she had recently cost him a considerable sum by letting out the neighbor's goat as a prank. The animal never returned, forcing him to offer monetary compensation. "You will either marry Tommaso or dedicate your life to God. The choice is yours to make."

"That's what I should have done at your age," Cecilia mused aloud.

Sabina frowned at her sister. "What?"

"I should have become a nun instead of getting married. They must enjoy a peaceful existence."

"Well, that kind of dull life may be appealing to you, but not to me."

"There's nothing wrong with dedicating your life to God," Don Antonio snapped. "It's a selfless and noble endeavor. Perhaps a convent would be a better choice for you, after all."

"Forgive me, Papa," Sabina said contritely. "I meant no disrespect."

His expression softened. "I can't continue to support you forever. Tommaso is willing to wed you without a dowry because he's desperate for an heir, and needs a strong young bride to provide him with one."

Sabina pursed her lips. "You expect me to be grateful?"

"You have no dowry."

"No, but I'm a Rossi. Does our noble name not account for anything? I'm sure our blood is purer than the common sludge coursing through Tommaso's veins."

"Our noble name is *all* we have now—a chance like this will not present itself again." Don Antonio was aware of his daughter's stunning beauty and how it drew the attention of the local men. Her chastity was in constant danger, so the sooner the girl was married, the better. "Tommaso is dining with us tomorrow evening."

"*Tomorrow*? When were you planning to tell me?"

The old man's patience was exceeding its limit. "I was on my way to tell you now, only Donna Francesca intercepted me at the gate. Tommaso wants to meet you before the official betrothal."

"Of course. All men wish to inspect a broodmare before making a purchase. I'm assuming it won't matter if I like him or not, will it?"

*"Sabina is going to marry Signore Tommaso! Sabina is going to marry Signore Tommaso!"*

Hearing her nephew's childish taunt, Sabina ran into the house and went straight to her small bedchamber, bolting the door. Going to the window, she gazed at the neat rows of olive trees growing beyond the stone walls of the courtyard. Her late grandfather, Bernardo, had planted those trees before her father was born. They were tall and thriving now, but barely producing enough crop to make a profit.

Sabina was in this miserable predicament because of her grandfather and his bad gambling habit. She couldn't be angry with him, however. In life, Bernardo had been a charming man whom she had loved dearly.

"Open up," Cecilia cried from the other side of the door.

Ignoring her sister, she looked past the olive trees to the distant hills of the sun-scorched landscape. The grass was the color of straw thanks to the unusually dry summer. Oh, how she desperately longed for rain.

The Republic of Venice was never scorched or dry. In fact, there was plenty of water in La Serenissima; the very streets there made of it! She could run away to Venice and...

*And what, you silly girl?*

Shortly after her mother's death, her father became ill. He eventually recovered, but his health was never the same. Money was tight and the lack of decent suitors put a strain on the Rossi finances. To make matters worse, Cecilia was forced to return home with an extra mouth to feed after her husband died. Her father was right; he could not support the four of them forever. She would have to marry Tommaso.

"Sabina, please open the door," Cecilia implored.

"Go away. Leave me alone."

"Papa is right. You won't get another opportunity like this one. Stop behaving like a spoiled brat and be grateful."

"If you feel so strongly about it, sister, then you should marry him!"

She expected an angry reply, but instead she heard Cecilia's frustrated sigh and retreating footsteps.

# CHAPTER 2

Sabina's contrary mood the following day prompted Don Antonio to threaten his daughter once again with a cloistered life in a remote convent. She was ordered to bathe and prepare for the evening's festivities while Cecilia and two kindly neighbors cooked an elaborate meal to impress their guest of honor.

Sabina spent a considerable amount of time fuming and pacing the floor of her bedchamber. Rather than wear something pretty for the special occasion, she chose a somber black frock with high neckline and long sleeves. Unmarried girls usually wore their hair loose—and Sabina was no exception, often allowing her thick, dark locks to cascade down her back. Despite this, she fashioned her hair into a severe style by coiling her tresses into a knot at the nape of her neck. When she was done, she smiled smugly at her reflection in the looking glass.

Cecilia pounded on the bedchamber door. "Make haste, Sabina! Signore Tommaso will be here at any moment."

"I'm almost done," Sabina replied in a cheerful voice.

Don Antonio and Cecilia exchanged a look of hopeful surprise, but when Sabina finally emerged from the room, their faces fell.

"You look like Mother," Cecilia commented.

Don Antonio was about to tell his stubborn daughter to change into something more suitable when he heard a carriage outside the door. "Santo Cristo, he's here." He gave Sabina a stern look and warned, "Behave." She rolled her eyes and crossed her arms. *That wretched girl*, he thought while opening the door for his guest.

"Buona sera! Your presence honors my humble home, Signore Tommaso. Please, come in."

Tommaso mumbled a polite reply, practically pushing past

the old man in order to get a better view of Cecilia and Sabina. The young women gaped in admiration of the Florentine's clothing, correctly assuming that his lavish outfit was worth more than both of their entire wardrobes put together.

Tommaso cut a fine figure in his knee-length black velvet robe trimmed with fox fur. Beneath the robe he wore a tunic fashioned from green silk with silver embroidery around the collar. He offered the sisters a gallant bow while studying each of them in turn. One was plump and rather plain, but she wore a decent gown of good quality linen. The other, although dressed like an austere matron in black, had an exquisite face with eyes the color of emeralds.

Tommaso turned to Don Antonio. "Which one is to be my bride?"

Before her father had a chance to answer, Sabina replied, "I am."

*Ah, the beauty is to be mine.* Tommaso masked his relief with a grimace. "She doesn't look hearty enough to bear children."

Sabina was about to take a step forward and give a sassy retort, but her sister restrained her with a painful pinch to her upper arm.

"I assure you, she's as healthy as an ox, Signore," Don Antonio gently contradicted. "Sabina will bear you many sons."

Feigning interest in Cecilia, Tommaso asked, "What about her?"

"Oh, my daughter Cecilia is a widow and has a small son."

The Florentine waved his hand dismissively and heaved a theatrical sigh of resignation. "I suppose Sabina will have to do."

"How dare you come in here and—"

Cecilia's hand clamped down over Sabina's mouth.

Tommaso raised an eyebrow. "I see she possesses a fiery spirit, Don Antonio. No wonder you wish to be rid of her."

The old man's face resembled the color of ripe pomegranates as he glared at Sabina, who stared back at him with fearless defiance.

Tommaso continued to study the untamed beauty with amusement. "Please remove your hand from your sister's mouth," he said calmly to Cecilia. "I would hear what she has to say."

Cecilia looked to her father, who nodded with obvious reluctance. Her hand had been so tightly cupped around her sister's mouth that rosy imprints of fingers were splayed across Sabina's cheek.

"Well?" Tommaso prompted. "Go on and speak your mind."

"How dare you come in here and inspect us as though we were farm animals that you wish to breed. How dare you comment on my appearance when you're practically old enough to be my father and—" Sabina was about to make a rude comment about his lack of good looks, but it would be untrue. Tommaso's face was lined, yes, but also strong and distinguished—almost handsome.

Tommaso eyed her expectantly. "And?"

Don Antonio stood aside, silently wishing for the earth to swallow him whole while Cecilia nervously bit her lip.

"You should know that I'm not the type who merely sits at home praying over rosary beads and doing needlework," Sabina warned. "I don't plan on changing my ways, either."

"Sabina!" Don Antonio cried.

Tommaso never broke eye contact with Sabina as he placed a hand on the old man's shoulder to restrain him. "I'm devout but not overly zealous, so I don't expect you to pray any more than you already do. Also, I don't need any more tapestries on the walls of my palazzo."

Sabina crossed her arms. "I dislike being told what to do."

Mortified, Don Antonio covered his face with his hands.

"That makes two of us," Tommaso admitted quietly as he patted the old man's back in a gesture of comfort. "Anything else, Signorina?"

"That's all I have to say...*for now*."

The relief in the air was almost palpable.

"It seems as though you and I have much in common, Sabina," Tommaso said. Turning to Don Antonio, he inquired cheerfully, "Well, when do we eat? I'm absolutely famished."

The three of them stared at him in surprise.

"What can we do about Sabina?" Tommaso asked in response to the curious stares. "Shall we thrash her within inches of her life? It won't change how she thinks or feels, will it? Besides, I like her spirit. I think she'll make a fine wife."

The old man's eyes widened in disbelief. "You still wish to marry my daughter?"

"Of course I do." Taking a step closer to Sabina, Tommaso whispered, "Hopefully, you'll grow to like me someday."

Don Antonio and Cecilia looked immensely relieved as they sat down at the table. Sabina was silent throughout the meal as Tommaso regaled them with tales of his travels. At one point he noticed a book on a stool, carefully bound in red velvet.

Reaching for it, he inquired, "What's this?"

Sabina stood. "Please, Signore, I insist that you give me the book."

Realization dawned on him when he noticed the pages were written by a neat, female hand. "This is your writing."

She was tempted to snatch the book out of his hands, but her father shot her a warning look. "Yes, it is."

"I would love to know what sort of things my future bride writes about." Sabina remained stoically silent. Not wanting to torment the girl further, he relinquished the book. "You have pretty penmanship."

"Thank you," she replied, clasping the book to her chest.

The evening soon came to an end and Don Antonio insisted that his guest spend the night. "After all," he reasoned, "you'll be my son-in-law soon, and I hope you will think of this as your home in Lucca."

"I appreciate the offer, Don Antonio, but I have urgent business early in the morning." Tommaso bent over Sabina's hand, and said in a low voice meant only for her ears, "*Goodnight, Tempesta.*"

Sabina received a thorough tongue-lashing from her father, then helped her sister clean up. Cecilia swept the floor while Sabina scrubbed the plates, lost in thought. She was relieved that Tommaso was not the ogre she had imagined—after all, she could do worse.

Three days later, a messenger from Florence arrived at the villa with a posy and a small wooden box.

Cecilia went to the kitchen door and called out to her younger sister who was picking rosemary in the garden. "Something has arrived for you! Come inside!"

Sabina took the box from her sister's hands once she entered the kitchen. "What's this?"

"Open it and find out."

Sabina opened the box and pulled out a string of pearls. Perfectly round orbs gleamed in the sunlight pouring in from the window.

"Oh, my!" Cecilia exclaimed. "There's a note and flowers, too." She shuffled inside and picked up a piece of vellum from the scarred wooden table. "Here, let me read it to you."

"I can read just fine," Sabina said, taking the note from her sister's hand.

" 'My dearest Sabina…Your beauty and spirit have enchanted me, and I look forward to our next encounter. Until then, enjoy the humble token I have sent you. Your servant, Tommaso.' "

"He's incredibly generous and kind," Cecilia pointed out. "You're a fortunate girl."

Sabina put the necklace on with her sister's help, then placed the flowers in a ceramic pitcher filled with water.

"Sabina? Are you home?"

Cecilia frowned as she peered out the window. "It's that good-for-nothing Marco! You should send him away. Signore Tommaso won't appreciate men visiting you now that you're officially betrothed."

Marco's tall, stocky frame filled the doorway. "I heard you're getting married to Tommaso Caravelli," he said sourly. "Is it true?"

Cecilia took it upon herself to reply. "Yes, it's true. My father has arranged for Sabina to marry—and about time, too!"

Sabina intercepted. "Come with me, Marco."

Cecilia moved to block her path. "Papa and Signore Tommaso wouldn't approve of you wandering off alone with Marco now that you're spoken for."

"I will handle things the way I see fit," Sabina retorted as she exited the house with Marco in tow. When they were out of earshot, she added, "My father is forcing me to marry him."

"What about us?" Marco asked, his brown eyes lacking their usual twinkle. "How will we continue to see each other if you're married and living in Florence?"

Sabina looked over her shoulder to make sure Cecilia was not following them. "Let's walk far from the house."

They followed the stream that snaked behind the olive grove and led into a wooded glen. Hidden beneath a thick canopy of trees, Marco gripped Sabina's shoulders and pulled her against him.

"You're hurting me, Marco."

Easing his grip, he noticed the expensive pearls around her neck for the first time. "Are those from him?"

"Yes."

"My God, what is your father thinking? He's too old for you."

She felt a strange urge to defend Tommaso, but refrained. "There's nothing I can do."

"Marry me, instead."

*"What?"*

"Marry me."

In all the time they had known each other, and throughout the many embraces they had shared, Marco had never mentioned the word 'marriage.'

When they were children, Marco ran with a pack of older boys who enjoyed making mischief and wreaking havoc on younger, weaker children. He was the imp, the bully who had teased her incessantly—sometimes even cruelly. The moment she blossomed into a young woman, his demeanor toward her changed from aggressive to possessive. At first, she resisted his amorous advances, but he was persistent. To make matters worse, her mother died unexpectedly. With her father overcome by illness and grief, and Cecilia caring for a husband and child, she had no one to turn to for comfort. Marco came to the rescue, filling the sudden, agonizing void in her life with his constant company and piquant humor. In exchange for this emotional salve, she had finally given in to his physical demands.

Although Marco was attractive, their relationship was far from the romantic ones described by troubadours.

"I can't marry you," Sabina stated firmly.

Taking hold of her chin, he bent his head and plundered her mouth. Unable to resist the familiar comfort of his body, she wound her arms around his neck and played with the dark curls at the nape.

"Are you ready to give this up," he asked against her lips, his big hands trailing down the length of her spine.

"I'll learn to live without it, and so shall you."

The house was far enough away to allow Marco to ease Sabina onto the soft grass and lift her skirts. His lovemaking was urgent, and he took his lustful pleasure as selfishly as a common stallion. She bore his considerable weight and hard thrusts placidly, knowing it was the last time they would ever be together in a carnal sense.

Satiated, Marco placed his head on her bosom afterward. Trailing a blade of grass along her collar bone, he said, "Don't marry him."

She stifled a yawn. "I can't disobey my father."

He raised himself on his elbow and stared at her in disbelief. "Since when are you the good, obedient daughter? The role of martyr doesn't suit you at all."

"Hush or I'll find a potion that will turn you into a toad."

"Be careful, Sabina," he warned, his face serious. "You'll end up burned at the stake someday if you continue to make such jests."

Despite Marco's blatant disregard for the divine admonition against the sin of fornication, he came from an extremely devout and superstitious family.

"Who said I was jesting?" she challenged with a twinkle in her eye.

Marco frowned at her in disapproval. He knew the love potions Sabina created for the village girls weren't real—or at least he hoped they weren't. "You try my patience at times."

"Then I've succeeded in my task."

To break the tension, he tickled her roughly. "Vixen!"

"Stop that, Marco Alfani!"

Lowering his head, he kissed her heartily on the mouth. "Marry me."

"I cannot," she replied, wriggling out of his grasp and smoothing the creases from her skirt.

"Let me speak to your father and ask for your hand in marriage."

"No!"

Marco's expression was one of puzzlement verging on anger. "Do you *want* to marry him?"

"Do you realize that you've never told me you loved me? What difference does it make if I marry you or Tommaso? Neither of you love me. I'm only a pawn to be used in a game played by men."

"Please, let me ask your father for your hand."

"Why? Is my marriage to another man an assault on your pride?"

Marco appeared wounded. "I do love you, Sabina."

\*\*\*

Marco arrived at Don Antonio's villa later that day. Cecilia and Sabina were both in the kitchen preparing supper while Paolo played at their feet.

"Don Antonio, may I have a word with you, please?" he said from the doorway as he fidgeted nervously with his hands. Despite the August heat, he had worn his best wool tunic in an attempt to look presentable and there was a sheen of perspiration on his brow.

Don Antonio eyed the uninvited guest suspiciously. He never cared much for the young man who eyed his daughter like a stud seeking to rut, but said, "Come in, Marco. What can I do for you?"

Marco cleared his throat. "As you know, sir, I'm a simple

man but I come from a decent family."

"Yes, your father is a good man and I've known him for many years."

Encouraged by this, Marco continued, "I don't have much now because I'm still young, but I'm a hard worker. I would like to ask—"

"—for my daughter's hand in marriage."

"Yes, I want to marry Sabina."

"She is already spoken for."

"But, Don Antonio—"

"I'm sorry, Marco. The answer is no."

Although his pride was deeply wounded, Marco inclined his head respectfully and gave Sabina a wistful glance before taking his leave.

Don Antonio sat down at the table and allowed his daughters to set a plate of steaming stewed tripe before him. "Have you been allowing Marco to court you?" he asked, staring pointedly at Sabina.

Sabina poured wine into his cup and re-corked the bottle. "You know how Marco has always been fond of me."

"That's not what I asked you."

"We are not courting."

Cecilia snorted. Don Antonio glanced at his eldest daughter before fixing his gaze on Sabina. "Well, whatever is going on between you two must end. *Now*. You're going to be married soon, and I will not have you sullying yourself or our family name, do you understand?"

"Yes."

"I'm serious, Sabina."

Placing a loaf of bread on the table, she said, "I know, Papa."

"Don't worry, Father," Cecilia said. "Sabina is not so foolish as to throw away her entire future."

"I hope you're correct," he said. "I'm entrusting her into your care."

Cecilia's eyebrows shot upward. "Into my care?"

"Yes. From now until the wedding day, don't let your sister out of your sight."

# CHAPTER 3
## FLORENCE, TUSCANY
## AUGUST 28, 1477

Was there ever a city more glorious than Florence? It was no wonder the royal courts of Europe recognized it as the epicenter of art, culture, and classical expression. Tommaso had sent a carriage to fetch his bride and her family a few days before the wedding. When the vehicle passed through the massive city gates, Don Antonio pointed out the Medici crest— a gold shield with several red balls. Since the Medici commissioned many public artworks and paid for structural repairs, the family's coat of arms was ostentatiously displayed throughout the city. This cunning strategy served as a visual testament to any foreigner entering Florence that Medici authority was both unchallenged and absolute.

The horses were forced to slow their pace within the crowded streets, thus allowing the occupants inside the carriage to marvel at the grand palazzos and public statues carved from dazzling white Carrara marble. The elegant piazzas teemed with Florentines, many flaunting expensive jewels and sumptuous clothing. The majority of people wore red, but not just any red; *Florentine Red* was currently the most fashionable color in Europe. Sabina mentally likened it to the color of blood— vibrant, yet deep, and extremely flattering to the complexion. Some wore Florentine Red in the form of plush velvet with a luxuriously thick pile while others sported brocade with decorative flowers and leaves fashioned from gold or silver thread.

"Red everywhere," Paolo chirped.

"What a clever boy you are," Cecilia cooed as she kissed the top of her son's head.

"Florence is overflowing with wealth and it shows," Don Antonio mused aloud, his gaze fixed on a well-heeled pair of gentlemen.

The city consisted of successful bankers, artists, sculptors, wool and silk merchants, carpenters—too many talented people to mention. The staggering net worth of some bourgeoisie families rivaled that of royal princes.

The carriage turned down an impossibly narrow street and finally came to a stop in front of a long stone wall with an iron-studded wooden door at its center. Above the door was Tommaso's family crest, marking the residence as the Palazzo Caravelli. The carved stone shield portrayed a cylindrical tower with an eagle poised atop Guelph crenellations. Two servants appeared, helping them alight from the carriage. Sabina and her family followed them into a courtyard surrounded by low stone buildings and a tower that appeared to be at least five hundred years old. There was a cistern in the center of the courtyard and a bronze fountain fashioned like a mermaid.

"Welcome," Tommaso said as he emerged from within the shadowy interior of the tower.

Greetings were exchanged, then Sabina eyes were drawn to the ceramic bas-relief sculpture of the Madonna and Christ child adorning the wall behind his head. The exquisitely carved figures, along with the boughs of decorative leaves and fruits framing the charming scene, were painted in brilliant white, yellow ochre, and blue.

Following her gaze, Tommaso smiled. "Do you like it?"

"It's lovely."

"You have good taste. Luca della Robbia's work is in high demand." Taking her hands into his own, he said, "I trust that you'll find your chamber comfortable. If there's anything you or your family requires, please don't hesitate to ask the servants."

She was charmed by his courteous hospitality. "Thank you."

Motioning to the servants, he instructed, "See that our guests are given some refreshment and show the ladies to their bedchambers."

Turning to Don Antonio, he inquired, "Would you care to take some wine with me under the shade of my fruit trees before going to your room, or would you prefer to rest first?"

"I would be delighted to have some wine with you."

"Very well," Tommaso said as he put his arm around the old man in a friendly gesture. "Ladies, we shall see you at supper."

The cool interior of the palazzo was a relief from the heat outside. Sabina, Cecilia, and Paolo ascended a long flight of stairs separating the servant's ground floor from the *piano nobile*. Sabina took in the attractive surroundings, liking her new home instantly. She smiled in delight when she entered her new private quarters, which were spacious and well-lit. The wide bed boasted a canopy fashioned from the softest yellow silk. The servants had carefully strewn lavender and tansy onto the comfortable straw and down-filled mattress in order to give the bed a pleasant scent while simultaneously repelling bedbugs. There was an antechamber for bathing and a sitting room with a small writing desk.

The Rossi family enjoyed the best of what Florence had to offer, including the hospitality of their gracious host. Sabina, who had always taken an interest in the arts, immediately noticed that the paintings and sculptures of Florence possessed a different style than those of Lucca. Many of the themes were the same—Annunciation of Christ, Madonna Enthroned or the martyrdom of various saints, but in Florence the figures seemed to be alive. The Virgin Mary was often depicted as a pretty young woman flaunting current fashion rather than a stiff matronly figure in traditional dark blue cloak. Instead of static religious effigies, Florentine sculptors adopted the style of ancient Greece and Rome to create idealized gods. One could easily imagine these impressive figures stepping down from their marble pedestals at any moment to walk among the people.

Interestingly, it was common for wealthy Florentine families to commission religious paintings for their private chapels with their own likenesses included in the holy scenes. Family members stood alongside Jesus or their patron saints dressed like royals and dripping in jewels. Sabina wondered if these people were trying to be seen as godly, or if they were attempting to drag God down to their level. Although unsure of the answer, she was certain that Florentine art was magnificent.

Artists, architects, sculptors, writers, philosophers, and musicians thrived under the patronage of guilds and generous commissions from wealthy families. Tommaso mentioned the names of the city's most prominent families and Sabina committed a few of them to memory: Strozzi, Pazzi, Rucellai, and Tornabuoni. Of these great families, none was more generous in their patronage than the powerful House of Medici.

The day before their wedding, Tommaso and Sabina attended Holy Mass in the church where they would be married.

"This is the Basilica of San Lorenzo, a revered church in the city," Tommaso stated proudly. "Brunelleschi, who is considered the most talented architect in the city, designed the basilica's interior."

"Did the Medici pay for this church?" she inquired, her eyes darting to the Medici coat of arms displayed throughout the church.

"Yes."

Sabina was again impressed by the wealth and power of Florence's leading family. "Will I have the honor of meeting them soon?"

"Most certainly."

After the service, Tommaso led Sabina to the front of the church. On the floor before the high altar was a big circle of porphyry, a rare and expensive Egyptian marble the color of mulberries—a stone normally reserved for emperors. "Lorenzo's grandfather, Cosimo, was buried beneath the circle upon which we are standing. So beloved is he by the Florentines that they've bestowed upon him the Latin title of *Pater Patriae*, or—"

"Father of the Fatherland," Sabina supplied.

"Correct," he beamed. "Cosimo adopted the turtle as his personal emblem during his lifetime, thus alluding to his infinite patience. He was a man who waited for the right moment to strike. The great grandfather of Lorenzo, Giovanni di Bicci, was buried in the sacristy beneath that communion table." Sabina followed his pointed finger. "His location is also marked by a circular slab of costly porphyry."

"What about that beautiful porphyry sarcophagus over there?" she asked, indicating the iron grate in the sacristy's wall.

"That's the final resting place of Lorenzo's father, Piero, commonly known as Piero il Gottoso. The Medici are plagued by gout, thus the nickname. Do you see how the sarcophagus rests on four turtles? It's an homage to Cosimo."

The precious materials and prestigious locations of the tombs hinted at the Medici family's enormous pride, but Sabina wisely refrained from voicing such an unkind speculation.

***

The last day of August dawned clear and predictably hot. Tuscany was still in the midst of a drought with no relief in sight. True to her father's words, Sabina would be married before the month was over. Tomorrow was the first of September and, by then, she would be the legal wife of Tommaso Caravelli. She was pleased that her future husband treated her and her family like royalty. She had even been allowed to bring Mendi, who was now calling out loudly from his wired brass cage near the windowsill. The bird took flight at whim throughout the day, yet always returned in the evening to roost.

Every fine lady in Florence possessed a talented lady's maid, so Tommaso had procured one for his bride as a wedding gift. A girl by the name of Teresa plaited Sabina's hair, expertly coiling the braids into two rolls at the top of each ear then tucking the rolls into templers adorned with pearls. She then pinned a length of silk as sheer as mist to the headdress, allowing a measure of the fabric to fall in front of her mistress's face.

Sabina admired her reflection in the highly polished looking glass. The long-sleeved gown she wore was cut from gold brocade with an intricate pearl design sewn into the front panel of a snug-fitting bodice.

A page eventually knocked on the door, signaling that it was time to go. Tommaso had arranged for a litter to carry his bride the short distance to the church.

Don Antonio began his familiar speech the moment he saw his daughter descend the stairs. "We have long since lost the family fortune—thanks to your grandfather's gambling—but our name is still one of great fame, going as far back as—"

"—the first fathers of Tuscany," Sabina interjected with a huff. "I know, Papa. The Rossi family were once the great Guelphs who possessed considerable wealth... *I know*... but we are not rich and we no longer hold any power, political or otherwise."

"Show some respect, Sabina," Cecilia snapped.

Sabina shot Cecilia a withering look before taking her father's hands into her own. "Don't worry, Papa. I won't disrespect our good family name," she assured in a gentler tone.

Hurt by Sabina's initial harshness, Don Antonio nodded sadly.

"Forgive me," Sabina offered before entering the litter.

Cecilia placed her arm around her father's slumped shoulders. "Come, our carriage awaits."

As a rule, Tommaso Caravelli avoided ostentatious behavior whenever possible. Unlike some noblemen who flaunted their wealth by strutting around like peacocks in the latest fashions, he preferred understated elegance. While he adhered to this personal code of conduct, he had no qualms bending the rules where Sabina was concerned. It was a popular custom in Florence for veiled brides to ride to the church on a white horse on their wedding day, but that was not good enough for Tommaso. He insisted that his future wife be transported to the basilica in a gilded litter with the Caravelli crest painted on the door.

Family, friends, and curious onlookers gathered to see Tommaso Caravelli get married—again. They stared at the golden litter as it was carried up the stairs of San Lorenzo by two liveried pages, then gaped as Sabina emerged from the velvet-lined interior with all the pomp of a queen arriving at her own coronation. She walked into the church, drawing the eyes of many lustful men and envious maidens. Tommaso stood by the altar looking handsome in a brocade tunic of deep amber, the golden beads sewn into the fabric gleaming in the candlelight.

The moment Sabina stood beside the groom, the priest began the long, monotonous marriage ceremony. Everyone appeared relieved when Tommaso lifted the sheer veil from the bride's face and kissed her cheek. Invited guests made their way to the Palazzo Caravelli in the blazing heat of the midday sun to partake of the marriage feast.

The lavish meal was served in the spacious main hall, which was airy and cool. The cooks prepared roasted fowl, stag, hare, and swan, each served with various sauces. Fresh breads, aged cheeses, and stewed vegetables accompanied the meats. Honeyed treats of every size and shape mixed with nuts, fruits, or rare spices were available in abundance for those with a sweet tooth. Acrobats and troubadours performed to entertain the many guests as minstrels sang songs of love to honor the newlywed couple.

Sabina sat beside her husband at the high table with a look of sheer amazement on her face. Never in her life had she attended such an extravagant affair!

Tommaso leaned over and whispered, "Are you enjoying yourself, my Tempesta?" She nodded and he smiled in satisfaction. "I did this all for you. I hope you are pleased, Sabina."

For a brief instant, Tommaso resembled a lovesick young man. Did this mean he could be easily swayed? She smiled at the possibility and said, "I'm very pleased. Thank you."

Later, after eating and drinking more than she should have, Sabina wandered away from her husband's side to a staircase located at the far corner of the main hall. Feeling excessively warm, she decided to get away from the revelry and cool off for a bit. Several of the florid-faced guests were already drunk and dancing merrily as she ascended the stairs. At the top was a spacious room with cream-painted walls and a red-tiled floor. There was a big window in the room, its green shutters thrown back to reveal the tiny orange grove in the courtyard below. The wide wooden bench beneath the window was piled high with soft cushions, and it beckoned invitingly.

Sabina sat down and pulled the heavy brocade skirt up past her knees, revealing a set of shapely bare legs. Teresa had tried to convince her to wear stockings for propriety's sake, but flaunting rules for the sake of comfort was nothing new for Sabina. She kicked off her shoes, relishing the deliciously cold tile beneath her toes. Resting her head against the windowsill, she closed her eyes and allowed the breeze to caress her clammy skin. The lazy hum of bumblebees in the courtyard almost lulled her to sleep. After several minutes, she felt a presence in the room and her eyes snapped open.

It was Marco, dressed in a black tunic and hose as if attending a funeral. "*Signora*, should you not be with your husband and your guests?" he inquired drily from the doorway.

She sat up straight, quickly slipping her feet into her shoes. "What are you doing here?"

"An old friend can't offer his congratulations on your wedding day?"

"I know you too well to believe this is your true intention."

His gaze swept over her bare legs, her cleavage, and finally rested on her full mouth. She let her skirt fall to the floor and adjusted her bodice as he sauntered into the room. "So, how does it feel to be the wife of such a wealthy man, *Signora*?"

"Stop calling me that!"

"You are now married, are you not?"

"Yes, but—"

"I'm merely giving a married woman the respect she is due."

He sat beside her on the bench and boldly traced the curve of her breast with his fingertip, compelling her to slap his hand away.

"Marco, I don't know how you got here—or even why you came—but you must leave right now." Ignoring her words, he leaned forward in an attempt to kiss her lips and she shoved him. "I'm serious. Go!"

"You know you'll always be mine," he whispered.

She stood and walked to the center of the room. "Leave now or I shall be forced to summon my husband's guards."

"You wouldn't dare," he said menacingly.

Tommaso walked into the room and looked from Marco to Sabina. "Some of the guests have been wondering where you went off to, my dear."

Her face paled. "Forgive me, Signore Tommaso. It was sweltering downstairs...I came up here to cool off."

"First of all, you must stop calling me *Signore* Tommaso. I'm your husband now. Secondly, who is this man?"

"Signore—I mean, Tommaso, this is an old family friend," she replied. "He is Marco, son of Signore Niccolò Alfani."

The men nodded to each other without saying a word.

Tommaso offered his arm to Sabina. "If you will excuse us, Signore Marco, my wife and I must return to our guests."

Marco did not move as he silently watched them leave.

"I never want you to be alone with that man again," Tommaso whispered as they descended the stairs. To drive his point home, he gave her arm a painful squeeze. "Do you understand me?"

She winced. "Yes."

He released his vice-like grip. "Good. We shall get along fine if you do as I say."

Obviously, her husband was no lovesick fool, nor would he be easily influenced by feminine wiles.

"Sabina! Come and dance with me," Cecilia called out when she caught sight of her sister.

Sabina allowed herself to be pulled away from Tommaso and into the throng of dancing guests. The smell of sweet perfume, wine, and perspiration permeated the air, making her feel nauseous.

"What in God's name are you doing?" Cecilia demanded.

"What are you talking about?"

"I saw Marco follow you upstairs. Please tell me you haven't done anything dishonorable on your wedding day."

"I'm insulted that you would insinuate such a thing. I didn't even know Marco was here."

"Well, no one invited him. Two of Signore Tommaso's guards just escorted him outside. What an embarrassment to our family."

"An embarrassment not caused by me, I assure you."

"Don't be stupid and ruin the wonderful opportunity you've been given. You could have married someone poor, like I did." Cecilia sighed. "If only I'd been blessed with your beauty, I would have fared better in life."

Sabina was tired of her sister's constant disparaging comments. "Enough, Cecilia!"

Some of the nearby guests tossed curious glances in their direction, causing Cecilia's cheeks to redden with shame. "How dare you speak to me in such a manner?"

"How dare you insult me on my wedding day! I've endured enough of your reproaches. Papa's too, for that matter."

Cecilia raised an eyebrow. "Now that you've married a man with prestige and wealth, you think you're better than me."

"That's not what I think at all—Cecilia, wait," Sabina protested, but her sister was already walking away.

First her father, then Tommaso, and now her sister. How many more people would she offend today?

Tommaso came to stand beside his wife. "Is anything amiss?"

"Not at all."

He knew harsh words were exchanged between the two sisters, and he was willing to bet they had to do with Marco Alfani. "May I have the pleasure of this dance?"

"Since when does a husband ask permission of his wife?"

"You have much to learn, my dear," he said as he slipped a hand around her slim waist.

Sabina was pleasantly surprised to learn that Tommaso was not only surefooted, but also physically fit for a man of his age.

"Are you feeling unwell?" Tommaso inquired.

"Why do you ask?"

"Your face is flushed."

"Perhaps it was the wine," she lied.

"Perhaps," he repeated. "Tell me, is Marco your lover?"

"Marco?"

"Yes, *Marco*, the man whom you were alone with upstairs

during our wedding celebration. Do not bother lying to me, Sabina, I'll know when you do."

"How will you know if I lie?"

"Your lips lie, but your eyes do not. I have dealt with enough people in my life to know when someone is being dishonest, especially women."

She looked away before admitting, "Yes, he was my lover."

"And now?" he demanded, taking hold of her chin and forcing her to meet his gaze.

"Now I'm married and have no lovers."

"Did you invite him here today?"

"No. I didn't know he was here, I swear."

"Are you still in love with him?"

Sabina hesitated. It would be improper either way she responded. If she said "yes," it would threaten her marriage, but if she said "no," she would seem like a whore. She decided to be honest. "I was never in love with him."

"You're telling me the truth."

She nodded. "I was a stupid girl."

He found her honesty refreshing. Of all the women he had known, and he had known many, Sabina Rossi was the most peculiar. She was strong and rebellious but possessed a childlike quality that was almost endearing.

"Good," he said, pulling her against him. "I prefer a stupid girl over a woman who is in love with another man."

Don Antonio tapped Tommaso on his shoulder. "May I have a dance with my daughter on her wedding day?"

Tommaso handed his wife to his father-in-law. Don Antonio beamed with pride. "Signore Tommaso is a fine man, Sabina. I'm certain he will make your life very comfortable and offer you many niceties that I cannot."

"You've given me everything I need, Papa."

"Yes, but you deserve more and I know you want more. You are nothing like your sister, Cecilia, who was content to marry a simple man and now basks in motherhood. Such a dull existence would kill your spirit. Life would have been easier had you been born male, but Fate can be cruel." He paused. "I wouldn't have married you to Tommaso if I didn't think he could provide you with what you need in life."

"What is it that I need?"

*"Excitement."*

She could not deny it. "Thank you, Papa," she said, kissing his cheek.

Don Antonio narrowed his eyes. "You may think me a simple old man but pay heed to the counsel I'm about to give you. Do not let your heart or your headstrong ways lead you astray."

Sabina rolled her eyes in anticipation of another onslaught of admonitions when her father took both of her hands firmly in his own and pulled her forward. His face was serious, his eyes fearful.

She frowned. "Papa?"

"Listen carefully to what I'm about to say, my child. Be wary now that you are a member of Florentine society. You should know who your friends are but, more importantly, know your enemies. Watch that tongue of yours; be mindful of what you say and to whom you say it. Control your temper. Never reveal anything you do not want repeated—speak little and listen twofold." Don Antonio cast a furtive glance over his shoulder and whispered, "And for God's sake, do not concoct any of your silly potions! Being accused of witchcraft is no trivial matter here in Florence. Signore Tommaso deals with important and influential people, and you would not want to jeopardize your husband's position in society."

Don Antonio's wise words hit Sabina with great impact. As she scanned the room, she noticed several sets of eyes watching her carefully. For the first time since her arrival in Florence, she felt insecure of her new role. She had been afforded a good education and learned basic court manners but never had the opportunity to actually mingle in high society until now.

"Papa, take me home. I don't want to stay here in Florence," she said, gripping her father's hands tightly.

Don Antonio saw the panic in his daughter's eyes and found her vulnerability disconcerting, especially since it was

310

something she rarely, if ever, displayed. "Now, now, Sabina," he said soothingly. "There's no need for you to fear. You are a lovely young woman and you know how to behave properly. You'll be fine as long as you heed my counsel."

She immediately straightened her shoulders. "You're right, Papa," she said, glancing around the room and coolly meeting the eyes of those who stared in her direction. "I know what to do. I'll be fine."

Don Antonio embraced Sabina and walked away, leaving her alone in the center of the room. With her head held high and several eyes following her, she walked to where Tommaso stood and placed a hand upon his arm.

He gazed down at her and smiled. "Come, dearest, there is someone I want you to meet," he said, leading her through the throng of guests. "Giuliano de' Medici has arrived from Milan only a moment ago and is here to offer his congratulations."

Sabina was led to a group of well-dressed men. The most exquisitely dressed was an attractive young man in his mid-twenties with brown, shoulder-length hair and a serene face. He smiled at Tommaso before embracing him with great affection.

"Giuliano, I'm so happy you could come," Tommaso said.

"I wanted to arrive earlier, but we were delayed," Giuliano explained. Noticing the stunning woman at his friend's side, he added, "Is this bella donna your new bride?"

"Giuliano, may I present to you my wife, Sabina, daughter of Don Antonio Rossi."

The dark eyes that studied Sabina were alert and intelligent. Giuliano stepped forward and gallantly kissed her hand. "It's an honor to meet you, Signora. You are living proof of Tommaso's impeccable taste."

She smiled. "You are too kind, Signore Giuliano."

Giuliano turned to Tommaso. "I congratulate you on finding such a lovely treasure."

"Thank you, my friend. Where is Lorenzo?"

"Unfortunately, my brother was forced to remain in Milan and instructed me to convey his best wishes to you both. He regrets not being able to attend your wedding today."

"I know the business he tends to is urgent; there is no need for him to feel any regrets. I shall see him soon enough."

"You must present your wife at the palazzo when Lorenzo returns," Giuliano said, winking at Sabina. "He will be charmed."

"It will be an honor. Now, please, I want you and your men to eat, drink, and enjoy the festivities," Tommaso said before quickly summoning his servants and instructing them to pay special attention to the Medici entourage.

Giuliano mingled easily with the guests since he knew everyone.

Sabina was duly impressed that her husband was on such friendly terms with the wealthiest and most politically influential family in Tuscany. "How long have you known the Medici brothers?"

"I was a good friend of their father, so I've known them since birth. Before that, my father and their grandfather did business together."

"Oh? What kind of business?"

"Why, banking, of course."

"I see. Do you regularly attend court at their palazzo?"

Tommaso stepped closer to Sabina and lowered his voice. "You must never refer to the Palazzo Medici as a royal court, my dear. It's offensive."

"Forgive me."

He waved away her apology. "You must always keep in mind that Florence is a republic, not a monarchy."

Her brow creased in confusion. "Oh."

"You will be presented to Lorenzo, who, although not being a prince, assumes the role of one." He paused. "Do you understand?"

"So I should treat him like a prince but never call him that to his face."

Tommaso nodded in approval. "Correct."

"And the Palazzo Medici is not an official royal court but it operates as such, although everyone pretends it doesn't because Florence is a republic."

"I think you'll learn how this city operates very quickly."

The wedding festivities lasted until nightfall. Don Antonio wished many blessings upon the marital union and kissed his daughter's cheek before retiring to his guest chamber. Cecilia also approached her sister and brother-in-law before retiring. She hugged her sister coolly, muttering a blessing on their marriage before heading off to bed.

Later that night, after the guests had gone home, Sabina sat at the dressing table in her bedchamber. Teresa had already helped her mistress out of the wedding gown and was now brushing her hair in the light of three flickering candles.

"You are very lucky, Signora Sabina."

"Why do you say that?"

"Signore Tommaso is a good man who gives with an open hand to those whom he loves. He is always helping people and never asks the cost, which is why God has blessed him with so much wealth."

"How do you know this?"

"My father was cousin to his first wife."

"Tell me about her."

"We're not allowed to speak of her because... Well, she fled with another man."

Sabina hid her surprise. "I see..."

"Signore Tommaso helped us very much after my mother died."

"I'm sorry for your loss, Teresa. My mother is dead, too."

"May her soul be blessed in Heaven," Teresa said before crossing herself and kissing the tiny gold crucifix that hung from a chain around her neck.

"How well do you know my husband?"

"Well enough to assure you that he loathes impropriety and does not tolerate disrespect," she replied candidly.

"I'll keep that in mind."

"He seems very fond of you, Signora Sabina. One of my cousins served as the lady's maid to his second wife, Signora Mariella." Teresa lowered her voice and added, "She and Signore Tommaso were never in accord. She died in childbirth.

The baby died, too."

"What happened to your cousin after her mistress died?"

"She was sent to another Florentine lady across the city."

How clever of her husband to get rid of the girl. It certainly prevented any gossip about the late Signora Mariella. "Anything else I should know?"

Teresa froze, her cheeks bright red in the reflection of the looking glass.

Tommaso stood in the doorway. "Leave us."

Teresa bowed her head. "Yes, Signore Tommaso." She laid down the brush, curtsied to her master and mistress, and started to walk out of the room when Mendi began to caw loudly from within his cage.

Tommaso frowned. "Take that damned bird with you. I know you love that wretched crow, Sabina, but there is room for only one male in your bedchamber tonight."

Teresa retraced her steps and picked up the cage. Mendi, unhappy at being moved, threatened to peck at the girl's hand, but Sabina's sharp reprimand kept him from doing so. Holding the cage as far away from her as she could, the maid hastily vacated the room.

"What do you think of Teresa?" Tommaso asked with feigned nonchalance.

"I like her," Sabina replied cautiously, wondering how much of the conversation he had heard before entering her room.

"Good. I want you to be happy." He stood behind her and placed his hands on her shoulders. "I don't expect you to love me." She stiffened at the unexpected statement and tried to turn around in order to face him, but his grip on her shoulders tightened. "I'm well aware your beauty and youth, Sabina. After seeing what your former lover looks like, I know you'll probably never love me."

"Tommaso, I—"

"Don't interrupt me again," he warned. "Unlike other men, I do not care that my bride is not a virgin. I'm no longer a young man prone to frivolous jealousies, nor do I wish to engage in any hot-tempered duels for the sake of your virtue. Time is

314

precious to me."

He moved her hair aside to expose her nape and bent to kiss the soft skin. "Now that you're my wife, I expect your loyalty and respect. I want you to provide me with a son and not make a cuckold of me. In return, you will be afforded freedoms that are usually denied most women. You can read as many books as you wish, learn any subject you desire—with my approval, of course. I may even share political views with you, but only if you adhere to my conditions. If you refuse to abide by my rules and decide to take on a lover, or dishonor me in any way through improper conduct, you will be cast out of this house in shame. Your reputation will be ruined forever." His hands fell to his sides. "Do we have an agreement, Sabina?"

"Yes, Tommaso."

Without further words, he led her to the bed. Sabina was surprised by the unexpected finesse of his lovemaking. Marco had been lustful and clumsy in comparison with Tommaso's expertise. When they finished, she stared at the exposed timbers on the ceiling. The act itself had been pleasant enough, which was somewhat of a relief.

"You must be tired," he said, kissing her cheek before getting out of bed. "I will retire to my chamber now. Goodnight, Sabina."

"Goodnight, Tommaso, and thank you."

"For what?"

"For everything."

He cast a wry smile over his shoulder and left the room.

Do you want to keep reading? SABINA is available on Amazon.